THE BROKEN WORLD

AN ELEANOR MORGAN NOVEL: BOOK FOUR

AMY CISSELL

The Eleanor Morgan Novels

The Cardinal Gate
The Waning Moon
The Ruby Blade
The Broken World
The Lost Child*

*Forthcoming

THE BROKEN WORLD
Amy Cissell

A Broken World Publication
PO Box 11643
Portland, OR 97211
The Broken World

ISBN 978-1-949410-08-2 (ebook);
ISBN 978-1-949410-09-9 (paperback)

Cover Design: Covers by Combs
Edited by: Colleen Vanderlinden

Over the years, I've been blessed with so many good friends
who've supported me and my writing.
This book's for you, Marcy
Thanks for ditching me in California.

ACKNOWLEDGMENTS

I'm grateful to my editor, Colleen Vanderlinden for her expertise, humor, and encouragement.

Special thanks to my cover artist, Daqri Combs, for her continuing excellent work on bringing Eleanor to life.

Thank you, RJ Blain, for your patience, advice, and formatting expertise.

My fellow authors are invaluable. Without the back copy advice, cover critiques, word sprints, and penis jokes, this book would not be what it is today.

Cat—you are the one who made this all possible. If you hadn't pushed me to send you the draft of The Cardinal Gate, lo! These many years ago, we wouldn't be here today.

And to all the friends who didn't get a mention on the dedication page: you are, every single one of you, blessed to know me.

Special thanks, as always for Chris. My partner, my love, and my first and last reader. Without your patience, support, enthusiasm, and incredible eye for detail, I couldn't have done this.

Lastly, thank you to my readers. Your continuing interest in Eleanor, Florence, Raj and the whole gang's shenanigans is more inspirational and gratifying than you could ever know.

CHAPTER ONE

I sat up slowly and tried to orient myself. The last thing I remembered was getting in the car just after sunset to drive west. I'd opened the gate in New Orleans, and the weak chains that'd bound me had snapped. Somehow, I'd managed to keep that information to myself. I'd passed out and woken up in Texas. Raj had been absent, but the others had been there. We needed to go to Bandelier National Monument—and I couldn't remember if I'd told the others where we were headed, or if I'd passed out before I had the chance.

This last gate had taken more out of me than any since the first, probably because of the stupid conspiracy Florence, Raj, and Marie had hatched up between them to bind my dragon with iron ink cut with dragon's blood—my blood, apparently. A wave of annoyance tinged with a hint of low-grade anger washed over me, and I squashed it down. What's done was done, and there was no use being upset.

Instead, I focused on the crick in my neck, the ache in my lower back, and the nausea that came from disorientation and motion sickness. The seatbelt was still strapped firmly across my lap, and I could feel it cutting into my side.

"Where are we?" I croaked.

"Almost to San Antonio," Florence said.

"We're still in Texas?"

"We will always be in Texas," Emma said. "Texas is huge and goes forever, and I hate it here."

I blinked a couple times. She wasn't usually so negative. "What's wrong, Emma?"

"I'm hungry, and Florence won't let me drive."

I cocked my head to one side. I'd obviously missed something because Florence hated driving, and Emma never copped to being hungry. "How long was I asleep this time?"

"Six hours," Florence said. Her voice was as serene as always.

"Why aren't you letting Emma drive?" I couldn't shake the grogginess. I'd done nothing but sleep for the past few days and would've liked to stay awake for more than a couple hours at a time.

"She speeds."

"There aren't any cops," Emma pointed out.

"There might be. Texas is different. There's power here. There are other cars on the road. There might be cops."

"I don't see any other cars," Emma groused.

"It's one-thirty in the morning," Florence said. "There was quite a bit of traffic earlier."

"You drive like an old woman."

"I am an old woman."

"Stop!" I said. "Both of you. Oh my god. Maybe it's time to take a short break. Get out, stretch our legs." My stomach growled. "Grab a bite to eat while we're not moving."

"That would be wonderful," Emma said. "Florence won't let me eat in the car."

"Seriously, Florence? Do you want a starving werewolf riding shotgun?"

"She gets carsick when she eats while we're moving."

I shook my head. "How far to San Antonio?"

"Less than ten miles," Florence replied.

A few minutes later I saw a glow light up the horizon. It'd been so long since I'd seen a city glow at night that it took me a moment to figure out what I was looking at. "They have electricity," I said. San Antonio wasn't lit up the way you'd expect a modern city to be, but it wasn't a skyline of dark, abandoned-looking high-rises like we'd seen the last few months, either. Wouldn't it be funny if Texas became the bastion of civilization?

"Florence just said that, duh," Emma said. She was in a fantastic mood.

"Do they have fast food?" I was feeling an excited tingle in the pit of my stomach. I would cheerfully eviscerate someone for a Crunchwrap Supreme.

"Probably not at this time of night," Florence said. "We'll be better off looking for an all-night diner at a truck stop."

"Don't you know about fourth meal?" I asked. My mouth started watering. I was going to get some Taco Bell. I did a little shimmy of excitement.

"I'm sure we won't be able to find one easily," Florence said. A sign appeared in the headlights advertising the food options at the next exit. Taco Bell was the first one listed. "Damnit," she muttered.

"Yay!"

Florence sighed, hit the blinker, and exited the freeway.

There was an open Starbucks next to the Taco Bell, and I screamed, "Hazelnut latte!"

I'd fallen a long way when I got this excited about a Starbucks. Ohhh...maybe if there was a Starbucks, there'd be other, better coffee shops around. I wondered how they were getting the supplies they needed to keep things going but decided that for some things—coffee beans being one of them—there must be shipments coming in from Mexico and Central America.

"Where would you like to go first?" Florence asked, interrupting my coffee-flavored reverie. "Taco Bell," I said after giving it some serious thought.

There was a "cash only" sign in the window, but other than that, it was exactly like every Taco Bell I'd ever been in. I bought a Crunchwrap Supreme, two burritos, and an order of nachos, then stood aside so Florence and Emma could order.

"Where you from?" the cashier drawled. "You look like you've been travelin'."

"New Orleans," I replied.

"What's been going on there, then? We're not gettin' a whole lotta news from outside Texas."

I thought back to what the President had said and not said regarding current events. I didn't want to give away any secrets, especially not secrets that would mark me as other. "Lots of unrest. No power. Martial law."

"That why you left?"

"It seemed time to move on." I was getting impatient; I wanted my damn food. This might be a good time to get some information since we hadn't seen a news broadcast in three months, I reminded myself.

"What's going on here?"

"You know what the President said," he stated. There was no room to believe that I wouldn't. "We're mostly tryin' to prepare in case we lose power, too, but I don't think we will. If we see any of those supernatural freaks, we'll take them down before they can mess us up, too."

"Have you seen any supernatural…uh…freaks around?" I didn't have to work too hard to sound nervous. "I wouldn't want to run into anything strange."

"Nah. Maybe they know to get out while the gettin's good. Everyone is armed with silver now. No freaks are going to take us on."

Our order was finally up, and I turned to go. "I appreciate the news," I called over my shoulder.

After picking up a coffee order, Florence found us a hotel and rented two adjoining suites. Petrina showed up as soon as we were settling in and stayed just long enough to exchange a couple sentences with Florence before taking off again.

Emma devoured her fourth meal, then she and Florence, hatchet buried over their mutual disdain for my dinner choice, retreated to the other room, leaving their barely touched coffee drinks.

I finished their coffees—leaving that much caffeine abandoned violated one of the major tenets of my religion—then got in the shower. All this hot water was spoiling me.

After I was clean, full, and caffeinated up, I climbed into bed. Only then did I allow myself to think about Raj. No one had mentioned him since I'd woken up. If something had happened to him, I was almost positive that someone would've told me, but I was starting to bounce back and forth between worried, disappointed, and angry. How was I supposed to work through my feelings about his pseudo-betrayal if he wouldn't show up to continue begging for forgiveness?

I didn't realize how worked up I was getting until I noticed the bedspread was smoking. "Damnit!" I yelled. I whipped it off the bed, dragged it into the tub, and turned the shower on. Apparently, weeks of no magic and a huge power surge had eroded my carefully fought for control.

I looked at the clock next to the bed. Seven. The sun would be up soon—the eastern sky was already lighter. I wouldn't get my answers from Raj today, if he even intended to give me any. I crawled back into bed and tried to slow my breath and my mind. I shouldn't be tired after all the sleeping I'd done, but I felt my eyelids drooping almost immediately.

I WOKE to the smell of food and hot coffee. I opened one eye and then the other, squinting through the sleep haze that still blurred my vision. Right there, in the middle of the chest of drawers, was a tray replete with pancakes, bacon, three kinds of syrup, bowls of butter, fruit, and whipped cream, and the largest carafe of coffee I'd ever seen next to a pitcher of cream.

"Florence?" I called, my voice throbbing with reverence. "Did you do this?"

"Yes. I hope you enjoy your breakfast."

"You are a goddess."

"I know," she said.

"This is the best day ever!"

"Better than your mating day?" Emma asked. There wasn't as much acid dripping from her tongue as there would've been if she'd asked the question six weeks ago, but I didn't think she was entirely kidding.

"Have you ever been through a mating ceremony?" I asked. I was being a little mean, because I knew the answer was no, due to her kidnapping and me being mated to the wolf she thought she'd end up with.

"No," she said, walking into the room holding a chocolate croissant. My eyes locked with her pastry and my mouth filled with saliva.

"My eyes are up here," Emma said, shaking her croissant at me.

"Until you can compare fluffy pancakes and hot, delicious coffee to the tedium of a ceremony that ended up with everyone naked but me, I'm not interested in what you think. Isaac would totally agree with me here."

"I had one of those," she pointed at the pancake that was rapidly disappearing into my gaping maw. "It wasn't very good."

I gasped dramatically. "Bite your tongue, Emma Melinda Wolfenstein!"

She tilted her head and squinted at me. "That's not my name."

"Way to ruin it for me. It occurred to me that I don't actually know your full name, so, until you told me differently, it could've been."

"It's Emmaline Petrova. I don't have a middle name."

"Well then, Emmaline Petrova, bite your tongue. This breakfast is fantastic."

She shook her head at me, not willing to concede, but not interested in pursuing it further.

I finished my pancakes and bacon, then leaned back with a second cup of coffee to rub my warm and happy belly. Life was good. "I am so happy right now. This was almost as good as the middle of the night Taco Bell."

Emma, who'd been watching me eat with something akin to horrified fascination, made a sound I couldn't identify. It was halfway between a cough and a laugh with a slight detour to hysteria-town. I grinned at her, "Anything wrong?"

She shook her head. "I don't understand you."

"I don't have a lot of small pleasures right now, but food is one of them. I can eat and forget that Isaac's gone, that I don't know what the next three months are going to bring, that the cashier at Taco Bell last night would cheerfully shoot each of us if he knew what we were, and that Raj is missing."

"Raj isn't missing," Emma said. "He's just not here right now."

"Emma, that's what missing is. He's not here, and I don't know where he is."

"No one knows where he is," she said.

"If you're trying to comfort me, you're going about it in a very strange fashion."

"He'll come back. He has to, right? That was the whole point with the sword?"

I sighed noisily and refused to acknowledge her pun. "Yes. He has to come back. But that's not the point. The *point* is I'd mostly forgiven him for New Orleans. Mostly. I'm still not pleased, but I'm not as angry as I was. And then as soon as I made that concession, poof! He fucking disappears. I don't want to sound like some overdramatic Twitter girl, but I cannot keep a man!"

Emma started laughing. "I don't know what Twitter is, but you are being completely illogical, and that's not like you at all. It's only been a few days since you opened the last gate and even less time than that since you woke up. Raj might have been your near-constant companion for the last few months, but that doesn't mean he doesn't have other interests and responsibilities. He owes allegiance to the Queen of New Orleans, has children scattered all over the world, and a large territory he's responsible for in the Pacific Northwest. Maybe he had to do something for Marie, or check on the kids, or take care of some business. The world doesn't revolve around you, no matter how much it seems to at times."

Her words hit me like a punch in the gut. She was right. I fucking hated it when she was right. "Argh!"

"What was that?" Emma asked.

I had no choice but to admit it. "You're right. Of course you're right. I don't have to like it, but you didn't say anything that wasn't true."

She reached over and patted my head like I was a good puppy. "Your life will be much easier if you always assume that I'm right and you're wrong."

I bared my teeth at her in a mock growl, and she laughed. The lightness lasted only a moment before I sunk back into my melancholy. "Emma, I don't know what to do."

"About what?"

"Raj. Isaac. Everything. Maybe I should become a nun."

"Are you Catholic?" Emma asked.

"Not in the least, but I don't know any other official ways to renounce the company of men."

"You could try not being a whore," Emma said primly.

I flipped her off, and she laughed again.

"Eleanor," she said. "I didn't see you with Isaac, but I've seen you with Raj. You guys are great together. I don't get it, but there's definitely something there."

"Of course there's something there," I scoffed. "He's an incorrigible flirt capable of sending all his perverted thoughts to me."

"He never did that to me," Emma pointed out. "He's not just chasing anything in a skirt. It's you he's after. I've seen the way he looks at you when you're not looking at him. He adores you."

"Pfffttttttt." I was eloquent today.

"We aren't friends. Well, maybe a little bit now," Emma conceded. "You know I think—thought—that you were betraying Isaac. And I'll be honest; it's in my best interest for you to break your bond with Isaac and stay with Raj. You might not believe it, but what Isaac and I had was real, too. I loved…no, I *love* him. I don't know if I would've been enough for him if we'd been able to stay together, but you're teaching me how to be enough for him now. I'm stronger because I've watched you be strong, and I think that if I can stop being so scared, I'll be able to be the kind of strong woman Isaac wants. The kind of strong woman he deserves. I want that chance with him, and you choosing Raj gives me that chance."

My mouth hung open. I hadn't been prepared for this level of honesty. It made sense, from a twisted perspective. There was one thing she'd said that really bothered me, though.

"Emma, you are already strong enough. You've been free for about three months, and you can handle yourself alone at a full moon, something Isaac couldn't do. You're fast and smart and sassy as fuck, and the more you learn to let go of your outdated opinions about sex and a lady's place in the world, the more awesome you're going to be. Isaac would be lucky to be chosen by you. I'm just not sure I'm ready to let him go. We are bound."

"Maybe he won't choose you again," Emma said. I could hear the hope in her voice, and I didn't know how to respond. I couldn't lie and say of course he'd choose me. I couldn't lie and say that he'd choose her. All I could do is look at her in mute sympathy, my heart aching in my chest, and try to smile.

SHORTLY AFTER DUSK, Petrina showed up, and we loaded the car. We camped the next day in Fort Stockton, deprived of the little luxuries like coffee shops and fast food joints, then made our way slowly west and north. We stopped in El Paso where I was able to get pizza and some good beer, then drove to Santa Fe. It was the last day of March. Seven days since I'd opened the previous gate, and eight nights since I'd seen Raj. Not that I was counting.

When we crossed the border into New Mexico, we also crossed the border of the Texas power grid. Although there wasn't power, some things were still working here as we were about as far away from a gate pulse as was possible in the continental US.

We found a hotel in Santa Fe. We were still a couple hours away from Bandelier National Monument, the site of the penultimate gate, but this was as good a place as any to set up shop. I had exactly one month before opening the seventh gate. There was one more after this one, but it was starting to feel like I was approaching the end of the quest. I looked at the women who were sharing this journey with me and reflected that they were ever so much more reliable than the men

I'd started with, or even the one that had wormed his way into my life halfway through.

As dawn approached, I sat alone in my motel room and thought about why I was alone. Petrina was preparing for her day sleep somewhere else. Florence and Emma were sharing a suite. When I started this journey, Isaac, Finn and I had always shared space. Florence didn't share unless it was necessary because Isaac and I were so new in our relationship and had trouble keeping our hands off each other. By the time Isaac left and Emma joined us, it had become habit. Also, there was some cuddling with Raj. Maybe a little making out, but not so much that we needed our own space. And now I was alone.

I'd never been the kind of woman who believed a relationship with a man would make me whole. I liked men, sure, but I'd never had any long-term romances, and I'd always been okay with that. So why now, after a few months of being with Isaac, and even less time with Raj, was I so fucking lonely? I didn't need to be held while I slept. I was not a cuddler. I was Eleanor Jane Morgan—*Ciara nic Mata*—and I would survive. Gloria Gaynor played through my head and resolve snuck in and straightened my spine.

I stood up and pointed at myself in the mirror. "Eleanor Jane Morgan, you are thirty-five years old, you are Fae, you are a motherfucking dragon who doesn't need anyone to keep you going, and you are going to get this done." I stripped off my shirt and bra and concentrated on my dragon wings, holding the idea of them in my head until they were free of their metaphysical bindings and pushed through my skin. They were gorgeous and didn't match the idea of what I would've guessed wings sprouting from my humanoid form would look like. If you'd asked, I would've gone with either the angel-variety of fluffy gold-tipped feathers or the shimmering dragon-fly wings I'd seen on story-book fairies. These were an almost-black purple membrane stretched over delicate bones that ended in claws. They were more reminiscent of batwings than butterfly. I moved them delicately and was rewarded with a large burst of air.

I was Eleanor nee Ciara, Dragon Queen of the Dark Sidhe, and I was here to get shit done.

AT DUSK, Emma, Florence, and I were ready for our field trip to Bandelier. I filled up the car with the gasoline we'd been toting for months. We'd refilled every can while driving across Texas and should be set for a while, no matter how much driving we had to do.

I got behind the wheel of the car and impatiently drummed my fingers on the steering wheel until Petrina graced us with her presence. We headed north out of town, but before too long our route headed west and then, once we passed the turnoff to Los Alamos, started zig-zagging south. I was so glad I was driving. There were few things I liked less than being a passenger on a dark and winding road.

It was nearly nine o'clock when I pulled into the deserted parking lot. The posted sign said the park closed at dusk, and it was well past that, but it didn't look like anyone had been there for a while. I hoped it was because of the weirdness of the last few months and not because a bunch of people had been blown up by surprise landmines.

We got out of the car and climbed over the entrance-blocking gate. "Florence, can you see okay, or should we get a flashlight?"

"I can't see much of anything, but won't a flashlight ruin everyone else's night vision?"

"I have a plan," I said. "Emma and Florence, you guys stay here while Petrina and I investigate."

"I can see fine in the dark," Emma said. "Probably better than anyone here."

"Even in human form?" I asked.

"Even so."

Interesting. "Next time, it'll be you," I promised. "But we're operating under the buddy system here, and you and Florence are buddies now. Back over the fence with you."

"I wish you'd come up with this plan before I climbed over the fence," Florence griped. "As Emma so aptly pointed out the other night, I am not a spring chicken."

"I wish she'd come up with this plan before we left the hotel," Emma said. "That drive was not my idea of a good time."

"Shut it, both of you," I said. I didn't think Emma knew my bindings were gone, and with Finn probably lurking about, it needed to stay like that.

"Petrina, could you grow back a leg if you lost it to a landmine?" I asked. I wasn't sure how far the regenerative powers of the vampires went.

She stopped and looked around carefully before answering. "Possibly. I've never lost a limb before. It would be excruciating and take a long time, though. I'd rather not experiment with it. Are they close?"

"I don't think so. I wonder if I would grow back a limb." I pondered for a while and then gave it up as a 'let's hope we never find out' question. "Maybe we should all head back. This is definitely the gate site, and Finn is likely in the area. I'd rather not go in if we don't have to until we know for sure what we're dealing with."

"And this couldn't have been a daytime trip?" Emma groused. "Or a trip that didn't involve me at all?"

I heaved a sigh. "I'm sorry, you guys. I made a mistake."

"Well, it wasn't the first one, and it won't be the last," Emma said pragmatically. I flipped her off, knowing she'd see it, even in the dark.

CHAPTER TWO

I escaped the hotel early the next morning before talking to anyone else. I wanted to scope out the city and get a feel for the land on my own, and I knew if I waited to discuss my plans with anyone else, I'd end up with Florence and Emma serving as unofficial bodyguards. Honestly, the nicest thing about currently being without male company was that my female companions were slightly less likely to overreact when I wandered off alone.

"Eleanor!" Florence yelled.

I winced.

Slightly less.

I turned around. Florence was standing two blocks behind me, arms akimbo, and although it was too far away to know for certain, I suspected that she was glaring. I sighed. At this point, I had two choices. The first was to go back, discuss my plans with Florence like a mature and rational adult, and accept whatever escort she thought necessary.

The second was to run away as fast as possible and hope that I lost her in the streets of Santa Fe.

I waved at Florence and started walking towards her. Halfway up the first block was a long, shadowed alleyway that led to who-knows-where. I darted into the alley, sprinted to the other end, took a right and ran until I saw another alley, ran through that, and continued until I was gasping for air and my thighs were burning with the effort. I slowed to a walk and tried to regulate my breathing. I looked around me and realized I was completely and totally lost. This city seemed to have a hatred of straight lines and nice, easy-to-follow street grids. I was at a triangular intersection. The street sign said I was standing on the corner of Cathedral Place and East Alameda Street. I walked north up Cathedral Place and took a sharp left towards the smaller of the two churches I could see.

Signs announced that I was gazing at Loretto Chapel and that it was open. I ducked inside to catch my breath and give Florence even longer to lose my trail. It was a beautiful little church with high arched ceilings, creepy Catholic sculptures, and gorgeous stained-glass windows. The weirdest thing, though, was the free-standing spiral staircase. I tilted my head to one side trying to determine how it stayed up and if it was just decorative or an actual method to get to the choir loft.

"You can walk on it if you want."

I jumped and ended up at least a foot away from where I'd started. The priest who'd spoken was trying unsuccessfully to stifle his laughter. I hated being laughed at, but I couldn't sense any malice coming from him. I stuffed down my hurt feelings and asked, "How do they stay up?"

He folded his hands and glanced upwards with an expression of piety. "God's will, of course."

"Seriously, though."

"You are not a believer?"

"Even if I was a Christian, I don't think that would preclude me from also believing in physics," I countered.

He smiled at me. "The way the stairs were built puts the pressure on the stair beneath in such a way that the entire staircase is held up by the pressure placed on the bottom stair."

"That doesn't sound stable."

"It's been there without incident since the late nineteenth century; I think it'll stand a little longer."

I looked around. "This isn't a real church anymore, is it?"

"No. It's a museum and wedding chapel now."

"And a gift shop?" I nodded towards the entryway behind us. After you paid the admission fee—although there'd been no one for me to pay today—you could enter the chapel or the gift shop. "Gotta sell your souvenirs to bring more people to the fold?"

"You are very cynical," he observed.

I shook my head. "I believe in a great many things that I've not seen with my own eyes. I'm even willing to concede that there may be divine beings out there worthy of worship. I just don't have a lot of faith that any church or organized religion has any relationship to a higher power. Most seem more intent on lining their pockets than fulfilling the tenets of their faith."

He laughed again, and this time, my hackles rose with his amusement. I cocked my head to one side and considered him. His glamour was fantastic, but when he laughed, it wavered a bit. Heat caressed my body, and the priest shook his finger at me.

"Don't try to look deeper, little girl. It will not go well with you."

Flames shot out from his body so quickly that all I could see were flashes of green light for several seconds as my eyes adjusted. "What are you?"

"I'm Father Clement," he said.

"I didn't ask for your name. I want to know what you are."

He smiled, winked, and walked away. Right before he disappeared from view, he dropped his glamor for a moment, and a vision of flaming feathers filled my eyes.

Holy fuck. I'd just seen a phoenix. I shook my head to clear my vision. I wondered if he knew who and what I was and didn't care. Was he really a priest? Or was he spying on me?

I made a mental note to discuss this with the others later that evening, knowing that bringing it up would further encourage

Florence to scold me for running off alone, but something about him seemed significant. I was sure that he'd sought me out. This chapel wasn't active and wouldn't have a priest assigned to it. Nor was it being used today. Tourism wasn't a big deal in mid-apocalyptic America.

After a last look around, I wandered back out into the street to begin my exploration of the city in earnest.

I walked down every side street and back alley I came across. Should something happen and I found myself running from someone with more ill intent than Florence, I didn't want to find myself in an alley with no exit and no choice but to fight or fly. I hated that we were still keeping my recovery on the down-low, even if I more or less understood the reasoning behind it.

When I'd committed as much of the city as I cared to to memory and mapped out every park within running distance of my hotel, I found a local brewery that was still open. They were doing all their cooking over large grills, and according to the bartender, the beer on tap was from one of the last kegs they had on reserve. They weren't doing much business anymore, so he expected to be able to stay open a couple more months—long enough that he could figure out next steps at a more leisurely pace.

I paid in cash, even though we both acknowledged that it was probably useless unless the new government agreed to back the cash system the way the old one had. At this point, how that'd be handled was anyone's guess.

After I left the Blue Corn Brewery, I meandered through dusks' lengthening shadows back to my hotel. Florence was waiting for me in the hotel bar, nursing a glass of whiskey and a sour expression.

"Hey, Florence," I said, trying for casual and achieving tentative instead.

"Did you have a good day?" she asked.

"It was interesting. I met someone."

"Another man?" Emma said from behind me. She wasn't even trying to be snarky anymore. I thought about pouring one out for the loss of our enmity, but decided against it, especially since I hadn't ordered yet.

"Possibly," I said. "He looked like a man."

The bartender had gotten closer during our brief exchange, and the glass he was holding was getting an extremely vigorous polish.

"Maybe it's a conversation for the hotel room once Petrina shows up," Florence suggested. She'd noticed the bartender, too.

"I'm here," Petrina said. She looked at the bartender. "I'd like a glass of your house red, please."

"Shirley Temple," Emma said when he looked at her.

"Seriously?" I asked.

She shrugged. "I really don't think you get to judge my choice of beverages."

"Fair enough." I turned to the bartender. "Hendricks martini. Dry with a twist."

He nodded and got to work.

Drinks in hand, we retired to a table in the back corner, far away from the nosy bartender, and I told them about Father Clement.

"A phoenix? Are you sure?" Florence asked.

"You must be mistaken," Petrina added. "They're extinct."

"I've never seen one before," I conceded, "and his glamour was amazing. But he was hot, and when he shed his glamour for me, his back was covered with burning red and orange feathers."

"Do you think it was happenstance that you encountered him or something deliberate on his part?" Petrina asked.

"Deliberate. Although I don't know why. We talked about the chapel and how organized religion is a crock of shit, and then he laughed at me, and I felt it. Something old and unworldly, and that's when I tried to see who he really was. Whatever and whoever he is, he's old, he's powerful, and he's interested in us."

Petrina drummed the fingers of her left hand on the table while taking a sip of her wine. "We should find out more about this priest. I don't want him meddling in our affairs."

Heh. English history joke. I cracked a grin and looked around. No one else looked amused. Guess there weren't a lot of Becket fans around. Whatever. "Wanna do some recon, Petrina? You're probably the sneakiest of us all."

"Father would be better," she noted.

"Yeah, well he's not here right now," I pointed out. I wasn't able to keep the bitterness from my voice, and I winced at how angry and hurt I sounded.

"He'll be back soon," Petrina said.

I couldn't say anything nice, so I decided not to say anything at all.

She offered me a half smile and said, "I will start 'sneaking.' Can you give me a physical description of his human form?"

I closed my eyes and went into my total recall headspace. "He was a few inches taller than me. Probably about five-foot-six. He had white hair and eyebrows, but his face was completely unlined. His skin was dark. Not as dark as Raj or Isaac, but reminiscent of someone from Turkey or Jordan. He had a long, straight nose with a hint of bulbousness at the end. His eyes were..." I trailed off. I couldn't remember what color his eyes were. That was weird. Every time I tried to focus on the color of his eyes, his entire face went out of focus in my mind's eye. I shook my head and continued. "He had high cheekbones and a full mouth with a bitable lower lip."

Petrina laughed. "I'll look for Middle Eastern men with sexy lower lips, then, shall I?"

I rolled my eyes at her. "I don't know why I can't remember what color his eyes were. Logic dictates that they be brown—it would match his coloring—but that doesn't seem right."

"You gave a good description," Petrina said. "When I find him, I'll make a special point of finding out his eye color so it won't drive you crazy."

I beamed at her. "Thank you. I would appreciate that."

She finished her wine and walked out of the bar. I took a sip of my martini and looked at the others. "If I promise not to leave the hotel grounds or get into trouble, can I go for a walk?"

"You don't need my permission," Florence said.

"Noted. I'll throw that back in your face every time you bitch about me wandering off on my own."

"It is, however, polite to at least inform people when and where you're going," she continued.

"Fine. I'll leave a note next time." I threw back the rest of my martini, gasped in pleasure at the burn of the gin as it warmed my stomach, and stood up. "I'll be back later."

I WANDERED out of the hotel and into the wild gardens that began almost immediately behind. The landscape was alien and beautiful. Cacti mixed with flower blossoms that were almost too brilliant to be realistic and silvery bushes dotted the in-between spaces. It reminded me a little of the Badlands I'd fallen so in love with in South Dakota, but instead of the starkness of death, this was almost too exuberantly vibrant; like it was trying too hard to make me believe that it was alive.

The early evening air smelled like perfume and ozone and the barest hint of rain. I walked over to one of the larger trees at the edge of the garden wall, sank cross-legged to the earth, and closed my eyes. I formed the picture of Arduinna in my mind and called to her. I hadn't spoken with her since before I'd opened the gate in New Orleans, and I wanted to make sure the Fae she'd sent had made it out alive and that everything was settled there. No more wars on my behalf. At least—I corrected myself—no more wars on my behalf that pitted ally against ally.

I don't know how long I waited, but I was drifting off by the time Arduinna interrupted my meditation.

"Eleanor," she said.

I looked her over. She was wearing a business suit—the first time I'd ever seen her dressed in that fashion—and it was ill-fitting.

"Did you come from a political meeting, Seth?" I asked.

She glanced down at herself, and a rueful smile ghosted across her face. "There are times I'm very easy to read, aren't there?"

"Only when you want to be," I replied. Arduinna never did anything without purpose—at least not as far as I could tell.

"What can I do for you, Your Highness?"

"I want updates. What's going on in the big world? What happened in New Orleans? How's this new government thing shaping up? And anything else you think I should know."

I thought about my last statement and then amended it. "Anything else you know I'd want to know."

"You are getting better at playing the game," Arduinna said.

I clutched my hands to my chest. "A compliment? Maybe the world really is coming to an end."

Arduinna laughed, but the look in her eyes didn't signal amusement. I wasn't good at reading expressions, particularly not those of the Fae, but it looked more like pain or sadness than amusement. It was gone so quickly; I thought I might be imagining things. I knew that regardless, Arduinna wasn't likely to share her inner turmoil. At least not right now.

"So?" I prodded. "Give me the deets. What's the sitch?"

"I don't think those words make any sense, particularly not with that inflection. Please don't use that kind of slang. It's hard to understand and makes you sound ridiculous."

I smiled at her. I did so like tweaking her. She was always so formal and proper. "Fine, Arduinna. Please tell me what's going on. Can you start with New Orleans and work your way bigger?"

Arduinna gestured towards a couple adobe benches that matched the architecture of the hotel. "May we sit? It's been a very long day, and I've been standing for all of it."

"Of course." I led the way over to the benches and settled myself. As per usual, the benches were just high enough that my feet didn't quite touch the ground, which meant that I'd either have to reconcile myself to numbness below my thighs, leaning inelegantly and uncomfortably, or sitting cross-legged on the bench like a child. I opted for a crisscross applesauce position, leaned back against the wall that jutted up behind me like living stone, and waited for her to start talking.

"You know what happened in New Orleans. You were there."

I rolled my eyes at her. "I was in one very small part of New Orleans, very much focused on the gate opening, and then shortly thereafter, passed out. You had agents on the ground, not to mention the whole Fae army that was—how did you get them here again? I'm beginning to think these gates didn't really need to be opened."

It was true. There were more and more Fae showing up all the time. Fae living everywhere, in all parts of government, and apparently entire armies. I started to get a nagging sensation in the pit of my stomach that I'd been had. If entire armies could get through the barrier separating the plane, why did the gates need to be opened, and what would happen when they were?

"You've known that there are places, carefully guarded, that allow free, if not easy, passage."

I found myself nodding. That was nothing but truth. I could hear it in her voice. Wait a minute. Every time she explained things, a lethargy preventing me from asking further questions settled over me.

"But the sheer numbers of Fae I've seen in the past months hint at more than a few carefully guarded passages," I said, struggling to stay on point. "There's something you're not telling me. Something big. Something I need to know."

"Carefully guarded doesn't mean small, and your father will spare no expense when it comes to keeping you safe, even if it means sending more people through a passage than the gateway can handle, causing it to collapse and become unusable."

I nodded again, and this time couldn't fight the haze that made my questions seem unimportant. I tried to find my train of thought, but it had left the station without me.

I stared blankly at Arduinna for a moment until she helped me out. "You were asking about the fate of your honor guard?"

"Oh yes, thank you! I'm still hazy from the post gate magic influx, I think. I completely lost the thread of the conversation. Did everyone make it out okay?"

"They did. There were no injuries to speak of, and they stand ready to defend you again at your word."

"I'd really rather not have them again, but I don't want to make that call yet. I'm not sure what waits for me at the next gate site."

"It is your call, Highness," Arduinna said, inclining her head.

"And the rest of New Orleans? No more fighting between my Fae and vampire allies?"

"Are they truly your allies?"

"At least as much as you are," I replied.

"And do you trust them?"

"As much as I trust you."

She grinned, showing a line of green-tinged teeth. "Maybe you aren't such a disastrous heir after all."

"So many compliments today! This unprecedented rain of praise might make me start to feel cocky!"

"Was there anything else?"

"Yes. I'm interested in how the government building is going. I know you said there were regional governors elected from the state governors, who form a type of parliament that works with President Murphy. Is that still the case?"

"It is, for the most part. Texas is refusing to have anything to do with their assigned region, saying they're big enough that they deserve their own seat at the table, and since they're the only ones with a functioning grid at this point, they're getting their way more than they ought to.

"California—at least the coastal regions—seceded. Alaska and Hawaii still have power and have been able to communicate via satellite phone, but I wouldn't be surprised if they end up completely left out of this new nation building. The major news of the day is the civil unrest. People are forming militias and taking up arms in an attempt to repel what they see as 'other'—in other words, us."

Since this wasn't much different than what I'd expected, I simply nodded at her to go on.

"General Mircea is working to consolidate the military's power and ensure that the local militias don't get out of hand."

"How's he doing that?"

Arduinna smiled—a broad, terrifying smile—and answered, "A

combination of threats and intimidation, coercion, and attrition in the militia ranks."

"And by attrition, you mean?" I asked.

"Those who are seen to be the most hostile, organized, hot-headed, and generally responsible for the increase in activity have been meeting with a series of rather unfortunate accidents should they prove to be immune to intimidation or coercion."

I was pretty sure that's what she'd meant. Mircea—or his delegates —were killing off the opposition, both in the regular armed forces and the start-up militias. I wasn't sure how I felt about that. I'd never been super pro-second amendment, but I'd never been solidly against it, either. I was almost certain that this was the exact type of situation the second amendment had been written for, though. I shook it off. Not having armed militias roaming the countryside trying to kill me was definitely a plus.

"Anything else?"

"The changes are not settling as quickly as Murphy'd anticipated. Despite having lived here for decades, the obstinance of humans to fall in line with what's best for them is surprising to her."

"And to you?"

"I've met you, and although you are not human, you were raised as one and until recently mostly thought like one. Your stubbornness in the face of truth was a...I think the term is 'eye-opener,' is it not?"

"I'm glad I could help form your expectations." I took a deep breath and forced my next question. "Any news of Isaac? Or Finn?" I tagged on the last as an afterthought, hoping it would signal that I was equally interested in the fate of both.

"I've not heard anything new of your werewolf lover recently. He is in the Dark Queen's domain, and few of the light go there willingly.

"Finn once again eluded capture," Arduinna said, her face twisting into a grimace. "That half-breed is slipperier than a salamander and twice as useless. Are you expecting him?"

"I'm always expecting him. He's like the proverbial bad penny."

"So nice to hear you're looking forward to seeing me," Finn said from behind me. I'd seen Arduinna's eyes widen slightly before he spoke, so I didn't jump as much as I might've otherwise. He was a sneaky bastard.

"Speak of the devil," I said, then was forced to correct myself, "or possibly his less popular and much less attractive third cousin."

"Aww, didn't you miss me, Ellie?"

"Like I miss bad coffee." My scathing retorts needed work.

"What are you doing here, Finnegan?" Arduinna asked.

"Just checking in on our girl, here."

"You have no right…"

"I have every right," Finn interrupted. "I was hired by her father to keep an eye on her, and as yet, he hasn't relieved me of that charge."

"You haven't shown up to report in a while," Arduinna said. "I suggest you go see Eochaid so you can keep up your end of the job."

"Since you're here, I'm sure you can carry my report by proxy," Finn countered. I'd moved a bit while they were bantering so that I could see them both at the same time. It was like watching a politely vicious tennis match.

Arduinna looked up at me. "Highness, if you require nothing else?"

"You may go," I said. "Although you'll owe me a favor for leaving me here with…him." I gestured in the general direction of Finn.

Arduinna looked at him. "Finnegan."

"Seth." The tension in the air grew even thicker. "What? Didn't Ellie know about your alter ego?"

"She knows."

"Then what's the problem?"

"I have so many problems with you, I don't know where to begin. Instead of listing them alphabetically, chronologically, or categorically, I will say farewell and leave you to the gentle ministrations of Her Highness."

"She can't hurt me. She's bound," Finn asserted.

"Of course," Arduinna said. "Nice ear."

Finn's hand rose unconsciously to the ear I'd docked in St. Louis, and a flush suffused him.

"Walk with me a moment, please?" Arduinna asked me.

I joined her, and we strolled down the street, away from the trees she'd come through originally. "What do you want, Arduinna?"

"Don't trust him."

I gave her major side-eyes. "That ship sailed a while ago," I said.

"I know you don't trust him in the way most people would mean," she clarified, "but don't trust that your knowledge of his treachery is accurate, either. Don't expect him to be who he's shown himself to be."

"Your clarity leaves something to be desired," I said.

Arduinna smirked, executed a graceful half-bow, then turned and walked back into the trees, dissolving from sight.

FINN WAS WAITING in the garden when I returned to the hotel. "Have a nice chat?" he asked. "You ladies are always talking about men when they're not around."

I stared at him in astonishment. *Oh my god. He really thought that, didn't he?* "As a matter of fact, this time we were talking about you. In fact, most of our conversation was about various men—although none of it had any romantic bent."

"Not even your inquiry about Isaac?"

"Let it go, Finn."

"I guess he wasn't the strong one, after all, was he?" The smug look on his face nearly did me in. I'd had a lot of negative feelings about Finn over the last few months. I'd threatened him. I'd cut off the tip of one ear and a couple fingertips. I'd named my sword "elf-stabber" in his honor. But this, this was the first time that I really, really wanted to punch him in his smug, stupid face. I could feel the rage coursing through me and knew if I didn't get a handle on it soon, I'd start smoldering, and then my whole façade of helpless binding would go up in —wait for it—smoke.

I snorted at my internal monologue pun, and that's all it took to dissipate the building anger and take a step back from the situation.

"Still can't shift, can you?" he taunted. "I guess the tattoo artist the

Voodoo Queen found was better than the late, not-so-great Harvey Dennehy after all. Maybe I should've kept one of them alive, though, just in case."

"You killed them?"

"Me? Oh, no. I have subcontractors for wet work."

"But they're dead?" I wasn't letting him word-wiggle out of this one.

"Very much so."

"Are you sure? Last time you reported a death, you were wrong."

Anger darkened his face and his fists clenched. I knew that he was using every ounce of self-control he had not to punch me, and the thought that I angered him as much as he angered me was almost as satisfying as the fact that he thought I was still bound.

"If I could shift, don't you think I'd be making your world a little hotter right now?" I asked. "Or at the very least, flying as fast as possible away from your unwanted presence?"

"You wouldn't, not in the open like this. You wouldn't want any of Medb's spies to tell her you could shift into a dragon. That's definitely a fact that would enrage the Dark Queen."

"You expect me to believe she doesn't already know? You've been her lapdog for years, Finn, and you think I'll believe you didn't tell her the minute you found out?"

"If Medb knows your alternate form, she didn't learn that fact from me. You'd already be dead, and that's not in my best interest."

"What are you talking about? What has all this been—" I waved my arms, gesticulating wildly "—if not a bunch of attempted homicides?"

"Are you dead?" Finn asked, crossing his arms in front of his chest and smirking at me.

"Obviously not, but that's because I'm competent."

"Whatever you need to believe to get through the day. Isn't it more likely that instead of competent, the attempts haven't been sincere? After all, you're thirty-five, and I'm several hundred years old. How does it make sense that you're more competent than I am?"

"You might be older than me, but I have self-preservation on my side, not to mention friends who are infinitely more powerful than you could ever hope to be."

"Friends like your little blonde wolf who's afraid of her own shadow? Or like the wolf who's in a cage now?"

"You kidnapped me and had me bound in Rapid City, and those bonds didn't last because of my friends. You've tried to start shit everywhere I go, and I'm still standing here, because of my friends. I have mages and vampires on my side who were able to stop your stupid sex slave spell from taking hold. And yes, even the wolves are stronger than you. They both lived through more torture than I can even imagine, and they were not broken."

"But you're broken, aren't you? I heard you say that the last gate was almost too hard because of the bonds I manipulated Marie Laveau into placing on you. How are you going to get through two more?"

His smirk was almost out of control now, and the growing sense of glee that he really was underestimating me almost broke through my contemptuous façade.

"Binding doesn't mean breaking," I said. "I'm stronger than you ever anticipated. I'm the catalyst, the worldbreaker, the fucking Dark Queen and I will never break for you."

Finn laughed. "Strong words for someone who doesn't even know what the Dark Throne is."

"I'm done with this conversation, and I'm done with you. I have only one question for you now. How did you know where the gates were before I did? You knew about the gate at Alpha in advance—enough to go there and get a bunch of violent jerks to move into the nature preserve to cause problems for me. And you were waiting for us in New Orleans, making deals with Marie before I got down there."

Finn winked at me, and I wished desperately for my sword so I could dock his other ear. "The location of every gate was in your mind the minute you opened the first one, and we were linked then. I lifted it all out of your mind and erased my tracks. After all, if you don't show up for a gate opening, half my work is done for me."

Sword or no sword, and Florence's warning be damned, I was

going to end this asscandle. I pulled back at the last second, remembering that he didn't know I was packing magical heat again. *Of course, if I kill him, he still won't know,* I thought to myself. In the time it took me to have that brief argument with myself, Finn disappeared. I hated it when he poofed out.

"Damnit," I muttered to myself, staring at the space he'd occupied a moment before.

CHAPTER THREE

I opened the door to the hotel suite. I'd walked around for almost an hour, trying to shed the skin-crawling disgust and stomach-churning anger coursing through me after my encounter with Finn. Florence was talking, and I paused to let her finish before interrupting with what was likely to be upsetting for everyone. Petrina laughed at whatever Florence said, and then I heard him.

"We should wait for Eleanor to return before I get into too much more detail. I don't want to have to repeat myself," Raj said.

My jaw dropped, and my chest tightened in excitement and nervousness, and my forward momentum was completely arrested. I felt a slow, stupid smile spread across my face, and my pulse accelerated. *He was back.*

My smile widened into a grin and forced myself to walk—not run—into the next room. Every last ounce of anger I'd been holding on to dissolved as the worry I didn't know had been overwhelming me disappeared.

"Raj!" I said. He turned towards me, but instead of the open-armed greeting I was expecting, I got a nod before he turned back to the others in the room.

"*Raj?*" I tried again silently. There was no answer. I tried to squelch the hurt that flooded my body, but humiliation and pain heated my cheeks.

"As I was saying," Raj said, "I've spent the last few days with Mircea, getting a general update on the state of the country."

"A general update," I said. "Nice one."

"Nice one what?" Raj asked.

"Nice pun? Because he's a general, so it had to be a general update?"

Emma laughed, Florence and Petrina grinned, but Raj remained impassive. "May I continue?"

My smile faltered. "Of course." I added mentally, *"But if you don't give me a good reason why you're being a dick to me right now, you can continue to stay the fuck out of my life when you're done with your news update."*

His mental voice sounded pained when he replied. *"Eleanor, I really do have important news to share with everyone. I assure you, I am not trying to be a...dick. I am merely trying to do my part to keep the group informed. Now, if you don't mind?"*

I heaved a loud sigh so that everyone in the room would know I was displeased, and answered aloud, "You do what you have to do Raj, but don't be surprised if I do the same."

"I hate it when they do that," Emma said. "At least if they were speaking in a foreign language, I could learn it and eavesdrop."

Werewolf Barbie was fast becoming one of my favorite people.

"Mircea is working with the other military leaders to quell the signs of civil unrest that are starting to pop up all over the country. There are bands of armed militias out there spouting about their Second Amendment right to shoot anything unnatural. Unfortunately, most of their targets are deemed unnatural by virtue of their race or class or sexual identity, and the militias apologize for 'trying to keep good Americans safe from the devil-spawned hell beasts roaming the streets' and hope that no one notices that they haven't managed to kill anything 'unnatural' except by sheer happenstance." Raj sounded bitter and angry, and I wondered for the first time if he'd ever found himself on the wrong side of a bigot or if his vampire nature had cushioned him from that.

"The country is currently operating under a system of six regional councils, each headed by a governor appointed from the states' governors that make up the region. There's a northwest region, consisting of Washington, Idaho, Oregon, Montana, northern California, and nominally Alaska. The southwest region is Arizona, Utah, Colorado, New Mexico, Oklahoma, Nevada, and southeastern California. The upper Plains is North and South Dakota, Minnesota, Iowa, Nebraska, and Kansas. There's a Midwest region that's Wisconsin, Michigan, Illinois, Indiana, Ohio, and Missouri. The southeast region is Arkansas, Louisiana, Alabama, Mississippi, Georgia, and Florida. The eastern seaboard is the rest of the states. They will likely split in two at some point."

"You didn't mention Texas, Hawaii, or most of California," Florence noted.

"Hawaii's been disinherited, more or less. They're too far away to do anyone any good, and we can't get there now, so they're on their own. Alaska is in much the same boat, only it's been less explicit. Texas is claiming they're their own region and don't want to have anything to do with any other states, and most of California has seceded."

"What does that mean for us?" Emma said. "I mean now, and not long-term. I can cross that bridge when we get to it."

Raj grimaced and rubbed his face tiredly. "For now, it means we need to be careful. There are people out there who'd attempt to kill us on sight if they knew who—or what—we were. Some of us are bigger targets than others." He shared a significant glance with Florence. "But even those of you with your lily-white skin can become a target if you're in the wrong place at the wrong time. Mircea urges caution, and I have to back him on this."

"We've already met a couple people who were all-too-eager to share their prejudices," I said. "We'll be cautious. Emma, that means that at the full moon, we need to be well out of the city before you shift. We'll have to find a place."

"Anything else?" Petrina asked. "You smell like sulfur and wood smoke, and that makes me think you've seen him."

"Him who?" Emma asked, nose wrinkled. She must be smelling it, too.

"Vlad," Raj answered. "Yes, I did stop in to see Vlad as well as check in on the staff that had been residing in New York, so I could make arrangements for them to come here and ready my home in case it's needed."

"And how is my dear, mad uncle?" Petrina asked.

"Still mad. He still searches for his lost love, but we had one of the most rational conversations I've had with him in decades."

"Really?" Petrina tilted her head to one side. "About what?"

"About my sire."

There was a long pause. Petrina clearly knew the significance of that as well as I did. From the looks on Florence's and Emma's faces, they did not. *"May I?"* I asked Raj silently. He didn't respond but nodded curtly.

"Raj never knew his sire," I explained. "He was made in secret after being left for dead on a battlefield. The only thing he knew about his sire was that she turned him in an unusual way, giving him strength well beyond that of a new vampire, that she signed her notes with the first initial "S," and that she'd see him again at the end of the world."

"And here we are at the end of the world," Florence said.

"Here we are," Raj agreed. "I'd been thinking of her—or him, it was Eleanor who insisted I use the feminine pronoun since my progenitor remains unknown—often lately. I told Eleanor the story on one of our rendezvous in New York. I confess that I'm nervous to meet the one who gave me this life."

I looked at him. He was being honest. He was nervous—more than nervous.

"If there's nothing else, I'd like to go for now. It was a long journey, especially transporting others, and I am hungry and tired. I will meet you back here at sunset, and we can decide where to go from there."

"I do have one more thing," I said. "I spoke to Arduinna tonight.

Much of what she told me was the Cliffs Notes version of what we've learned from Raj, but Finn showed up at the end of the conversation."

Everyone was immediately on high alert, and Raj's hand dropped to the sword he wasn't currently wearing. Interesting. I would've thought he'd keep it on his person at all times after regaining it.

"Is he still alive?" Florence asked.

"Yes," I tried to keep the disappointment out of my voice, but the knowing grin that briefly ghosted across Raj's face let me know I was unsuccessful. "I was contemplating killing him when he poofed out."

"Did he have anything useful to say, or was it all empty threats and grandstanding?" Florence wondered.

"I actually got some information out of him this time. Both Harvey Dennehy—the Rapid City tattoo artist—and Daniel from New Orleans are dead. The reason he knows where all the gates are is that he lifted that information from my mind when I passed out after the first gate was opened, leaving me with only the ghosts of memories to lead me, and Medb doesn't know I'm a dragon."

"Some information?" Emma asked. "I'd hate to see what would qualify as a lot."

"He was talkative tonight," Raj observed.

"He had to be letting most of that slip deliberately," I said. "He wants me to underestimate him."

"But why? Why not tell Medb?"

"I think he believes he has a shot with me still. I don't understand it. He goes from threats and insults to creepy flirting and gestures he thinks are much nicer and more generous than they are. He's not well."

"That's an understatement," Florence said. "Thank you for not killing him."

"It took a lot of self-control to not use my magic to fuck with him a little. I was working myself up to rationalize that I'd have to kill him to keep my secret."

That earned a grim chuckle from everyone except Raj. "I really must go," he said. He looked exhausted, which made me feel bad for him, but not bad enough to let him off the hook.

"I'll walk you out."

I CAUGHT up with Raj in the lobby of the hotel. He was fast when he wanted to be and didn't care if anyone noticed, but so was I. "Don't walk away from me, Raj. Not this time. Not if you want to come back."

He turned to face me. "I'm tired. I'm hungry. I do not want to fight right now."

"I don't either, but I want to know where you've been and why it took you so long to come back."

"You know where I was."

"Raj, c'mon. You ignored me in there. You knew what I was thinking, and you ignored me. I thought you wanted me to forgive and move on."

"I do. I was giving you time and space."

My jaw dropped. "Seriously? You think going AWOL is going to help? I didn't know if you were ever coming back!"

Raj looked confused. "Of course I was. I told you I had to be at the final gate, and we said we'd hash everything out after New Orleans."

"You could've changed your mind or been killed or who the hell knows! You can't disappear like that."

"Were you worried?" His silky voice wound its way around me, and I countered the seductive effects by taking a very large breath of air.

"That's not the point." I sounded silly, even to my own ears.

"I'm here, and since you're obviously not going to let me eat and rest until you've had your way, let's talk."

I wanted to rail at him, tell him again how the betrayal was not that he'd traded me for a sword, but that he'd made the plan without talking to me. I was tired of the people in my life withholding information from me. I couldn't live like this. Finn had withheld so much about who I was and why he'd shown up in my life. I could've had years to prepare, instead of days. Isaac…I sighed. Between his pigheaded decision to leave me to save Emma without discussing it and all the secrets from his past, I wondered if he'd loved me as much as he'd said, or if the mating ritual was for some other purpose entirely. And now this. I'd been prepared for betrayal, but not for lies.

Raj looked helpless, an emotion I was guessing he didn't often feel. I wasn't sure if he was staying out of my head for once, if I'd finally learned how to block him, or if my racing thoughts were too difficult to follow, but he hadn't once commented on my internal monologue.

"I'm trying to have this conversation without further antagonizing you," he said through gritted teeth. This was the most emotion I'd ever seen from him, barring lust. "Also, some of the things you're thinking about me aren't terribly complimentary."

He just couldn't help himself. "What do you want, Raj? Really and truly, what do you want from this?" I waved my hand to encompass the space between us.

"I want you. I've told you that more than once. What do you need to hear from me to believe it?"

"I believe you want me," I said. "I just don't know if your lust is enough." I nipped my errant thoughts in the bud, hoping he didn't hear the continuation of that sentence in my mind. *I want more than that.*

"What I feel for you goes beyond lust. I like you."

I didn't know how to say what I needed to say without yelling or angry-crying.

"You can yell at me if you need to," Raj said. "And I don't mind if you cry."

"I do, though! I don't want to cry. I want to be strong without you, without anyone!"

"Eleanor, my sweet." I teared up at the endearment and angrily dashed them away. "No one is strong alone. Anyone who claims to not need the support of others is either delusional or lying. Every time in my life I've tried to go it alone, I've ended up falling further than I would've had I sought out or accepted the strength of those who cared for me."

"But I don't need a boyfriend to be strong."

"Of course you don't," Raj said. "You are already strong. And beautiful. And independent. But you don't always need to be the strongest. You don't need to hold everyone up all the time. One of the best things about having people who care for you is that sometimes they can take the burden."

"That is not the point."

"Then what is? I don't know where you're going with this."

"Why don't you read my mind?"

"I'm trying!" he yelled. I took a step back. Raj never lost his temper. "You don't know where you're going with this, either. I am trying to be here for you, to let you have your say. I am tired and hungry. I've not eaten in weeks. I have been all over this damn country multiple times in the last few days, transporting people here and there and using my power and influence to keep my stupid, mad grandson from lighting the world on fire because he thought he saw a spider. I don't want to fight. I just want to rest and eat and come back refreshed and be whatever it is you need me to be, if you ever figure that out."

His voice was quiet by the end, and I couldn't meet his eyes. I didn't think I deserved his anger, but maybe he didn't deserve mine, either. I knew why he'd done what he'd done in New Orleans, and I understood the reasoning. Either I was going to have to forgive and move on, or I was going to have to walk away. I didn't know if I could do either of those things right now.

"I don't know, Raj," I said.

"That's painfully obvious."

I was taken aback. First yelling, and now biting sarcasm? I lost my temper.

"Fine. Go, if that's what you'd rather do. I'm sorry I can't articulate my every thought clearly and separate my day-to-day emotions from the millennia-long plan you're a part of, but I'm only thirty-five. I don't know how to walk away from my humanity the way you do. Give me a few centuries, and maybe I'll be able to justify being a dick to the people I purport to care about, too!"

"Is that the way you truly see me?"

"I don't know," I said again.

"Let me know when you do."

Raj turned and stalked out of the room, slamming the door so hard I was afraid the generic pictures that graced every hotel lobby in the world were going to come off the walls. After the echo of his epic tantrum faded, I walked back to my room and gently closed the door behind me.

I heard a tentative knocking at the door that separated my suite from Florence and Emma's. They were both standing on the other side of the door.

"That went well," Florence said.

"Bite me, witch."

"I'm not the biting sort," She replied primly. "I think your chances of being nibbled on today may have quietly snuck out of the building."

"You'd never guess a guy who'd reached his eleventh century could throw such an epic fit, would you? That was emo-teen worthy."

"Are you going to forgive him?" Florence asked.

I sighed. "I don't know. I want to, but I feel like I'm making a bad decision. He betrayed me!"

"So did I," she pointed out. "Have you forgiven me?"

I stared at her. "Of course. I get why you did it, even if I don't agree."

"So why can't you forgive him?"

"It doesn't feel very Gaynoresque," I explained.

"What?" Emma asked.

I tried to explain the song "I Will Survive" to her, but in the end, nothing else would do but to grab my hairbrush and do some a capella karaoke. I have a lot of talents. Singing is not one of them. Emma and Florence were both laughing by the time I finished.

Florence eventually pulled herself together and offered one more piece of advice. "It does not make you weak to forgive a man a sin. You have recognized what he did and where the real crux of the betrayal lay. My betrayal was bigger, I think, because we are friends. You forgave me. Do not hold this against him merely because you are in love with him. Love does not make you weak. You do not need him to complete you, but you want him. You are also not blind to who he is and what his shortcomings are. Forgiveness doesn't mean you're compromising yourself."

My mouth was still hanging open from her assertion that I was in love with Raj. I wanted to argue that point but found I couldn't. Damnit.

The tightness grabbed my chest again. "You know what you're going to do. You might as well admit it to yourself," Florence said, then she and Emma left.

I MOPED for a few minutes before deciding that moping wasn't very Gaynoresque, either. Raj might deserve an apology. Maybe. I'd have to find him, first, though, and his manner of exit left me doubting my ability to track down an angry vampire. Maybe if I wandered the streets with my neck on display, I'd be able to lure him in.

"Or maybe you'd lure in a vampire with no conscience and greater strength than you're expecting and end up drained dry in a minute," Raj said from behind me.

"Damnit! I am getting you that bell. You can't keep sneaking up on me like that."

"I came back to apologize."

"You don't have to—"

"Yes, I do. Please let me finish." He paused for a moment, and I nodded at him to continue. "I am impatient," he confessed. "It is not a feeling I am familiar with. Patience is something I usually have a great talent for, as is a remarkable control of my temper. I am not proud of the words I said or my actions in storming out of the hotel like a child. Please, forgive me for that, and for the choices I made in New Orleans that resulted in your betrayal. But I am tired and was very hungry, and I lost my temper."

"You were hangry," I said, nodding sagely. "We've all said things we didn't mean when we were hungry."

"Hangry?"

"Hangry—like hungry-angry. I feel that way a lot."

For the first time since Raj returned to me—*to us*, I corrected myself—he cracked a grin. Relief washed over me. Maybe this was salvageable.

"Of course it is, my sweet," he said. "Almost all things are salvageable if enough effort is taken."

"Do you think this is worth the effort?" I was almost whispering. Silence stretched between my question and his answer and my breath caught in my throat.

Raj took two steps forward and grabbed my face with both hands. "Eleanor, you are the only thing in my life that is."

"Except your sword." I bit my tongue before the words were even out of my mouth. His hands clenched on my jaw very briefly before they relaxed. "Shit, Raj. I don't know why I said that."

"I know why. You're still hurt, and you will probably be for a long time. I'd appreciate it if you could limit the number of times you choose to remind me of the time I chose my sword over you to once a month or so, though."

"I will do my best, but I cannot guarantee it. Sometimes my temper gets the better of me, too."

"I'll keep you well-fed, then. No hangry Eleanors around here!"

"Thank you, Raj," I said, opening the gulf of debt between us.

"For what?"

"Coming back."

"You knew I'd be back, didn't you? Even if you didn't trust my feelings for you, you knew I had to be at the final gate opening."

"I meant coming back tonight. You didn't have to."

"I needed to do something to keep you from trying to lure me to you by exposing your neck in the seedy side of Santa Fe."

"Does Santa Fe even have a seedy side?" I asked.

"Everywhere has a seedy side if you know where to look."

"And you know?"

"It's one of my many gifts."

I smirked at him. "Tell me about some of your other gifts."

"You mean beyond my Bollywood good looks, almost irresistible charm, and razor-sharp wit?"

"Did you forget to mention your staggering humility?"

"I'm much too humble to mention my amazing humility."

I laughed out loud. "Yes, Raj. Beyond those fine qualities... anything else?"

He slid his hands down to my shoulders and leaned in close. "I have it on very good authority that I can do things with my tongue that most men wouldn't even consider attempting," he whispered against the skin of my neck before flicking his tongue out and over my suddenly pulsing carotid. I sucked in my breath as a bolt of electricity shot through my body. "Raj..." I murmured.

"Yes, my sweet?" He brushed my lips lightly with his.

"I need..." I didn't get to finish my sentence. He pulled me roughly into him, and all thoughts fled my mind as his tongue plundered my mouth. My hands tangled in his hair and I pushed my body closer to his, wanting to eliminate all space between us. His hands slid down my arms and found my waist, wrapping around me. He tilted my head back and trailed kisses down the side of my neck, pausing to bite down hard on my collarbone. I gasped and arched into him, pressing my breasts against his chest and hoping he'd take the hint.

Whether it was my body language or my mental urgings didn't matter; he took the hint and slid around enough that he was able to untuck my shirt and slide a hand up and over the silky fabric of my bra. The positioning was awkward, and I stepped sideways to give him greater access. Unfortunately, I stepped on his foot and then tripped into him.

"I'm so sorry," I gasped.

Raj was laughing so hard that pink-tinged tears were streaming down his face. "Oh, Eleanor. You are a continual surprise."

I chuckled a bit ruefully. "That is not the best make-out session we've ever had."

Raj stroked my cheek with one finger. "It was perfect. It was passionate and a bit silly, just as I hope we'll always be together."

I leaned forward and kissed him lightly. "I want you. I want this. But even more than that right now, I want some sleep. You can stay if you want, but I am exhausted, even though I've been doing nothing but sleeping."

"If I stay, you may not get much sleep."

"Trust me when I tell you that there is nothing you could do to keep me awake at this point."

He arched an eyebrow at me. "I desperately want to take that challenge, my sweet. However, I will content myself with a good-bye kiss and a promise that you'll consent to a date with me tomorrow night where we can reestablish our baseball parlance and maybe get to—where were we again?—third base?"

"It's a deal," I said, stepping into his arms and raising my lips to his. This kiss was slower and gentler and stirred longing deep in me for something I couldn't put a name to. I ached in pleasure and anticipatory loss. I was sure the Germans had a word for what I was feeling, but I didn't.

"It might be love," Raj's voice whispered in my head.

I closed my eyes, leaned my forehead against his, and thought back, *"That is a possibility."*

He took a step back, kissed my forehead, and disappeared.

CHAPTER FOUR

Florence waved Emma and I off claiming she had business to take care of and didn't want us underfoot, so we went for a walk. Other than my run through the city and visit to Loretto Chapel, I hadn't seen much of Santa Fe, and most of what I had seen had been under cover of darkness. The late afternoon sun of early spring caused long shadows to sprawl across the streets and warmed the ubiquitous adobe buildings until they glowed amber.

Santa Fe was beautiful, and I wish I'd seen it before. Even with the lack of power and the amenities we'd all grown used to, the shops were doing a decently brisk business. There were art galleries and jewelry stores interspersed with food carts hawking fire-roasted corn, fresh tortillas, and warm, corn tamales. A wine shop was offering free wine tastings with the purchase of a bottle, and I dragged Emma over to partake. I bought three bottles of red with my dwindling cash and wondered—not for the first time—how long it'd be until paper money became worthless. I filed that away as a question to ask Arduinna next time I saw her and turned to Emma to clink glasses as our first sample was poured.

Emma wrinkled her nose as she took the first drink. "I'm not sure I like this," she whispered.

"Haven't you had good wine before?" I asked, keeping my voice low as well.

"I seldom drank anything. Occasionally a cocktail, but that's about it."

"Huh," I said. "Wine is probably a bit of an acquired taste, but I like it. It's not beer, of course, but what is?"

Emma took another sip. "Maybe it's not so bad."

"You're acquiring at record speed," I teased.

She stuck her tongue out at me, finished her wine, and held her glass out for the second pour. "That was wonderful," she said to the wine pourer.

He flushed a little under her gaze and poured her the second wine in the flight. "This is a local wine, a Chenin Blanc." He started telling Emma about the history of the grapes and the local winery, but after he poured my taster, I tuned him out and focused on the crowds. Something felt off, but I couldn't put my finger on it.

The sun was angling sharply down as dusk approached, and there was an energy in the air that made me nervous. I glanced towards the west, expecting to see storm clouds on the horizon, but the sky was a clear, pale blue barely marred by puffy salmon-colored clouds beginning to show off for the evening's sunset.

"Are you ready for your next pour?" the guy interrupted me. I looked down. I'd barely touched the wine, although it was delicious.

I gulped it down, earning a disapproving look from Emma. "It's meant to be savored, not guzzled," she said. "It's not a beer."

I rolled my eyes at her, and she smiled. "Ready!" I said to the guy, while still keeping my attention on the crowds.

He filled my glass with something pink. I gave it a skeptical glance and the wine guy—

"What are you called?" I interrupted him before he could tell me about the wine I was about to drink. I laughed at myself. I'd gotten so accustomed to not asking for people's names directly it'd become habit. I hoped he didn't think I was a weirdo. I mean, I was a weirdo, but I didn't want strangers knowing that—especially not in this political climate.

He blinked three times before answering, "Gabriel Zamora, ma'am." Ma'am? Seriously? I was only thirty-five.

"Thank you so much for pouring our wine for us. Do you think I could skip this one and get right to the good stuff?"

"The good stuff?"

"I'm here for your reds."

Emma took a sip from her glass. "Oooh, this is good."

Well, if werewolf Barbie liked it, I guess I could give it a shot. I took a careful sip. "This is much better than I was anticipating," I admitted.

"Do you damn me with faint praise, Highness?" he asked. I took another look at him, then through him. His glamour was exceptionally well-done, but now that I knew what I was looking for, I could see around it.

"I would prefer you not bandy that word around," I said. "You never know who might be listening, and there are those who would see me dead."

"As you wish," he said. "Would you care for a glass of Cabernet Sauvignon?"

"Now you're talking," I said. He poured a generous glug into each of our glasses and I inhaled the aroma—first through my nose and then through the back of my throat. I closed my eyes in pleasure. Beer might be my first love, but there was nothing quite like a bottle of good, red wine. I took the first sip, eyes still closed, and wished that I had the experience and knowledge to describe the tastes that were cascading over my tongue. I tipped my glass up for a second sip, but before I could savor it, an elbow hit me between my shoulder blades, jostling me and spilling my wine.

"Hey!" I yelled, spinning around. "Watch it! You spilled my wine." I was face to face with an enormous—abdomen, I guess. It was too low to be the person's chest. I tilted my head back and looked up. And up. The guy in front of me was at least a foot and a half taller than me, and twice as broad. He was dressed like a lumberjack—or a Portland hipster—and reminded me more of Paul Bunyan than anything at all. His energy roiled around me, and now that he was right in front of me, I knew he was the disturbance I'd felt on the streets earlier.

"What do you want, shifter?" Emma asked, scorn dripping from her voice. "Or should I call you Teddy?"

"Do you know this guy?" I asked.

"For a clever woman, sometimes you're awfully slow on the uptake," Emma said. "I called him Teddy because he's a bear."

"A bear? Oh. Oh my god. He's a fucking were bear?"

"Yes. And not a very polite one."

Teddy was getting tired of being ignored and shoved forward between us, spilling Emma's wine and knocking over a couple bottles in the display.

"Are all the bears around here such clumsy, uncouth jerks?" Emma asked, delightfully mixing her old slang and my new.

"You don't belong here, wolf," he growled. If I'd had hackles, they would've risen at that bass rumble that started deep inside him and vibrated everyone within five feet. "You didn't come to ask permission to visit, and now you have two choices. Get out, or come with us and join our pack."

"You're not a wolf. There aren't any wolf packs in this area," Emma said. "I am breaking no rules. Now shoo!"

"Isn't the proper collective for a group of bears a maul?" I asked. Emma and Teddy looked at me.

"What? I'm exceptionally good at pub trivia, but have no real, useful knowledge that can benefit us in this situation."

"Pack is also acceptable," Gabriel interjected from the ground where he was picking up broken glass.

"You will need to pay for the bottles you broke," Emma said.

"I will pay for nothing. You are trespassing on our territory, and you have twenty-four hours to leave town or join us."

"I'll go ahead and save you the trouble of checking in tomorrow. I'm not going to do either of those things."

"You will, or I will make you."

"You and what army?" Emma said.

Damnit, Emma. Now you're just asking for trouble. I sighed and said, "Why don't the rest of you come out now. I know you're there."

Three more people slunk forward and joined Teddy. One of the men was a great hulking brute like our bear shifter, but the other two were smaller and lighter on their feet. "You're not bears," I said.

Emma curled her lip. "Cats. I hate cats."

The woman hissed her displeasure, and Emma laughed. "Did you need a saucer of milk, kitty?" The woman's arm swung so quickly it barely registered, but Emma caught her before her open palm made contact with Emma's cheek.

"This is neither the time nor the place for a fight," I said. "But make no mistake, if it's a fight you want, it's a fight you'll have. No one forces Emma to do anything against her will."

Teddy looked around the crowded street. We were drawing a crowd, and although some were merely curious, others were openly unholstering guns. A bullet probably wouldn't kill a shifter, but it would hurt a whole hell of a lot, and mistakes happen. I didn't want anyone on the street to get hurt if I could help it.

"Fine," Teddy growled. He grabbed my arm just above the elbow and started walking. "We'll go somewhere else."

SEVERAL DOZEN BLOCKS later we reached a mostly empty park, and Teddy let go—or rather, shoved me very roughly to one side, causing me to stumble gracelessly. "Are you sure the two of you want to fight us? There are four of us and only two of you." He looked me over dismissively. "Only one. What are you?"

Excellent! Someone from the magical world who didn't know who I was. Of course, he still wanted to kill me, but I felt like I was making progress.

"She's nobody," Emma said. "Just some chick I'm stuck with." I felt my face scrunch a bit as I took offense before I could control my expression. I smiled, hopefully vapidly, and stayed silent.

"Can she even fight?"

Emma laughed. "Depends on what you mean by fighting." I shot her some serious side-eye. What's the point of being able to lie to your enemies if you don't take advantage of it? She'd spent way too long with the Fae.

"So, it's just you against us, cupcake?" Teddy asked, laughing.

"Not exactly," Florence said, stepping out of the shadows. Raj and Petrina were close behind her. "Looks like it's an even match now."

"Bloodsuckers?" Teddy asked. "I thought you smelled funny."

"You should talk, you overgrown, discarded child's toy. When's the last time you bathed? When you tripped and fell in a mud puddle after a three-day whiskey bender?" Emma taunted. My eyes bugged out. What the hell was she doing?

I drew my sword and readied my stance. "Are we going to fight, or are you two going to hurl insults at each other all day."

"Let her take the lead in this," Raj said in my mind. *"She needs this victory."*

I stepped back behind Emma. "Let me know if you need my help," I said to her.

She turned her back on the other shifters, fucking patted me on the head, and said, "Oh, honey. That's sweet of you to offer. I'll let you know."

I bit my tongue and smiled at her. We were going to have words later.

She turned back to Teddy. "She's not wrong, though. Unless your clever plan is to talk until I pass out from boredom and then kidnap me, we should probably get to it."

Teddy raised one hand in the air and crooked his fingers. The other three shifters were joined by five more, making it nine against five—or four, since I was being discounted. We'd won against worse odds before, but that didn't mean I had to like it.

"Emma doesn't want us to interfere any more than necessary," Raj informed me.

"What does that even mean?"

"We'll keep them off her, guard her back, and alert her if any more show up, but other than that, this fight is hers."

"I won't let them hurt her."

"None of us will, but let her prove herself."

"Okay," I said. I took another step back and, with Raj, Petrina, and Florence, created a protective perimeter around Emma's back.

"Let's do this," Emma said. She launched herself at Teddy before the words were out of her mouth, and he drew back his arm to backhand her. I took a step forward, and Raj grabbed my arm, holding me back. A few of the newcomers were coming for us, and suddenly we had our hands full.

We were surrounded by flesh and fur as some of the shifters—mountain lions for the most part—shed their human selves and came at us with fangs and claws. It didn't take long for us to disarm the five shifters that'd come for us, and I was almost certain they were all unconscious and not dead. I spun around, trying to spot Emma so we could go to her aid against the four that had targeted her, and my jaw dropped.

There were two bodies down, one still and one slightly twitching. Teddy and the female lion who'd tried to slap Emma earlier were the only ones still standing. Emma didn't look like she was in any danger. She was bouncing back and forth between the two of them like a perfectly controlled pinball, shifting back and forth between human and wolf form from one breath to the next. She swiped at the throat of the cougar with a claw, then landed on two human feet and swung her leg out to trip her before shifting back to wolf and using her teeth to tear at the huge bear shifter's hamstring. The other shifters were still in human form, but their control looked like it was wavering. I wondered why they hadn't shifted yet. They were clearly losing.

"They are trying to stay human so they can take her out and capture her rather than kill her," Raj said. "They fear that with the viciousness of her attack, they'll be unable to maintain the control they need to leave her mostly undamaged."

Whatever their reasoning, it was working in our favor, or rather Emma's favor. The cougar was still on the ground when Emma shifted back to human once more and jabbed an elbow into her throat. She slumped and was still. The bear roared in anger and started his shift, but it was too late. Emma was back in her wolf form and used the advantage of his temporary inability to fight and the fact that his high leather boots were splitting off his massive ankles as he grew fur and even more mass to grab his Achilles and rip it from his leg. With skin and tissue hanging from her jaws, she watched him go down on one knee, then spat and shifted back once more. "Do you surrender?" she asked.

He growled at her and she smiled. "I can take the other Achilles if you want."

"I surrender," he said.

"And you'll leave us alone?"

Raj strode forward, Petrina a half step behind him. "I think we should formally negotiate the terms of this pack's surrender and do so when their Alpha's had a chance to assess the casualties and heal enough to talk without spraying spittle and blood. Meet us at this address in three hours." Raj handed the bear shifter a slip of paper. "If you have a pack lawyer, I'd recommend bringing them with you. You'll need all the help you can get."

I PACED BACK and forth waiting for the pack—or whatever they were —to appear. Raj and Emma seemed confident, and I wished their feelings were contagious. "What are we going to say?" I asked for at least the tenth time.

Emma sighed audibly, but Raj just smiled, brushed my cheek with his hand, and patiently repeated, "We are going to negotiate a complete cessation of hostilities, and, if Emma decides she so desires a pack to run with at the full moon, they will provide that without rancor, coercion, or violence."

I nodded. It wasn't the first time he'd gone over it, but I liked that he was willing to allay my nerves by going over it again with no sign of impatience.

I resumed pacing. "What time is it?"

"They have ten more minutes to show up," Raj said. "They're not late yet. However, it's probably best to move your anxiety to an internal monologue. You don't want anyone else to know how much this is stressing you out."

"Why not? They already think I'm some helpless human Emma's babysitting."

Emma laughed. "I can't tell you how much it delighted me to imply that you were an incompetent hindrance."

Florence spoke up for the first time. "Children, if it's not too much trouble, I'd appreciate some calm and silence, so I can finish setting the wards."

"What wards?" I asked, also not for the first time.

Florence answered—again—but her cadence was much less smooth than usual. She was getting fed up. "Silence and distraction. People won't be able to hear the conversation unless they're within the confines of the wards, and anyone wandering by will feel a sudden urge to be elsewhere. We will not be interrupted by any anti-magic fanatics."

I grimaced, started to walk the length of the park again, and then stopped myself. I shifted from one foot to the other, then took three deep breaths, reminded myself that if all else failed, I could fry them where they stood, finally finding a little zen.

I was still practicing my deep breathing when Teddy and friends entered the park.

"Teddy," Emma greeted him.

"My name is Chad," he said.

"Why do all my enemies have such white-boy douche-bro names?" I asked.

"We are not your enemies," Chad said.

"Of course not," I murmured.

"I don't even know who you are, if you're anyone at all," Chad said, chadily.

"Why are we wasting our time?" Emma said. "We are here to negotiate the terms of your surrender."

"We are here to negotiate your stay in our territory," Chad corrected.

"Did you need another ass-kicking?" Emma asked. "I went easy on you the first time, but I won't be so generous the second time around."

"Easy on us?" one of the other shifters squeaked. "You killed Aaron!"

"We killed one person in a fight with two to one odds against us," Emma corrected. "We were merciful. If you want me to continue to be merciful, you'll negotiate the terms of your surrender."

"Or we shall taunt you a second time," I said.

"Stop helping," Emma said. She turned back to Chad, "Did you bring your pack lawyer?"

"We don't have one," he said, sounding altogether sulkier than an adult grizzly shifter ought to. "Our accountant will handle negotiations."

A slight man with a twitchy nose and tiny glasses jumping at the tip of his proboscis came forward. Raj and Emma stared at him for a moment and then looked at Chad. He nodded tersely.

"Okay," said Raj. "Do you want to go sit over at that picnic table and do some negotiating?"

"That one over there?" he asked, pointing a shaking hand at the nearest bench. I was pretty sure he was seconds from pissing himself in fear.

"Is that okay with you?" Raj was at threat level zero, and the poor shifter was still terrified.

"That'll be great." I could hear our narrator's voice: "He didn't believe it would be great."

Raj, Emma, Chad, and the nervous shifter walked over to the table. I trailed behind, trying to remain subtly unobtrusive.

Once they sat down, Emma reached out her hands and took the accountants in hers. "What's your name?" she asked, looking up at him and fluttering her eyelashes coquettishly.

"St-St-Stanley," he stuttered. "Please don't kill me."

Oh my god. He is going to die of heart failure. How on earth did Chad think he was a good person to negotiate a truce?

"Stanley," Raj started. "We are here to negotiate a truce between your pack and our werewolf, who is currently her own pack."

"That's not allowed," Stanley said.

"What part?" Raj asked.

"Ladies can't be outside of a pack structure," Stanley said. He pulled his glasses off and polished them on his shirt tails. His hands were shaking and as soon as he realized that, he put his glasses back on and hid his hands under the table. He tried to stare defiantly at Emma but couldn't meet her gaze. I hid my grin behind my hand and faked a cough.

Emma gave him her hard Alpha stare and the acrid scent of urine permeated the air. "I am no lady," she said. "I am an Alpha and your better. I am the better of everyone in your pack."

He tried again but failed to meet her eyes. Chad cuffed him.

"Hey!" I yelled. "Don't abuse the man you brought to negotiate for you. Unless you pulled him off the street on your way here, you knew who he was. And because you were in the fight with us earlier, you know who we are. It is not his fault he's not the match of our Alpha."

Chad glared at me. "Do you wanna go, doll face?"

Oh no. No, he did not say that. I took a deep breath, expanding my chest and trying to dampen my ire. "Did you call me doll face?" I asked.

"Oh, shit," Florence muttered from somewhere behind me.

"What are you going to do about it?" Chad sneered.

"She doesn't have to do anything," Emma said. "It's me you need to worry about." She hopped up on the table, grabbed Chad's shirt collar, and pulled him close. "Do you think what happened earlier was happenstance? I can assure you it wasn't. Either you negotiate your surrender in good faith, or you and your pack mates can die right here, right now."

By all the gods, she was a badass once she let herself go. I was bursting with pride and couldn't stop the smile from spreading across my face.

Chad backed down, letting everyone present know he recognized Emma's dominance. He flushed, but didn't say anything further, just sulked behind Stanley, making the accountant increasingly nervous—something I didn't think possible after he'd peed himself.

Raj sat down at the table, folded his hands, leaned in conspiratorially, and said, "Listen, you and I know that most of the work isn't done by the Alphas." He rolled his eyes towards Emma, and I heard her spine crack as she straightened in irritation. "Let's you and me ignore our big bads and work something out. How much authority do you have for this truce?"

Stanley gulped, glanced over his shoulder at Chad. "Not that much."

Raj looked at Chad. "Will you authorize your proxy to make a deal in your surrender?" The way Raj emphasized the last word made me squirm, and I wasn't even the one yielding.

Chad's fists clenched, his knuckles whitened, and the veins in his temples popped. "Yes," he ground out through his clenched jaw.

Emma smiled at him and saccharine dripped from her words, "I think it would be nicer for Stanley and Raj if you and I moved away from the table, don't you?"

Chad did not look like he agreed, but he didn't argue. Emma shot Raj a look before she walked away, and the grin he smothered was likely only visible to me.

"She gave you instructions?" I asked.

"Guidelines. Rules meant to be skirted."

I rolled my eyes, knowing he'd get the gist even if he couldn't see me. *"Negotiate then, oh wise one."*

"Stanley," Raj said. "We are men of the world..." What I wouldn't give for the vampire's ability to lie... "And you know as well as I do that your Alpha has lost this fight. My Alpha has no desire to punish him. She will not take his lands, nor lay claim to his mate. She merely wishes free passage for her and hers."

"Women can't be Alphas," Stanley said, stubbornly sticking to his guns.

Raj laughed softly. "Oh, Stanley. You have seen the way she cowed your Alpha. Do you want her to come here and prove her dominance to you?"

Stanley gulped visibly but repeated the party line. "Women cannot be Alphas."

I stepped forward and opened my mouth to argue, but Raj cut me off. "You must know that's not true. I've met the Alpha of the Black Hills pack, and she's a woman. True, female Alphas are rare in North America but in the European packs, they outnumber the men by almost two to one.

"I ask you again, do you want Emma to demonstrate her dominance, or will you negotiate in good faith?"

A sickly smile plastered itself on Stanley's face. He was about fifteen seconds from vomiting, and I wasn't sure I could handle that odor on top of his piss-soaked pants. "I will negotiate."

"Item one, Emma and her companions, both those here now, and any future people she chooses to claim, are welcome in Santa Fe."

"Everyone who is here can be claimed as part of her pack."

"And anyone else who shows up and she claims."

Stanley was not pleased but gritted his teeth and worked through it. "And anyone else she publicly claims."

"Good enough," Raj said. "At the full moon, Emma will run with your—" Raj stopped briefly, smirked, and then amended, "If Emma decides that your pack needs further surveillance, she will run with you at the full moon without challenge."

Stanley inhaled deeply and the cords in his neck stood out. "I am not author—"

"Either you can negotiate, or you can't," Raj said. "If you're not authorized to say that one werewolf might run with an unfamiliar pack, then can I trust your word on anything?"

Stanley sat up straighter. "My word is binding."

Raj produced a piece of paper and a pen. "Fantastic. If you sign here," he indicated a line, "and here, we can get this wrapped up. This contract merely validates your claim that you can speak for your pack and that you agree we can stay in this territory and Emma can supervise your full moon if she so desires."

"I wouldn't mind the option of gate protection," I sent.

Raj picked up the pen and wrote briefly in a graceful script. "I've added a clause that your pack, if called upon, will provide protection to Emma's on Beltane. You will protect those recognized here, as well as anyone else Emma claims, from all other comers, including Fae, vampires, mages, or shifters. You may not be called on, but if you are, you will respond quickly and in good faith."

Stanley glared at Raj and picked up the pen. "Fine," he muttered. "But I'm adding a clause that you have to leave."

"We'll be out of your territory by May fifth at the latest," Raj said.

Stanley scribbled a few words and passed the contract back to Raj. They both signed. Raj grabbed Stanley's hand, nicked first the accountant's finger and then his own, then squeezed one drop of blood from each on the contract. "Done."

CHAPTER FIVE

The next evening, I paced in the parking lot waiting for Raj to arrive. After the minor fiasco the last time, I didn't want to risk Emma or Florence, no matter how much they protested. I knew pacing wouldn't bring Raj any faster, but I was impatient. After solidifying our surveillance plans for the next evening, he'd brushed a kiss across my knuckles, inclined his head, and left.

After one exciting, but ultimately dissatisfying make out session and the brief exchange of what might have been the "L" word, I'd kinda hoped for more. Especially since we were supposed to have had a date last night.

"Believe me, my sweet; I would've much preferred to round the bases with you than what we ended up doing," Raj said.

I spun around and felt a ridiculous grin begin to creep across my face. "Hey," I said, reaching out to touch his face.

"Are you ready?" he asked. "I would like to get this out of the way so we can get on to the better parts of our date."

"This is part of the date?" I teased. "I was expecting dinner and movie before the making out, not a trip to check out some landmines."

"I do so hate to be predictable," Raj said. He wrapped his arms around me, and I buried my face in his chest.

"I hope you don't mind me crashing your date," Petrina said, striding out into the parking lot.

Raj sighed dramatically. "Always interfering with my love life, daughter."

"Florence asked me to make sure you two stayed on task and didn't get carried away making out on a landmine."

"That sounds both wildly impractical and extremely hazardous," Raj said.

She smiled and didn't answer.

"You can come," I said.

"Like you could stop me," she scoffed.

"Let's go, guys," I said. "We don't have all night."

"Actually, my sweet, we do," Raj said. He pulled me close and flew up into the air. The familiar rush of air battered me, and I inhaled in a combination of exhilaration and sheer joy. I missed flying—a fact that would've caused me to laugh in disbelief a year ago.

Raj set me down, and dust whumped around my feet. "That was amazing!" I said, kissing him hard. Then I felt the gate energy start pouring through me and the exhaustion I'd felt was washed away as I was replenished.

"I smell blood. A life has been lost." Petrina's gaze was unfocused. "It was a child." Her words yanked me out of the combined euphoria of flying and standing at the gate site.

"Any sign of Finn?" I asked, ignoring Petrina for the moment.

Raj closed his eyes, rose up into the air, and hovered about ten feet off the ground. He stayed there for longer than I was comfortable with, and I was starting to fidget when he returned to the earth. "If he's around, I cannot sense him," Raj said. "Still…"

"I know. I'll be good."

"I hope not *too* good," he said, smirking at me.

"Have you forgotten that a child died where you stand?" Petrina asked. I jumped, then ducked my head in shame. I had forgotten.

"Trina," Raj said, reproof evident in his tone.

"It's okay," I said, placing a hand on his arm. "She's right. I was overcome, and I forgot."

"Based on the slight disturbances in the earth, the landmines start about twenty-five yards out from the center, which will make it impossible for anyone to approach on foot while they're still there. Do you think that will be too far for Florence?" Petrina asked.

"That's farther than I'd like, but I'm sure Florence could make it work."

"I'm more concerned leaving them there will make you vulnerable," Raj said.

"I can get to the gate with no problem," I said. "The gate will be opened just before dawn, so you can get me there."

"It's not the getting in that I worry about so much. It's the getting back out. Someone may need to fetch you, and I might be busy."

"Also, you'll be more vulnerable in the air if there are snipers," Petrina said. That was true whether I was a dragon or the passenger of a vampire. I conceded the point.

"The ideal situation would be to disarm the mines before we open the gate," I said. "It's possible to open the gate with them there, especially since we know about them, but I'd rather not. Too much room for error. I vote we reconvene at the hotel and call a team meeting." I paused. "Hearing no argument, I declare the motion passed. Let's head back."

I OUTLINED the situation for Florence and Emma.

"How do you disarm a landmine?" Emma asked.

"I don't know," I admitted. "Petrina? Florence?"

They both shook their heads, but Florence added, "I can find someone who will know. I still have contacts in the military."

"What do you mean still?" I asked. "I didn't know you were in the military."

She winked at me but didn't answer. I looked at her through narrowed eyes. Someday, I was going to get her whole story.

"I'll drive out to Los Alamos tomorrow and see what I can do."

"Do you have clearance?" I asked. Again, no answer. Damnit.

"Okay, I guess that's all we can do for right now. Raj, can I walk you out?"

"I'll go now. Send word through my father if anyone needs my assistance," Petrina said.

"What's with her?" Emma asked.

I considered carefully. "I think knowing that one of the landmines had killed a child got to her. I think she's going to go feed and fume. Or possibly search for Finn and kill him, regardless of the no-kill order we have right now."

Florence shifted in her seat. "I wish..." she started.

"It's okay. Someday," I said. "Plus, we need to get him to unbind himself from Werewolf Barbie."

It was a measure of how much the reminder of her connection with Finn upset her that she didn't even protest the insulting moniker.

I STOOD in front of Raj in the parking lot where we'd met earlier that evening. Even though things had been going well, I still felt out-of-sorts. Something was wrong, and I couldn't put my finger on it. Maybe it was just me?

I sighed and pasted a grin on my face. It faltered almost immediately, though. I was almost as bad at lying to myself as I was at lying to others. I'd thought everything was fine, but apparently, I wasn't quite there yet.

Damnit.

"I believe you owe me a date and some heavy petting," Raj said. He must've been picking up my thoughts because he sounded more tenuous than usual.

I flushed. "I did agree to that."

"What's wrong, Eleanor? Things have been strained between us. I thought you understood my actions post New Orleans and weren't holding a grudge."

“I’m trying!” I yelled. I ducked my head to the left and looked at my feet. I hadn’t meant to yell. What was wrong with me?

“Eleanor?” Raj sounded genuinely confused. “I thought we’d gotten through all of this the other night.”

“I thought we had, too. I’m all mixed up.”

“Talk to me.”

“Here?” I looked around the dark and mostly empty parking lot.

“Why don’t we take a walk.” He held out his hand, but I ignored it. Gah! What was wrong with me? Isaac’s face formed in my mind’s eye and tears began to form at the corner of my eyes.

“I feel like betrayal is the theme of my life,” I said. Raj started to speak, and I held up one finger. “Let me finish. Finn was my best friend, and he betrayed me because I couldn’t return his love. Even after discovering that he’d never been the nice guy he pretended to be, I can’t erase the years we spent together as friends and the dejection I felt when he chose to be a vindictive ass-clown over being my friend.

“Isaac was the first man I ever cared for as more than a friend. I agreed to mate with him because it was the only way we could truly survive according to the prophecy—which, by the way, is a phrase I use a lot more often and less ironically than I ever would’ve guessed. But even with the prophecy, I wouldn’t have agreed to it if I didn’t care for him and believe that he cared for me. And even with all that, he left. He chose his stupid sense of nobility over me, and worse, wouldn’t even talk to me about it. The betrayal from him came when he walked out without saying good-bye, and not when he walked through the gate to save Emma.

“And New Orleans. You and Florence made decisions you shouldn’t have made without me. You let me believe that it was a true betrayal. I understand why you guys did that, but it doesn’t erase the hurt. You, Florence, Isaac—you all had reasons for what you did, but it still feels like a betrayal.

“And now? Contemplating a real relationship with you feels like I’m betraying Isaac, but in a much more fundamental and much less noble way than he betrayed me. Before New Orleans, when we were dating and making out, it didn’t feel real. There was a line I wasn’t going to cross, but that line is gone now. Everything," I waved my hands around, trying to encompass Raj and me and the memory of Isaac, "seems less fun; more serious. I'm confused and mixed up, and I don't know if I should pursue what I want because I don't know the long-term consequences of my actions."

My voice had increased in volume the longer I talked, but now that I was done, the sudden silence squeezed in on me, and I hunched my shoulders as I deflated. Raj held out his hand again, and this time I took it. He drew me to a nearby bench, and we sat. My head leaned on his shoulder as he settled an arm around me.

"Eleanor, I have something to tell you, and I beg of you to let me finish just as I let you finish."

"Okay," I said, closing my eyes.

"I've had opportunity to converse with Isaac."

My head shot off his shoulder, and I twisted around to look at him. "What now? When? How?"

He pulled me back into his body. "I will explain. Because of your mating bond, when you are in great distress or pain, he is pulled closer to you. Isaac and I shared blood three times, which gives me the ability to find and converse with him anywhere on this plane. And the connection that I have with you is far greater than anything I've shared with anyone in my long, long life. Those three ties, combined with the boost your blood gave me from my second drink, are enough to allow me to talk to Isaac when he is pulled to you. This shouldn't work, but the three of us are connected in ways I never would've guessed possible."

"That answers the how, so what about the when?"

"We spoke while you were being tattooed. Your distress pulled his consciousness onto this plane. He told me he'd dreamed of you once, and you told him you were falling in love with me."

I gasped. "I thought it was a dream."

"He also told me that in that dream he said you needed to do what you could to find happiness."

A cool breeze kicked up, and I shivered. "Was that all you talked about?"

"He is going mad. His mind is fragmenting, and I don't know how much longer he'll be able to hold on. I tell you this not so that you will give him up as lost and forget about your plan to rescue him when this is all over, but to let you know that after we do rescue him, he may not be the same Isaac you remember. He is beaten, used as target practice, and kept in a silver cage to prevent him from shifting with the moon. If this was the first time, or if his previous imprisonment had been shorter, his sanity would probably last longer. As it stands, I don't know how much longer he can hold out."

The knife that had stabbed me in the gut when I thought of Isaac earlier twisted itself around. I doubled over on myself as my metaphorical pain became physical.

Raj's arm around my shoulder tightened, pulling me closer. "Eleanor, I didn't tell you this to cause you pain or to make you feel guiltier than you already do." Confusion laced his words, and I tried to pull my thoughts into a coherent enough structure to explain.

"I'm glad you told me, I am. It's all just so much to process. Isaac, you, relationships. I need to concentrate on getting through this gate opening without anyone else getting hurt, then finding the last gate and opening that one. Maybe then I'll have enough time for other stuff."

"Do you think there will ever be a point when you're not too busy? After the last gate opens, you'll take a long vacation and have some me-time?"

I shook my head. I knew he was right, but didn't that make it all the more important to not have more romantic entanglements?

"My sweet, if you truly don't want this, I will back off, and we will be friends. But don't push me away because you're afraid of what this could be."

"I am not..." I couldn't even finish the sentence. Damnit. "I need a little time. Some space. Breathing room to think about this all."

"Wasn't that what I gave you after New Orleans?" Raj asked.

My temper flared. "No. What you gave me was an unexplained and unasked for absence. I didn't know it was space and time because that's something that should be decided by—or at least known by—

both parties. Now I'm asking for it. This time we'll both know what this is. So please, Raj. Please."

Raj stood up and looked down at me. "Will you be okay here?"

"I'll be fine."

"When can I come back?"

"You'll know I'm ready when you find me in the seedy part of town with my neck on display."

A smile ghosted across Raj's face as he walked away. He'd gone only a few steps when he turned around and looked at me. "I have to ask. Are you?"

"Am I what?"

"Falling in love with me?"

I couldn't answer, couldn't say the words out loud, but my thoughts betrayed me. "*Yes.*"

"Then I will give you the space and time you need. After all, we're neither one of us getting any older." He disappeared into the darkness.

I WALKED into the lobby of the motel. I'd spent hours on the bench analyzing, reanalyzing, and overanalyzing every aspect of my relationships with Isaac and Raj. I cared for Isaac—so much. And when I concentrated, I could still feel him there, but whether it was the difference between our planes or something else, it seemed less prominent. Sadness caused an ache in my chest, compounding the guilt that already sat there.

I knew what I was going to do. I'd known for a long time. The reality of it smacking me in the face was hard to take. I was going to finish this quest, protect my people, and save the world, possibly breaking it a little in the process. Then, I was going to Faerie to find Florence's sister and Isaac and rescue the shit out of both of them. At some point, I was going to have to do something about Medb—she had to stop trying to kill me. It was getting more than a little annoying.

And I was going to do it all with Raj by my side. I was falling in love with him. I couldn't fool myself anymore. I would always care for Isaac, but I'd never been in love with him—something he'd known from the beginning.

I'd paused in the middle of the lobby, standing there long enough that it was probably weird. Luckily, the hotel lobby didn't get a lot of traffic, particularly in the wee hours of the morning. I headed towards the stairs and then heard the murmur of voices. I paused to listen. Something seemed off about the conversation, so I wandered surreptitiously towards the people conveniently hidden behind a large, potted palm to listen in.

"Trina," Florence said. My jaw dropped, and I decided now was the time to unwander my ass away from this. I didn't want to be caught eavesdropping by a couple of witches, particularly on a conversation private enough to have inside a shrubbery. Before I could make good on that goal, Florence continued. "I don't know if this is a good idea."

"Baby," Petrina purred, "You know it's a good idea, you're just afraid to jump in."

"Last time I jumped in, I ended up getting burned."

Petrina laughed softly, and there was a small gasp that I did *not* want to know the cause of. "You're mixing your metaphors. You only do that when you're flustered."

I didn't hear Florence's response, but Petrina laughed again. "I like flustering you. You're gorgeous when don't know what to say."

I took a step backwards, but right then, they shifted position enough that if I took another step, Petrina would see me. It was either own up to the spying or stay put until they moved again, so I could make my escape. I put the tightest lockdown I could on my thoughts, hoped Florence was *flustered* enough that she wouldn't detect me and prayed to all the gods Petrina wouldn't smell me. Was there a god for olfactory senses? And a term for not being able to smell things? I missed the internet. I hoped my mental babbling would be enough to keep me from noticing what was happening mere feet from where I stood like a forgotten but stubborn victim of freeze tag.

"It's a little public right here, isn't it?" Florence said.

"We're hidden from view, and it's the middle of the night. And this is much, much more fun."

Florence sucked in a breath and said, "Exhibitionist."

"Is it really if there's no one watching?"

Now I fully understood why Florence had been so irritated with Isaac and me. This was not fun. I didn't mind a sexy movie, but these were my friends. I screwed my eyes closed so I wouldn't see anything I didn't want to, but then realized that would prevent me from spotting a good time to make my escape. I opened them again while attempting to remain stoic in the face of watching my best friend get lucky in a hotel lobby.

Petrina had one hand on Florence's face and was caressing her cheek. Their eyes were locked on each other and the depth of emotion I saw rocked me back on my heels. I'd been so worried about my own love life that I didn't even stop to think about the other connections I'd gotten hints of. I'd known they were flirting. I'd seen glances and too-casual touches, but I'd never considered it might be more than that. I was so selfish. Florence lowered her head, and their lips met.

It started out gently, but moments later, Petrina's arms were twined tightly around Florence's neck. I watched as Petrina released the clip that bound Florence's hair allowing it to tumble freely down her back. She threaded her hands through the hair and tugged back, exposing Florence's neck. "Are you sure?" she asked.

"I'm sure," Florence gasped as Petrina grazed her fangs along her neck. Petrina sunk her fangs in, Florence cried out, and I took the opportunity to make my escape. Instead of heading up to my room, I fled the hotel and didn't stop moving until I'd put a mile between me and my accidental voyeurism.

I was really happy for Florence. I didn't know how long ago it'd been since she and Savannah broke up, but I knew she'd been alone for a long time. She'd told me once that she saw how the people she loved would die when she first met them, and that's how she knew they'd be important to her. I wonder what she saw hanging out with a bunch of immortals. Did she see my death? Petrina's? Raj's? I wanted to know, but knew I'd never ask, nor would she tell. That was too much a violation of privacy, and after the violation I'd just committed, I was planning on giving her all the privacy possible for the rest of forever.

I should probably get her an "I'm sorry" card for all the times she overheard my thoughts and fantasies about Isaac. I hadn't realized exactly how uncomfortable that could be until I was on the receiving end. I was such an ass. I turned around and started walking back towards the hotel, determined this time to head straight to my room, make as much noise as possible, and pretend I was returning for the first time. I looked around and realized I had no idea where I was and which direction to walk to return.

"You're in the seedier part of town," Raj said behind me.

I jumped and cursed. "Damnit! I've asked you to stop doing that!"

"I know, but every time you jump like that, it causes interesting things to move under your clothes. I rather like watching it."

"You could just ask me to jump for you," I groused.

"And you'd say, 'How high?' I doubt it."

He had a point. "What are you doing here?"

"You said I'd know you'd had enough time and space when you wandered the bad part of town with your neck exposed. Here you are."

Oh. Right. I had said that. Oops.

"You're not here for me? Why then…" he must have caught my thoughts because he choked on a laugh. "I see. Well, I can get you headed back in the right direction, and we can resume this when you're ready."

CHAPTER SIX

Raj left me in the parking lot. I entered the hotel lobby, deliberately ignoring the large potted plants against the back wall and headed upstairs. I wasted no time in stripping off my clothes and crawling into bed. The last couple days had been physically and emotionally exhausting. My magic stores might be refilled, but I hadn't even tried to use them and didn't know how—if at all—I'd leveled up after opening the New Orleans gate. I supposed it was possible that all the gate energy washing through me had merely broken the bonds and not increased my power level like at the previous gates, but I wouldn't know until I tried. I needed to shift, to weave air into shields or weapons, to make more potted palms for Florence and Petrina to skulk behind. Something. Anything.

I sighed.

I didn't want a burst of power to signal to anyone that was probably lurking nearby that I wasn't as helpless as I seemed, even though I wasn't sure this was the best plan. Blah, blah, blah, underestimate the enemy, blah. He always underestimated me anyway, with or without my powers intact.

I closed my eyes, resolutely put all thoughts of flying as a dragon out of my head, and tried to fall asleep.

After counting a few hundred sheep, I gave up. If I was going to spend the rest of the night navel-gazing, I might as well be comfortable. I dug through the supplies piled in one corner until I found the cooler I'd been hiding from the others. I opened it and retrieved the last six-pack of Oregon beer I had in my possession. I'd come across it at a convenience store in San Antonio—it was the only one they had left—and although it wasn't my favorite local brewery, it was still better than almost any other beer I'd had.

I popped open the top and took a long, slow pull from the bottle. I closed my eyes and let the bitter taste of the hops meld with the mellow sweetness of the malt before swallowing and taking another sip. I hopped back into bed, leaned against the headboard, and got started with the self-reflection.

There was only one question in my mind that I couldn't settle; one thing that was keeping me from telling Raj I was ready: Isaac. He'd practically gift-wrapped me for Raj before taking off to be a big, damn hero. But I was going to save him—I had no doubt in my mind. I'd promised, and I would deliver. And then what? He was my mate, but I was in love with Raj.

Not *falling* in love. I'd already fallen, and nothing I could say could claw away the guilt I felt about falling in love with someone else when my mate was being held prisoner somewhere else. If the dream I'd had was more reality than sleeping fantasy, he'd given me his blessing, but I wished we could have a real, honest conversation about it now before I did something irrevocable. He'd said then that he'd loved Emma, bought the ring he gave me for her, and had intended to perform the mating ceremony, as well as probably a wedding, with her. But he loved me, too, and had mourned Emma for decades, not knowing she was alive.

It was weird to think about whether or not they'd get back together, leaving a guilt-free path for me and Raj, and it did them both an injustice. They'd both changed in the decades apart, and neither of them owed me an easy path. I was an adult, and if I chose Raj, I needed to do it with the full knowledge of what the consequences could be.

Worst case scenario was that I broke Isaac's heart, and with him so close to the edge, he succumbed to insanity. Pain squeezed my heart, rendering me breathless, and I struggled to regain my equilibrium. I was giving myself too much credit. Finn might've gone off the deep end a bit when it finally hit home that I was never going to be in love with him, but he was already a few sandwiches short of a picnic. It was not my fault he was a psychopath.

Isaac was not a psychopath. He might not be the most mentally stable guy at the moment, and he might love me, but he would not jump off a bridge because I chose someone else. He was stronger than that. He might be skirting the border of crazy-town, but he wanted me to be happy. Me choosing someone else might hurt him, but it wouldn't break him.

I hoped that was the truth and not merely wishful thinking. I should ask Florence if she agreed, but she was having a happy relationship interlude right now, and I didn't want to throw my love triangle angst into her burgeoning romance. I drained my beer, leaned back, and finally let my thoughts settle on Raj.

I'd tell him my decision tomorrow night, and maybe, if I played my cards right, I could finally round the bases. My lips curled up into a smile and heat simmered low in my belly. After months of teasing, flirting, and heated kisses, I was finally going to see if he was as good as he wanted everyone to believe he was.

"Raj!" I cried out, waking myself up. I'd just woken, seconds too soon, from the most erotic dream I'd ever had, panting and more aroused than I'd ever been before from a dream. I throbbed and ached, needing a release.

I closed my eyes again and let the images from the last moments of the dream flood over me. I arched my back with the memories of Raj's fingers and tongue and let one hand slide down my body until it was cupping my sex. I was so wet that a touch had me gasping on the cusp of orgasm. I slid my fingers against the wetness and stroked my clit lightly. I didn't want to rush over the edge and tried to go slowly, but it was no use. I gave up on slow and thrust two fingers of my left hand inside while continuing to rub my clit with my right. Less than a minute later I was moaning my release.

I lay panting and flushed for a second and then became suddenly and embarrassingly aware that there was someone else in the room. I opened my eyes and turned my head. Raj was standing by the window staring at me with a heat that left me gasping. He looked hungry, and I knew that all it would take was one hint of welcome and he'd be on me; inside me.

"More than one hint," he said, his voice caressing me with warm sensuality. He slid home the lock on the door leading to Emma's room and then added aloud, "I want our first time to be slow, not a quickie born out of uncontrolled heat."

I watched him stalk towards me and made no move to cover myself. I was embarrassed that he'd watched me pleasure myself, but also extremely turned on.

"Why are you here?"

"I was in the neighborhood and heard you call my name."

I flushed as the memory of the dream washed over me. "You should probably knock next time," I said.

"I wouldn't have missed that for the world," he replied.

"What about for your sword?"

And yeah. That broke the spell. He stopped a couple of inches from the bed and looked down at me. The heat in his gaze faltered, and his eyes flashed red. "How long will you hold that over me? Will I pay for it for the rest of our time together?"

I kicked myself. I hadn't meant to say that. I wanted nothing more than to take Raj into my bed and let the past go.

"I'm sorry, Raj," I said, an ocean of debt opening between us. "I'm trying."

I sat up and ran my fingers through my hair. I didn't bother to cover myself. I chose my next words carefully. "I think I'm having more trouble forgiving you because although Florence is my best friend, you are the man that I've fallen in love with." I cringed and peeked at Raj through my eyelashes. Talk about going for the all-out vulnerable! I'd bared my body and my soul to this man. I just hoped it wouldn't come back to bite me in the ass.

He looked incredulous and then a slow smile spread across his face, and his eyes glinted ruby red again. "The only ass biting that's going to happen due to that revelation is what I'm going to be doing to you in approximately five minutes."

I grinned and flushed with renewed arousal. "Five minutes? Why's it going to take so long?"

"Because first I am going to kiss you senseless."

We still had things to talk about, things to hash out between us, and trust needed to be rebuilt; but finally, after months of waiting, it was on. I spread open my arms and welcomed him into my bed. He was still fully clothed and resisted my efforts to change that. "Soon, my sweet. Soon."

He settled on me, fully clothed, and kissed me. Every kiss we'd shared before paled in comparison to this one. Months of longing and teasing came to the surface. I was desperate for him and from the way he was returning my kisses, he felt the same way. I wrapped my legs around him and pulled him deeper into me. Our mouths opened, and I ran my tongue over his teeth, flicking his fangs because I knew it would make him crazy.

He groaned as I knew he would and pressed his hard center into me. The denim of his jeans rubbed across my wetness, and this time it was me who moaned.

"I need you naked. Now." I gasped out. He just laughed at me. This must be what true evil sounds like.

He slid down my body, pausing long enough to flick my nipples into attention with his tongue, and then settled at the juncture of my thighs. I couldn't contain my scream of pleasure as his tongue reached out and stroked me. His voice was thick with need. "I have dreamed of this since the minute I laid eyes on you."

His tongue began a full-scale assault on my clit, and I arched into him anxious for more. Suddenly, he thrust three fingers into me at the same time that one fang pierced my clit. The moment of pain quickly receded behind the waves of ecstasy that rolled over me, and I bucked into his face with a violence that was shocking.

As soon as I was coherent again, Raj rolled me over and bit down gently on my left butt cheek.

"There's the promised ass biting," he said.

I rolled back over underneath him and said, "You need to take your clothes off now. I'm not going to wait much longer."

He stood and stripped quickly before rejoining me in the bed. "Better?"

"Much," I said. I wanted to take my time, too. There were so many parts of his body that I wanted to taste and explore, but there'd be time enough for that later. Now I just wanted him inside me, filling me, making me whole.

He obliged and thrust into me. He paused and looked into my eyes. "I love you, too."

"Bite me," I said.

He took me then with his cock and his mouth. He thrust into me over and over while I matched his rhythm, and his teeth pierced my neck. The dual pleasures sent me spiraling into orgasm again and again. He pulled himself from my neck and sealed the bite. Two more thrusts and we fell into the abyss together.

Afterward, we lay content and panting in the afterglow. I rolled up onto one elbow and looked down at Raj. I didn't say anything, just kissed him. He pulled me down until I was half sprawled over his body. "Told you we were inevitable," he whispered.

I DOZED for a bit and woke up to Raj suggestively nibbling on the inside of my thighs.

"Again?" I asked, trying for a censorious tone.

"We need to make up for lost time. Was it worth all the waiting?"

I thought back over the events of the last months. "Yes. It would've taken me much longer to forgive you if we'd already slept together and exchanged I love yous."

This statement seemed to puzzle him. "Why?" He punctuated his question by thrusting his tongue between my legs, and I gasped.

It was a few moments before I could pull my thoughts together enough to answer. "If you'd told me you loved me, and we'd slept together, and then you'd left me out of plans that important with no indication I meant anything to you while I was imprisoned, I don't think that is something I would've come back from. It may not have been logical, but it would've hurt more."

"Florence's warning was just a way to ensure that we ended up together instead of as a brief fling that ends with tears and recriminations? She's a clever witch," Raj murmured against my most sensitive skin, causing it to vibrate in pleasure. "Remind me to get her a thank you card."

"Can we not talk about her now," I said. "It's a bit distracting."

"I like you distracted," he said before his tongue took a long, leisurely trip over my clit, causing me to jerk against his face.

"Presumably, not distracted with thoughts about your daughter's sex life," I said between gasps. His tongue halted its journey.

"Did you have to say that?"

"You started it."

He moved up the bed to settle next to me. "I'd like to hear a little more about the dream you were having."

"Which dream?" I asked.

"The one that made you yell my name so loudly I was drawn instantly to your side."

"Oh. That dream."

"Presumably, I had a starring role." His fingers began a slow dance over my skin, pausing here and there to tease and caress and pinch.

"Maybe I was yelling at you to get rid of you," I suggested.

He slid his fingers over my clit, flicking it with his fingernails, and I gasped as sensation and heat exploded over me. He rubbed slowly back and forth until I was panting with need. "I think you were telling me something else." The rhythm in his fingers sped up, and I writhed beneath him. I was so close to the edge, and I knew what I needed to fall over.

"Raj! Please."

"Please what, my sweet?" he whispered. His hand roamed up to knead one of my breasts, and he pinched the nipple into a hard peak.

"Inside me. Please."

"You had merely to ask." He rolled over me in one smooth motion and entered me, stroking back and forth until I came, seconds later. "Is that what you needed?"

I whimpered a bit with the aftershocks. "Yes."

"Good, because now I am going to get what I need." He rolled over, pulling me along with him until I was straddling him. His hands were on my breasts, and his eyes were closed.

I rocked back and forth, oh so slowly, a teasing grin on my face. His hands slid down to my hips and pushed me into a faster rhythm. "Harder," he murmured. I ground myself into him faster and harder. Every forward stroke ground my clit into him as he was pushed further into me, and in seconds, I was gasping my second orgasm. I tried not to let it disrupt my rhythm, and whatever I did, I was successful, because Raj groaned and came beneath me. I collapsed on top of him, his cock still inside me, and he smoothed back the sweat-dampened hair on my brow.

"Worth it," he said.

I kissed him lightly below his jaw. "Definitely."

ISAAC

INTERLUDE

Isaac's back arched, and he woke gasping and panting on the verge of orgasm. His vision was blurred, but he knew very well he had an audience. The next thing he noticed was his hand stroking his cock. He tried to stop, but it was too late, and he arched again as the orgasm jolted through him. The loose sweatpants that were his prison uniform developed a growing wet spot, and he withdrew his hand, trying to surreptitiously wipe it on his sweatpants before exposing it to the open air and his audience—not that they wouldn't know what'd just happened.

It'd been a long time since he'd had a wet dream, and it was depressingly appropriate that this was where it happened.

He couldn't put it off any longer. The muffled laughter would soon become something harsher, and he wouldn't put it past them to "wake him up" by uncomfortable means. He opened his eyes all the way and propped himself in a sitting position.

"Good dreams, freak?" asked one of the guards, a creature who looked like a cross between midnight and an upright, reindeerish human. When she stood still in the shadows, she was nearly invisible, but when she moved, the darkness of her form, enhanced by a swirling cloak, seemed to suck the light from the room and fear from his heart. He speculated that maybe fear was the meat that fed her.

Isaac wasn't sure she had any room to call him the freak, but he wasn't going to argue. She had a temper that matched the fiery red of her eyes, and she outweighed him by at least eighty pounds.

He stood up. "The dreams were apparently good. May I have some clean clothes?" He didn't gesture towards the stains marring his light-grey sweats, but he didn't have to. Everyone in the room was staring at the wet spots with various degrees of amusement and disgust.

"Not today, I don't think," the guard said. "You're not due a change of clothing for another week."

Isaac took a deep breath and reminded himself not to argue with her. There were only three possible outcomes. The first was that she'd punish him, and her punishments, although swift, were harsh. The second was that she'd leave, and for whatever reason, he felt sanest when she was watching him.

A third outcome was that she'd punish him and then leave, which was the least desirable.

He didn't want to unpack the knowledge that her presence kept him anchored to sanity, but he did know when he'd first noticed it.

After Eleanor had opened the last gate, the one in New Orleans if Raj was to be believed, the backlash of magic that wrung through him from her was so strong he started shifting uncontrollably from wolf to human and back again. He wasn't supposed to be able to shift in his silver cage, but the power that bounced back and forth between the two of them burned through the slow silver poisoning he was experiencing and pushed him through what seemed like every shift he'd missed in the entirety of his very long life.

He was writhing in pain, panting from effort, and slicked with sweat when strong, cool arms lifted him to a sitting position. He couldn't pry open his eyes, but he felt the cool, damp cloth blot away the sweat and blood from his brow. The arms held him through every change he made, and a low, strong voice whispered comforting words to him. The shifts got further between, and he felt the protective magic being woven around him by the person holding him together both physically and mentally.

For the first time since he'd found himself back in Michelle's cage, he felt like sanity was within reach. When he had finally stayed in his human shape long enough to catch his breath, he forced open his eyes and looked up at the one who'd used her wild, green magic to protect him from Eleanor and himself. Her eyes, green and brown like the sun-dappled forest floor, grounded him as nothing else had. He stared into her eyes, and she looked back before her gaze shuttered and she dropped him back to the floor of his cage and stalked out, slamming the door behind her. That's when he noticed her antlers.

"He'll be fine," she said as she walked out of the room. "Let me know if you need my services again."

"Who was that?" he asked, his voice shaking and weak.

One of the remaining guards tossed some towels and clean, dry clothes into the cage then barked a harsh laugh. "You don't want to know. You certainly don't want her to know who you are, although it's a bit late for that now, isn't it?" He laughed again.

After that, she made regular appearances on guard duty. Those were his best days. The more often he saw her, the saner he felt until the moon madness started fading into the background and the effects of the silver poisoning seemed to lessen. No longer did he feel like he was covered in a rash just under the surface of his skin. His headaches faded, and he began to entertain the most dangerous of feelings: hope.

Now, he looked forward to her next rotation on guard duty, although her turns didn't come as regularly as the others and had no predictable frequency that he could tell. The other guards didn't seem to enjoy her presence as much as he did and were jumpier, more paranoid, and crankier in general when she was around, although they were always careful to be nothing but polite to her face.

"She gives me the creeps," he heard one of the guards—a slender man whose eye sockets shone with an eerie light, and who Isaac had dubbed Will—say to his companion, a dark, grumpy and exceedingly ugly trow Isaac privately called Bollockface.

"Shhh," cautioned Bollockface. "She's as like to hear you as not. Those ears don't miss a thing."

"Prey ears," dismissed Will. "She's a creepy old reindeer, but still prey."

"Have you ever seen one of those big deer fight?" Bollockface asked. "They don't prance around and paw at each other 'til supper time. They are brutal and vicious, and only one walks away alive. Your gut tells you to be afraid, and it's the first good thing your gut's ever told you."

Isaac couldn't keep still any longer. "But who is she?" he'd asked. He'd earned a flaming arrow to the thigh for that, and the guards were careful to keep their gossipy conversations out of earshot from then on.

And now she was here again, looking at his cum-stained sweatpants and avoiding his eyes. She was the only one whose expression he couldn't read. Since she wasn't showing overt disgust, he was going to take that as a win.

"Please?" he asked. "A change of clothes would make the next week slightly less miserable."

"I am not here to make your life less miserable," she sneered at him. "You are a dog in a cage. Your entire purpose is misery."

He hung his head. He knew better than to appeal to her mercy. The other guards might not talk in front of him much, but he'd learned enough about her reputation to know that mercy was not part of her repertoire. She was slumming on guard duty. The only time she made appearances in the dungeons was when her talents were needed for enhanced interrogation techniques.

Isaac didn't know where she spent the rest of her time when she wasn't extracting information from other prisoners or taking her turn on guard duty with him, but he wanted to know that almost as much as he wanted to know her name.

A bundle dropped at his feet, and he looked down at clean, gray sweatpants, a tank top, and boxer briefs. He considered the clean clothes for a long moment before looking up and meeting her gaze.

He knew what he was about to say was ill-advised, but he couldn't stop himself. "Thank you."

He didn't feel the debt between them, but he knew she would. She met his gaze, and the brown-green of her irises swirled slowly clockwise, making him a little lightheaded. She nodded slowly, acknowledging his debt, then turned and left the room.

CHAPTER SEVEN

I woke up alone, but the pillow next to me was still dented, so I knew I hadn't been alone long. I headed into the shower, reminded myself to write a new thank you card for Petrina for the constant supply of hot water, and got dressed for the day. We needed to do more recon on the landmines, and Florence had had some ideas.

When I walked back into the bedroom, Raj was waiting.

"Where were you?"

"I have a home nearby. I went to make sure Jeffries and Salem were settled in and retrieve a few items."

"How many homes do you have?"

He paused for a moment. "I own about twenty residences scattered all over the world, but there are only five places that I would categorize as homes."

"Where are they?"

"It would take too long to tell you where all my residences are, but the places I consider home are: Portland, southeastern Belgium, Uttar Pradesh, Holmvik, and outside of Albuquerque."

"Why Albuquerque? It seems a little more deserty and sunny than most vampires would enjoy."

"That's the gist of it. Someday, I'll tell you the whole story, but now…" He kissed me. The kiss was light and sensuous and full of promise. It was sweeter than the passion-laced kisses we usually shared, and that both frightened me and made me resolve to put thoughts of the betrayal out of my head. It was in the past, it was done, and it shouldn't be distracting me during the kissing parts.

Raj pulled back abruptly and pulled a jeweled knife out of a sheath low on his calf. It looked to be a relative of the sword I'd just been thinking about. His eyes flashed again, and he pulled the blade of the dagger across the palm of his hand.

I gasped in surprise. That is certainly not where I was expecting this to go.

"Eleanor," Raj rasped. "Look at me."

I looked up at him and met his ruby gaze. They flared more brightly, and I knew that if I wasn't immune like all Fae, he'd be mesmerizing me right now. Even with my blood-born immunity, I was feeling extremely suggestible.

"Eleanor. I swear by my blood that I will never knowingly cause you harm again. Not for the sword of my family. Not for the children of my line. Not for those I consider my people."

The blood began to drip from his palm even as the cut healed before my eyes. I watched the drops of blood hit the motel carpet, and I moved to kneel to blot the blood before it stained.

"Leave it," Raj said. Then he sighed. "It seems we must talk. I was hoping to delay a bit longer as I am desperate to taste you again."

My hand went to my neck almost unconsciously.

"Not your blood, my sweet, although that is delicious. However, I think it best if I abstain from drinking of you again. I was talking about tasting you elsewhere. I cannot seem to get the vision of you writhing under my tongue out of my mind."

Strangely enough, that's all I could think about now, too.

He smirked at me, so I shot him the bird. He gestured towards the leather sofa, and when I sat, he crossed to the bar that had been mysteriously stocked while I slept, selected a bottle of red, and poured two glasses.

"I feel like we've spent a lot of time talking over the last weeks," I said.

"And not nearly enough tasting," he agreed.

I gulped my wine, trying to once again remove that image from my head so we could talk.

"You're trying to distract me," I accused.

"Is it working?"

"Almost, but I don't want this hanging between us. I want clear air. I want to be able to think about the damn sword without freaking you out. I want to get to a place where I'm not worried about you betraying me again, and you're not worried about me never letting it go."

Raj was sitting there with his vamp face on, which meant there was absolutely no expression whatsoever. Even his eyes were back to the beautiful chocolate brown that could melt the panties off a woman. For a second, I was sure that stray thought was going to at least warrant an upwards lip twitch, but he remained inscrutable. Whatever. Ignore my blatant flirting now. Since I wanted to talk anyway, that was probably for the best.

"I think we have two items up for discussion." That did get a response. One elegant eyebrow rose inquiringly. Damnit. Another motherfucking person who could raise just the one eyebrow. Was I seriously the only person in the whole world, natural and supernatural, who couldn't do that? Raj's lips quirked. I narrowed my eyes. Was he actually laughing now? Not at my panty melting comment, but at my real and legitimate pain over my uncooperative body parts? Ass.

I decided to ignore him.

"Item the first, the new super powers you probably got from drinking me again. Item the second, the extra surprise that you wanted to tell me 'later.'" I added air quotes because it seemed appropriate.

Raj stood and retrieved the bottle of wine we'd already breached and snagged another one. It was going to be one of those kinds of discussions.

"If you don't mind, I will take those questions in the order you asked them," he said.

"Whatever order pleases you is fine with me, as long as we get through them in the next," I made a big show of checking my wrist for the non-existent watch, "however many hours until you need a little vampire nap."

"What are your elemental powers?" he asked.

"You know this answer," I said.

"Humor me." I wasn't sure if it was my imagination or not, but his accent, which was usually a faint mix of Asian subcontinent and British, was stronger.

"Earth," I said. "I can make plants grow. Air: I can create shields of air to cut off sound waves and have used it to suffocate people—well Fae—who are misbehaving. And fire: I'm a dragon, after all. Fire is the easiest for me to wield and control."

"Not water, then. That's odd."

I tilted my head to one side. "Is it? I didn't think much of it. I have enough going on as it is."

"So you do." He paused. "In my first drink from you, I developed a powerful resistance to silver and a partial immunity to the threshold laws—I have since found that with those who are psychically gifted the threshold laws still apply. In my second drink, I learned how to bend air to travel faster as I flew and the genetic pyrokinesis that most of my line share finally manifested in me. Those skills are obviously much flashier than the skills gained with my first drink, although that is not surprising considering how much more I took in the second drink than in the first.

"My third drink, as you will recall, was in the throes of passion and was not nearly as controlled as the second. I took more than I would've—perhaps more than I should've. My control over Earth is nearly complete. I could will the ground itself to move for me if I so desired. The other gift I got is something I cannot speak of to anyone else. Everything else that I have received from you is enough to make the other vampires wary of me, and there are those who would like me destroyed already. But if this becomes known, both our lives will be in immediate danger."

This was not sounding good. What the hell else could he have gotten from me that had already manifested and was so dangerous that we'd both be killed on sight if anyone knew? My eyes were wide, and I was on the edge of my seat. I took another fortifying drink of wine as I waited for his next words.

Raj stood, set down his wine, and walked to the middle of the room. Then he looked at me with a grimness I'd never seen on his face. He closed his eyes, and his body seemed to turn to smoke. A moment later instead of Raj there was a...bat?

"Did you just turn into a bat?" I asked.

"Come closer."

I did as instructed. On the floor was a fruit-bat sized dragon.

"Oh my god, you are so cute!" I couldn't help myself. My voice rose to a pitch that I usually reserved for kittens, snakelets, and sneezing baby pandas.

The miniature dragon disappeared into a curl of smoke, and a moment later Raj was back with me, sans clothing. I bit my lips together trying not to laugh. He certainly wasn't giving me his impassive face now.

"Go ahead and laugh," he said.

I did. Once I'd recovered enough to talk again, Raj had already dressed, which was a bit disappointing. "Ummm, so I can't tell anyone, or they'd kill us both?" I asked.

"It's embarrassing," he bit out.

"At least it's not actually a bat," I said. From the look on his face, my reassurance wasn't that comforting.

"Okay, then. I can see why you didn't want to share that with the others. I'll reassure them that your second gift isn't a big deal and that I do, in fact, know what it is." I giggled again.

"And now for answer number two," Raj said, obviously eager to move on.

I nodded, trying to get myself under control.

"I found the other night—the night I surprised you in your room—that when I think of you hard enough, I appear directly at your side."

"No flying and bending space?"

"None. I was at home, trying to figure out what I needed to say to you to get you to forgive me, and poof! I was in your room. My sudden appearance must have awoken you, because before I could get back out, you woke up and, well, you know what happened next."

"Well, that's slightly better than a pre-meditated showing up while I was sleeping," I said. "How's it feel to be leveling up so quickly after so long?"

"Pretty fucking good," he said. I grinned again. He didn't swear nearly as much as I did, and I really enjoyed hearing him bust out the saltier language.

"Really," he purred. "If I'd known that, I'd have been talking dirty to you months ago."

I shivered. "If you keep it up, you can do whatever you want to me," I said.

"Promise?"

"Pinky swear."

WE GATHERED in Florence's room to hear what she'd learned from her military contacts.

On the table in Florence's room were three cups of coffee. I smiled at Petrina. "You're still my favorite."

I grabbed my cup and settled myself against Raj on one of the beds.

"Surprisingly, demining the area is not the military's top priority," Florence started. "They know it's littered with landmines which is why it's closed; they just don't particularly care. The person I spoke with suggested that they could send in an unmanned—" her lip curled derisively at the term— "vehicle to attempt to set all of them off if that's what we wanted, but that's not what I am interested in for two reasons.

"One: that would let Finn know we were onto him and give him enough time to come up with something else and two: that was the home of The People at one point, and I do not want to blow it up if I don't have to."

"Where does that leave us, then?" I asked. "Even if I could just get to the middle to do the opening, you'd be pretty far away for your part, and it doesn't leave a lot of room for error."

"Can a path be cleared with some individual disarming?" Petrina asked.

"That is possible but time-consuming."

Raj looked thoughtful for a moment. "They are pressure-activated, correct?" At Florence's nod, he continued, "What if someone went in and picked them up, one by one, and carried them out?"

There was a moment of stunned silence before Florence said, "They are extremely sensitive. That would take inhuman control."

He grinned at her. "I think I know someone."

"No," I said, much more sharply than I'd intended. "That's ludicrous."

"It would be time-consuming and dangerous," Florence said. "I went back to the site yesterday afternoon. There are hundreds buried just under the surface. You'd have to dig them all up."

Raj smiled rather grimly. "That wouldn't take very long."

Florence narrowed her eyes at him. "You've been drinking again, haven't you?"

Raj winked at her.

"What did you get this time?"

"I can control earth," he said.

"Your first drink gave you immunity to silver and the threshold barrier, your second drink triggered your pyrokinesis and allowed you to skip through space when you're flying," Florence said. "Do you think it's likely that the only gift of your third drink is control over Earth?"

"Not with the amount of blood that was given," I muttered, heating up at the thought of what we were doing when the exchange happened.

"There's more," Raj answered. "But the earth moving is the most relevant at this time. The other gift is incidental and not particularly useful."

"Your sudden shifts in power make me nervous," Florence said.

"Me, too," Raj said.

"Really?" I asked.

"Not really. It's kind of exciting. Nothing new has happened for centuries. I like it."

I rolled my eyes at him. I wished I could tell lies. *"You should tell them what else you got."*

"I would prefer to never tell another soul."

"At least tell them you can jump to me instantaneously. That is immensely useful information for our posse to have."

"Our posse?"

I didn't let him argue. "Raj can now jump to me instantaneously. He doesn't need to bend air."

Florence leaned forward and rested her chin on her tented fingers. "Does it work for anyone else?"

"I haven't tried it with anyone else," he admitted.

"Did this manifest before or after your third drink?" she asked.

"Before," he said.

"Before your drink and before the sex, too?"

"Yes," I answered. Why does that matter?"

"Because it isn't the power in your blood that allowed him to come to you, so maybe he can travel to the side of anyone he knows well."

"It could be her blood," Raj argued. "It might be a residual effect from the second drink that I hadn't noticed."

"And it still might be something you can do for anyone you think of that you know well enough," Florence said.

"I have an idea!" I announced, cutting off further argument. All eyes turned towards me. "Why don't we test it?"

"So rational," Petrina observed drily. I started to preen, but then she added, "Especially for one so young."

I flipped her off before I could think better of it, and then snatched my hand back as if I could rewind the obscene gesture. I cringed. "Sorry, Petrina."

She laughed a deep, throaty chuckle. "It was well-deserved."

Raj stood, mock-glared at everyone, and then stepped off the balcony and flew off. I shot him an image of an eensy-weensy dragon, and he replied with a bird of his own.

The rest of us sat and waited. And waited. After almost ten minutes, Raj popped into the room at my side. "It's only Eleanor," he said. "I couldn't even travel to Trina, and she and I have been bound for centuries."

"At least we know," Florence said. "Now back to the matter of the mines."

"Raj, do you think you can uncover all the landmines and get them out and to a safe place quickly enough that Finn won't be suspicious, and they won't explode? I assume exploding wouldn't be good for you."

"If we can identify a location that I can toss them into, I can do it," Raj said. "Florence, can you be more specific on the number than hundreds?"

"Nothing exact, but an educated approximation would be close to three hundred."

Raj seemed to be doing some rapid calculations in his head.

"I need a good place to dump them. Somewhere that no one's likely to stumble over them and that isn't too far away."

"What about a currently active volcano, now that you're not flammable?" Petrina suggested.

"That should work. Where's the closest one to us?"

"Probably Colima in Central Mexico," Petrina said. "That's still something like 1,100 miles away, though."

I did the math in my head. It was hard. I was just about to announce my calculations—I said it was hard, but I didn't say I couldn't do it—when Raj broke in. Damn him and his supernatural calculating speeds.

"When I brought Eleanor back to Alpha from Brooklyn, I was going about 370 miles an hour. She's a bit heavier than your standard landmine, but I'm also stronger than your average human, so it shouldn't make too much of a difference."

"That's still three hours one-way. Even if you took two at a time and jumped back to me, you'd still not have enough time to do more than four a night," I said. "It'd take you more than two months to clear the site. That's not going to work. We have a month."

"I have an idea," Emma said.

I tried not to let my surprise show on my face. It was tough.

"What if, instead of tossing them into a remote volcano, Raj took them all to a remote desert location around here. There have to be some deep canyons near the Grand Canyon that are less likely to have people in them right now. If it was like a hundred miles away, it'd be less than thirty minutes round trip. Take that times two mines per trip times nine hours, and you could do about sixteen a night, getting through the three hundred in less than twenty days."

Now I wasn't the only one staring at her in surprise.

Raj was the first one to get over his surprise enough to talk. "They'd still be there; dangerous."

"Most of them would explode when you tossed them in, and those that didn't you could destroy at the end of the mission, either by bringing down a landslide with your fancy new earth powers or by using your pyrokinesis to melt them."

"I am impressed," Petrina said, looking over Emma with genuine interest for the first time. "That is simpler and more effective than anything we were thinking."

Emma gave a little half shrug. "I'm not much of a big thinker," she admitted.

Petrina looked at her, her eyes flashing red. "Simple and effective is much better than grandiose and doomed to fail," she said. "It shows a lot more wisdom to come up with a workable plan on a small scale than to waste time coming up with a big plan that cannot be implemented. Why do you persist in putting yourself down? If you keep doing that, people will start to believe you."

A faint pink stained Emma's cheeks. I think she was pleased but couldn't admit it. We hadn't quite yanked her all the way into the twenty-first century yet, but we were getting closer. I felt a sudden urge to break into a rousing rendition of "Anything You Can Do, I Can Do Better," but thought better of it.

Raj unsuccessfully stifled a snort of laughter, and I glared at him. Everyone else just ignored us.

"When do we start?" I asked.

"Three nights hence," Raj said. "I'll use tomorrow night to find a good location and ensure that it's free of human and animal life and the following night to study the landmines and their pattern. I'll start at dusk on the third night while there's still enough light to see when I use my power to move the earth."

"If it takes nineteen days, that's cutting it pretty close," Emma said. "You won't finish until the twenty-sixth of April."

"The morning of the twenty-seventh, actually," Raj corrected.

"That's four days of buffer," I said. "The gate opens just before dawn on May the first."

"Will that be enough?"

"I think so. I might get faster with practice," he said. "I haven't been practicing too much. Also, I do have an idea that might speed things up."

"What is it?" I asked.

"I'll tell you later. I don't want to spoil the surprise."

"It's pretty early yet," Emma said. "Not even midnight. Why not get started right away? You could at least find the drop zone tonight."

"I have other plans for the rest of the evening," he said. The look he raked over my body made my toes curl. "Saving the world will have to wait another day."

That reminded me that I wanted to ask a few questions about the role of the now-hated sword in this upcoming world saving, but I decided that it could wait. After all, we'd have four days of leisure at the end of the month, right?

Raj didn't wait for a reply from any of the others, just grabbed my hand and dragged me back through the door that adjoined the rooms. He grabbed my backpack and shoved a few items in it.

"What are you doing?"

"Packing." *Duh,* his tone said.

I rolled my eyes.

"Why are you packing my stuff? I thought we were coming back here to have crazy sex."

"I am tired of leaving you at dawn."

"The sun can't really hurt you. Stay with me."

"It can't really hurt me, but it does make me uncomfortable and vulnerable."

"Where are we going?"

"You'll see."

"Let me guess. It's a surprise."

He shot a quick grin in my direction. "You catch on pretty quick."

"Now that I'm not half starved and cut off from the source of my power, my brains are working pretty well."

He stiffened but continued scanning the room for anything else I might need.

"Ummm…how long am I staying in this mystery spot? Because you've packed a lot of stuff."

"Twenty-six days."

"Hmmm," I said, studying my fingernails. "I know we've accelerated the pace of our relationship. I was okay with moving to 'first overnight trip' but not sure I'm ready for 'moving in together.'"

His eyes flashed red, and the look on his face was almost incandescent rage. I took a step backwards. "What the fuck, Raj?"

Almost immediately the rage and the ruby glow faded. "Sorry," he muttered.

"Not so fast, mister. You can't just give me a look like you'd cheerfully eviscerate me for teasing you and then walk out of it with a half-assed apology. I didn't say anything that should've made you mad at all, much less homicidal. So give."

"Give you what?" he cocked his head to one side.

"It's cute when you pretend you don't understand modern slang, but I know you not only watched all seven seasons of Buffy but have them on Blu-Ray and have watched them multiple times. I'm guessing that's just the tip of the iceberg. Don't make me ask Petrina whether or not you own the Twilight series."

He looked a little sheepish but didn't argue.

"Fine. I'll explain. Will you come with me?"

"I'll come with you for tonight. Whether or not I stay depends on what you say."

"Fair enough."

He grabbed my bag and me and hauled me to the window. "Close your eyes."

I did, and he jumped. I knew there was nothing to worry about. Even if he dropped me, it was a three-story drop. I'd be fine if my wings didn't unfurl in time. But still, that initial drop left my stomach behind and me struggling to reclaim it without vomiting.

"That was mean." I thought.

"Sorry."

"No, you're not."

He squeezed me a little tighter and hugged him back. I pulled the shields I'd been practicing with Florence over my mind. I wanted to think, and I didn't want Raj to know what I was thinking about. Something was going on with him, and I was betting it had something to do with that fucking sword.

"You can't block me out," he said. He actually did sound a bit apologetic this time. *"Now that I've drunk of you three times, there are no shields that can keep me from your mind. If we weren't touching, I wouldn't be getting everything the way I am now, but even distance won't keep me out if I don't want it to."*

Motherfucker. *"You didn't mention that before."*

"Must have slipped my mind."

Riiight. Well then, I guess my musings on his stupid sword could wait until Monday when he was too busy flying explosives around to pay constant attention to what I was thinking about.

We'd been in the air for about ten minutes, skipping almost imperceptibly every couple minutes, when Raj began to slow. By my calculations, that meant we were about sixty miles outside of Santa Fe. He set me down on a stone patio in front of a beautiful and sprawling adobe home that appeared to be built into the side of a mountain.

"This is yours, isn't it?"

"It is. The front rooms all have windows, and there's a courtyard off the kitchen with an outdoor eating area and a pool, but the west wing is built into the mountain, sealed off with reinforced stone doors, and there are no windows there."

"So, a custom jobby, then?" I asked.

"I added some modifications to the original plans," Raj said. "The architect was most…agreeable. Decent chap. Great artistic vision and was delighted to work on something that was both challenging and unique. Other than my few specifications for the back bedrooms, I gave him free rein with the rest of the house. I think he did a good job."

Raj opened the door and ushered me in. I looked around my mouth agape in awe. It was gorgeous. "Yeah, I think so. I hope he got a lot of business from this."

"I wouldn't let him publish the full floor plan and all the photos, so it looks as though part of the house doesn't exist, but I think it helped his career a bit. It also helps that he doesn't remember that there was anything odd about the job anymore, either."

"Probably for the best," I said as I looked around the expansive living room. There were skylights through which I could see the waxing moon, and the ceiling had large exposed beams half covered with white-washed plaster. The effect was breathtakingly simple. The house was furnished simply with a mix of modern and traditional southwestern decor.

"Where's the bedroom?" I asked, trying for casual.

"There are bedrooms off that way," Raj gestured. "And you're welcome to one of those if you'd prefer to have windows. But if you'd like, you can share mine." Now the exaggerated casualness was his.

"I'd like," I said.

He walked towards the windowless stone wall on the western side of the dining room. He pressed one of the irregularly shaped stones, and there was a mechanical noise that preceded the entire wall shifting and moving to reveal a doorway.

I grinned. "I love secret passages more than almost anything in the world," I said.

Then he took my hand and led me into the dark passage. Moments later, the creak of gears and bang of stone signaled that the door had closed, and we were shut into the mountain.

Lanterns regularly spaced along the passageway provided enough light to see by. There were only two doors. "What are they?"

"The right is my bedroom; the left is a bathing room."

I veered to the right, and he laughed. "Eager, are you?"

I turned towards him. "Always with you, vampire."

I'd intended to pull him into the room and take him quickly, before grilling him on his mini-freakout, but the room gave me pause. I hadn't much thought about what it was going to look like. Hobbitish. Comfortable. After all, we were in a hole in a ground; and not a nasty, oozy, wormy one nor a dry, bare, sandy one. But oh! It was so much more than just comfortable. Raj sent some sparks towards the large fireplace that took up the entire—I paused to orient myself—west wall and soon the room was filled with a welcoming orange glow. There was a large Persian carpet that took up most of the stone floor, and one wall was lined with bookshelves. I longed to spend some time running my fingers over the spines and figuring out what kinds of books Raj had in this home.

"It's time," he said.

I must have looked vaguely alarmed, although I couldn't think of a solid reason why I would be.

"I mean, it's time to explain why I was so discomfited when you stated you weren't ready to live with me."

"Good, because I'm going to be honest; that was a little on the weird side."

Raj gave a completely unnecessary sigh. "It's going to upset you," he warned.

"The reason your eyes turned red and you tried to kill me with your glare is going to upset me more than the actual action did? Please enlighten me."

"I am not human," he said.

"Me neither! Go Team Supernatural!"

Raj glared at me for my interruption, but since this was a normal, brown-eyed glare, I wasn't worried.

"Panty-melting brown-eyed?" he asked.

"Whatever," I replied. "You didn't react earlier, so you can't use it now. Those are the rules I just made up."

"Fine. I am not human, and although I work very, very hard at keeping many of my qualities as human as possible, every once in a while, there is a…glitch…in the system. This glitch was unexpected, so I wasn't prepared to dampen it. That's all."

"That's all?" I asked. "What kind of glitch was it?"

"Apparently we mated."

"Quite a few times," I agreed.

"No, Eleanor. We're mated. Joined. Bonded. Wed in the custom of my race."

"But I'm already all those things with someone else." I wasn't protesting, necessarily. I just wasn't sure I was ready to be a bigamist. Or a woman bigamist. A wigamist?

"It's just bigamist," Raj interrupted my runaway train of thought. "However, there are no laws against it in our world, so it's not illegal. Polygamy is extremely uncommon in the supernatural world. Most people do only bond with one other; I've only heard of a couple cases where a person mated with two different people."

Before I could ask for clarification, Raj continued. "In both of those cases, the second bonding happened after the death of the first mate."

"Isaac is still alive."

"I know."

I took a moment to digest.

"When I teased you about not wanted to spend the rest of my life with you, your mate bond with me was triggered, and it pissed you off?"

"What if I'd slept with my meal earlier this evening before I came to you? What if she'd given me the same pleasure you gave me before I drank from her?"

I wanted to say that it was fine, but between my inability to lie and the sparks flying from my fingertips, I didn't have a chance.

"You're feeling a bit possessive, too?"

I unclenched my fists and willed the fire to dampen. "Did you fuck her?"

"No. I cannot. I am not sure I could rise to the occasion for anyone but you now."

"Good." I sent a very clear picture of my dragon biting the head off any others that caught his eye.

"I'm not saying I won't look," he said.

"I won't eviscerate any pretty people you want to eye fuck, but you keep your parts to yourself," I said.

"The same must go for you, then," Raj said.

"What about Isaac?"

"I don't know," Raj admitted. "Right now, he doesn't feel like a threat, but I'm not sure how I'll feel once he's on the same plane again." He rubbed his fingers through his hair. "I guess that's a bridge we'll cross when we come to it."

I scooted closer to Raj, and he tucked me under his arm. "Is the air clear?"

"Enough for tonight. Wanna show off your dirty-talking skills?"

"I'd be delighted."

CHAPTER EIGHT

Raj tessered us back to the hotel to meet the others at dusk the next evening. I was exhausted, not having gotten a lot of sleep during the day. Apparently being that deep underground, Raj didn't feel the pull of the sun and only needed about thirty minutes of sleep. He saw to it that I got a little more than that, but not much.

"We have to make up for lost time," he said. "I've been waiting for you for a millennium."

"We only need to make up a few years," I said. "Anything beyond about ten to twelve years gets into a creepy realm where you cross over from cradle robber to pervert." That's how I got my nap.

Petrina arrived about the same time we did, and I decided that now that she was my daughter-in-law, I should treat her as such. I didn't know how to do that, though. Should I ask her to make me a sandwich? Provide me with grandchildren? Or should I just be a cold bitch?

Raj laughed, and I grinned up at him and then pulled him down for a kiss.

"Petrina and I are going to scout for an appropriate location to drop the landmines," Raj said. "We'll meet you at the gate site at midnight."

"I'm not doing that jumping thing with you, father," Petrina said. "Let's just fly like normal people."

All of a sudden, the vision of a tiny flying dragon popped into my head, and I had to stifle my giggle. Raj glared at me. "*Tell no one.*"

"Fine," he said to Petrina. They walked to the balcony and took off.

AFTER RAJ AND PETRINA DISAPPEARED, the rest of us prepared to drive back out to the gate site. I internally grumbled about flying to the gate site, careful to keep the knowledge of my dissolved bonds from Emma. It didn't sit well with me. We'd deliberately included her before, even knowing that Finn was linked to her, and that had made her feel part of the group. Even after—*especially* after—my own betrayal by my best friend and my lover when they didn't think I'd be able to keep the truth from those that needed to be in the dark, I still didn't want to be that person. I knew why Finn needed to stay ignorant of my restored condition, but I hated lying to someone I'd come to regard as an integral member of the team. How could I still feel betrayed about what had been done to me if I was doing it to someone else?

I dropped my mental shield a little, and Florence looked over at me. "Your thoughts are leaking," she warned.

"I know. I'm doing it on purpose so you'll read my mind." Oops. That was a little more biting than I'd intended. Florence didn't seem to take offense.

She followed my train of thought, and I could see that she agreed with my logic but wasn't sure if she agreed with the outcome. Well, fuck it. Was I or was I not the intrepid heroine of this damned quest?

"Florence? Is there a way for Emma to block the bond that Finn made to her? So that he can't read her mind with such ease?"

"Not that I know."

"But from everything we've observed, he can only read the mind of someone when he's in physical proximity to that person, correct?"

"Correct, but he can use the bond to find that person anywhere."

"I think I have an idea. I'll tell you all when we get to the gate site. Can you drive?"

"I knew that your idea was going to involve you not driving."

"I can drive," Emma said. "I'm beginning to enjoy it."

Emma got us to the parking lot at Bandelier National Monument in white-knuckled record time. "You are out-of-control," I gasped out.

"What?" she laughed. "We're all immortal."

"I'm not," Florence said. "I'm just very well preserved."

"I'm sorry," Emma said, actually sounding apologetic. "I forgot. You seem just as immortal as the rest of us."

"I will take that as a compliment and warn you to never drive that way again," Florence said, climbing out of the car.

I was a little shaken, too, but at least I was actually immortal—or at least as immortal as the rest of my supernatural gang. I hadn't quite sussed out what would kill me yet, other than decapitation which was a pretty sure bet for most of us.

"Now, Eleanor," Emma said, sounding way too cheerful for an angel of death in disguise. "What was your idea?"

I didn't run it by Florence first, even though I probably should've. Instead, I drew on the gate power and filled myself magically. In my head I imagined my tiny mana gauge turning completely blue. I concentrated and for the first time in what seemed like weeks set full shields around us, complete with my fly-paper early warning system. These shields were so tied to my signature that if anyone walked into them, it would be a sign I was at full power again, which is why I hadn't reset them before. This time, however, I did something different. I reached out to Florence, physically and magically, and linked with her. Fortunately, she didn't fight me, and I was able to tie her into the shields. She caught on quickly and once she was tied into the structure, she wove her own magic in, strengthening and overlaying them with her signature as well as enough flash and flare that it would completely mask how much of my power was invested.

"Clever," she said.

"I learned from the best."

We grinned at each other. Emma looked at us impatiently. Fair enough, so far everything we'd done had been invisible. Now for the showy part. I drew myself up to my full height—which was admittedly not very full—and concentrated on my in-between form. My beautiful purplish-black wings sprang free from my physical being and for the first time I felt scales erupt over my skin. An itchy, almost painful sensation on my forehead sent my hands up to investigate: Horns had sprouted from my temples. I concentrated on *not* growing a tail.

"Holy shit," Emma said.

Florence was also staring at me in shock. I guess she'd never seen my half form either. To be honest, I didn't know it was anything but wings. I hoped my tongue was still normal. I didn't want to talk in sibilant hisses.

"So, Emma," I said, relieved that I didn't sound like a Disney villain, "I broke the chains that held me."

"I guess you did," she said. "And you couldn't tell me because of Finn."

"You guessed it."

"Sorry," she said.

"Please don't apologize. He did the same to me. But next time he gets close enough to us to hear your thoughts, we should be able to catch him and force him to break the bond."

"He got away from you last time," Florence reminded me.

"That is true, but hopefully he won't be expecting me to be at full power this time."

"He has to leave still not knowing you're at full power."

"And that's why you are woven into my shields so thoroughly that it looks like you're merely reinforcing the broken-down shell of my shields. I will do nothing, but Emma cannot be kept in the dark any longer. It is not fair to her to be a member of this team and yet be kept ignorant. Perhaps it puts us in danger, but I'd rather have everyone come to the table with the same knowledge and understanding. We'll work together better that way. Who knows, if we'd approached our problem in New Orleans that way, maybe we could've avoided me starving in a dungeon for a few weeks."

"Still pissed about that, huh?" Florence asked.

"A bit. At least if I'd been in on the plan and agreed to it, I could look back on the experience with the knowledge that I entered of my own free will. How long has it been since New Orleans?"

Florence blinked at the unexpected question, but answered quickly enough, "Just over two weeks."

"And how are my mental shields now?"

"I haven't been pushing," she said.

I put up the walls I'd been working on. "So, push me, witch."

After a couple of minutes, a line of sweat broke out on her brow. It was five minutes more before she looked at me and said, "I'm in."

"Two weeks of half-assed practice without guidance and it took you a bit of time to break through. Imagine twice that time with focused sessions led by you and Raj."

"I've already admitted we were wrong," Florence said. She sounded pissed. "What do you want? And can you put your wings away? They're kind of creepy."

"The wings stay out until Raj and Petrina get here. I want them to see what we've got going on here, so no one is startled if I ever need to change forms unexpectedly."

"Probably a good idea," Emma said. "Florence is right. You are creepy. You know your eyes are purple and look wrong now?"

"Wrong how?"

"Reptilian I guess. The pupil is a vertical slit instead of a circle. It is really, really weird."

I grinned. "Awesome." I looked back at Florence. "What I want is a promise that you will not withhold information again. If the information affects any member of this team, it is to be shared with that member and she—or he if you happen to come across something about Raj—will decide if the rest of the team needs to know. If decisions are going to be made about anyone on this team, that person has a right to know. No more hiding information for someone's own good, or because they are too weak to be part of it. No more. I have had it." A small tongue of fire burst out of my nose at that last statement, singing off all my nose hairs in the process, and making Emma laugh.

I pointed a finger at her. "Bite me, wolf."

Before she could answer, I felt someone hit the outer edges of my perimeter spell. I knew instantly that it was Petrina. Oops, I hadn't recalibrated to include her.

Raj landed in front of me moments later. "Could you release Trina, please?" he asked. He did a double-take at my appearance but didn't say anything.

"On it," I said. It took Florence and I working together to release her and add her to the whitelist, but a couple minutes later, she was on the ground in front of us, looking annoyed if no worse for wear.

She glared at me. "That was highly unpleasant."

"My apologies, Petrina," I said. "It won't happen again."

She looked slightly mollified after I explained what I'd done, and I think my half-dragon form impressed her a bit.

"Did you find a good place to drop the mines?" I asked. I wanted to change back to my more human-looking self but had neglected to bring an extra set of clothes. My wings had torn out the back of the shirt and my scales had rubbed holes in the rest of my clothing. I was pretty sure that without the impressive dragon features, I was going to look like a nearly nude homeless woman.

"Nearly nude is a very good look on you," Raj said.

It was at that point that I began to worry that my half form was unattractive. I got so caught up in a weird spiral of self-doubt about my appearance that I missed most of what Raj and Petrina relayed about the location they'd scouted.

It was only when I noticed everyone staring at me expectantly that I figured out that I was probably supposed to be making a decision or giving a pep talk or something equally important from a leadership standpoint. "Uhhh," I said, rather cleverly.

Emma gave an exaggerated sigh. "Do you think that you, Petrina, Florence, and I should be here guarding the landmines while Raj makes the trips back and forth to keep an eye on things in case there's trouble? Or should we be elsewhere? Or should we split up?"

Raj said, "I'd rather not have anyone else here in case something goes wrong. It's close enough that I won't need the time savings of jumping to Eleanor."

"I'd feel more comfortable if I guarded the drop site," Petrina said.

"Good idea," I said. "Any other suggestions? If not, that's the plan!"

I took everyone's silence as consent.

"Where are we for time? Raj, did you still want another night after tonight to prepare before beginning?"

"Yes, I'll come back out here tomorrow night and uncover everything and make some calculations. Right now, I'm exhausted and hungry. The next three weeks are going to take a lot of energy—using my new skills does—and I'll need to feed more deeply and more frequently than I'm used to doing."

"Not from Eleanor," Florence said.

Raj glanced over at me, his expression shuttered. "No," he agreed. "Not from Eleanor."

I kept my thoughts locked down as tight as possible, even though I knew that nothing could keep Raj out. Between my self-doubt about my appearance and my current feelings of jealousy about his future meals and my unsuitability to be that for him, I was not having a very good evening. I wasn't used to self-esteem issues, and it was making me feel a little extra bitchy.

"Are we done for tonight? I'd like to get some sleep." I walked back to the car and opened the driver's door. I started to climb behind the wheel but ran into a snag—literally—when my wings got tangled up in the seatbelt.

"Goddamnit!" I yelled. I bumped one of my horns on the door frame trying to get free sending a weird jolt of pain down into my head. I pulled free of the car, stomped away a good fifty feet, and then sat down causing a puff of dust to rise around me. I could feel the tears trickling down my cheeks and was embarrassed that I was crying. In addition to not being plagued with an overabundance of self-doubt, I was also not much of a crier. At least I hadn't been before this trip. Now it felt like I was bursting into tears every other time I turned around.

I heard the car start and then the sound of gravel crunching indicated that it was pulling away. They were leaving me?! My temper tantrum hadn't been that bad, had it? The tears were doing more than trickling now. I scrubbed at my face and tried to slow my breathing. I concentrated on my shape and pulled the dragon back inside. Now that there was no one else to see me, it didn't matter if my human skin showed through my ripped clothes. I'd have to turn fully anyway if I was going to fly back to town, but I wasn't ready to do that yet. If I was going to be abandoned in the middle of nowhere, I was going to have a good long sulk first.

"Why would you think I abandoned you?" Raj asked.

I hadn't heard anyone approach, and I jumped about four feet in the air and very nearly lost control of my bladder.

"Jesus Fucking Christ! You can't do that!" I yelled.

"Why are you so upset?" he asked. "I was trying to figure it out, and I couldn't pinpoint what was wrong."

I couldn't articulate what was wrong; it sounded ridiculous when I tried to put it into words. I struggled with what to say for a while and finally, since my only two choices were to tell the truth or stay silent, I went with the truth. "I am tired, both physically and emotionally. I am uncertain as to where I stand with you. I know you say we've mated, but everything is still so new. I've been in approximately two long-term relationships when I actually cared what the other person thought about me, and it's driving me crazy. All I could think of was whether or not my half form would be too unattractive for you and would ruin the desire you felt for me, and then later, I was jealous of the loads and loads of blood you're going to have to drink to stay peppy for the next weeks.

"Also, it hurts my feelings that you don't want to drink from me again." I closed my eyes. I couldn't look at him after all that soul baring. That was a lot of exposure that went beyond my hulked-up clothing.

"Eleanor," Raj said. "Look at me."

I kept my eyes closed and shook my head.

I felt a finger under my chin. He tilted my head up towards his and brushed my lips in a soft kiss. "Open your eyes."

I kept them stubbornly closed.

"Do you know how much it delights me that you feel so vulnerable with me?" he said.

Now I did open my eyes. So that I could glare.

He smiled. "That you feel enough for me to allow yourself to be vulnerable, and then to confess as much. It is meaningful to me that you trust me with your feelings." He sat down on the ground next to me and pulled me into his lap. "Now, let me reassure you. You are beautiful to me, whether human-skinned or bewinged and purple-scaled. I will always find you attractive.

"As for the blood. I would much prefer that you were my only donor, but that is not possible. I cannot take the amount of blood from you that I will need without severely weakening you. I also cannot add anything new to my arsenal at this time—not until I feel comfortable with the gifts you've already granted me. I do not wish to become too powerful too quickly. If it would make you feel better, we can work out a compromise for the blood drinking."

"What kind of compromise?"

"You could be present for the feedings to see that there is nothing but a meal happening, much like I have watched you consume countless tacos and slices of pizza."

"Or we could rob a blood bank," I suggested.

Raj shuddered. "I am not drinking dead, plasticky-tasting blood if there are other choices."

"Animal blood?"

"Gross."

It was such an American teenage girl thing to say that I giggled.

"Live human or bust?" I asked.

"It's the best way to go," he replied.

"I don't want to watch," I said.

"Then you must trust me."

I leaned back into his arms. "I do. Can we go home now?"

I felt his surge of delight at my request to go home, and then he stood up, pulling me with him, and shot up into the air.

FOR THE SECOND afternoon in a row, I woke in Raj's bed. We'd been up past dawn "making up for lost time" as Raj put it. I sat up, stretched, and then glanced at the other side of the bed where Raj was still resting. I couldn't exactly call it sleeping because it wasn't exactly. Nor had he fallen into a corpse-like state as I'd half expected from too many vampire movies. It seemed more like a deep meditative state. It reminded me of seeing people from my yoga classes really get into their savasana.

"That actually means corpse pose, you know," Raj said. He still wasn't moving, but apparently, he was aware of his surroundings.

"I know. I've done a fair amount of yoga. But there's a difference between corpse pose and being a corpse."

Raj's eyes fluttered open, and he smiled at me. My heart stuttered in my chest, and I knew I loved this man.

His grin widened, and I cursed mentally. It was really hard to guard my thoughts when I hadn't had any coffee. Raj reached up and pulled me down for a kiss. "I like knowing what you think of me," he said against my lips.

"It won't always be complimentary."

"Of course not, but I can do my best to ensure that it is the majority of the time, and at least I'll always know why you're upset so I can tell you why you shouldn't be."

I rolled my eyes. "Really?"

He rolled me over underneath him and slid between my legs. "Well, if I can't, at least I can find other ways to distract you at least. I'll always know what you like." He punctuated the last statement by gently nipping the underside of my right breast before continuing his journey down to the juncture between my thighs.

I felt my eyes roll back in my head as he flicked his tongue slowly over and around my clitoris. Soon I was writhing and moaning under his ministrations and then he slid two fingers inside me, crooked them back towards him in that universal "come" gesture, and within moments, I did.

He slid back up my body and then inside me. This time it was I who rolled him over. I straddled him and rose off him until he was barely inside me. He strained up instinctively, trying to sheath himself more completely, but I held myself just out of reach.

"Tease," he growled.

I smiled. I loved having this power over him. Then he grabbed my hips and slammed me down onto his rigid cock. I bit my lip and smiled at him and then began to move. "Grab the headboard," I commanded.

He looked at me but didn't obey. I stopped moving.

"Headboard. Now."

Raj reached up and grabbed the headboard. The action caused his taut abs to ripple and I watched with possessive pleasure. Once he was holding on, I began moving again. I rode him slowly, one breast in each of my hands. I pinched my nipples to tight peaks and then brought first one breast and then the other to my mouth. Raj's movements under me got more frantic, and one hand left the headboard. I stopped moving and looked at the rogue hand.

He glared but complied.

I continued to move over him slowly, teasing him with my breasts, until I couldn't take it anymore. Then I dropped the tease and started moving faster. His hands grabbed my hips and I didn't object this time. He moved me into an even faster rhythm that he matched, and I leaned forward until my nipples were brushing his chest and my clit was grinding against him. I felt his movements change from smooth to jerky and then he came beneath me. Moments later I followed him over the cliff screaming his name and then collapsed against his chest.

Raj kissed my hair as I rolled off him and slid out of bed. "Where are you going?"

"Bathroom."

I headed across the hall to pee and wash up with the magically heated water—courtesy Petrina—then headed back to our room for clothes. There was a large tray with a basket of pastries, a coffee carafe, an enormous cup, and a pitcher of cream waiting for me. Jeffries had been by. I inhaled the steam, and my eyes rolled back in pleasure.

"I think you're enjoying that more than you enjoyed me," Raj teased.

"Nonsense," I scoffed. "I enjoy you just as much as I enjoy coffee."

He laughed and watched me finish my breakfast.

"Are you headed to the gate site immediately or do you need to feed first?" I asked, trying for a neutral tone. I wasn't okay with it even though I knew it was necessary.

"It doesn't matter in which order I do things tonight," Raj said. "I will need to feed at sunset every night before transporting all the landmines, though."

I swallowed my jealousy and reminded myself it was okay that he fed from others. Preferable even. I could only supply so much blood even if we weren't concerned about all the new powers he was siphoning from me. There would likely be a point when he'd gotten as much from me as was possible, and feeding would be purely nutritional. Or erotic. Or both. But we weren't there yet. He was right. Now was not the time to be adding to his arsenal on a daily basis. It was hard to deal with leveling up every five minutes—at least if you wanted to be effective at any of your new abilities.

"Eleanor, my sweet," Raj said, pulling me into his arms. "This jealousy seems very unlike you. What is going on?"

I fought back a flash of rage. He was right. I was not a jealous person and jealousy over where he found his next meal was unlike me. "I don't know," I said. "I felt a little jealous when I met Isaac's ex-lover Rebecca, but nothing like this." I tried to be logical. It wasn't working.

"Something is weird," I said.

Raj quirked an eyebrow at me. I stuck out my tongue. "You know what I mean."

I'd spent a lifetime of not being jealous. I was mated to a werewolf for fuck's sake and I still managed to avoid feeling excessively possessive. What was it about this vampire that aroused these avaricious feelings?

"Ordinarily, I'd delight in arousing any feelings in you," Raj said. "However, since this is so out of character *and* because I don't actually want to cause you discomfort by performing the necessary feedings, I think we should examine what's going on."

"Maybe I'm just jealous. This is a thing. It happens. There have been epic poems and ridiculous movies based entirely on the premise that women are jealous shrews."

"But this isn't you."

"True, this is unusual for me, but maybe it's just because you're superior to any of the men I've dated before."

"That is obvious. I don't think it explains it though."

"When did our bond settle?" I asked. Was it my imagination or did Raj's eyes widen a bit in surprise?

"When did the jealousy set in?" he replied.

I thought about it. It'd been pretty severe lately, but there'd been uncharacteristic twinges before New Orleans.

"When did the bond settle?" I asked again.

"I knew it was happening in Brooklyn," he answered. "It became permanent when we made love for the first time."

"So, my jealousy started when you first sensed the bond," I said.

"Yes."

"How possessive do you feel about me?" I asked.

"Not terribly," he replied.

"Really?" I answered. "You'd be okay if I slept with someone else?"

I felt a surge of rage and his eyes flashed red. "Absolutely," he said through clenched teeth.

"You wouldn't mind if you came across me on my knees with another man's cock in my mouth?"

This time it was more than just a brief wave. The tsunami of anger that washed over me was almost strong enough to knock me down.

"Vampire," I said. "What exactly is this bonding?"

Raj groaned and looked away.

I stared at him and tapped my foot.

Finally, he answered. "It's impossible," he said.

"Okay then. Tell me about this impossible bond."

"It is only possible between two vampires, and it doesn't work because two mated vampires drain each other to the point of death. What is happening between us is not real. It cannot be."

"Sweetheart, you turn into a twee, miniature dragon. Let's not talk about impossibilities."

He glared at me, but this time without the menacing ruby glints. I laughed. He really was an adorable mini. "We could turn into dragons at the same time. You're my mini-me."

He didn't find this as funny as I did. Whatever. I was totally the Dr. Evil of the Fae world.

I decided to change the subject. "What you're saying is that the strength of the bond between us is vampire strength?"

"And you're not a vampire."

"Do vampires mate—bond—with other supernaturals?"

"No."

"Who do vampires bond with then? Where is this body of knowledge coming from?"

For a moment, Raj was completely nonplussed. "You know, I'm not sure. We seldom mate with anyone. I guess it's just lore."

"Lore?"

"You know, canon."

I nodded solemnly like I knew what he was talking about.

"Do you know any bonded vampires?" I asked.

"Mehmed and Radu were bonded before Mehmed turned him. After, well, that didn't work out so well."

"Obviously."

"So, a human and a vampire bonded. Is that typical?"

Raj thought for a moment. "In everything I'm familiar with, yes."

"You don't know of any vamp/shifter or vamp/witch bondings?"

"No, nor any vampire/Fae bondings."

"We're unique."

"*You* certainly are," Raj muttered. I was pretty sure I wasn't supposed to have heard that.

"You love it," I stated. He just looked at me, but I felt a surge of affection that confirmed my assertion.

I got back to the point. "The vampire bonding usually settles on vampire/human pairs, but only the vampire feels the full strength of it, is that correct?"

Raj nodded.

"Our bonding seems to be pretty strong—as strong as it would be if two vampires bonded. That bonding is rare because it generally results in the eventual death by starvation of the vampires in question. Am I right so far?"

"Yes."

I tapped a finger against the corner of my mouth. "Do you think someone's fucking with us?"

Raj thought for a moment. "I think the bond is real. We both felt it start to settle into place earlier. I've never bonded before, so it's surprising but not impossible. I think that it's possible that someone is amplifying it to throw us off our game."

"Why would someone do that?"

Raj looked at me, "What would you do if you sensed I was in danger?"

I tried to think about it coldly—academically—but the minute it became a possibility in my mind, it felt like my vision was overlaid with red.

"Eleanor, I'm not," Raj interrupted. "Could you put out the sparks?"

I looked down at my hands, which were coated in a layer of fire. "I guess it's a good thing you're fireproof," I said. I was a little embarrassed at the strength of my reaction.

"If it's any comfort, I feel the same way," Raj said.

I smiled at him, "It helps a bit. But how is that nefarious?"

"What if you were opening the gate? Would you abandon that to save me?"

I started to automatically say 'no, of course not,' but the words stuck in my throat. "Oh holy crap," I whispered. "I'd do anything—give up anything—if I thought you were truly in danger."

"And if someone threatened your life in the middle of the opening,

I would interrupt, no matter the cost to me or the world, if it meant a chance to save you."

"This is going to be a problem," I said.

Raj nodded. "Even if this is completely real—and I believe our bond is real—it's still an issue. I need to feed," I again had to suppress the wave of jealousy at the thought of his mouth on another woman, "and you need to be there, doing your thing. I don't ordinarily object to you putting yourself in danger because I trust you to get yourself out."

"Maybe Florence can help," I said.

"Or Petrina. She's a witch and a vampire," Raj reminded me. "She might have come across something like this before."

"In the meantime, maybe just being aware of how irrational we're being will help."

"It has been helping," Raj said. "I've managed to let you out of my sight for several hours at a time."

"I didn't get weird when we were separated last night until you saw me in my half-dragon form. But I think that's mostly because I was really distracted by what I was doing. How are we going to do this going forward?"

"How about a don't ask don't tell for the feeding?" Raj suggested.

I mulled that over. "That should be okay. I mean, I'll still know it's happening, but I won't have to obsess about it at least. How far does our mind bond stretch? You said before that there was nothing I could do to keep you out. Is that always? Or just when we're together physically?"

"I'm not sure as we haven't been too far apart while awake recently. What are you thinking?"

"Regular check-ins. Like, 'Hey! Not dead and in no danger! Carry on!'"

Raj laughed. "And what if you are in danger? I can lie to you about my danger level, but you can't return the favor."

"Telling me that you're planning on lying about it is really going to negate the whole purpose of the check-ins."

"Let's go find Petrina and see if she has any suggestions. If not, we'll loop in Florence."

"One more question, Raj." He must have picked up a sense of what I was going to ask before I opened my mouth again, because I felt a surge of emotion through our link. "How do you feel when you think about me and Isaac?"

I couldn't identify any of the emotions that were washing over me. It felt like a crazy and overwhelming mixture of anger and jealousy and lust and resignation and grief.

I put my hands over my head like it was going to help stem the tide. "Please, Raj, lock it down."

The buffeting of emotions stopped, and I felt nothing. I lowered my hands and looked at him. "A bit conflicted," he said.

"I see. We'll just wait to revisit that one at a later time, then."

"Good idea."

I wasn't quite sure how to phrase the next question, so I just barreled ahead. "Can I stay here tonight? I mean, while you go out to do what you need to do?"

He considered me. "Why?"

"I don't want to be near you after you've fed. I can smell other blood on you. Also, I haven't done a lot of flying lately and I'd like to stretch my wings."

"Can you fly in your half form?"

"Yes, but it's easier as a dragon and I'd really like to get some air. It's been a long time since I've had time to myself to do that."

Raj appeared to be mulling it over, and I thought I'd better interject before he got the wrong idea. "I'm not asking for permission to be alone and fly. I'm asking permission to do it at your place."

He shot me an amused glance. "Oh, I know. I would never presume that you were asking for my permission to do anything."

"I'm not that kind of woman."

"I wouldn't want you to be."

"Are you sure? I've read the books and seen the movies. You old folks are supposed to long for the acquiescent ladies of your youth and be incapable of suppressing your male instincts in the face of a strong, independent woman."

Raj snorted. "I may have been born over a thousand years ago, but I wouldn't have survived sanity intact if I failed to adjust to the times. I've known plenty of strong, independent women over the last centuries; none of them would've thanked me for keeping them sheltered or denying their autonomy. I will protect as much as necessary, but you need very little protection. After all, you are—as you put it—a motherfucking dragon."

I smiled at him. "Your attitude is surprisingly progressive, vampire."

"I would like to progress back into bed with you later, and this seems a better way to do it than to threaten to lock you in an ivory tower for your own good."

"So, no more lying to me for my own good?"

"Touché," he said.

"I'm not getting that promise, am I?"

"No. But I will not make assumptions about your abilities in the future. If I do lie to you, it will be for different reasons."

"Ummm, okay then. Go before I get pissed off." I flapped my hand at him. He pulled me into his arms and kissed me until my knees buckled.

"I'll be back well before dawn," he said.

"Brush your fangs, first. I don't want to taste anyone else."

"You won't."

He brushed another light kiss across my lips and then strode out of the room. Watching him go was almost as much fun as watching him come, and I sighed in satisfaction.

After Raj disappeared, I headed to the kitchen to see if I could talk Jeffries into some more food. He made me several sandwiches—apparently, he remembered the strength of my appetite—and produced a pitcher of cool, delicious water to wash it down. I ate, drank a few glasses of water, then went out to the backyard. The yard was sparsely landscaped and dotted with sagebrush, agave plants, and other types of chaparral. It wasn't what I was used to in Portland, but it had its own wild beauty. The sky was resplendent with stars. Without any nearby light pollution, it felt like I could see into eternity. I stripped off my clothes and pulled the dragon into myself then out.

It didn't take long to shift, and it was amazing to feel whole and not have any obligations. For this night, anyway, I was alone and had no agenda. I wheeled up into the sky and did lazy circles in ever-widening spirals away from Raj's home. I tried not to think too much about Raj. I knew that he was likely feeding and the thought of that made me angry enough to cause fire to spew forth from my mouth. It was best to think of other things. Like Isaac. And what it was going to mean to be bonded to two very strong-minded supernatural creatures at the same time.

The surge of rage that triggered the fire breath this time didn't come from me.

Okay, then. Not the time to think about that, either. I guess this small distance wasn't enough to affect the strength of Raj's mind-reading capabilities. Good to know.

I focused on the feel of the breeze flitting over my scaled skin, the look of the half moon, and the glowing Milky Way that was brighter than I'd ever seen. I thought about the coyote I saw running below and froze when it stopped running and looked right at me. Before I could fall too far, I remembered who and what I was and started my wings again, but that was certainly one of the weirder encounters I'd had. I wondered if the coyote had been a shifter, or maybe it was Coyote.

That sent my thoughts down a wild forest path of philosophy and religion. I'd never thought much about God or gods or any of that, but if this new world I lived in with vampires and werewolves was all real, did that mean that all the stuff I'd attributed to cultural mythology were real?

I spent a very satisfactory few hours flying around the desert southwest thinking about old gods and new and wondering if I should try to get in touch with Neil Gaiman to find out how fictional *American Gods* really was.

My wings were starting to get tired, so I headed back to Raj's place. It had only been about four hours since he'd left, so I wasn't expecting him back for a while. His errands—I decided that was the safest way to think of what was going on—and his trip to the gate site, not to mention travel time to and from, should take another couple of hours.

I went down the private hall, closing the security door behind me, and entered the library—a room with even more books than the bedroom. Jeffries had lit the lamps for me, and although it wasn't as easy to see as by electric lights, it was enough.

I hadn't had a chance to read for pleasure in a while, and I was going to take advantage of his collection while I was here. I perused the shelves for a bit, trying to figure out how everything was organized, before determining that everything—fiction, non-fiction, poetry—was mixed up together and sorted by author's last name. I wandered through a bit, overwhelmed by the sheer number of volumes available, and eventually pulled out Stephen King's *The Stand*.

I was lost in the book when I heard the gears of the hidden door engage. I sat up, smoothed my hair, and waited for my lover to return.

CHAPTER NINE

Arduinna was waiting in the courtyard of the motel when Raj and I returned early the next evening.

"I must speak with you," she said.

"It's nice to see you, too," I replied.

She bowed her head almost fast enough to hide her rolling eyes, but not quite. "My apologies, Your Highness. Greetings. How are you? Isn't the weather lovely today?"

"I am well, and I appreciate you asking. The weather is quite nice. If I wasn't afraid that it'd get wicked hot in the summer, I'd consider setting up camp here permanently. How've you been?"

Arduinna sighed noisily. "I have been busy. Things are happening at a more rapid pace than we predicted, and I would appreciate the opportunity to apprise you of global events."

I waved my hand as majestically as I could. "Please do."

Arduinna pasted a pained smiled on her face and asked, "May I sit?"

"Of course." I led the way to a pair of small benches facing each other.

"Eleanor, my sweet, do you need me to stay for this conversation, or is it okay if Petrina and I get the location set up and secured?"

"Go ahead. If I need you, I'll call."

He dropped a kiss on my upturned lips and left the courtyard so fast I expected a comic book blur to appear in his wake. I turned my attention to Arduinna. "What news of the big world, Arduinna?"

"The United States government is fracturing, and the power of the current government isn't enough to hold things together. There are more independent militias than previously known, and they are organizing against the central government. They've found a new group to serve as a target of their hatred and bigotry, and that target is us."

"Us, as in the Fae? Or us as in all supernaturals?"

"All supernaturals. Pamphlets are being distributed on 'how to recognize Satan's demons' and the best ways to kill us."

"Satan's demons, eh?" I asked. "I wouldn't have guessed that's the direction they'd go, but now that I've heard it, it isn't surprising at all. How accurate is their propaganda?"

"It varies. They are pulling a lot of information from old movies and books, and so there is a brisk underground market in silver bullets and wooden crossbow bolts right now. They can't identify us unless we show our supernatural selves off, but a lot of assumptions are being made by these groups on what constitutes the 'look of evil.' You, the wolf, and the younger bloodsucker will be safe, but the witch and the old one will be suspect."

"The hate groups not quite ready to get rid of their racially-based hate?"

"It seems not. They are stating that minorities have been secretly hiding their association with the Christian devil, and that is what has 'tainted' their skin color."

"This is horrifying. How is this playing out?"

"As you'd expect. The level of racially-motivated violence is at an all-time high in the name of purging the country of supernaturals."

"What's President Murphy doing to combat this?"

"As of now, the militia is killing very few actual supernaturals. Mostly, they are impacting poor, minority humans."

"That didn't answer my question unless the answer is 'nothing.'

Are you trying to tell me the government won't act unless the violence is perpetrated against supernaturals?"

"The government would never endorse a stance of that kind."

"Unofficially, then?"

"There are too many sects and factions to quell right now. We are concentrating on solidifying power in the central government and the regions on the eastern seaboard. The violence is less there than in western reaches of this country."

I could feel my temper fraying. "Arduinna, a straight answer. Are they ignoring the violence against human minorities because they're human, even though they're being targeted due to their supposed supernatural status?"

"Yes," she said. She didn't volunteer anything more.

"That isn't right."

"What do you propose to do about it?"

"I propose that you get your green ass back to President Murphy and tell her to knock it off. If she wants to pull together a unified government, she can't ignore the elements that are powerless."

"If they are powerless, how could they threaten her standing?" Arduinna asked.

"Are you stupid?" I couldn't even gather my thoughts together enough to mount a coherent argument. "Leading a country while shitting on a large segment of the population is not a recipe for success. It's a recipe for discontent and rebellion. If she wants to be the one featured positively in the history books, she'll find a way to protect and uplift those who are downtrodden. Maybe it's not the United States anymore, but we don't have a new name yet, and some of the founding statements should be upheld. Are we not all created equal?"

"No," Arduinna said flatly. "We are not all created equal. The president is a Fae, not born on this plane, and therefore not even qualified to be president under the terms of the constitution. We are powerful and full of magic. Even the supernatural entities tied to this plane are superior to the average human. What can an ordinary person know of magic, of the earth, of a future with real consequences? They spend a few score years on this planet and do their best to break their home in the name of profit. They are not the equal of those of us who will outlive them by centuries and have to deal with the results of their carelessness. They do not deserve protection."

"Not every human participates in activities that harm the earth. Many of them are fighting to preserve it."

"They are all complicit. If they cared, things would've already changed."

I tilted my head and looked at her. "How long have there been Fae in the upper echelons of the federal government?"

Arduinna didn't answer, but she did look away.

"It's been a while, hasn't it? With the number of Fae I've met out and about, I know that many were trapped on this side when the gates slammed shut. If I had to guess, I'd say there's always been Fae in power here and in every government in the world."

Arduinna nodded.

"Don't talk about complicity, then. The Fae haven't done anything, either. And since we're so *fucking* powerful, it should've been easy to get our way over the clamor of the powerless humans, right?"

No response.

"So how about you tell the fucking president that she needs to get to work! If she's not interested in leading all the people, then she needs to step down in favor of someone who is."

"And is that someone you?"

"Fuck, no. I'm not old enough, for one thing."

"You are. You've recently turned thirty-five."

Oh, right. I waved my hand dismissively. "Doesn't matter. I'm too busy saving the world to lead it. She's the one who wanted the power. She needs to use it wisely."

"I will convey your message."

"Anything else I need to know?"

"The leylines are still not safe for travel. They blink in and out without warning, which has a rather unfortunate effect on anyone trying to use them. Sometimes they end up with parts missing. The last gate didn't have as devastating an effect when it opened. The damage was almost imperceptible initially. However, the magic wave is picking up strength as time goes on, and the expansion is showing no sign of stopping. It's a slow burn, but destructive. It'll hit Texas soon, and likely with enough power to take out the last working grid in the former United States."

I sighed. "It's too bad the leylines aren't reliable yet. That would be handy."

"Even when they don't randomly remove the odd organ or limb, it'll still be a while before they're fully mapped and ready for general use."

"Mapped, staffed, and taxed?" I guessed.

"The government needs revenue, and people need reliable transportation."

I tried to muster a smile, but inside I felt defeated. I'd gotten through life pretending that politics didn't affect me. And for the most part, I'd been right. I'd written letters to my elected officials every time someone tried to take away birth control and the right to choose, but overall, I'd stayed in my bubble, dutifully voting in every election for the candidate that seemed most likely to have compassion. Now, I was in a position to effect real change, and I was already exhausted.

"Unless there's anything else..." I trailed off and looked at her, hoping she'd say no and bow her way out.

She inclined her head, we stood, and she walked into the trees.

I WAS HALFWAY across the hotel lobby—headed for a hot shower—when I saw him.

"Finn." I tensed and prepared to call Raj, just in case. Better to ask my boyfriend for help than reveal to my stalker that I wasn't as powerless as he thought. No need to blow my cover in a fit of pique.

He was leaning against the far wall with that stupid, fucking, insufferable smirk on his face. "I've been waiting for you."

"If I thought it'd do any good, I'd take out a restraining order." I kept my distance and drew my sword.

"You don't have to be afraid of me," he said. "I'd never hurt you."

My burst of laughter was so sudden I startled myself. "You have got to be kidding. You've kidnapped me, had me magically bound —*twice*, sent groups of homicidal supernaturals after me, set a trap in Ringing Rocks to make me your mindless sex slave—"

"It wasn't about the sex. It was about love."

"Bullshit. If it was about love, you wouldn't be interested in forcing me."

"Don't you see? I'm just trying to protect you. You thought you had something with that dog, but he didn't stick around very long once he had an opportunity to go back to his old girlfriend."

"Are you serious right now? You do know that kidnapping someone and keeping them against their will isn't how relationships work, right? He's not off making time with Michelle any more than I'm planning on eloping to Vegas with you. Kidnapping is never romantic."

"Didn't your bloodsucker try to have you kidnapped? And didn't he succeed in getting you imprisoned and bound? Yet, you seem to be getting along fine with him. I don't understand why you deem him worthy and not me. I was there for everything over the last few years. I earned this."

I took two steps back and brought my sword up. "You can't earn a woman, Finn. I am not a vending machine; you can't put in niceness and get sex in return. I spent time with you because I liked you and considered you a friend. That didn't give you the right to my body or my heart."

"You've shared your body with me."

"Yes. I did. But that wasn't an open-ended contract."

"You're just punishing yourself for betraying me with the dog. It's okay; I'm not angry with you. We can make this work." He took a slow, gliding step forward and every hair on my body rose in protest. I lowered the point of my sword. "Stay back."

He laughed again and suppressing the urge to run him through with my sword took every ounce of willpower I had. "Why are you here?"

"I caught the tail of Arduinna's trip here and decided to tag along.

In about ten minutes, she'll walk through that door, buzzing like a hornet nest, demanding to know what's blocking her from returning."

"That's how not why."

"I know you're not as strong as you were before. I just wanted to make sure you were okay."

"Bullshit," I said again. "You don't care if I'm okay."

A wounded look settled on Finn's face. "That's not fair. You know I love you, Ellie."

Must not stab. I reminded myself, as I adjusted my grip on the sword I'd named *Elf Stabber* after he'd kidnapped me in South Dakota. *Must not stab.*

"I need you to leave," I said. "You are unwelcome and unwanted. Crawl back to your mistress like the lapdog you are." In retrospect, maybe that was taking things a bit too far. Finn had proved both his fragile ego and his irrationality more times than I cared to count. I wish Florence would tell me what use he had so we could brainstorm a way around it. Fucking psychics and their hesitance to influence the proper course of events.

The change in Finn was instantaneous. His fists clenched, his eyes narrowed, and a slow, dull red flush covered his neck and face. "Make me."

It was so ridiculous and unexpectedly juvenile that I laughed before I could stop myself. Again, a mistake. I might as well poke a mama bear with a short stick. He strode towards me and pulled his sword from the invisible sheath where he usually kept it. Before I could even brace myself properly, he attacked. I stumbled back a few steps and barely managed to get my sword up in time to counter his first strike. His onslaught was aggressive and quick, but his anger made him sloppy, and he wasn't difficult to counter once I got my feet firmly planted beneath me.

I slowed my breathing, concentrated on watching his eyes more than his hands, and calmly met every parry with a block, slowly backing him towards the door that led to the hotel courtyard. Although the staff were fairly understanding of the odd hours and habits of the few guests they had, I didn't think that acceptance would extend to a fencing match in the lobby.

By the time I forced Finn outside, he was breathing so rapidly he was practically hyperventilating, and I was still calm and in control. I dropped my guard a bit, and he took the bait, stepping forward and committing himself to an ill-advised thrust at my midsection. I sidestepped his attack, grabbed his wrist with my left hand, pulled him close to me, then rammed my knee into his groin. He dropped the sword at the same time he collapsed to the earth moaning in pain. He really ought to be more careful—that must have been the third or fourth time he'd had his package returned to sender with great prejudice by me or someone I knew.

"Bitch," he hissed out between clenched teeth. And there they were —his true colors. He might claim to love me and to be here to protect me, but all it took was a little taunting—and a kick in the balls—for him to want to hurt me. I wiped my sword on my pants and resheathed it. I took his sword, saluted him with it, and walked back into the hotel.

I TOOK a seat at the hotel bar—which served mostly straight liquor and wine, leaned Finn's sword against the wooden frame of the bar and waited for the underworked bartender who doubled as the bellboy to notice me.

"Jameson. Neat."

I almost never drank whiskey—I was more of a gin girl—but desperate times, and a martini-hampering ice shortage, called for desperate measures. The glass appeared in my field of vision interrupting my unfocused concentration on the scratched and stained wooden bar. The hand holding the glass was gray and smooth and the slightly webbed fingers ended in darker gray claws instead of the expected fingernails. I looked at the bartender. For a second his glamour wavered, and I saw a selkie in his human form.

"What the hell are you doing in the desert?" I asked.

His glamour solidified instantly, and he returned to the short, round, pale-skinned bartender I'd seen earlier. He glared at me. Before I could decide if I wanted to press the issue—and I almost certainly did because I didn't want any unknown Fae to be aware of my location—his eyes widened, and he took a step back.

"You'll pay for that," Finn said. Something cold and pointy slid its way around my neck and rested in the hollow of my throat. I froze. I didn't think he'd kill me—I didn't know what his endgame was, but I didn't think it involved my corpse. My mind went to a very bad place, and I shuddered in disgust. The knife—for that's almost certainly what it was—pricked my skin, and I felt a drop of blood well up to the surface.

"Hold still," he hissed.

I held, wracking my brain for a way out of this mess. I'd turned my back on him after wounding and taunting him. That was not the smartest thing I'd done in a long time.

"Stand up." The knife pulled up, leaving me little choice but to obey if I didn't want a slit throat. "Walk with me." He shoved me forward which pushed me a too far into his ridiculously sharp blade—seriously, did he get it from one of those late-night infomercials? Could it effortlessly slice a tomato?—and a fresh cut burned my skin.

"I can't walk like this," I said from between clenched teeth.

Finn heaved a sigh, but the knife traveled around to the back of my neck, and then down to the middle of my back. I heard the sound of footsteps behind me and hoped that Raj hadn't felt my distress and zoomed in to save me. This was embarrassing enough as it was, without needing my boyfriend to rescue me.

I strained my ears, but didn't hear any more steps, and decided it'd probably been the selkie making a break for it. The point of the knife dug into my back through the layers of leather and fabric. "Move it."

I started walking back to the courtyard, knife digging into my back. I hoped I wasn't going to be kidnapped. Again. I had a reputation to maintain.

The knife jolted into my back hard enough to elicit a gasp and then disappeared, the clattering signaling that it'd hit the ground. I turned around without thinking and saw the most inspiringly awesome thing I'd seen in a long, long time.

Emma was firmly attached to Finn's back. Her legs wrapped around his waist, and a look of grim determination was plastered on her face. One arm wrapped around his chest and under his arms, the other was in a modified sleeper hold with four gleaming claws splayed across his throat.

Seriously. Ninety-nine percent of Emma was human, but the sharpest wolf claws I'd ever seen were growing from her fingertips and threatening his jugular. I wanted to slow clap in awe but was afraid I'd distract her.

I picked up the knife he'd dropped, wiped my blood from the blade, and stood back, ready to help if she needed me. She drew a line across his throat and blood welled to the surface. She licked her lips, her eyes glowed amber, and she lifted her head and howled at the ceiling.

Every hair on my body stood up, and it took everything I had in me to not take another step back.

"You deserve to die," she said after the echoes of her howls dissipated. "You are a monster."

"Look who's talking," he gasped. "Where's your high horse now?"

"I don't need a fucking high horse."

I raised my eyebrows. Emma'd gotten some great speech pointers from me. I was so proud.

"Don't kill him," Florence said, striding into the room.

"Why not?" Emma growled. "He deserves it."

"More than anyone I know," Florence agreed. "But he still has a part to play."

"Fine. I'll let him live."

No one else could see his face—and even if they could, they didn't know his expressions as well as I did—but he was relieved. He'd really believed she'd kill him.

"I can leave," he said.

"You will leave," Emma said. "But first, you will remove the bond."

"What bond?" he asked.

Four claws punctured his throat, carefully avoiding anything vital. "You know what bond, elf."

He gasped, and tears streamed down his face. "There is more than one."

"You will fucking remove them fucking all."

I winced. She needed a bit more coaching to fully hit appropriate cursing. It was okay. I'd work with her.

"I can only remove the ones I set."

"Then we will start there, and you will tell me who set the remaining ones."

"I need to touch you to remove the bonds."

"You are fucking touching me, asshole. I'm on your back with my claws in your throat." Emma was losing patience, and I worried that the loss of patience would be followed by a loss of control.

"I need to take your blood."

Emma looked over at me. "That's what he did when he removed the bonds he placed on my mind," I confirmed. "No matter what he wants anyone to believe, he can't lie."

Emma nodded, pulled her claws out of his throat, and dropped off his back.

Finn dropped to the floor.

"Do it," she said.

"I need your blood."

"Do you need to draw it yourself or can I?" she asked. Damn. Good question, and one I wished I'd asked when it was my turn.

"You can draw your own blood, but I'll need to touch it."

"Fair enough. Eleanor, can you hand me the knife?"

I passed it to her and she made a shallow cut on her left forearm. "Do it."

Finn reached out and ran a finger through her blood. "Nire odolarekin, lotura hori apurtu dut. Sever konexioa. Nire odol prezioa da.

"It is done."

Emma took a couple steps back and looked at Finn. "Do you swear you have removed every bond between you and me?"

"I swear."

"How many remain?"

"Two," he replied.

"Who created them?"

"One was created by Michelle and one by Medb herself."

Emma's chin jutted up. "I've never been close enough to Medb for her to create a bond with me."

"You don't remember. That doesn't mean it didn't happen."

"Can you remove the other bonds?"

"No."

I interjected, "Can you remove your bond with Arduinna?" She'd walked into the room during Emma's heroics, but hadn't drawn attention to herself. She must not have gotten very far before feeling Finn use their bond to follow her again.

"No," Finn said. "I didn't create those bonds. Arduinna did."

I looked over at her and she nodded.

"Can I take him into custody now?" she asked.

"If you like," I said. "It seems he's been surfing your psychic wake. Is there a way you can prevent that?"

"Possibly," she admitted.

"If you can't promise me you'll prevent it, I'll be forced to do without you for the duration of this quest," I said. "Things are hard enough without him showing up every time we talk."

"I will close the channel," she said. She grabbed him by his elbow, but before she could leave with him, he disappeared. I glanced towards the corner where I'd leaned his sword and wasn't surprised to see it had poofed out, too.

Arduinna cursed and stalked out the door. I shook my head, unsurprised. That elf was slippery as fuck.

"Fucking hell, Emma!" I said once I was positive they were gone. "That was amazing. *You* are amazing. I had no idea you had that kind of control. You are an Alpha."

She grinned, ducked her head, and said, "Maybe."

CHAPTER TEN

Emma bounced into the hotel lobby where I was making the bartender extremely nervous by having an almost-cold martini and staring at him surreptitiously. I was growing to like the werewolf, but I still didn't know why she found it necessary to be so fucking perky all the time.

I glared at my not-cold-enough martini, stabbed one of the olives with my toothpick, and chewed it up with great prejudice.

Emma ordered a glass of water, elicited a put-upon sigh from the bartender, and sat down next to me.

"What do you want?" I asked.

"It's lovely to see you," she said. "How was your day?"

I growled at her, and she laughed. She clasped her hands and rested her chin on them, gazing at me through fluttering eyelashes.

I rolled my eyes. "I had an uneventful day," I said. "Now, tell me what you want."

"Tonight is the first night of the full moon," she said.

"Oh, shit! You're right! I'd completely forgotten."

"I can't forget."

"I don't suppose you can. Did you want to contact Chad's pack and run with them?"

"No. I might get carried away and accidentally kill Chad."

"No great loss," I said.

"Agreed, but I don't want to take over this pack. I have places to go and no desire to be tied to Santa Fe. Besides, I've been doing well without a pack the last couple moons. I'll go a little ways out of town and be fine. I merely wanted to inform you that I'll be heading out soon."

"Why not tell Florence?"

"I don't know where she is," Emma admitted. "Petrina and Raj are off doing their thing with the mines, and Florence is nowhere to be found. All I've got is you."

"Do you want me to come with you?"

She thought about it. "Not particularly, but it's probably not a bad idea."

"How much time do we have before moonrise?"

"Less than an hour."

I downed my martini and hopped off the barstool. "Let's go, then. I'll be slower than you, so we should get started."

We headed east towards the mountains and away from Bandelier. I was no slouch, but even in human form, Emma was a machine. We were in the foothills and out of civilization in a half hour, and by the time the moon began to brighten the sky, we were well away from any humans. I wish I'd thought to grab a hoodie, but I'd have to make do and hope that the chill of the spring night didn't send me into hibernation.

"Emma, I need your clothes," I said. My teeth were already chattering.

"Darn it," she said. "I didn't even think about what the cold would do to you. You should go back."

"I'll stay for a bit since I'm already here, but toss me your clothes as you strip. If it looks like all is well, I'll head back to town to get more clothes."

As she started shifting, I sorted through her clothes. I put on her socks, t-shirt, and long-sleeved flannel. I wasn't as warm as I'd like to be, but I'd last long enough to ensure Emma was going to be okay.

I finished putting on the extra clothes at the same time Emma finished her shift. I'd seen her shift faster, but apparently, she wasn't in a rush today. She stretched, her snowy white fur gleaming in the light of the rising moon. She bared her teeth at me, and I flipped her off. "Bring it wolf," I said. Her tongue lolled out in what I assumed was wolfy amusement.

She lifted her muzzle and howled to the moon. Every hair on my body stood on end, and I shivered—but not from the cold this time. Emma was amazing, and I couldn't wait to see her take her own pack. I didn't know if the packs had a structure like the vampires, with one wolf to rule them all, or whatever, but if they did, Emma was going to be a contender for the top spot. She had more control than any…my thoughts trailed off as she turned back towards me and bared her teeth again. This time, the light in her eyes wasn't playful, it was mad.

She growled. The low rumble made my guts clench in fear, and I stood up, facing her and not lowering my eyes. She might be dominant as fuck as well as an apex predator, but I was still a motherfucking dragon, and there was no way I was going to roll over for her. She paced forward, and I held my ground. I reminded myself that shifting was always a possibility. We might want to keep everyone in the dark about the state of my fancy New Orleans binding, but if it was a choice between saving my life and the lives of possible innocents or letting the cat—or dragon, rather—out of the bag, I was voting for the big reveal.

"Raj! If you can hear me, now would be a good time to practice beaming yourself up." I sent him an image of Emma and put the full force of my fear into my mental call for help. I didn't get anything back and wondered if we had a distance limit for communication. I straightened my backbone, looked her in the eye, and said, "Emma. Sit!"

It worked just as well on her as it had for my annoying neighbor's even more annoying chihuahua. Emma was probably a lot less likely to bite my ankles. Although, the way she was looking at my throat made the lessened threat of ankle-biting not as comforting as it could've been.

Shit. I shivered. The temperature was dropping rapidly, and if I didn't do something soon, I wasn't going to be able to do anything at all. I started stripping off my clothes, hoping the movement would keep me warm enough to shift and compel her to behave herself. Isaac hadn't needed me to be in my dragon form to fall under the sway of my dominance, but Emma was a hell of a lot stronger than Isaac.

Before I could finish taking my clothes off, I felt Raj's presence behind me. "Get dressed," he said. "I have a place we can take care of this."

I didn't ask questions, just did as he said. I was already shivering and starting to feel the effects of the cold on my body. Emma was stalking closer and closer to us, and I wasn't sure how much time we had left.

"What are we going to do?" I asked Raj, my teeth chattering so hard I thought they might break.

"We'll take her to my place. I have plenty of land there, and latent wards that will be easy to raise with the help of a witch."

"How are we going to get her there?"

Raj paused for a minute and looked at me, clearly stumped. "I hadn't gotten that far," he admitted. "Do you have any ideas?"

I thought about it. The only viable idea I could come up with still involved leaving Emma alone for a few minutes, and that might be long enough for her to get into trouble. "Only one," I said, "but it's not a very good one."

"It's better than the lack of ideas I have, and yours has a possibility of working."

I rolled my eyes. There were never private thoughts. "Let's do it, then," I said. "The sooner, the better."

Raj rose straight up in the air and disappeared. I kept my eyes on Emma and attempted to raise my body temperature by adjusting the levels in my hypothalamus. It didn't work, but at least it kept my mind busy and off the possibility of falling asleep in front of a possibly wild werewolf.

It felt like hours but was in reality probably only a few minutes before Raj returned with Petrina. He set her down and picked me up, rising back up into the air with a whoosh. I shivered against him, his lack of body heat intensifying my chill, and tried to concentrate on not falling asleep.

My feet hit the ground and jolted me awake. Raj handed me to Jeffries who wrapped me in a blanket and set me on a padded bench in front of a fire pit.

"Th-th-thank you," I stuttered. He handed me a mug of steaming tea, nodded, and disappeared.

Moments later, Raj reappeared again with Emma in his arms wrapped in some kind of netting and Petrina riding piggyback. She hopped down, glared at her father, and walked off, presumably to activate the wards Raj had lying dormant.

"What will they do?" I asked through my chattering teeth, narrowly avoiding biting my tongue.

Raj didn't look at me when he answered. All his attention was on Emma as he backed away from her, one corner of the netting in his hand. She whined, then snarled at him, snapping her teeth and slavering.

"It will keep all sentient beings within the perimeter of my property and will mask the presence of magic. No one outside the barrier will be able to see what's happening—on a magical scale, at least —within.

"Handy," I observed.

"Get ready to run," he answered.

"Where to?"

"Behind you, to the house. Go now."

I turned and stumbled towards the dark mass that must be his cavernous hobbit hole of a house. The torpor was coming on quickly, and I was clumsier than usual. Every branch and pebble in my path was an obstacle to trip over. I was about halfway there when someone scooped me up and flew me the rest of the way.

In seconds, we were inside, and the sturdy door was bolted behind us. I heard the angry snarls of a wolf on the other side and shivered.

"What's happened?" I asked. "She's done so well the last few full moons."

There was some more growling and scrabbling at the door, and even knowing that together Raj and I could take her with no problem whatsoever, I still shrunk away from the sounds.

"I don't want to speculate, but given the timing, I can't help but wonder if the bonds Finn forged with her mind gave her an extra modicum of control."

It sounded plausible, or at least as plausible as any theory I could come up with.

"Will she be okay?"

"I caught and released a few rabbits just a couple yards away," Petrina said, striding into the foyer. "She'll catch their scent as soon as she gives up on the door, and once she runs off into the woods to chase them, she'll have a more normal full moon night. The only humans in the vicinity are Jeffries and Salem, so she won't inadvertently harm anyone. I'll keep an eye on her tonight so that I can make sure she gets back to shelter once she shifts back to human form, and we can make a better plan for the next two nights."

Petrina blurred out of view again, and I realized the sounds at the door had disappeared. I sagged as the tension went out of my shoulders. Raj wrapped an arm around me and led me to a small and cozy sitting room lined with bookshelves on three sides and a large, roaring fireplace on the fourth. Jeffries was waiting for us with a plate of sandwiches, a tray of brownies, and two glasses of wine.

I fell on the sandwiches like a starving werewolf and only came up for air after licking—literally—the last crumb. I looked up and saw Raj and Jeffries both staring at me with something akin to horror. Jeffries quickly schooled his features back into their usual polite disinterest, but Raj didn't bother. "I was hungry," I said. I picked up one of the glasses of wine and a brownie and settled onto the loveseat positioned in front of the fireplace.

I suddenly remembered what Raj and Petrina had been doing when I called him to my side. "Shit! The landmines! I can't believe I interrupted that. You shouldn't have come."

Raj gave me a look that could politely be called incredulous disbelief. "And what? Leave you to either betray the full range of your abilities to anyone lurking nearby or be eaten by a hungry werewolf when you fell asleep? The mines will be there tomorrow, and now, so will you and Emma."

That made sense, and I nodded at him. My nods must have been a little more serious than I thought because the next thing I was aware of was being carried. Images and sensations happened disjointedly. My clothes were peeled off. There was a bed, soft and warm, and then a cool kiss on my forehead.

"Good night, my sweet."

EMMA WAS in the kitchen when I made my way there the next—I glanced at the clock over the stove—early afternoon.

"How are you?" I asked as I poured myself a cup of coffee.

I turned back towards her in time to see her face turn scarlet.

"Fine," she muttered.

"There's no reason to be embarrassed," I said. "We've all made miscalculations before."

"Who says I'm embarrassed?"

I rolled my eyes and poured cream into my coffee. "You're blushing like a virgin bride on her wedding night."

"What would you know about that?"

Oooh...she was not interested in talking if she was already going for the slut jokes. Too bad. "I've read about it in stories," I said. "We don't have to talk about what happened last night right now, but we do need to talk about it if only to make sure it doesn't happen again. You can decide the exact time, but it will happen, and it will be today."

I took a cautious sip of my coffee and nearly groaned in delight. I wondered if I could add Jeffries to my entourage. After all, if I was to be queen someday, I should probably start amassing servants, right? I'd need one person whose sole responsibility was beverages. Or maybe that was a two-person job? One for coffee and one for beer and wine?

"Fine." One word, torn grudgingly from Emma's mouth, interrupted my reverie of traveling with a herd of people whose only jobs were to see to my comfort.

"Now?" I asked, setting my coffee down and joining her at the large, farm-house style table. Sunlight streamed in through a skylight enhancing the white, wood, and chrome furnishings and making me feel immediately at home.

"Might as well," she grumbled. "Get it over with."

I waited. And sipped my coffee. And waited some more. When my second cup was halfway gone, I broke the silence. "No one blames you," I said.

Her head jerked up, and she glared at me, eyes flashing with temper. "I do."

"This was your what," I did some quick calculations on my fingers, "third full moon since rejoining this plane?"

"Fourth."

"After being trapped on another plane and prevented from shifting for fifty years."

"It wasn't that long for me."

I waved away her objections. "Regardless. A very long time. Your control is extraordinary. Either you are a very young wolf who's had only a few years to learn that control, and you're amazing. Or, you're an older wolf who spent most of her life trapped and unable to shift, and you still have great control. You pick which you're most comfortable claiming."

She was glowering at me, and her eyes were more amber now than baby blue. "I had perfect control in New Orleans," she growled, and the timber of her voice made every hair on my body stand up in fear. I didn't want to float the theory Raj had come up with the night before, but it seemed even more plausible in the light of day.

"It might be possible that the bonds Finn forged without your knowledge or consent lent some control. After all, he is old, and although recent events tend to belie this, he has a lot of mental control."

"He is a..." her face contorted as she sputtered through half-formed curses looking for the right epithet. "He is a ratfucker."

I stifled my laughter and agreed. "Yes, but he is a very old half-elf ratfucker who can exhibit inhuman control when he chooses to. Maybe some of that was available to you either with or without his intervention. Now that you know it's going to be harder, you can shift tonight with that knowledge and be prepared. It was too easy before. You need a challenge."

Oh, she was pissed off now. Her eyes were starting to glow, and if she didn't tamp down that temper, she was going to sprout fur right here at the table. I leaned back, sipped my coffee, and drove it home. "Even if all the control wasn't yours, you're still doing pretty well for a werewolf Barbie. Definitely meeting expectations, although you may have been right when you insisted you weren't Alpha material."

She sucked in a breath between her teeth, clenched her jaw, and wrestled her temper back into place. The glow faded from her eyes, and within seconds they were back to their regular sky-blue. She stopped shaking with anger, picked up her coffee cup, and said, "Tonight will be better."

Heh. She was so easy sometimes. Might be time to throw her a bone. "You are so strong, Emma. When you lost control last night, I couldn't cow you in my human form. My presence was all Isaac needed, but you're much stronger than he is. If you can maintain control without me flying overhead breathing fire at your ass, I will personally sponsor you in whatever pack you decide to take over. I wasn't kidding earlier when I said given the circumstances you were doing extraordinarily well."

A small smile ghosted across her face and was quickly replaced by a hard line. "And just now? Were you trying to goad me into losing my temper?"

"I was trying to goad you into reining it in," I corrected.

"That was cruel."

"It worked," I pointed out. "You regained control in record time, even though it's a moon day and you were already upset."

"I did, didn't I?"

"You absolutely deserve to be proud of that. Tonight, when you shift, remember how it felt to pull back from growling at me today. You can do it."

I WATCHED from the magically reinforced window while Emma shifted. I'd watched other wolves shift—mostly the St. Louis pack and Isaac—but I'd never seen anyone make it look so effortless and almost beautiful.

Emma stood in a bright patch of moonlight amid the carefully landscaped xeriscape, and I could see her shaking from here. She turned a slow circle, and the light caught the amber in her eyes. Something caught her attention, but whatever it was it was too small or too far away from me to see. Her hackles rose, and she bared her teeth. I couldn't hear her, but I was pretty sure she was growling.

She closed her eyes, lowered herself to the ground, and held very, very still for so long I had to fight the urge to knock on the glass to see if I could get a response.

After what seemed like ages, she stood up and somehow managed to perfectly position herself in the brightest shaft of moonlight. Her pale coat glistened silver as she raised her muzzle to the sky and howled. She glanced towards the window where I was waiting—alone—and padded over to me. Even knowing the glass was theoretically unbreakable, I still tensed. She pressed her wet nose on the glass, leaving a smudge, then let her tongue loll out of her mouth in a wolfy grin.

I let out a breath I hadn't known I was holding and smiled back at her. She dipped her head in acknowledgment without breaking eye contact, and I followed suit. A meeting of equals, then. This was the first time I'd ever experienced the in-control Alpha Emma on a full moon, and I found that I quite liked it.

She turned and trotted out of sight, and I sighed a breath of relief knowing that all it took for her to maintain her control was the knowledge that she needed to. Now that she wasn't surprised at the difference, she was able to pull herself together in one night.

I walked back to the library where I knew Jeffries would've left me a bottle or two of the cheaper wine, and I'd have my choice of books ranging from history to biography to a surprising amount of vampire romances. I mulled over Emma's control and strength as I sipped a glass of wine and browsed the paranormal romance section of Raj's library. A sudden thought stopped me cold, and I almost dropped my wine.

"What if Emma wasn't just bait or punishment or whatever it was we all believed her to be? What if she was just as much a target as Isaac?"

A noise behind me made me jump, and I finished the job my earlier thought had started and dropped my wine.

"Fuck!" I said.

Jeffries bowed, somehow managing to convey apology with that action. He disappeared—he was almost as fast as a true supernatural—and reappeared with a rag and some cleaning solution. I was happy the rugs in the library were dark enough that the red wine stain would remain nearly unnoticeable.

Jeffries stood, held out my unbroken glass, and when I took it, he refilled it. He then handed me a notebook on which he'd written, "the wolf is the most powerful I've seen, and I've heard the master talk. He's never yet seen her equal, either. She would be a prime target for the vampire known as Michelle."

"Do you know Michelle?" I asked.

He took the notebook back, turned that page, and then in an elegant script wrote while I looked over his shoulder, "I've known her my whole life. She's a collector. She gathers things that are pretty or powerful. If she'd sensed the Alpha power in a wolf as young as Miss Emma was when she was first taken, Michelle would've coveted her. If the young wolf also held Isaac's attention as his interest in Michelle waned, she would've been doubly interested in obtaining her."

Something wasn't quite right, but I couldn't figure out what. To buy myself time, I asked a question. "How long have you been with Raj?"

He smiled, shook his head, and topped off my wine glass.

Strike one.

"If you have known Michelle your whole life, it follows that you've been associated with vampires your entire life. Did you always know what they were?"

Jeffries looked at me a moment, and then wrote, "I serve the master's family, as did my mother before me."

Not a lot of information, but better than nothing.

"Who's Michelle?"

He looked at me for a moment, then turned the page, and wrote, "She is the unstable vampire of whom we've been speaking. Are you tired? Have you had too much wine?"

And then the jerk drew a winking emoji. I looked at his face; he was laughing soundlessly.

I pointed at him. "You are a jerk, Jeffries."

He smiled, bowed, and exited the room, but not before uncorking another bottle of wine and leaving it next to me.

My stomach fluttered uncomfortably. I was nervous and didn't know why. Florence had driven out to fetch us after Emma woke at sunset since Raj and Petrina were still busily disarming the gate site. Between an Alpha werewolf, a wi—I caught Florence's side eye out of the corner of my own—mage of incredible power, and a decently powerful Fae, we were pretty safe.

"You are not decently powerful," Florence said. "You are a helpless little fairy who has to rely on us to protect you."

"Bite me, witch," I said.

"You know why we are doing this."

"Blah, blah, blah to keep Finn complacent and from setting even more traps for us. Whatever." I heaved a loud put-upon sigh.

"Don't worry, Eleanor," Emma piped up from the backseat. "We'll protect you."

I buried my face in my hands. My life had gotten so weird.

"Shit!" Florence yelled. I jerked my head up in surprise. She almost never swore. I was just in time to see three robed figures in the road in front of us before Florence slammed on the brakes. The seatbelt cut into my chest, and I braced myself against the dashboard. There was no way we could stop in time. My old car might be decent, but it wasn't made of magic.

Florence spat out a word I didn't understand, but it made every hair on my body stand up, and a chill washed over me. The car stopped inches from the women, and I breathed a sigh of relief that while my car might not be made of magic, my bestie for life was.

"Who are they?" Emma asked.

As if they heard her, the three women tipped their heads back so their hoods slid back, revealing the blood red material inside.

"Necromancers," Florence said the same way I might say "cheap American lager."

"What does that mean?" Emma asked as a row of figures appeared in the darkness.

"I'm going to take a wild guess and say zombies?" I hazarded.

"Ghouls," Florence corrected. She hadn't let go of her grip on the steering wheel, and her knuckles were turning white. "There's no such thing as a zombie—not the way pop culture would have you believe, anyway."

So many questions, but from the way Florence was glaring at me, I got the sense that now was not the time.

"Ghouls like Marie had in New Orleans?" I asked instead.

"Approximately," Florence said. "But instead of...whatever she is... these are necromancers. They have a lot less control than Marie does, and their morals are even more suspect than Madame Laveau's."

The ghouls were shambling closer, and the looks on the faces of the necromancers were approaching a frightening level of ecstasy. "What do we do?" I asked.

"I will talk to them," Florence said.

"Is that a good idea?"

"Probably not, but unless you have a better solution..."

"Run over them and their weird undead freaks and get back to town?" Emma suggested.

"I like it," I said.

"What if they're on our side?" Florence said.

"Is this typically how necromancers make friends?" I countered.

"It could be. I don't know that many."

"Do you think the ghouls are bringing the wine and cheese?"

Emma clapped her hands together. "Oh, I hope one of them can make me a pink squirrel!"

"What the fuck is a pink squirrel?"

"Cream, crème de cacao, and some other ingredient that tastes like amaretto."

"That sounds revolting," I said.

"Oh, it is! It was so popular with the kids in my set. I never understood it."

"Children," Florence chided.

"What? We're just preparing our drink orders in case they are here to throw us a welcome party!"

She closed her eyes and heaved a heavy sigh. I'd heard that sigh before—it'd been years, but that's exactly how my mother sounded about 30 seconds before I got sent to my room. I did my best to appear contrite: widening my eyes and blinking up at her. "We'll be serious."

"Don't make promises you can't keep, Eleanor."

"What do you want us to do?" Emma asked. She hit contrite-sounding better than I did.

"You two stay here, but have your doors open so you can get out and back me up if I need it."

"How will we know if you need help?" I asked.

"If you see a few dozen ghouls tackle me and I don't come up swinging within thirty seconds, that'll be your sign."

Sometimes her wit was so dry I needed a glass of water just to talk to her. Wait a minute... "A few dozen?" I looked up, and where before there'd been ten flesh-eaters, now there were close to fifty. "I'm beginning to think this isn't the welcome wagon."

"Give me five minutes; then you can come out with metaphorical guns blazing. They may want to talk and are just using the ghouls as an intimidation tactic."

"It's working," I muttered.

Florence patted me on the arm. "Don't worry, dear. Emma and I can handle this."

I narrowed my eyes at her. "Don't get cocky, witch."

She opened the door and strode over to the trio of women. Arms akimbo, she stared at them while I opened my door so I could eavesdrop.

"Why are you blocking our path?"

"You have no right to be here."

"I thought witches weren't as territorial as shifters and vamps," Emma whispered.

"I don't know. You probably know as much about it as I do at this point. Shhh...I'm trying to listen."

"...will not host the world breaker and her companions. This goes against everything we stand for."

"How?" Florence asked.

There was a moment of silence, and looks of consternation floated across all three women's faces. "The Fae traffic in our kind."

"Necromancers have long been known to commit the same crimes, and more. You upset the natural order of things more than most Fae I've met."

"Our magic is of this earth." Necromancer number one stretched up to her full height—which was, admittedly, fairly impressive—and tried to look down her nose at Florence.

"Your magic is born from pain and blood and death," Florence said. "You are more unnatural than any Fae. They have no tradition of blood sacrifice to achieve their aims."

"Only kidnapping, torture, and murder."

"If that's what you truly believe, then it sounds like you'd be right at home with them. You cannot dismiss the foulness of your acts by pointing fingers in other directions. The misdeeds of others don't justify your own."

And with that, discussion time was over. The three necromancers stepped back, and I took a moment to be impressed that they could walk backwards without seeming to worry about tripping over their trailing cloaks. Then the ghouls attacked.

Fortunately for us, ghouls are not the swiftest foot soldiers, so Emma and I had plenty of time to get out of the car and get to Florence before the first wave hit. "Need backup?" I asked.

"Probably not, but if it makes you feel useful," Florence said. I rolled my eyes at her. Every once in a while, she tried to horn in on my idiom, and I tried not to let her know how much it amused me.

I drew my sword and swung it around a few times to warm up my wrist. Emma began removing her clothing, taking the time to fold everything neatly and place it in a tidy pile on the hood of the car. The necromancers were staring at us, but not in the awe and fear that I hoped. At this point, they seemed unconcerned by the presence of my sword, Emma's boobs, and Florence's…I glanced over at her, and the smile on her face was enough to make me take a step back. Clearly, the necromancers were looking at the wrong people. If they'd been watching Florence, they'd have turned tail and been in the next county by now.

"It is our three against your three," Florence said. "Do you think you can beat us?"

"We are more than three," middle necromancer said. She was much shorter than the other two and had a pleasing roundness to her pretty face. She also emanated power like heat from the world's most powerful space heater. She was the one to watch. Unlike them, I wouldn't make the mistake of taking my eyes off the strongest person in the room. She gestured behind her, the skin of her arm blending almost seamlessly with the black cloak and blacker night. One long, pale fingernail caught the light of the waning moon, and I followed her gesture. The shambling hordes—they weren't going to win any land speed records—were almost upon us.

"Question?" I asked.

The necromancers' turned towards me in spooky unison, and I shivered involuntarily. They didn't say anything but didn't tell me to shut up, either, so I plowed ahead.

"I can't help but notice that your ghoul army isn't that fast. Why are you convinced that you'll beat the people who are willing to stand and face them rather than hop in their car and zoom off?"

"We have more than enough power to keep you from fleeing," Shorty McScarynails said.

"That's not the point," I countered. "The point is you don't have to keep us from fleeing. We're not trying to get away. Doesn't that tell you anything about the people you're messing with?"

"You've been neutered," the statuesque goth one said. "And the wolf is too young to be a threat. The only one with any real power is the earth witch, and they are healers, not killers."

My jaw dropped. These three had no business challenging strangers to a game of ping pong much less a pitched battle the night after the full moon.

"I'm getting cold; may I change?" Emma asked. I admired her ability to take the backseat to Florence as easily as she'd taken the lead with the equally incompetent local shifters.

"Of course," Florence said.

"Is anyone in this part of the country working with a full deck?" I demanded. In the space it took me to ask, Emma had changed, and unless I was hallucinating, she was bigger than she'd been last time I'd seen her up close. She sat at Florence's side and bared her teeth. Tall and creepy turned even paler.

"You still have three score ghouls to fight as well as us," the hitherto silent one announced. I understood immediately why she'd remained silent. She was cursed with one of those voices that would have people mistaking her for a child long into her dotage.

Florence laughed, and a chill breeze rose up and swirled around us. "You are gravely mistaken. I only have to defeat you, and they will sink back into the dust from which they were formed."

A few of the ghouls had flanked us and Emma and I stepped away from Florence to take care of the first wave. I wanted to compliment her on her grave pun but decided now wasn't the time. Fighting ghouls was both easy and annoying. They were slow and easy to mark, but they couldn't die, even with my rapier slightly—and hopefully undectably—enhanced by air magic. Watching a headless corpse shuffle towards you with arms outstretched was an experience I never wanted to go through again. I cut through them, thankful that their speed didn't compromise my adequate but not fantastic swordswomanship and concentrated on cutting off legs rather than heads. Crawling corpses bothered me slightly less.

The chill behind me grew more pronounced and goosebumps spread across my body. I sliced off the head and legs of the ghoul nearest to me and turned back towards Florence just in time to see all three necromancers impaled with what looked like super-sized icicles.

The bodies crumpled, and as the life bled out of their prone bodies, the ghouls started to rot and fall apart, the stench of the grave washing over me and triggering my gag reflex.

"Holy shit. Guess your girlfriend's been telling family stories. That was some quality impalement." When in doubt and holding back vomit, my go-to was awkward jokes and revealing poorly kept secrets.

CHAPTER ELEVEN

Petrina and Raj met us in the hotel courtyard a couple hours before dawn, both a little put out that we hadn't called for backup. "It is better to be safe than right," Petrina said to Florence, reaching out to tuck a strand of hair behind her ear. Petrina's hand lingered on Florence's face and dusky pink stained Florence's cheeks.

"We were fine," Florence protested. She smiled up at Petrina. "Just a few ghouls. Nothing I couldn't handle."

"Plus, she had backup," Emma pointed out. "I was there."

"And me!" I announced. "I dismembered quite a few ghouls before Florence the Impaler took over."

"Florence the what?" Petrina demanded.

Florence glared at me. Oops. We hadn't gotten to that part of the story yet, and from the shade she was throwing my way, she may have been planning on glossing over that part. Either that, or she was still pissed at me for calling out her not-so-secret relationship.

"How did you think we defeated an unkillable ghoul army?" Emma asked. "We didn't have the right kind of magic to cut their connection and removing and burning each and every ghoul brain would've been dangerous and tedious." Florence had given us everything she knew about ghouls on the trip back to town and Emma had just summed it up for us.

"Florence is a badass," I informed the vampires. "If she ever exhibits the full range of her abilities—abilities she's been honing for half a century—she could probably take us all out. Don't discredit her because she's human."

Petrina's eyes widened, and she took a half step back before she caught herself. "This is truly what you believe?" she asked me. "That a human is more powerful than any of the rest of us?"

She was trying to get under my skin with her 'mere human' talk, and it wasn't going to work. From the chill permeating the room, though, it was getting under Florence's skin. "Don't be an ass, Petrina. You know me well enough at this point to know I am not anti-human. The only person you're pissing off is your girlfriend, so tell her you're just poking the dragon, and then take her back to her room so you can apologize properly."

Petrina grinned at me, fangs on display. "You are cleverer than you look."

"She'd have to be," Emma muttered, just loud enough to ensure we all heard her.

"Anything else of note happen?" Raj asked. He'd been silent through the whole exchange, not even throwing suggestive thoughts into my head.

"Nope," I said. "Unfriendly necromancers and a ghoul army pretty much sums up the night."

"Do you have plans for the next hour or two?" he asked.

"I'm going to bed," Emma announced, rather more loudly than necessary. She tromped out of the room with none of her usual shifter grace. Florence and Petrina followed her, and then it was just Raj and me in the empty hotel courtyard that was conveniently heavily foliaged and had a scattering of benches about.

"What did you have in mind?" I asked after a quick scan verified that we were, indeed, alone.

He raised my hand to his mouth and pressed his lips against it. "I had a few ideas of how we could pass the time before I must seek my rest."

I pulled him to a bench and pushed him down before settling myself on his lap. "What kind of ideas? Are they the kind of ideas that mean we can stay out here and enjoy the night air?"

Raj's hand skimmed up my side and brushed against my breast. My breath quickened, and he smiled at me. "If that's the game you want to play tonight, I don't mind indulging you."

I found his lips with my own and kissed him, opening my mouth to him and running my tongue over his fangs. I shifted on his lap until I was straddling him and pressed myself into him, rocking against him, until we were both breathing heavily.

"You are a devil woman," he said against my throat before biting, careful to not break the skin. "You tempt me in ways I've not been tempted for hundreds of years."

"Good," I whispered. "You deserve a little temptation."

His hands found the hem of my shirt and he pulled it over my head. I shivered against the suddenness of the chill air against my skin, but the fire in my blood kept me warm. We took turns kissing and touching and stripping until we were both naked and aching with need. I resumed my position straddling him on the bench and eased down oh-so-slowly onto his erect cock, teasing us both as long as I could.

"Eleanor, please."

I smiled at the pleading in his voice and let myself go. I rocked against him, faster and faster, bringing myself to climax within minutes, before settling into a harder, more steady rhythm. His hands were full of my breasts, and I looked down to watch him take each nipple into his mouth in turn, teasing them into erect points. I started to lose control of my rhythm and Raj's hands slid down to my hips, urging me faster and faster. I cried out my orgasm seconds before him and collapsed against him in a boneless, sated heap.

I don't know how long I lay against him, but soon the chill of the pre-dawn air overcame the residual heat of our frenzied love-making, and I shivered. "Probably should get dressed anyway," I said. "Someone could be along any minute."

"I thought that's what you were hoping for," Raj teased as we cast about for our discarded clothing.

"Someone walking by while we're mid-coitus is altogether different than someone seeing me after," I said. "Not the same thing at all."

I dressed in record time and as I pulled on my boots, I noticed the eastern sky was tinged with the barest hint of pink. "I suppose you need to go?"

Raj pulled me into his arms and kissed my upturned lips. "I do, but I'll see you tomorrow. Petrina and I are nearly finished."

"Have a good day," I said, trying for nonchalance and failing miserably.

"You, too, my sweet," he said. "Do you have plans?"

"I might contact Arduinna, take a nap, pester Florence. The usual."

"I love you," he said. Before I could answer, he was gone.

"I know," I said to the empty courtyard.

I WOKE A FEW HOURS LATER, if not refreshed, at least not as cranky and restless as I'd been before my nap. I stretched, dressed, went on a quest for coffee. The hotel bar was always open, and the selkie bartender was always there—day or night—and the fact that he didn't like me made me much more likely to want to order from him. I wasn't sure if the contrariness was part of my Fae heritage or something I'd inherited from my human parents.

I bellied up to the bar, waited for him to glare in my direction, and then said in my perkiest under-caffeinated voice, "Coffee, please! With cream, no sugar."

He grunted in acknowledgment and five minutes later a steaming cup of coffee and a mini pitcher of cream were slammed on the bar in front of me. Coffee sloshed over the side onto the saucer and the selkie stared at me as if challenging me to say something.

"Thank you so much! Is the kitchen open?"

He didn't respond, just tossed a hand-written menu down in front of me and walked off. The only item on the menu was a green chile-smothered breakfast burrito, and I didn't even have to think about it. "I'll have the breakfast burrito," I called out. "Extra green chile!"

There was no reply, but he did stomp through the doors that led to the kitchen, so presumably, my order had been received. I sipped my coffee and thought about what I needed to talk to Arduinna about. Mostly, I wanted an update on the political machinations of the President and her minions, including my boyfriend's grandson. Now that I was more or less directly responsible for the downfall of the union, I felt that I owed it to the rest of the country to take an interest in politics—especially since the folks in charge were not necessarily as nice to the downtrodden as I'd believed when I'd voted.

After devouring the best damn breakfast burrito in the history of breakfast burritos—seriously, green chiles are a gift from the gods—I headed out into the courtyard, smirked at the bench Raj and I had defiled that morning, and reached out for Arduinna.

I hadn't even opened my eyes when Arduinna snapped, "What?"

I jumped back a half step. She never appeared this quickly, and she never showed how much I irritated her. Part of me was irritated as fuck that she dared speak that way to me—the Dragon Queen, heir to the Dark Throne—and part of me was appalled that I had such a visceral reaction to her disrespect. I backed my brain up five steps and tried for mild. "Did I catch you at a bad time? We can always chat later if it's inconvenient." I pushed the full force of my truth into my words, knowing somehow that she'd hear it.

She deflated somewhat. "Apologies, Highness," she said. "I was in a meeting with the President and General Mircea."

"You need a busy signal," I said. "I wanted to talk, but it's not urgent."

"The next gate opening isn't for two more weeks. What could you possibly want now?"

"An update on the state of the union?" I asked. She was being incredibly and out-of-characteristically rude. “Is there something else bothering you?”

“May I sit?”

Rude, maybe, but still instinctively on protocol.

“Of course.” I sat first, knowing it made her more comfortable. I wanted to reassure her again that she could go if she had to, but I didn’t. Mostly because I was the queen here, even if I was trying to suppress that part of me, and a little bit because I’d given her an out and she hadn’t taken it.

“May I speak frankly?” she asked, surprising me out of my internal bitchiness.

I tilted my head to one side and looked at her. “Of course, but are you sure that we’re alone?”

“Can’t you ensure we won’t be overheard?”

Fair point. “I can put up a shield, but if you’re still linked to Finn, I can’t guarantee he can’t listen through your mind. I don’t understand how that link works.”

“The link between my mind and the half-breed’s was implemented by me. I control the link, and he cannot access what I don’t wish him to access as long as I’m paying attention.”

“Okay, but remember, I was bound in New Orleans, and that greatly affected my magic.” I had to bite my tongue to stop myself from continuing.

“I will come closer so that the range of your magic doesn’t have as far to stretch.” Arduinna came and settled next to me. She had almost a foot on me but still managed to sit with her head lower than mine. I pulled the magic to me and pushed it out, doing my best to seem weak and incompetent, but not sure how well I was succeeding.

“It’s up,” I said.

“I have a dilemma,” Arduinna said.

“Please, tell me about it.”

“I am a double agent and work for the Dark Queen.”

That was a blow I didn’t see coming. My breath left me in a whoosh and I stared at her. She refused to meet my eyes.

"If you're a double agent, you must have a side you're really on," I said, not knowing what else to say and trying to buy time.

"Do you remember when you asked me about how a Fae could be a spy?"

I wracked my memory and came up with the vague ghost of a conversation from several months before. "Kind of? But a reminder would be appreciated."

"You asked me how a Fae could work for both your father and the Dark Queen and not be caught. I told you it wasn't easy. That the double-agent would have to be even more skilled than most in deceptive truths to never lie but to continue to serve two masters. That if they were asked, "Are you a spy?" it would not be enough to answer, "Why would you think that of me?" or "How could you accuse me of such a crime?" because a competent questioner would continue to drill the person until they got a definitive answer. Instead, the person must be so successful the question of guilt would never come up—they would have to divide their allegiance and be loyal to both parties. Not many are capable of such things."

"I remember now," I said. "I also asked how one could ever trust a double agent—for certainly at least one of the masters must know—if you knew their loyalties were divided."

"Do you remember my answer?"

"Yes. You don't."

Arduinna sat, head bowed in silence, for a long time while I tried to think of something to say. "Why are you telling me this now?"

"Because I have betrayed you."

"Okay, so there's that. But why tell me? And if you're a double-agent, whose side are you on? Is your first loyalty to Eochaid or Medb?"

"Do not say their names," Arduinna hissed.

I rolled my eyes. "Fine. Is your first loyalty to the Light King or the Dark Queen? You say you betrayed me, but was that in your role as a double agent who works for the King, or as the spy in the service of the Queen?"

"Both believe me to be a double agent for them."

"Christ on a cracker, Arduinna. If you're not going to fucking answer any questions about this, why even bother telling me? Get to the point. Tell me why you decided that today was the day you were gonna come clean, or get the fuck out and get back to the meeting you were bitching about leaving when you first showed up."

Arduinna met my eyes. Her irises were swirling greens and browns, and I noticed that her human glamour was wavering, too. She was about thirty seconds and one more stressor away from revealing her true form as the Green Man. Or Green Woman.

"Lock it down, Arduinna. You're losing control."

She flexed her fingers which now resembled twigs more than human hands, and visibly stiffened. Her skin flashed between the faintly green-tinged flesh that she usually sported and the mossy bark of an ancient deciduous tree. I swallowed back my nausea and averted my eyes.

"You can look now," she said, her voice deeper than usual.

She was no longer Arduinna, but Seth, in all his political lackey glory. Short brown hair in a standard cut, even teeth, tan skin...the kind of vaguely handsome politician that fades into the background at every political gathering. He took a minute to straighten his cuffs and then looked at me. "This form is easier for me to maintain."

"Why?"

"Is that the why you want, or would you like me to answer your earlier questions?"

I really wanted him to answer all my questions, but if I had to choose... "Fine. Why are you revealing your double-agent status now?"

"Because it's exhausting, frankly. Spying for two thrones as well as setting up a new government with a bunch of supernaturals who all want to believe they're the ones in charge, and then showing up whenever you want to talk...it's getting tiresome to maintain so many façades."

Suddenly I knew exactly whose side he was on. "You're in this for you, and that's why you don't have any trouble convincing either ruler that you're really on their side. You're on your own side and will do whatever it takes to advance your cause. If that means you follow the Light King's orders to protect me and the Dark Queen's orders to sabotage me, there is no internal conflict, because all you're doing is advancing your agenda."

He nodded at me, the early morning light glinting in his eyes that were exactly the wrong shade of green. "Guessed it in one. And that's why I decided to confess my role to you."

"Because you suddenly think that loyalty to me is going to be the most beneficial to you?"

"Precisely. You have little patience for the political machinations of the Fae and don't appreciate misleading truths nearly as much as others born to rule. By being honest with you now, you will trust my word more in the future."

"You were the one to tell me to never trust a double agent," I reminded him.

"But I won't be a double agent anymore."

"You'll quit your jobs in the Dark and Light courts?"

His mouth opened in a wide grin; his teeth were a little sharper looking than was typical for a human. I shuddered. "Of course not," he said. "Don't start being naive now."

"Oh, gods. You want to work for all three of us, but keep the other two ignorant of the fact that you're also taking orders from me, too, don't you?"

"Now you've got it."

"You're split into too many pieces, Seth. At this point, my interests largely align with the Light King's. Why not just include me in that camp?"

"You're the heir to both thrones. You are the only living issue of the Light King, and I've heard you lay claim to the Dark Throne, a fact that the current queen is extremely upset about, which makes me believe there is some credence to your claim. Why wouldn't I tether my star to someone with such an intriguing future?"

I sighed. "The Light King intends to give me this country to rule over, too, as a consolation prize for him not abdicating in my favor. I really do have a lot of prospects."

"Is that a yes?"

"Can I stop you?"

"You could refuse to speak to me any longer, and the command that I cannot approach without your permission still holds."

"But then I'd be without news of the outside world," I pointed out.

"Indeed you would. Such a conundrum." He leaned back, crossed his legs, and folded his hands over one knee. Motherfucker. He'd backed me into a corner, and he knew it.

"What do I get out of this, other than a continuation of the news feed?"

"My loyalty, of course."

"Right now, that doesn't count for very much."

"My word that when you decide to take the thrones, I will fight at your side."

"What if I only decide to take one?" I asked. I hadn't missed the pluralization.

"Then, of course, I will help you take the one of your choosing," he said, so smoothly that I couldn't tell if he was self-correcting quickly, or if that had been his intent the entire time.

"And in the meantime?"

"I will report back to you on all the schemes plotted by both thrones, as well as those of the half-breed."

I considered this arrangement. It seemed too good to pass up. I was about to agree when I realized there was one important question I hadn't asked. "What do you want from me, in exchange for agreeing to this?"

He smiled, and the predatory gleam that lit up his eyes caused the hair on the back of my neck to stand on end. It took all my self-control not to shift and light him on fire. Even if he was nominally on my side, he didn't need to know I wasn't still bound and weakened. "I want your assurance that you will allow me to stand at your side. I want you to recognize me as your advisor. I want power."

"I will not give you power if you will abuse it. There will be rules in place."

He waved away my caveat, "Of course. Your moral code is well-known if a bit odd."

I let it go. My insistence on treating humans like people worthy of respect was unFae-like. "Fine. I agree." I reached my hand out to shake on it, but instead of a firm handshake, there was a knife against my palm, then his, then he clasped our hands together and said, "Horrek ez du lotura indartsu bat."

Fuck. What had I just gotten myself into? *Oh well, what's done is done.*

"Tell me what you said," I demanded.

"It was just binding words," he replied.

"Translate them. Exactly."

He smiled, barely showing his teeth this time. "It translates as '*This is an unbreakable bond.*'"

"So, no way out, then?"

"Only death can break this bond. We are tied together forever. My loyalty lies foremost with you."

"And have you sworn this vow with anyone else?"

"Unbreakable bonds are discouraged."

"How are they discouraged?" I asked.

"There is a penalty of death for entering into one if it's discovered."

I hid my face in my hands for a moment. "How often are they discovered?"

"Only if one of the parties discloses it, or if they're overheard making it or discussing it. To that end, I suggest we never speak of it again. To anyone."

Eventually, I'd need to tell Raj, but for now, that made sense. "That's an eminently sensible suggestion. Now talk. Tell me everything."

I FOUND myself that evening in the unenviable position of once again defending my actions to Raj. This time, Florence joined in on the recriminations, although when I reminded her and Petrina that she'd been gallivanting around the Santa Fe area impaling necromancers just twenty-four hours earlier, she caved and lapsed into a judgmental silence, which was better than her much, much louder judgment.

"What would've you done differently?" I asked Raj. "Because the information I got today was pretty good, and it's an ongoing deal."

"You had to promise her a prominent seat in your government to get it."

"And? Arduinna or Seth or whoever they choose to be at any given moment is the only person I know from the Fae realm besides Finn. It was pretty likely that if I ever did take the dark throne, I was going to need an advisor anyway. Arduinna was the most likely candidate."

"There are likely things you didn't think of to ask."

"There likely were, Raj," I said. I could hear impatience shortening my voice and I took a deep breath to temper it. "There weren't good choices, and I hope I made the one that benefited me the most. Why don't you hear the intelligence I gathered from her and make up your mind from there? I am an intelligent adult, capable of making my own decisions, and while I appreciate your concern, you are starting to piss me off."

Raj crossed his arms, which made my thousand-year-old boyfriend look like a pouty emo teen. I laughed before I could stop myself, and he must have picked up my thoughts, because he doubled down on his sulk for a moment before straightening up and saying, voice tight with tension, "You are definitely an adult. It is one of the many things I appreciate about you. I will try to hold back judgment, but I wish you would've talked to me first."

I took a deep breath, bit back the retort I wanted to make. Now wasn't the time nor the place to argue. I was too emotional, there were too many spectators, and if I lost my temper, I'd reveal too much. I'd told my friends about my bargain, but had conveniently left out the part about the unbreakable bond punishable by death. "I appreciate your willingness to listen."

"So," Emma interrupted. "Are you ever going to tell us what Arduinna told you that made you think it was all worth it?"

I grabbed the beer Petrina proffered, popped the top, and settled down. "Medb has known I named myself the Dragon Queen since I opened the second gate. Finn brought her that information in exchange for her assistance in getting rid of Isaac. She is behind Finn's incompetent attempts to end my life, as well, but doesn't want me dead until after I open the final gate. She has designs on this world as well as her own. For some reason, she doesn't want to fight Eochaid for his throne, but thinks this plane will be a good prize.

"She believes me to still be bound, which isn't surprising because Arduinna also believes that to be so. Finn's memory has been tampered with so many times in the past decades that he's no longer playing with anything resembling a full deck. When he came to Medb before the fall equinox, he believed it to be the first time. His obsession with me wars with the commands of his queen, and that interferes with his competence.

"Also, Isaac knows that Arduinna has been working with the Dark Queen, as does Finn. Finn believes Arduinna's loyalty to be first to the Dark, then to the Light. Isaac regards Arduinna as a traitor. And the Queen has issued a command to Michelle that Isaac not be killed, although there's no ban in place on anything else. One last thing—the Queen has allowed Finn to live because, without him, the final gate cannot be opened. This belief is what's kept him alive on our side, too, am I right, Florence?"

She nodded but offered no verbal response.

"If both sides believe it true, then I guess we'll continue to tolerate his existence."

"Did Arduinna have any idea if Finn had other plans for this gate besides the landmines?" Petrina asked.

"She swore to have no other information."

"And what of Eochaid?" Raj asked. The sulk was out of his voice and he sounded genuinely interested. "What news of him?"

"His motivations seem as uncomplicated as they've been from the beginning. When I was born, I was presented to the court as his daughter and the heir to the Light Throne, then Arduinna took me, found a couple with few familial ties and unable to have children, and left me with a note and a bank account. Almost three decades later, he captured Finn sneaking into the palace, although no one knows what purpose he had—Arduinna believes he'd been sent by Medb, but had had his memory so thoroughly messed with that he couldn't reveal his intentions—and agreed to commute his death sentence if he'd sneak through one of the many holes between the worlds—it's apparently easier for the half-Fae than the full Fae—to keep an eye on me."

"So, your father did send him?" Emma asked.

"The Light King may have sent him, but Arduinna suspects that Medb had a hand in it as well."

"And since then? How has he been acting?" Florence asked.

"Like any concerned, but completely ruthless parent. Thrilled for my successes, disappointed in any failures or shows of humanity. He has no intention of giving up his throne to me and tells the courts that although I'm up to the task, my power levels aren't enough to rule in his stead."

"What does that mean?" Emma asked.

I sighed. "I got a crash course in Fae succession, but I'm not certain I understand. Eochaid needs to name an heir, or he appears weak. The Fae are near-immortal, so the heir isn't that exciting of a position, but necessary. His progeny would be considered to have an advantage when filling that position, but it's not a foregone conclusion. The heir must be the most powerful Fae in the court, and the child of a king is often the most powerful, but not always. He's painting me as less powerful because of my youth, inexperience, and 'human taint.'"

"Taint?" Emma asked. "Aren't you one hundred percent Fae? How could you be tainted?"

I raised a hand to cut off whatever Raj had been planning on saying and answered Emma. "I was raised by humans with no knowledge of my true parentage and came late to my powers. Therefore, I am likely weaker—or at least less experienced and less controlled—than anyone else in the Court with a claim to the throne.

"All that being said, though, Eochaid will happily accept me as heir if I can pass whatever test his court decides is necessary but has no intention of ever stepping aside to give me the throne. Arduinna believes he intends to offer me this plane to rule as his regent. She also believes that President Murphy has no intention of stepping aside and once the gates are open, that she will declare this plane not subject to the Fae thrones."

"That only makes sense," Petrina said. "This plane has far more resources than Faerie. Why would the minority population think they can rule?" She tilted her head, shook it ruefully, and added, "Never mind. Of course, they think they have the right to rule. They believe themselves to be the most powerful and the purest of all supernaturals and regard humans as little more than serfs. Forget I said anything."

"Bottom line," I said, "is that the information I got from Arduinna was interesting and valuable. She will also serve as my advisor and guide when I go to the Fae Plane to find and rescue Isaac, as well as advise me on anything I need to know when entering the Dark and Light courts. It was worth it." I glared at Raj, who dipped his chin to acknowledge my point. That wasn't enough for me. "Say it."

"You were right, Eleanor."

"And?"

"And I was wrong to doubt you, especially before hearing the entire story."

"Thank you. You know, a man who can admit when he's wrong is sexy as hell."

"That's our cue," Florence said. In seconds, my room was empty of everyone but Raj and me.

"Now what?" I asked.

"I have some ideas."

CHAPTER TWELVE

The need to clear the mines reached a critical point, and Raj and Petrina called in reinforcements to act as eyes and ears so they could concentrate on their part of the job without worrying about interference.

The next days passed in a blur. Each evening, Raj flew me to the gate site since I was not supposed to be able to fly myself. I would wait at the site for Emma and Florence to show up, and the three of us patrolled the site, hoping Finn wouldn't show up, while Raj flew the landmines to the old canyon Petrina guarded and then reappeared at my side.

It was boring for everyone but Raj—for him, it was exhausting. After a tense moment he refused to go into details about on the second night, Raj decided that his idea of speeding things along by carrying two instead of one wasn't worth the risk, even if it was faster. Because he didn't have to tesser back since he could reappear at my side, even with the other things that needed to be done each night, Raj was still getting rid of almost twenty mines a night. *We were absolutely going to make our goal.*

I tried not to let the next part of that thought creep into my mind...*if nothing goes wrong.*

It was hard to believe that everything would continue to go smoothly. There'd been problems leading up to every gate opening. Gate the first—I couldn't find it. Gate the second—werewolf fights, vampire attacks, and stubborn witches. Gate the third—more werewolf attacks, not to mention the witch attacks, and the whole Grigori thing. I spared a moment to wonder what Marie was doing with his head.

I shook that thought away.

Gate the fourth—Isaac the asshat, and the attacks at the opening itself, including getting shot.

Gate the fifth—the set up in the preserve, including getting shot again, not to mention the rune stone spell that Finn had set.

Gate the sixth—imprisonment and binding. Also, the Fae army attacking.

It stood to reason that something else would happen here. I couldn't imagine Finn putting all his eggs in one exploding basket.

I tried not to think too much about what else he might have up his sleeve.

Florence was withdrawing more and more into herself and resisted all my efforts to draw her out. She even ignored me when I called her Flo. I knew I'd need to address that soon, but we'd have time. In the meantime, I might as well complete this 'making friends' thing I was doing with Emma. We'd fallen into an easy repartee as we patrolled the gate site.

I'd never really had a girlfriend. Or any friends. We talked about growing up and the differences between Portland in the fifties and Portland in the new millennium. We assiduously avoided talking about boys, since her last boyfriend was my mate, and that topic was still confusing as fuck for everyone.

I teased her about being a goody-two-shoes, and she teased me about being easy. Neither of us meant it anymore, and it was nice to have moved on to that place where you could call a woman a bitch and have her say thank you.

I told her about the feminist movement and equal pay and legal abortion and birth control. She told me of the Fae court and what she'd observed and what I'd need to do if I wanted to fit in.

She was much stronger than anyone—including herself—had ever thought. Her beach blanket bingo body hid a keen intellect and—now that she was more comfortable with her place in the group—some very strong positions. She needed a pack, though. We were a makeshift one, but she hadn't spent much time with normal modern werewolves. I decided not to count the pack in Alpha since they'd turned out to be double-crossing asshats, and the pack here was not any sort of useful.

I'd never thought I'd be the kind of woman who, when happily in love, wanted everyone else to have the same thing, but it turned out that I was a bit. Or, what I actually wanted for Emma was some mind-blowing sex so that she could get some and have her last sexual memory be *not* my mate. But mostly for selfless reasons. Everyone should be getting laid on the regular if you asked me. She didn't, though, which was disappointing. The only thing I enjoyed more than actually getting laid was talking about getting other people laid.

However, as open as Emma was to just about every other subject I brought up—including my lectures on how there was a woman president, so she could be anything she wanted, dammit—she refused to talk about sex. It's too bad I couldn't set up a profile for her on Match.com. Or Tinder. I took the beer I was drinking and poured one out for Google.

I WAS ON HIGH ALERT. It was our last time here until the morning of May first, and I was not going to let the elf take me by surprise. By the time Raj disposed of the last landmine, and he and Petrina used their combined pyrotechnic skills to destroy the cache, I was so wound up that an errant breeze had me jumping out of my skin.

Raj appeared by my side, and I yelped.

"Done," he said. He was even paler than usual, and for a vampire, that was saying something.

"Do you need to eat again before we go home?"

"It depends on what you want from me for the rest of the evening," he said.

"Can you even get us both home in that state?"

He laughed, "Probably, but I'll probably pass out before I even get in the door, and you'll have to carry me across the threshold."

I sighed. "Go. Eat. I'll ride back to town with Emma and Florence. You can pick me up at the hotel when you're done."

"Thank you," he said.

Raj picked me up at the hotel about an hour after we arrived, and he must have showered because he didn't smell of anything but soap and water and his signature scent of exotic spices, sandalwood, and smoke.

It was three days until the gate opening, and although I'd been doing nothing but patrolling—and having a lot of incredible sex—I was exhausted. I shouldn't be. I wasn't using my powers much at all, saving it for the big show—or even longer, if I could get away with opening a gate sans anything but gate magic.

As leader, I gave everyone the next night off, and we agreed to meet at sunset the night before the gate opening to finalize plans.

"We should call the pack," I said.

"Ugh," Emma said.

"You should call them, Emma. They're your bitches now, and it wouldn't hurt to have backup. We've been attacked at every opening, and I'd love to have a few extra hands on deck for this."

"Fine," she groused. "I'll do that tomorrow."

I looked at Florence, "I'll check in tomorrow. Send Petrina if you need us earlier. In the meantime, Raj needs to get some rest."

She smirked, looking for a moment like the Florence I'd first met and not the brooding Florence that was biding her time for the kill. "I'm sure Raj will be getting *plenty* of rest," she said.

I opened my eyes up as wide as I could, going for innocent school girl. "Whatever do you mean?"

She snorted and waved us away. "Get out of here, you degenerates. I'm just glad I don't have to hear you two resting."

"See you in a couple days," I said as Raj picked me up and shot straight into the air.

WE SPENT the next day and a half in bed at Raj's secret hideout. There was a kind of frenzied desperation to our lovemaking. I wasn't sure if it was coming from him or me or both of us, but there was this niggling feeling that we might not both survive the next few weeks.

A couple hours before we were to leave to meet the others, when we both had called a timeout, I asked him the question he hadn't yet answered. "Raj, why did you need the sword?"

"For the final gate. It has to be there, and I need to be the one wielding it."

"But why?"

"It has been foretold."

"Was it also foretold that you were going to be a giant ass?"

Raj closed his eyes and intoned, "There would come a man, born under an auspicious moon, who would rise to power in the time of myth. He would live for centuries, learning, biding his time, until the day he was declared the world's biggest ass."

I snorted and threw a pillow at him. He grinned and pulled me onto his lap.

"It's almost time," Raj said. "Are you ready?"

"As ready as I can be, I guess. We have a bit of time, though, before we need to leave."

He kissed me. "Aren't you tired yet?"

"Of you, vampire? Never."

AT SUNSET ON APRIL THIRTIETH, Raj and I met the others at the hotel in Santa Fe. Everyone was subdued. Emma reported that she'd called the pack, and they'd agreed to show, as per the terms of their surrender.

We arrived at the gate site at three in the morning. Florence and I began weaving the weir that would slow the trickle of magic into the world. She'd warned her contacts at Los Alamos, and they'd ensured that anything that needed to be protected was far away.

By five, I was exhausted, but the weaving was done. I extricated myself from the weir and went to stand on the eastern edge of the small stone circle that marked the site. Emma came to stand beside me. "What do you need me to do?" she asked.

"Raj and Petrina will patrol the perimeter. They'll need to take off almost immediately after the gate opens since the sun will be rising but should be there to ward off any trouble until then. If you could guard Florence's back, and coordinate the pack, that'd be great. She's not completely unaware of her surroundings, but it is more difficult for her to pay attention to everything when the magic starts flowing."

"Of course. You can count on me."

"I know. I wouldn't ask you to guard Florence if I had any doubts."

She smiled at me, a brilliant flash of white in the darkness.

"When does the pack arrive?" I asked.

"They should be here any minute," Emma replied. "I said five-thirty."

"Okay. Tell them to watch for trouble, not to interfere, and keep an eye on them."

"As you command." She sketched a loose salute, went to stand near Florence, and began to shift.

Raj and Petrina were already roaming the perimeter, alert for any sign of life that wasn't the five of us.

"Raj," I called about a half hour later. "Can you drop me in the middle?"

We'd decided that even though the area was clear, we were going to avoid walking in it if at all possible, in case we'd missed any of Finn's other tricks. Raj glided over, picked me up, and deposited me in the center. He kissed me and said, "Good luck, my sweet. I'll see you tonight."

"I probably won't see you," I said. "I'm usually unconscious."

He kissed me again and returned to his post.

Soon after, I felt the surge of energy erupt out of the ground. It didn't hurt like it had in New Orleans; it was exhilarating. I opened myself to embrace the rush of power and worked on channeling the overflow into the weir that I'd constructed with Florence.

The eastern sky was stained pink and purple when the main swell of magic poured out. I snapped into the hovering X that had marked each of the previous openings and let myself be the instrument to bring forth this gate. I was ecstatic by the time the stream began to slow to a trickle. I felt my feet hit the ground, and I opened my eyes in time to look through the gate.

I gasped in awe. The sky was crystal-blue, and I looked into a forest clearing that was so peaceful I couldn't help but absorb the serenity it was casting off. And then I saw it. A pure white creature walked into the center of the clearing. The golden sun glinted off the silver of its horn. In the blink of eye, it was gone.

I watched the gate fold in on itself and snap back into waiting non-existence.

I knew at that moment that every one of the previous gates had momentarily appeared as well and that as soon as I completed the final task, they would all open permanently, if not quite so visibly. I smiled. I was so close to being done.

I looked around. Raj and Petrina were nowhere to be found, and I guessed they were already heading to cover. I felt a brief mental caress from Raj and then nothing. They were safe. I started across the circle towards Emma, who'd shifted back to her human form, and Florence, who was untangling herself from the spells we'd woven.

"Where's the pack?" I called. I knew I was starting to slur my words but couldn't help it.

"They didn't show," Emma growled. "I will destroy them for this betrayal."

"Oh well. Looks like we didn't need them. That was easy."

"Too easy?" Florence asked.

"Stop!" Emma screamed. I whipped around, trying to figure out who she was yelling at. I turned back towards her in confusion. There was no one else here. She started running towards me and changed in mid-stride.

My mouth dropped open. This woman was going to rule the world.

I didn't move, not sure what had alarmed Emma, but not wanting to move until I figured it out. She hit me at full speed and with full werewolf strength. The wind was completely knocked out of me and flashes of blinking light appeared in my vision.

"What the fuck, Emma?" I gasped as soon as I could. She was standing *on me* and looking around. This was making me incredibly nervous. Then she was off me again and racing back towards where she started.

I stood slowly, trying to catch my breath. I could feel the exhaustion threatening and knew I'd be out of commission soon, but I fought it. I didn't know what was going on, and I didn't want to pass out if there was still a threat.

I watched Emma race back towards Florence, and that's when I saw it. There was...something...rising out of the cleansed earth between Florence and me. Emma had sensed it was there and assumed I was the target. Now I could see that it was aiming a gun at Florence.

"Florence! Down!" I yelled.

She looked at me, still dazed from the magic and dropped the rest of the way to ground.

Emma tackled the shooter, causing the bullet to go wild. She began ripping at him with her claws, but before he was destroyed another shot rang out. Blood spread on her cream-colored belly, and I started running. She finished ripping the shooter to shreds, and no others rose to take its place. By the time Florence and I got to Emma's side, she was already changing back to human. I knew that was a bad sign.

"Silver bullet," she whispered, a trickle of blood staining her porcelain cheek. "I'm sorry."

"If you don't live through this, you will be sorry," I said.

She laughed and then groaned. I looked down. Gut shot. That couldn't be good. If only Petrina were here, she could heal her.

I must've said that last bit out loud, because Emma said, "I don't think even healing magic could help me now. Thank you. Tell Isaac thanks for saving me. But thank you for showing me that I was more."

Florence still hadn't said anything. I looked at her, hoping that meant she was performing some complicated magic to contain the worst of the damage until we could get Petrina here to heal her, but she was just staring, tears streaming down her face.

"He was a human," Emma said. "He said he'd collect the bounty."

Fuck. This had gone further than I'd thought. "Hold on, Emma. We'll get help."

"Good-bye," Emma whispered.

"Damnit!" I yelled. "This is not how it works. I just started liking you."

She closed her eyes, and I felt more than saw the breath leave her body. No breath came in to take its place.

Grief and rage swirled through my mind, and I felt the wind whip up.

"Eleanor," Florence said. "You need to control yourself."

Her face wavered in my vision. I was almost at the end of my strength. I needed to get to the car, take Emma's...body...to the car. My vision grayed out, then flared red. The body of Emma's murderer lay in pieces beside her. There was nothing more I could do to him. He was beyond pain, beyond punishment. I wished I could bring him back, so that I could kill him again slowly.

"Eleanor!" Florence yelled from far away.

Everything went black.

I CAME to in the middle of a firestorm. A wall of flame encircled me and curved up and over, making an almost complete dome. I felt the heat on my face, and I roared my rage and satisfaction into the fire.

Why was I so angry? I tried to calm myself long enough to find the source of all this. I'd been opening the gate. It'd been successful—the easiest yet—and then Raj and Petrina left. The pack hadn't come, and Emma was pissed.

Emma was…dead.

Another wave of rage rolled over me, and the flames rose even higher. My wings flared behind me as the heat-breeze swirled around me.

My vision was tinged with red, but when I glanced down, I saw her. Saw Emma. Still and lifeless. Blood roared in my ears, dulling the sound of the inferno. Emma was dead.

"Eleanor." The voice came to me, piercing my mind. That voice was familiar. I searched my memory until I latched onto a name. Florence. I didn't want to hurt Florence.

"I'm going to touch you, Eleanor," Florence said. She kept saying my name like it was supposed to mean something to me.

Her hand touched mine, and I shivered. She was the ice to my fire. Her rage was cold and slower than mine, but it was there. I let her ice temper my heat and knew she was drawing my warmth in to balance her chill.

"A human did this," I said. My voice was strained and inhuman in its timber.

"Yes," Florence said.

"He should pay."

"He has paid. He is dead."

"It isn't enough!" I roared, and the flames shot up another twenty feet.

"It will never be enough," Florence agreed.

"They have done this, with their bounties and their fear of otherness."

"I know better than you ever could," Florence said. "It will never be enough."

"I will kill them all." Resolve grew in me, and my spine straightened. I drew more power from the earth and felt it whither beneath me.

"You will kill the land and us if you don't stop. I can't let you do that. This is sacred land, and we have a job to do."

"You think to tell me what I can and cannot do?"

"I think I'm the only one who can."

I tried to pull my hand away, but it was frozen to hers. A ring of ice rose up in the middle of my firestorm. The fire melted the ice as fast as it grew, and the air became wet with steam. Constant hissing from the melting filled my ears, and heat started leaching from me faster than I could send it out. I tried to draw more from the earth, but that pathway was blocked.

"Control yourself, Eleanor," Florence said. Goosebumps rippled over my skin and the red-tinted haze that obscured my vision started to recede.

Movement in the corner of my eye caught my attention, and I turned, ready to take on this new danger.

Raj walked through my wall of flames. Something wasn't right. Vampires were flammable. A ray of sunshine illuminated him. He didn't even flinch. The last of my resistance faded, and the flames sputtered and died.

"How?" I asked.

"You needed me," he answered.

"I'm sorry, but I'm going to pass out."

"Can you get her to the car?" Florence asked.

"I'll take her home and come back to help."

"No," Florence said. "I will do this on my own. Take care of Eleanor."

"I'm sorry, Florence. I'm so, so sorry."

"I know, Eleanor. It will be okay."

It wouldn't, and we both knew it. At that moment, I envied her ability to tell a comforting lie.

"I'm sorry," I said again.

"Go. I'll take care of Emma."

I let go of her hand and turned to Raj. I hoped Florence would be okay. I hoped she was strong enough to get through this day.

The landscape grayed around me as my consciousness receded. His arms wrapped around me as I lost the fight against the darkness.

ISAAC

INTERLUDE

Isaac woke with a start. He'd been dreaming again, but at least not the kind that required a change of clothes when he woke. Everything was ecstasy and magic and beauty. The sun was rising in the desert, and it was noon in New Orleans, and he and Eleanor joined hands under the light of the full moon to be bound to each other, and he said goodbye knowing it would be the last time, and she was shot and bound and freed and afraid and in love and in the throes of passion.

He shook his head and looked around. Every time he woke, it took longer to remember where he was. Who he was.

He'd had a dream, but everything he'd seen with Eleanor and experienced with her, both in person and through their bond was dissolving together until he couldn't tell one day from another. Was that sexual pleasure from their time together or an echo from her time with Raj?

But this, this had been now. And real. And true. What was it? What had he seen?

"The gate has opened," a voice said near him, but not to him. He wasn't sure how he knew, but he knew that no one talked to him. Except for her. The one everyone was afraid of.

"Do you think he saw it?" another voice asked. It wasn't one he recognized. He turned his head and came face-to-face with two squat, grimy figures, both well-armed and alert.

"None of our business," dwarf number one said. He had a serious air about him, but also looked like he'd just as soon kill Isaac and get back to whatever murderous plans he had for the rest of the day than continue looking at him. *Grumpy,* Isaac decided. Giving nicknames to his various captors and guards was his only amusement.

The second dwarf—*Dopey*—opened his eyes wide. "Don't you want to know?"

"Not as much as I want to keep my head firmly on my shoulders."

Isaac wanted them to ask. Wanted to share what he'd seen. Maybe saying it out loud would make it real. Make it stick. Add it to the real timeline instead of the tangled ribbon that time was in his mind now.

"Out," a new voice said.

Not a new voice, Isaac thought. *It's her voice. One of the many scary hers that came to see him, but the least and most scary of them. The one with the antlers and the swirling green eyes. The one that had shown brief moments of kindness.*

A clatter of footsteps announced the guards' departure.

"Are you well?" she asked, crouching beside him and passing him water in a silver cup. Even this was torture. He steeled himself, took the cup, and tossed it back, doing his best to avoid touching his lips to the rim of the cup. He handed the cup back, and unlike her usual habit, she took it with no delay.

"No, milady, I am not well." His voice was hoarse with disuse.

"Would you like to share your dream?"

"Only if you wish to hear it."

"It will ease your mind, will it not?"

He narrowed his eyes. He knew he was going mad. Knew his mind was fracturing. The timelines weren't right, but he'd crossed through the gate at the end of December, and it was probably early May. That was four months. Four moons. And time moved differently here. He could feel the pull of the twin moons that illuminated the night sky on the Fae Plane, but they weren't as powerful as the moon on Earth. Too much silver. Too few changes. And now this creature, this intriguing woman, was offering kindness.

"Why do you seek to ease my mind? It is mostly gone."

She tilted her head and the ghostly antlers tilted with her. "A mad wolf has no purpose. No one will seek to rescue you if it's known you are beyond help. And if you truly go mad, you will have to be put down. That benefits no one."

He sensed she was holding something back, but couldn't trust his own mind, so he let it go. He closed his eyes and tried to pull the dream back.

"The sun rose in the desert. Eleanor stood in the middle of a rough circle. She was radiant. Emma was there, guarding her back, and Florence was there, protecting the magic. The vampires were there, but in the shadows, ready to flee. Neither of the traitors were there.

"The magic flowed through Eleanor, and for the first time, she channeled it as easily as breathing. It was beautiful. She was beautiful. It destroyed hidden things in her, things that were holding her down, holding her back. She opened the gate and *looked through it*. I don't know what she saw, but it made her happy. She nearly wept with joy at the sight."

Isaac paused.

"And then?"

"What is your name?" he asked.

"You know I won't tell you that." She smiled to lessen the blow.

"What shall I call you?"

After a moment's thought, she replied. "You may call me Diana."

Isaac smiled. It wasn't as much of a gift as her true name would've been, but no Fae would give their true name to a shifter, much less a madman. "Thank you, Diana. My name is Isaac."

"I know your name, wolf. Continue your story."

Isaac tried to gather his thoughts, but they kept floating just out of reach. "Where was I?"

"Eleanor had opened the gate and looked through."

"That's not her real name, you know."

"Of course, it's her real name. It's just not her true name."

Isaac looked around, then leaned close to the bars. "I know her true name," he whispered. Diana froze, and Isaac delighted in having surprised her. He grinned. "I can't tell you what it is, though."

"How about you just tell me the rest of the story. We can talk about Eleanor's true name later."

That made sense. He nodded. "After that, the gate disappeared, and the vampires disappeared, and Eleanor was happy and tired. Then she was angry, and then she was scared, and then she was furious. After that, it's all fire. And then I woke up."

"What do you mean, it was all fire?"

"Eleanor was fire. The world was on fire. It was hot and angry and dancing."

Diana reached a hand through the bars and caressed Isaac's face. "That was well done. Sleep now. Sleep a dreamless sleep."

Isaac's lids drooped, and he felt the fog of sleep steal over him. "Will you visit again?"

"Of course." The rest of what she said was lost to Isaac as he fell asleep.

THE LANDSCAPE WAS stark and barren. Isaac recognized it from his vision of Eleanor opening the last gate.

"She promised me no dreams," Isaac said aloud.

A figure appeared in front of him. "This isn't a dream," Raj said. "I've been trying to get in touch with you."

"Why are you here instead of her?"

"My psychic powers are far superior to Eleanor's, and I'm able to use the bonds we both have with her to connect with you. I've explained this before."

"I don't want to see you," Isaac growled. He turned his back on Raj.

"I have news for you."

"I don't want your news."

"You need to know this." Raj's voice sounded almost gentle, and Isaac turned back around.

"What's wrong? Is she okay?"

"Eleanor is okay. She's sleeping, as she does after a gate opening."

"I saw her surrounded by fire."

"She was angry," Raj said. "Something happened. Something bad." He paused and searched Isaac's face. "It's about Emma."

"Emma is dead," Isaac said.

"She is. Did you see that, too?"

"What do you mean? She's been dead for ages. Michelle sent her to me, and I killed her."

Raj took a deep and unnecessary breath. "That's not what happened. That's what Michelle wanted you to believe. You traded yourself for Emma, remember? That's why you're here."

Isaac screwed up his face trying to remember. It sounded wrong, but Raj spoke with such assurance, and why else would he be here?

"Emma isn't dead? But you said she was."

Raj shook his head in frustration. "I am phrasing this poorly. Emma did not die so many years ago when you thought she had. She was held prisoner by Michelle in much the same way you're currently being held. You traded your freedom for hers at Yule. Emma has been the companion of Eleanor ever since, but after the gate opening, she was shot and killed."

"I felt her. She was angry but okay."

"That was Eleanor. Eleanor is angry but okay. Emma is dead."

"I loved her."

"Who? Who did you love?" Raj asked, peering intently at Isaac's face.

"I don't know!" Isaac yelled. "Why are you still talking to me? Why are you here?"

"I wanted you to hear about Emma from a friend before Michelle taunted you with that information. I wanted to give you a chance, to give you time."

"You're not my friend."

"We are friends," Raj said. "You just don't remember now."

Isaac lunged towards Raj, jaws gaping open, and went for the throat. Raj took a step back, and Isaac fell, bound by invisible silver chains. "You killed her!"

"Eleanor is alive and well," Raj soothed. "Emma was killed by a human but got her revenge before she died."

"You did this. Without you, none of this would've happened. They call her the catalyst, the world-breaker, but you are the linchpin on which everything stands or falls. Your sword is the sword that breaks the world. She is just your sacrifice."

Isaac stepped backwards until the invisible chains no longer burned him, then closed his eyes and willed himself back.

CHAPTER THIRTEEN

I woke slowly to the sound of murmuring voices. I stretched up, trying to unlock the kinks in my body and then rubbed my eyes. My face was wet. Why was my face wet? I blinked them open, which was always hard to do after being unconscious so long. Then I remembered. The human. Emma. One bullet. The tears streamed faster now, and the murmuring of voices grew quieter.

I looked around. I was in my hotel room in Santa Fe, so the voices must be coming from Florence's and Emma's—the thought choked on a sob—Florence's room. There was no light streaming from the seams in the curtain—that and the fact that I heard voices—led me to believe that it was night. They must know I'm awake. I hoped no one would come in yet. I needed some time. The door didn't open, and the murmur grew louder again. Raj must have heard me. *"Take your time, my sweet,"* he said.

I sat up, fought off a wave of dizziness, and swung my legs out of bed. A few wobbly steps later and I was in the bathroom. I turned on the water in the shower, reminded myself for the hundredth time to buy a gift basket for Petrina, and stood under the hot shower. The water masked my tears, and I stood until the magical water heater gave out.

I walked back to the main room. My strength was returning rapidly, and I no longer felt like a newborn foal. I dressed, not paying much attention to what I was pulling out of my pack, only ensuring that everything passed the sniff test. I hated the lack of laundromats almost as much as I hated the lack of Google. I did a quick glance in the mirror and smiled grimly. I was dressed for war. Blue jeans, a utilitarian black tank top, black boots that were accented by the throwing knives strapped to my arms and legs, and my sword sheathed behind my back. I pulled on a blue button-down shirt to try to appear slightly less aggressive and wished for some coffee—and maybe a couple shots of tequila for liquid courage.

"I have coffee," Raj said. *"But you'll have to ask Florence if you want anything stronger. She's in charge of the liquor."*

I girded my loins and opened the door separating our rooms.

Our small band was all there. Raj was leaning against the far wall and Florence and Petrina were sitting next to each other on the bed closest to me. I did my best not to think about who wasn't there and why I couldn't keep my shifters with me.

"How long?"

Petrina and Florence looked at me uncomprehendingly.

"How long was I out?" I clarified.

"Two full days," Raj said. "It's three-thirty on the morning of May third."

"Any news from Arduinna? I think she prefers to show up when I'm unconscious."

"She stopped by yesterday," Florence said, her mouth twisted in distaste and her voice rough. It sounded like she'd taken up a pack a day habit—for the last fifty years.

"What did she want?"

"The same as always, a report."

"Did she come by after New Orleans?" I asked. No one had told me, but I hadn't asked.

"Yes," Florence said. "She's shown up after each of the last three gates were opened. I do not like her."

"She's made a deal. She will uphold her end of the bargain."

"She's dishonest," Raj said.

"She's Fae," I said. "She's completely honest."

"She doesn't lie," Raj countered. "That doesn't mean she's honest."

I conceded that point. I looked around and then asked the question I should've asked the minute I entered the room. "Emma?"

Florence and Petrina stood up and parted to give me a clear view of the distant bed. Emma was lying there. Her skin was no longer porcelain. Instead, it had the waxy pallor of death. Someone had cleaned her up and dressed her, so the gut wound wasn't visible.

"What do we do?" My voice cracked, and I had to take a deep breath and consciously reined in my grief.

"What are the funeral customs of her kind?" Petrina asked.

"I don't know," I said. "It never came up."

"Cremation and scattering the ashes to the four winds," Florence said. She sounded sure.

"Where? And when?" I asked.

"Bandelier at sunrise," Florence said.

"I will stay as long as I can," Petrina said. She reached her hand out to Florence who took it without looking. I hoped this was something real for them both.

"We'd better get started, then," I said. I avoided Raj's eyes. I didn't want him to touch me right now.

Petrina carried Emma down to the car and placed her in the backseat. I got in the driver's seat. If Florence had had to drive Emma back here, this was the least I could do.

"We'll meet you there," Petrina said.

I drove slowly because I was afraid a quick turn would send Emma's body tumbling off the backseat, and I thought that touching her to put her back might send me into hysterics. We didn't talk. What was there to talk about? I couldn't decide if Florence blamed me or blamed herself or was just grief-stricken. She'd made Emma a surrogate sister and just like last time, she'd lost her sister because of the Fae.

It was just after five-thirty when I pulled into the parking lot at

Bandelier. I wasn't sure what we'd see at the gate site. Would the killer's body still be there? Would it look like a crime scene?

Petrina and Raj appeared by the car, and Petrina took Emma and vaulted over the fence. Raj carried Florence over and I was left to scale it on my own. I did and followed them to the gate site where two days ago Emma had died.

The site was pristine. The body was gone, and there was no sign of even a struggle, much less a murder. It didn't even look like Raj had cleared the earth to remove the landmines. I looked at him and he nodded slightly. He'd been here to clean up.

Petrina placed Emma in the center of the circle and we gathered around. I didn't know what to say. The last time I'd been at a funeral was for my parents. Florence looked at Emma and touched her cheek. "Good-bye," she whispered. Tears started streaming down her face and Petrina pulled her into her arms.

I looked at Raj. "Is it not our custom to say a eulogy," he said.

I looked down at Emma. "You should've ruled them all. I'm sorry." That was all I could get out before I, too, was overcome with grief.

When the first rays of sunlight broke over the horizon, I stepped back, grabbed Florence's hand, and sent out a burst of flame to light the pyre. I kept the fire as hot as I could until there was nothing left but ash, then I pulled on the air and sent her out on the wind as the sunrise stained the sky.

"I will come to you tonight," Raj said. He brushed a kiss on my forehead and then he left. I looked around. Petrina had also left at some point. I tugged on Florence's hand until she turned towards me. Then I hugged her. After a moment's hesitation, she hugged me back and we cried in each other's arms as the sky turned from pink to lavender to blue.

It was close to noon before Florence and I made our way back to the car and drove back to Santa Fe.

"I'm so sorry," I said. I felt helpless and useless, and those were not feelings I was used to anymore. "I should've stopped her."

"If you had, then I'd probably be dead," Florence said. "I would trade my life for hers, but you would still be mourning."

"That's very pragmatic," I replied.

"It's all I've got left. Pragmatism and the dim hope we will find my sister."

I fell silent and concentrated on driving. We were so close to finishing this journey. I felt like it'd been going on forever, but I'd only known Florence for nine months. I'd known Isaac for less than a year, and I'd already lost him. The only friend I'd had going into this madness had betrayed me. Raj had been with me for seven months. How could I have this life with people I barely knew? How could they trust me; count on me?

I stomped a little too hard on the brake pedal at a stop sign and felt the seat belts tighten painfully on our chests. "Sorry," I muttered. "I was trying to stop the spiral of self-doubt and got carried away."

"It's okay," Florence said, rubbing her sternum. "If you could work on separation of metaphorical and literal in the future, that would be great."

I grinned for a second and then faltered when I remembered there was nothing to smile about. We'd just said good-bye to Emma. She and I hadn't been friends yet, but we would've been before too long. I was afraid I was going to have to say good-bye to everyone before this was over.

Once we were back in Santa Fe, neither of us wanted to go to the hotel. We hadn't spent much time sight-seeing, and sight-seeing in this in-between magic and technology age probably wasn't much to speak of, but we decided to give the town a shot.

I couldn't concentrate on the street hawkers who were out to sell jewelry and artwork, but the smell of cooking meat caught my attention. I grabbed Florence's arm and led her down the street towards that smell. I found an entrepreneurial family who'd set up an open fire grill and was serving street tacos with warm, homemade corn tortillas almost too hot to touch stuffed with a mix of shredded chicken, onions, and cilantro and garnished with radishes. I bought a dozen tacos and a couple of bottles of water then followed the scent of green and growing things to a nearby park for a makeshift picnic.

"These are so good," I moaned. "Maybe better than Taco Bell."

Florence just shook her head. "They are most definitely better than Taco Bell. This is authentic. Taco Bell is a cheap imitation with no real flavor."

I gasped and put my hand over my heart, striving for as much drama as possible. "Florence, you wound me! To the quick! Taco Bell is the epitome of fine dining experiences."

Florence gave me a withering glance and went back to her tacos. She ate three of the dozen which left nine for me. I wasn't sure it was going to be enough, but by the time I finished the last one, I thought I had enough to make it until a late dinner.

We carefully picked up our mess and found a garbage can. It was overflowing, and I wondered how the public service sector was coping with all the changes. Apparently, garbage pick-up was not a top priority, but the city didn't look filthy, so something was still happening. There were so many things that I didn't think of on a day-to-day basis. I'd always regarded garbage day as a necessary hassle. I never thought much about where the garbage went and what would happen to the landfills and giant composting heaps without power. I thought about it for a moment before realizing that without accessing Google, there was no way I was going to figure it out, and since there wasn't much I could do about it now, other than making sure my refuse was getting into the proper receptacles, I decided to let it go.

Florence and I wandered back to our hotel. I opened the smuggler's hatch under the trunk and snagged a bottle of really good whiskey. Tonight was going to be rough. Florence glanced at my liquor but didn't comment. She was probably ready for a drink, too.

The sun went down, but Raj didn't appear. About an hour after dusk, Petrina arrived. I looked at her and started to ask, but she shrugged. Petrina was not much of a conversationalist.

"Whiskey?" I asked. I didn't wait for an answer but poured three glasses. We sipped in silence and were almost done with our second glasses when there was a knock on the door. I shifted uneasily. Who would be knocking? Raj usually appeared on the balcony and let himself in. Everyone else was already here.

I pulled my rapier from the scabbard and crept to the door. There was no peephole, so I opened it cautiously, sword at the ready.

The woman who stood on the other side of the door looking decidedly uncomfortable was dressed head to toe in flowing robes of variegated green. Her hair, which had a mossy green tinge, was pulled back into a tight braid exposing her pointed ears. She looked less put together than I'd ever seen her.

"Arduinna," I said. "What are you doing here?"

"May I come in?"

Her question threw me for some reason.

"Why are you here?" I asked again. Something wasn't right. I shook a throwing knife into my left hand and resheathed my sword. Once I had a second knife in my right hand, I nudged the door open wider with my foot. Without taking my eyes off Arduinna, I strained my senses, trying to find the source of her unease. I looked her in the eyes and asked, "Are you alone?"

"Of course," she laughed, but her eyes narrowed slightly and darted to her left, down the dark hallway.

Not alone then. Whoever it was wasn't close enough for me to sense. I tended to not extend my defenses out as far when we were in hotels since I didn't want to catch any fellow visitors or hotel staff in my web. I winced slightly at the memory of the maid that I'd caught a couple weeks ago.

"Why don't you tell me what you need to tell me here, and I'll talk to you again when I can get to some good trees."

"I'd rather come in," Arduinna said. She was starting to sweat, and it smelled like pine sap on a hot summer's day.

"I'm afraid I can't let you come in. We're in mourning, and it's just family."

"Please," she sounded desperate. It was eerie hearing her plead this way. Arduinna was a sword of justice, not a lapdog for anyone. It had to be Finn. How he'd captured her, I had no idea.

"What if I don't let you in?" I was testing the waters, trying to figure out the pathway to the least damage possible. I didn't want anyone else to die.

She jerked and then straightened as if she'd been prodded in the low back with something giving off some pretty strong electricity. She reached slowly to her hip, and I watched curiously. My curiosity turned to alarm when she produced a gun. "Holy fuck, Arduinna! What are you doing? You can't shoot me."

She raised the gun and pointed it straight at my face. "Let me in," she growled.

I took a step back. This was beyond weird. Her arms were shaking with the exertion of holding up the gun, and they shouldn't be. She was Fae, and one of the strongest I'd ever met. Then I realized that it was iron. This was probably extremely painful and further reinforced my suspicions that she was not operating under her own free will.

I took another step back and moved to the side so that she could come in. The moment she cleared the threshold, I slammed the door shut with my foot and without taking my eyes off her, slid the deadbolt home. She kept the gun aimed at my head, but the tremors were getting worse.

"You're in," I said. "And I pledge not to harm you. Will you put the gun away, please?"

She stood staring at me for what seemed like hours but was in all likelihood just a couple of seconds, before lowering the gun and reholstering it. I darted forward and grabbed her wrists, turning her hands palm up. Her hands were red and blistered.

"Do we have any ice?" I asked the room. "Florence, can you cool her hands?"

"No, but maybe Petrina will help," Florence said. I turned to her to ask but before I could open my mouth, a throwing knife sprouted from the center of Arduinna's forehead with a wet and meaty thwack.

Arduinna's eyes opened wide and just before she collapsed, I saw awareness return. I caught her before she could hit the ground and lowered her gently down. The blade sticking up from her forehead like an accusatory exclamation point was one of my silver ones and not one of the iron ones. Whoever had thrown it did not intend to kill her. I looked down at my arm sheaths and was not surprised to find one missing.

"Hey baby," I said as Raj stepped out of the shadows.

"What did I miss?"

Petrina moved Arduinna to the bed while Raj went out to scout the halls for Finn. He came back a few minutes later empty-handed.

"Do you think she'll come to if we pull the knife out?" I asked. I was fascinated. She was still breathing and didn't seem to be injured or in distress, other than the impromptu unicorning Raj had given her.

"That makes sense," Petrina said. She'd done something to Arduinna's hands while she was out, healing the worst of the iron burns.

"Raj, do your hands need any healing from the silver knife theft?" I asked.

He held his hands up and I noticed they were gloved.

"Do you always carry gloves?"

"You never know when they'll come in handy."

"How long were you here? I didn't hear you arrive."

"Neither did I," Petrina said, pursing her lips as she turned around to look at her father.

"I can be very quiet when I want to be," he said smoothly. I knew then that he'd taken advantage of the miniature dragon shape. "I sensed that something was wrong, so I arrived as stealthily as possible to avoid alerting our enemy. Once here, everyone's attention was on the Fae; it was easy to steal a knife and wait for an opportune moment to throw it."

"Thank you," I said. "It seems to have broken the hold Finn had on her."

"Temporarily at least. Shall we wake her now or after dinner?" Raj asked.

"Now," I said. "I'm planning on drinking heavily tonight, and it'd be better to do this sober."

Raj smiled at me, white fangs briefly flashing against his dark skin. He reached forward with his gloved hands and pulled the blade out in one swift, sure tug. Arduinna blinked rapidly, then looked at the four of us hovering over her. She elbowed herself up into a half sitting position and I winced as a trickle of blood started seeping slowly down her forehead.

She reached up and touched it, then looked at her fingers. "You stabbed me in the head?" she said to me.

"That was me," Raj interjected.

"Thanks for using silver," she said.

"What happened?" I asked.

She sighed in disgust. "I let the half-breed bastard snare me. I wasn't paying attention and was crossing through a large area that was rock and metal and not living earth. I'm weaker without a direct connection to the earth and I should've been more alert. Before I knew what was going on, he'd grabbed me and put on iron bracelets to prevent me from accessing my magic. Then he used the tricks that I'd taught him to take advantage of our mental bond."

"Is the reversal permanent until he lifts it or one of you is dead?" I asked. "Can he hear you right now? Or can you wrest control back from him?"

"The silver knife weakened it enough that I'm back in control now. I don't know if he can reassert himself more easily, or if he'd need to capture me in the same way again."

"Wait, the bond you taught him not only allows the creator to read the victim's mind when they're physically close, locate that person wherever, but also allows him to *control* the victim's actions?" My voice was rising steadily and I finished with a shriek. "You taught him that? He did that to me. You gave him the means to control me. How could you?"

"And if he could control you, why didn't he?" Raj asked. That was probably a better question than mine, but I still wanted answers.

"How do you know he didn't?" Arduinna asked.

"I don't remember being controlled or doing things I didn't want to."

"You acquiesced rather quickly to the whole idea of this quest, did you not?"

"It didn't take much convincing. He saved me from a vampire..." I turned to look at Raj. "Are all the vampires in Portland yours?"

"No, but most are. And those that were not mine checked in when passing through."

"Jonathan Deacon?" I asked.

"Not mine, nor do I recognize the name," Raj said.

I looked at the group. "After the vampire attack, I told Finn I needed time. He gave me a night, explained everything to me the next day, and I was all in from that moment. After the attack, it seemed foolish to resist. Dammit." He'd violated my mind even more than I'd suspected. I flexed my fingers. Someday I was going to kill him.

"Why are you here?" I asked. "I mean why did Finn send you?"

"To kill one of you. It didn't matter which one."

"We already lost Emma. Wasn't that enough?"

"Apparently not."

"We're going to need the gun," I said.

"Of course."

Florence stepped forward and gingerly removed it from the holster. She checked the safety and then emptied the clip.

"I was coming to see you anyway," Arduinna said. "I have information about the final task."

I sat down on the bed with rather more force than I'd intended. "Spill it."

"The final task is, as I'm sure you've suspected, the last gate. It's in Portland—back where it all started for you."

"Why can't I feel it?" I asked.

"You will soon, I think. It must be opened on Midsummer at the exact moment of the solstice. It will be very early; pre-dawn. This gate does not open the way the others did, though. This one will require a blood sacrifice on the blade of ancient kings."

"Like a fatted calf?" I asked.

"Did you only read the grimmer parts of the Old Testament?" Raj asked.

"No. Human sacrifice," Arduinna said.

"Human as in not supernatural?" I asked. "I'm not going to do that."

"No, human as in humanoid. Any of us would work."

I grinned slightly as I imagined the perfect candidate for this. I wondered what Finn's plans for this midsummer were. He probably wouldn't be throwing another one of his famous parties.

"Eleanor," Florence said. "You are looking a little darker than I'd like."

The grin dropped off my face. Killing Finn was still on my bucket list, but Florence was right. Sacrificing him like the fatted calf was not me.

"What if I don't?" I asked.

"Then all your work over the last months will have been for naught and the world will collapse. You will truly earn the name of world-breaker."

I looked at Raj and knew that this is why he had the sword. It was to sacrifice me at the final gate. He looked as stricken as I felt.

"There has to be another way," I said.

"There isn't." She rose from the bed and I noticed that the wound on her forehead had faded to a thin, white scar. Soon, even that would be gone. "Thank you for your hospitality and the knife to the head. I will see you in Portland at midsummer. Do not do anything foolish." She strode out to the balcony and jumped off.

I wondered why Medb was so worried about me if I was supposed to die once the gates were open. There was no way I could take her throne if I'd been decapitated.

I looked at Raj and then at Florence and Petrina. I grabbed my whiskey bottle and walked into Raj's arms. "Take me home?" I asked.

His arms tightened around me. "Of course."

"We'll be back tomorrow night," I said to the others. "And then we'll make some plans."

I WOKE LATE the next afternoon and Raj was already absent from our bed. From the faint sounds of pacing and rustling pages, I guessed he was in the adjacent sitting room. I hopped out of bed but didn't bother dressing. After a quick trip to the bathroom, I went to lure my lover back into bed. It was likely our last night truly alone; maybe ever.

I opened the door and strutted to the middle of the room. I struck a pose and then looked at my admiring audience. He wasn't looking at me. He was pacing, holding an open book with his left hand and swinging his sword absently with his right. This was my first up-close look at the sword that he'd traded me for; the sword that was supposed to end my life. It didn't look like much. Old. Well-made. I couldn't tell much else since it was twirling too fast to get a good look. I could see the rubies that were supposed to hold the life essence of Raj and his ancestors and descendants. I wondered how that worked.

"They're blood rubies," Raj said, still not looking at me.

"Like blood diamonds?" I was wondering how slave-mined rubies made them mystical.

"No. They're not actually rubies. They're mystical stones that were forged in fire and tempered in blood. My people believed that rubies are the king of all gems and were born from the blood of demons. They were not wrong, although few believe that now. It is why rubies are so rare, even more rare than diamonds. They are blood stones, and the rubies on this sword were made from my blood, the blood of my forefathers, and later the blood of my children."

Okay, then. Raj was usually more practical and less mystical. I didn't often see this side of him. I wasn't sure what to think.

"And what is there to think?" Apparently, he was going to keep reading my mind. "You asked about the rubies. Can't you feel their power?"

I thought about it and realized that the power emanating from Raj was more than I was used to feeling from him. I guess the rubies were probably the best explanation. I sighed heavily. If he was reading and swinging swords, my nudity wasn't going to be fruitful, and I was getting a bit cold. I turned to go back to the bedroom in search of clothes.

Raj's head snapped up and he looked at me for the first time since

I'd walked in. For a brief moment, his eyes flared more crimson than the gems decorating his weapon and I was suffused with heat.

"My apologies, my sweet," he said. "I shouldn't have kept you waiting."

I tried to wave it off, "No problem. I know we've got some big events coming up."

"And they will march towards us inexorably. This opportunity, us alone in a very comfortable bed, when will that come again?"

"I don't know."

"Neither do I, and it's my motto to take advantage of large beds and willing, naked people whenever the opportunity presents itself."

I backed towards the door as he stalked towards me. I wasn't cold anymore.

I'd barely crossed the threshold to the bedroom when Raj caught me and lifted me into his arms. I wrapped my bare legs around him and ran my fingers through his hair, pulling his face close to mine.

He kissed me lightly at first and then with growing intensity. One hand slid under my ass to hold me against him; the other began a slow exploration of my right breast. He caressed and pinched until my nipple was throbbing with pleasure. Raj dumped me unceremoniously onto the bed, then stripped his clothing off before climbing in after me.

"Raj," I gasped as he nipped his way up my thigh. "Please..."

"Please? What are you asking for? A quick consummation? Or this?" He licked my center and fluttered his tongue over my clitoris until I was writhing beneath him. He grabbed my thighs, hiked them over his shoulders, and settled in to drive me crazy. Just as I thought I'd go mad from being held on the cusp of pleasure for too long, he plunged two fingers into me. That was all it took, and I screamed his name as I orgasmed wildly. Even before I'd recovered, Raj slid up my body and took me again. He kissed me, and I exulted at the taste of myself on his tongue. I raised my hips to meet him and spiraled out of control again. This time, Raj followed me over the abyss and then collapsed in my arms.

It was some time before either of us moved again. "That was

magnificent," I said.

"It was, wasn't it?"

"I supposed we should get going soon." I sighed in regret as I looked around the room. I liked this place and was sure I'd never see it again.

"Never say never," Raj said. "Who knows what the future holds?"

"Do you see a way around you sacrificing me?"

"Not yet, although I wouldn't mind using Finn as a substitute."

"That would be ideal, but I don't think we can count on that."

"Well, let's go forward. We have about six weeks before the last gate. We'll figure something out."

I kissed him and headed to the bathroom to clean up and dress. When I returned to the sitting room, Raj was already dressed and it looked like he was ready to go. Before I could precede him out of the room, though, he stopped me.

"I have something for you." He held up a small box. It wasn't the right shape to be something too scary, so I took it.

"Scary? An engagement ring would be scary?" I couldn't tell if he was amused or affronted, so I just opened the box. It was a key that had been made into a beautiful pendant and strung on a ruby and gold chain.

"Blood rubies or regular rubies?" I asked as I slipped it over my head.

"Blood, but these are my blood alone."

I stopped messing with the key and looked Raj directly in the eye. "This is kind of like an engagement ring, isn't it?"

He smiled. "Kind of. That's a key to this house. The coordinates are etched in the shaft of the key."

I settled the key between my breasts and took Raj's face between my hands. "Thank you." I kissed him. "Whatever happens, thank you for this time."

"We'll come back together," he said. I closed my eyes against the pain of imagining why I'd be here without him. When I could breathe without a hitch in my throat, I opened my eyes and kissed him again.

"Together," I promised.

CHAPTER FOURTEEN

"Motherfucker," I swore, kicking the tires of my car. My car that was decades old and had made the trip from Chicago to St. Louis to Savannah to Alpha to New Orleans to Santa Fe and finally to Durango Fucking Colorado. It wasn't out of gas. The battery should be fine. There was nothing wrong with the car.

"I think it's just too many supernaturals for too long," Florence said. "Our magic broke the car."

We were on the second night out from Santa Fe. We'd been making terrible time, anyway, since the highways were twisted and randomly littered with broken down vehicles.

"There's so much magic in the world right now that even this old engine is having trouble," Florence said. "It should settle down in a few years, and cars—at least non-computerized ones—will run again."

"Fat lot of good that does us right now," I muttered. "How much farther is it to Portland?"

"About twelve hundred miles," Raj said after consulting the map and measuring with his finger.

"That's too far to walk," I said. "We'll have to fly."

"You can't fly," Florence said. "You're supposed to be bound."

"This is ridiculous. Who cares if Finn thinks I'm still bound at this point? It's almost over. Besides, I had a power flare at the last gate. No one who was in the vicinity will believe I'm still bound."

"I can't fly," Florence said.

"Petrina or Raj could carry you. For that matter, so could I. You could ride me like a pony."

Florence looked a little pale and a tiny bit green.

"Florence, are you afraid of flying?" I asked.

"No. Not in airplanes."

"I bet Petrina is much safer than an airplane."

"At least when it comes to flying," Trina agreed with a throaty laugh.

"We have a lot of stuff to carry," Florence said, gesturing at the car. "How will we carry all of that? Your coffee and wine and our food. We need to wear packs and hike it."

"How long will it take to walk twelve hundred miles across the desert in spring?" I asked. "Won't it be faster to fly and then come back for our supplies if we need them?"

"If anything is still here," Florence argued. "We're not in the middle of nowhere. If we abandon the car here, it'll be stripped of everything useful before we could come back."

"Is there any way I'm going to convince you that walking is a ridiculous idea?"

"No."

"Do I have to walk?" Petrina asked.

"Yes," Florence snapped. "Now load up some backpacks with camping supplies, water, and food."

I grumbled but did as she asked. I was thrilled that I was preternaturally strong because that meant I could carry a few wine bottles and not have to leave them behind for scavengers.

Raj and Petrina took everything we weren't going to bring and took it to the General Store. Seriously, that's what it was called. I felt like we were truly in the wild west. They traded the leftover liquor and gasoline for warm clothes and canteens full of water. Then we found an abandoned motel, nailed boards over the windows in a couple of rooms and prepared to wait out the day.

Raj and I pored over the maps, trying to decide if there was an easier and less visible route than taking the roads we'd planned on when we were driving. It was about eight-hundred and fifty miles as the dragon flies, but the terrain would probably add more time than following the highways. In the end, we decided to take the highway, since we knew we'd find shelter along the way which might be lacking in a cross-country trek.

As soon as it was dark enough for Raj and Petrina to walk comfortably, we took off. It was May fifth. We had six and half weeks and just under twelve hundred miles before the solstice. We'd have to average almost thirty miles a day to get there in time.

Petrina rose at dusk much less disgruntled about our big hike than she'd been earlier. We plotted on the map and decided that our first day's goal was to get to Hesperus, a very small town about fifteen miles away. That should be a fairly easy day and a good way to break in our feet and bodies for this kind of activity. The first three nights should be short ones, all less than twenty miles with a town, however small it might be, at the finish line. The fourth night would be longer but still end somewhere that might be willing to give or sell us water if we needed it. There would also likely be ready-made shelter available. After the fourth day, there was only one more town between us and Moab, and we'd reach it on the sixth night. We might be on the road without guaranteed shelter for a total of four nights, three if Florence turned out to be a race walker. I was not looking forward to bedding down in the middle of nowhere with two vampires and no protection from the sun. After that, we'd plot out the next week, and the next, until we were in Portland—or until Florence gave in.

"I can easily make us places to sleep in the earth," Raj said, shrugging off my worry. "It won't be the first time that either Petrina or I have spent the day in a shallow grave."

I hoisted my pack on, tried not to let my thoughts dwell on sleeping through the day exposed to anyone who cared to look, and shuffled resignedly out the door. My biggest hope at this point was the Florence would find the whole ordeal so miserable that she'd agree to be carried the rest of the way.

It was the second morning out from Durango before Florence voiced anything but enthusiasm for our cross-country backpack. We'd just arrived in Cortez, Colorado, and I was delighted to see that this was an actual town with actual hotels. Sure, they were closed, but they existed. I was less thrilled to see hand-lettered lawn signs sporting anti-supernatural slogans. "Go home, demons!" worried me for a moment. I hadn't known there were demons around mixing it up. Then I saw the next sign, "Vampires and werewolves are demons!" Raj probably wouldn't win the next mayoral election. I saw a few signs with the infamous "Thou Shalt Not Suffer a Witch to Live" verse on it and thought maybe Florence wouldn't want to move here, either.

She was looking around at the signs that were barely visible in the gloaming light. "Let's find an abandoned motel to break into," she said. "My feet are killing me."

Truth be told, my feet weren't thrilled with having walked forty-five miles in two nights. The road wasn't flat, and it wasn't as arid as I'd expected. We were walking through a small mountain range, and the elevation changes were hell on my quads.

Another sign, this one a colorfully illustrated one with a witch in traditional Halloween garb burning at the stake, straightened Florence's spine. "I wonder if these people would despise me more for my magic or my heritage?" she asked in a voice I thought I wasn't supposed to hear.

Raj answered her, "They would pretend it was your magic that was a threat because that prejudice is currently more acceptable than judging us based on the color of our skin, but they would look harder at us than at them," he waved towards Petrina and me. "It will be easier for them to believe that we are the evil they are looking for than it would to believe the same of Trina. She looks like the American ideal of everything that is good and right in this world, does she not?"

Petrina looked like she would be right at home in beer commercials and on the cover of swimsuit magazines. She certainly didn't look like an evil, blood-sucking creature of the night. But then of course to me, none of my companions looked like an evil anything. If Raj was right, then that meant that the kind of people who put up signs like this were more likely to see Raj or Isaac or Florence as a threat than Finn—someone who was pretty evil.

"Let's find a place to hole up before the town wakes completely," Florence said. "I don't want to answer any questions about who we are and why we're here and on foot."

We did as she suggested. There was an abandoned Super 8 on the far edge of town that was already boarded up. Raj and Petrina pried off some boards on the side not visible from the road, and we slipped inside. Raj and Petrina both lay down and were out almost immediately. It made me feel a little bit satisfied that this walk was exhausting for them as well. Then I realized that neither had eaten since Santa Fe. Since this was our last population center for a couple days, maybe longer, they'd probably have to eat tonight.

I quelled the wave of jealousy. I knew it was irrational and hoped that this whole mating jealousy would settle down soon. Then I remembered that it might be irrelevant in six weeks, and I wished for more time and a private room. Since neither were likely to appear, I helped Florence reinforce our temporary wards, drank some water and ate a mouth-drying granola bar, then climbed into the bed Raj was occupying and curled up next to his statue-still form.

AT DUSK THE NEXT EVENING, Petrina went out to fill our canteens. She reported that a few people had approached her, but no one seemed to think her a threat. Instead, she received some pamphlets on how to avoid vampires and werewolves and several offers from local men for shelter for the night.

"I'd like to go out later with the same purpose, just to see how many offers I get," Raj said. "A social experiment."

"Let's just go," Florence said. She was rubbing her feet and eyeing her hiking boots with trepidation.

"Do you need help to get those on?" I asked.

"No. I just don't want to do it."

"We can always fly," I said. "If I shift, I bet I can carry all these supplies *and* you."

Florence paled and shoved her feet into her boots. "I'm good," she announced.

We slipped out through the boards Raj had pried away and had a torch-bearing crowd waiting for us. Petrina must not have been as stealthy as she'd thought.

"Give us your demons!" someone yelled. I looked at our welcoming committee a little closer and noticed that in addition to tiki torches and a scattering of garden implements, they all had matching, homemade t-shirts with a cartoon demon behind an "X." They were organized then.

A few figures broke from the rest and took a step forward. It was hard to make out their faces, even in the flickering light of the tiki torches, but they were all white, almost all male, and all holding rifles or shotguns.

The one who stepped out the farthest was presumably the leader of this make-shift demon-hating militia. "Ladies," he said, although his eyes were on Petrina. "We can help you." I wasn't sure if Florence and I were to be included in the rescue attempt, but I wasn't particularly interested.

"No thank you," I said. "We're okay."

Leader guy, who was sporting a mullet that hadn't been in style since 1983 and hadn't been fashionable ever, glanced over at me, took in the lines of my body, and swung his attention back to Petrina. He kept his eyes on her but directed his words to the whole group—or at least the presumed evil members of our group.

"The rest of you demons or whatever evil you are, step away from the ladies or we'll shoot you in front of them."

"Excuse me?" Florence asked. "Am I to consider myself a demon or a lady? Do you have a special line for demon ladies?"

"You're no lady," someone from the crowd spat.

"Burn them!" another voice rang out.

I couldn't help it. I burst out laughing. "What are you laughing at?" Mullet asked.

"She's probably hysterical from fear," a woman's voice said. "Poor dear, being held captive by these demons for so long."

"No," I managed to gasp out. "I was just reliving a Monty Python sketch and was so hoping that someone had a duck."

A couple chuckles echoed through the crowd and were quickly silenced. Mullet glared at me. "Maybe you're not as innocent as you look. You have a witchy air about you."

"Why? Because I talked back to you? Because I'm a woman? For that matter, what made you assume that I'm one hundred percent human and not a demon who's captured these three to take back to my lair and eat?"

"Yes," Florence said. "Please tell us how you determined the guilt and innocence of each member of this party. I'm ever so curious to learn how you identify demons at a glance."

"You stayed holed up all day and only sent your human out after dark," Mullet said.

"That might answer—if correlation and causation were indeed the same thing—how you decided there were demons among us, although witches can go outside day or night, you know. It does not, however, tell me how you decided which of our party were demons. Perhaps our 'human,' as you called my friend, is the one who couldn't go out until dark."

"Enough!" Petrina's voice rang out over the crowd. "You are pathetic. So scared of the dark that you have to hunt for monsters everywhere you go. So scared of the evil inside each of you that you have to find a name for it in other people."

I glanced over at her, and my jaw dropped. Her eyes were glowing red, and her fangs had dropped. She was going full-on Queen of the Damned on their asses. I took a step back, my hand seeking Raj's, but unable to tear my eyes from his daughter. He pulled me into his arms—none of the townsfolk were looking at me, now. Everyone's attention was riveted on the vampire they'd tried to rescue.

"Every member of this group you threaten is someone you would kill given a chance. The fact that you tried showed how little you know of what a supernatural is. I have lived among you for centuries, and you have been safe. My love," she gestured towards Florence, "plays a role in actively keeping all of you safe. You are not in danger because you found out we exist. The biggest threat to humans is other humans. One of you idiots killed another of our party only last week. You would've welcomed her into your town with open arms, for she was young, and blond, and beautiful.

"Open your eyes. You are steeped in prejudice and bigotry, but the only ones threatening lives here are you."

She strode forward, and the gun-toting idiots in front stepped back into the crowd.

Her eyes blazed, and fire appeared in her hands. "You tried to burn me once, and you will not be allowed to do it again. I am watching you. This reign of terror is over."

Flames shot up into the night sky, illuminating the town for a moment, before dying down.

"I will be back in two months. If you haven't transformed yourselves into a town of welcome, a haven for wanderers, and gotten rid of your hateful signs, I will be less kind. I am the vampire Petrina, and you will bow to me."

She strode through the crowd that parted in front of her like the Red Sea.

"We should follow," Florence said.

"Right." I shouldered my back, firmed my grip on Raj's hand, and followed Trina out of town.

THE NEXT MORNING, we set up our small tent out of sight from the highway just across the Utah border, and I stood back while Florence wove some camouflaging spells over it. It would still be visible to anyone who was looking for us, though not to anyone who wasn't.

"I'll take first watch," I said. Florence's wards didn't work as well without walls to attach them to, and the tent was too much a temporary structure to anchor them. My alarm system was still there and would alert us if anyone walked into it, but I'd been anchoring that to Florence's wards, so it was weaker, too.

Florence didn't argue, and I wondered how much this trip was taking out of her. She was, unlike the rest of us, mortal if extremely long-lived. I studied her carefully, looking for signs that she was more than merely exhausted, but I didn't find any.

I woke her mid-afternoon so I could get a few hours of sleep. She berated me for letting her sleep more than half the day until I told her that if she was interested in me getting any sleep, she'd have to shut up.

When Florence shook me awake, it was full dark. "Why didn't you wake me earlier?" I mumbled, rubbing the sleep out of my eyes.

"I thought it was better that you were well-rested than we get an early start."

"Where are Raj and Petrina?"

"They stopped in at sunset and when they saw you were asleep, said they'd be back in a couple of hours. Errands."

"Dinner, you mean."

"Yes. And speaking of, I made you some."

Florence handed me a bag of prepared freeze-dried stroganoff. "Mmm, that looks interesting," I said, trying hard to modulate the sarcasm.

I finished eating, and we broke camp, destroying any evidence that anyone had been here. Fortunately, between the time of year and my kick-ass sleeping bag, I wasn't getting too cold. Sleeping during the day helped, too. The nights were chilly, but all the walking kept my blood flowing. I hoped that we'd get to sleep in something with walls tomorrow. I knew it would be our last stop in civilization until Moab. I was deliberately not thinking of our trip past there. One leg at a time was as much as my brain—and my feet—could handle.

We'd just finished pulling our already noticeably lighter packs on when Raj and Petrina returned. Neither smelled of blood or humans to me, and I was glad they'd taken the time to wash. Raj kissed me lightly, but before I could turn it into something more serious, he pulled away. "Shall we?" he gestured to the rise that hid the highway from view.

I sighed. "If we must."

Our stay in Monticello, Utah was an almost identical repeat of our time in Cortez, Colorado with the small exception that these signs had more of a Mormon bent. We were just over fifty miles from Moab, which would be our next town. We were planning on dividing the walk into two nights. I was anxious to be there, but even with her swollen and aching feet, Florence refused to let someone carry her.

"Maybe we could find you a broom, and you could fly under your own power," I suggested.

I grinned at the look she gave me. It was probably a good thing there wasn't any power behind it. I had no doubt that Florence could kill with a glance if she wanted to.

It was just after sunset, and Florence and I were reorganizing our significantly lighter packs while Petrina went to find water to fill our canteens. Raj was lying on the bed staring at the ceiling. He'd been quiet since we'd left Cortez. I wasn't sure what was bothering him, but if it went on much longer, I'd find a way to prod him out of his mood.

Petrina returned with full canteens and a grin. "Guess how many men offered to take me in to protect me from the "evils out there" tonight?" she asked.

I rolled my eyes. "You are having way too much fun with this. Did you turn on your scary eyes and hiss at them tonight?"

"I do not hiss. C'mon. Guess."

"Twenty-seven."

She pouted for a second, and then grinned. "Six."

"It helps that you look like a twenty-year-old Swedish bikini team model," I said.

"That has almost always helped," she replied.

"Not always?"

"Not when I wanted to be taken seriously. Oh, and not when I wanted the women of my village to not burn me as a witch," she said.

"Ah, jealous were they?"

"Like I had any interest in their smelly, hairy men," Petrina said, tossing her blonde braid over her shoulder and handing out canteens. Florence waited until it looked like everyone was ready to go before pulling on her boots and lacing them up. I saw her try to suppress a wince and knew her feet probably hurt even more than she'd let on. I looked over at Petrina and wondered if she could use healing magic to make this easier.

Petrina caught my glance and correctly interpreted it. "Not until we're done walking for a bit," she said.

Florence looked confused as she glanced between Petrina and her cryptic statement and me. Then she realized what we were talking about, lifted her chin, and said, "They're fine."

"They're not fine, Florence," I said. "Frankly, mine aren't in very good shape, either. Can you do another thousand miles of this? Honestly? Or should we take a break here? If we push later, we might have time for an extra night."

"I'd rather push through now on my damaged feet and have time to rest and heal there than wait and then have to start walking again," Florence said.

"There are other options," I said.

"No."

Someday I was going to figure out her objection to taking the easiest and fastest and most foot-friendly way to our next destination. Apparently today was not that day. I sighed and hoisted my pack onto my back.

We walked until Florence was stumbling from fatigue and pain. Raj left the road to find a place to set up camp. He was still going for the title in this year's "Mr. Strong and Surly" pageant. I tried to reach out to him with my thoughts, but although I was positive he could hear me, I wasn't getting anything back. After sending questions about his state of mind, trying to cover everything from annoyance at our slow pace, annoyance at Florence's refusal to fly, and annoyance at my belief that he was going to have to sacrifice me at the final gate, I gave up. Then I started thinking about some of the more…adventurous…things we'd done in his home in Santa Fe. I was just up to the part with the handcuffs, silk blindfold, and candles when he appeared in front of me, eyes glowing red.

"You need to stop that," he growled. I was pretty sure I was supposed to be shaking in my utilitarian yet completely unattractive hiking boots, but all I could do was let my thoughts progress to the next stage. Hot wax. His skin. My tongue. I looked up at him from under my lowered lashes, knowing the light of the waxing moon and his superior vampiric eyesight was enough to signal how coquettish I was being. He picked me up, slung me across his shoulders, said something to Florence and Petrina that I didn't catch, and whisked me off in a fire-person's carry.

A few minutes later, well out of ear and eyeshot of the rest of our party, he set me down.

"What the hell are you playing at, Eleanor?" His voice reverberated through my body until I had to wrap my arms around myself to still the echoes.

My mind fled from flirt to furious in a heartbeat. "What am I playing at? You're the one who's been sulking for days, refusing to talk to me; to touch me. You haven't talked to me mind-to-mind, you haven't kissed me. I don't know what you're thinking, and it's driving me crazy."

He turned to look at me, his face an impassive mask. "Why would I share my thoughts with you? What do you think is between us?"

I rolled my eyes. "Seriously, vampire? And you ask me what *I'm* playing at? I can't just forget the last weeks. We are more than friends. More than lovers. You cannot deny that now, not after everything we've shared."

He sighed; gustily and completely unnecessarily. "Why do I even try with you?"

Now I was uncertain. "Try what? What do you mean?"

His lips quirked up at the corner in the barest imitation of a smile. "Why do I even try to dissemble. I thought to protect you from my thoughts and feelings. To spare you the turmoil I feel. To hide from you the plans I'm making."

"Yeah, that worked so well last time." I was pretty sure that I could be arrested for sarcasm abuse with the bite I'd infused into that last statement, but I didn't care.

He walked the few steps to me and pulled me into him, wrapping his arms around me. He whispered into my hair, so softly that I was sure I wasn't supposed to hear him, "My love, my heart. I would do anything to spare you pain."

I tilted my head up and brushed my lips against his. "Our love should be about pain shared and not hidden. I am strong, as you know, and I can take it."

He kissed me back briefly before stepping back. He didn't let go of my arms, but he put a healthy distance between us. "My sweet, I am old."

"Oh, I know," I jabbed.

He smiled again, but this time it was forced. "I am old. I have loved before."

I squelched the burst of hurt.

"I have lived over a thousand years. There have been others who have captured my mind and my heart. I thought you would be another for me to love, to worship with my body for as long as you'd have me. Another that I would mourn when you died too soon. In all those years, through all those relationships…" I was ready for him to stop referencing his numerous past loves in this recitation of his love for me. This time the smile that ghosted across his lips was genuine, if a bit grim. "I've never bonded. I've never felt this pull. I've always cared, but never did my love for the other surpass my will to survive."

My eyes narrowed. Where was he going with this?

"I cannot sacrifice you. You will need to turn the blade on me."

His pronouncement hung on empty air. I stared, positive that I hadn't understood. This was completely insane. *He* was completely insane.

He looked back at me, his face a placid pond again. I could no more read his true intentions than I could tell a fortune in my coffee grounds.

"Tea leaves," Raj said.

"What?"

"You tell fortunes in tea leaves, not coffee grounds."

"Maybe *you* do," I retorted. I didn't know how to address his pronouncement. I fought for words. "I thought the prophecy stated that *you* had to wield the sword if you wanted your people to survive?"

"That was my prophecy," he said. "Yours just said that the sword had to be wielded and that you and I would be involved. If you sacrifice me with the sword, that should satisfy the terms."

I tilted my head to look at him "So it would somehow be better for me to kill you than vice versa?"

"Of course." He seemed surprised that I would even ask.

"Why would I agree to this? Why would I do that?"

He stared at me before answering. "Because you have someone else to live for. You still have Isaac."

I was struck dumb. I'd read that phrase numerous times, but never really grasped how that could be true. Even my mind was at a loss for complete thoughts. Finally, my body decided for me. I formed my hand into a fist and punched him in the gut as hard as I could.

"Ooof," he gasped. Part of me reveled in the fact that I'd affected the big, bad vampire with my puny fist and part of me was still so angry that I was considering doing it again.

"Fuck you, asshole," I said, willing my fists to stay coiled at my side.

"Why'd you hit me?" Raj sounded genuinely bewildered.

"You think that because I'm mated to Isaac I'd be okay losing you?"

"It was a fair assumption. You've brought up the 'what happens after we find him?' more than once."

"Yeah, the 'what happens after.' Not the 'I guess I'll fuck you 'til we rescue my mate.'" I was livid. "I wanted to know how you thought we'd balance my love for you with my bond with him, not how you were going to quietly disappear when I had my one true love back."

"Your one true love?" Raj's voice was rising to an alarmingly loud level. I was a little afraid that regardless of how far we'd moved from the road that Petrina would be able to hear us.

"By all the gods, Raj!" I exploded. "I love you, you stupid undead asshat! I love you. I'm mated to Isaac, but I love you. That's what I thought we were going to work out."

Raj's shoulders slumped, and he looked defeated. "I love you, too, my sweet."

I felt tears begin to leak out of the corners of my eyes. I'd cried more in the past year than in the previous thirty-five years put together. I needed to get back to my default state of strong Eleanor.

"I like emotional Eleanor," Raj said.

I half-smiled. I wasn't ready to let it go yet. "Raj. I am not going to use your sword to kill you."

"I can't use my sword to kill you."

"Then what do we do?"

"Fuck until the world burns around us?" Raj asked, a grin ghosting across his face.

"Neither of us are that person, are we? The person who sacrifices the many for the sake of the one?"

"I never thought I was until I met you," Raj said. "It has to be this way."

"What if we find another?" I whispered. I didn't think anyone was around to hear us but switched to mental communication anyway. *"Finn."*

"Can you do that?" he asked.

"I don't know. Sometimes I think I can. When I think of Emma, I know I can."

"And what if you can't?"

"You'd be the one to wield the sword, right? Could you?"

His smile was deadly. *"Absolutely."*

I shivered a bit.

"Florence seems to think that he's necessary in the future," Raj said.

"Fuck the future," I exploded. "I'm tired of waiting around for whatever possibility Florence sees but won't explain. I'm tired of hanging on by a string for things that no one will bother to tell me about. I just want it to be over. I want these goddamned gates to be open, so I can complete my obligations and rescue my stupid, too noble mate, and then figure out how I'm going to live my life."

"Do you think Finn's survival is necessary to complete Florence's quest?"

I stilled. Now that Raj had mentioned it, I couldn't think of another reason that Florence would advocate so strongly for his continued existence if it didn't have something to do with her sister. Hell, she'd practically adopted Emma as a surrogate little sister, and still wasn't willing to kill Finn to release Emma. That had to be it.

Raj continued, *"So the question remains, how much weight do we give her quest over our own survival?"*

Well, if that wasn't the shittiest question that had ever been raised. Doom myself or doom Florence's sister? Doom my lover's future happiness or my best friend's?

"Fuck," I said.

"Exactly."

"We should get back."

"We should have Petrina compel her to sleep and then carry her the rest of the way. I'm tired of her stupid hang-ups."

"She'll be pissed."

"I don't care," Raj said. "My feet hurt."

CHAPTER FIFTEEN

Petrina flat out refused to glamour Florence. Something about "morals and ethics and lies in relationships and blah blah blah." When neither Raj nor I seemed convinced by her arguments, she wrote us off as immoral fools and went off to tell on us.

Florence eyed me reproachfully as I dragged my sorry ass back to our little camp. "What?" I asked, a bit more defensively than I'd intended. "I was thinking of you! Your poor feet! And if you were glamoured, you wouldn't even notice that you were flying!"

She regarded me with hard eyes.

I dipped my head down and looked up at her under lowered lashes. "Surely you can't believe I'd ever wish you harm?"

A muscle at the corner of her mouth twitched, and I knew she wasn't really mad. That was good because I was pretty sure that my next question would send her there. She must have caught a hint of what was coming next because she stiffened almost imperceptibly. Petrina looked up from where she was quietly arguing with Raj and glared at me. I hadn't even done anything yet. I blew out my breath, braced myself mentally, and went for it.

"Do you need Finn alive only because you've foreseen he is necessary to your sister's rescue?"

"Since when are you so eager to commit murder?" she asked. There was a decided chill in the air.

"Since I found out that I was going to have to kill one person or destroy the whole world."

"So, kill the vampire. Arduinna said it would work."

I narrowed my eyes at her. "It would make more sense for him to sacrifice me. It's his blade, after all. And the act would have paranormal symmetry."

She hesitated before blasting forward. "You know he'd let you borrow the sword."

"So, I'm necessary for your sister's rescue, too? But Raj is not. Good to know. What if we throw Petrina into the mix? Can we sacrifice her?"

The hesitation was longer this time. I wondered how obsessed she was with her sister's rescue. Would she agree to sacrifice her lover? Her expression grew shuttered. I reached out to touch her; to stop her before she said something that would irrevocably damage her burgeoning relationship with Petrina.

"We'll find a way," I said. "But I thought we had a deal. No hiding vital information from the intrepid heroine."

"It wasn't vital."

I swear she sounded like a teen in the midst of an epic sulk.

I raised my eyebrows at her. "It is to me! I agreed that we'd go after your sister. I need a sacrifice. I want everything to work out with the least amount of pain and suffering. If I could figure out how to avoid killing someone to complete this mission, I would. I'm afraid we've gone too far to back out, but that doesn't mean I'm looking forward to standing by while Raj kills for me."

"But you'd let him do it," she—and there was no other word for it—sneered.

Raj chose that moment to stride forward. I could feel his irritation—it hadn't yet advanced to anger, which meant that she was picking a fight with me to piss me off for some reason—rolling off of him in waves. I held up a hand. I needed to finish this on my terms without anyone burning bridges they'd cry about later.

"If the choice is Raj wielding the prophesied blade to kill me and save the world or me wielding said blade to kill him, I will absolutely let him do it," I said. I tried to inflect as much chill into my tone as she was managing, but I was a creature of heat and fire, and I sounded more impassioned than frigid.

"You can't let him do that," she said.

"Why?" I asked. "Because I'm vital to your sister's possibly unwelcome rescue mission, or because I'm your friend?"

She dropped her eyes, and I had my answer. Now I didn't have to try to be cold. I felt a strangling ball of ice form in my esophagus, and I willed myself to hold it together. I knew we were friends, but I guess in my inexperience, I'd overestimated how deep that bond went with her. Why would she regard me as her bff? She was decades older and much wiser than me. I touched her arm, and she flinched. "It's okay," I said, willing it to be so. "You've known me for a few months. She's been missing from your life for decades. Of course, she's more important than me. I know that doesn't make me unimportant, and I know I'm more than a means to an end—" I sincerely hoped, anyway. "Instead of fighting about this, let's work together to get where we need to be so we can move on to the next phase of this crazy adventure."

Florence bowed her head, and I saw tears roll slowly down her lightly lined cheeks. "I am sorry," she said.

I debated for a moment before listening to my rusty human instincts and pulling her into a hug. She froze for a second before throwing her arms around me and holding on tightly. I felt her body heave a few times with suppressed sobs. I looked up when I sensed eyes on me and saw Petrina glaring at me.

"Tell her it was necessary," I said to Raj.

"She's not glaring at you," he replied.

Oh. That was unfortunate.

"She'll glamour her and carry her to Portland," Raj said.

I winced and hoped Florence didn't notice.

"How long until dawn?"

"Forty-five minutes."

"They should talk," I said. *"If they're going to make it through, Florence needs to explain to Petrina that her hesitation was more about her unwillingness to sacrifice Petrina than about saying it out loud."*

"And is that true?" Raj asked.

"Yes. And if you could tell Florence that truth, I'd appreciate it."

I felt Florence stiffen in my arms and then pull away. Obviously, the message was getting through. I saw the stricken look on her face before she masked it.

"Go," I said to her. "Tell her how you feel."

"Thank you," she said to me.

"That's what besties are for," I said as lightheartedly as I could.

She almost grinned before walking away and snagging Petrina's hand.

Raj pulled me into his arms. "You are a brave, brave woman," he said.

I tilted my head up and pressed my lips to his. "Damn skippy."

He kissed me back with interest, and I was breathing a little faster when I pulled away. "Will they be okay?"

"I don't know, but it's good this is out there now when there's still a chance to talk things through."

"Speaking of," I said. "What are we going to do? I don't want to kill Finn, even if we were to catch him, if it means destroying Florence."

Raj didn't say anything, just kept trying to distract me with his lips and hands. I let him for a bit, then sighed deeply against his neck. "It has to be me," I said.

"That will doom Florence's quest as much as killing Finn would, and it would be much less satisfying."

"There is no one else that I feel comfortable putting into that situation."

"What if I found a criminal-type?" Raj asked, running his teeth along my pulsing carotid.

"Really? That's your solution? Kill a random guilty-ish human? That doesn't seem right."

"When nine hundred years old you get, as moral you'll be not."

I rolled my eyes. My thousand-year-old boyfriend was misquoting Yoda.

"Raj. It has to be me."

"No. End of story. I will not do it."

"You were willing to let me be imprisoned and tortured and starved for the stupid blade to save the world. At least this would be fast!" He flinched at my low blow.

"I knew you'd be okay," he hissed. Christ, was I going to pick a fight with everyone tonight?

I ran my hand up his cheek and into his hair. "I love you," I said. "But I think this is what's supposed to happen."

"Fuck what's supposed to happen. You. Are. Mine."

I backed out of his arms and folded mine. "Excuse me?" I tapped my foot.

Raj ran his fingers through his hair with an aura of exhaustion. "You know what I mean."

I softened. I did. And to be honest, I felt the same. He was mine and the thought of not finding out what the next chapter held hurt me.

"What else can we do?" I asked.

"I don't know," he admitted.

It was another hour before I heard signs of Petrina and Florence returning. I was getting a little impatient; we had a long way to go tonight if we were going to end up walking. When footsteps approached, I stood up, brushed off my backside, and hoisted my pack.

Petrina ran into our camp and skidded to a halt, Florence on her heels. "Someone's coming," Petrina said. "A lot of someones."

"What kind of someones?" Raj asked. He'd been pacing in the desert, and I hadn't heard him return. I jumped and glared.

"Shifters," Florence said. "Their thoughts are familiar, yet not."

"That is not as much information as I'd like," Raj said.

She shrugged. "It's the best I can do. My nose isn't as good as Emma's, and we ran back to warn you rather than stand and fight."

Emma's name elicited the now-familiar pang of pain, and I started to fold in on myself before I could stop.

"Do we run or stand?" Raj asked me.

"Stand," I said after only a moment's thought. "But let's make sure we're close together and our packs are easily reached in case you two have to grab us and fly out."

I felt Florence's glare. "Only in case of emergency," I said. "Just far enough to be safe. This is not a ploy to get you in the air."

She muttered something uncomplimentary about my heritage but grabbed her pack and leaned it against mine. The vampires did the same, then flanked us for an easy grab and go.

I heard them not long after. I hoped whatever they wanted didn't take long. Being this far behind schedule made me incredibly nervous. A small pride of lions materialized out of the darkness and came to a stop in front of us. They parted and revealed a shifter in human form. He was panting from exertion. He must not be able to shift quickly so had to stay human to talk. They should've stopped just out of earshot to let him catch his breath, then enter at a jog. He would've looked better, and I wouldn't have had to suppress laughter while watching him suck air until he could breathe normally.

"Can I help you?" I asked, well before he was capable of speech.

He held up one finger and shook his head. I couldn't suppress the laughter anymore. This was beyond ridiculous.

The flush that had started to fade from his cheeks reappeared as I laughed at him. I tried to stifle my laughter, but by this time, Raj and Petrina were chuckling, too.

After what seemed like ages, he straightened and looked at me.

"We were formerly of the southwest pack but have formally separated from the bears," he announced.

"And?" I prompted, when his pause seemed to indicate that he expected a response.

He appeared flustered, glanced behind him for support, and then faced me again.

"We are here to formally apologize for not appearing as commanded by the wolf you call Emma. My former Alpha forbade our presence, and I wasn't strong enough to formally resist."

He was awfully punctilious. I wondered if I could prompt him into using the word formally again.

"Too little, too late," I said. "Your apology doesn't right the wrong that was done."

He bowed shakily and clumsily. "Perhaps the wolf would accept my formal—" *jackpot!* "—apology. It is intended for her, after all."

"She's not here," Florence said before I could reply.

"We will wait."

"What's your name, cat?" I asked.

He puffed up his chest. "John Randolph III. Alpha of the SW Pride."

"John, Emma is not here to accept your apology. No one here will accept it, no matter how formal you get. Please take your pride and go."

John flushed. "We won't go without her. She is part of our pack now."

I laughed in his face. "You're interested in losing your Alpha status already? Too much responsibility for you?"

"What do you mean?" he sputtered. "She would be in our pack, not lead it."

"Did you learn nothing of her showdown with your former Alpha? She schooled him, and she would've wiped the floor with you." I was mixing my metaphors, but I was too incredulous to keep them straight. "She was the strongest shifter I've ever met. It doesn't matter, though, because she's not here. Your inaction at Beltane—your direct opposition to the terms of the treaty signed between your Alpha and ours—resulted in her death. Now take your sorry bunch of kitties and get the fuck out of here."

"You're lying," he said.

"I'm Fae, you idiot."

"Not a very good one," John said.

"What do you want?" I was suddenly tired. "Go home, John.

There's no wolf to try to abscond with, and I'm not in the mood for your bullshit today."

"I challenge you," he said.

"What? Why?"

"I will fight you, and the winner gets the wolf."

"For fuck's sake. She is dead. And even if she wasn't, she's not a prize to be won. She was strong, powerful, and more than capable of fighting her own battles. If she'd wanted to be a part of your pack, she would've taken it."

"She's a girl. Girls can't be Alpha."

"Listen to me, John. I'm going to tell you this one last time. Emma is dead. Your pack could have very well saved her, but you didn't show up. No woman is ever a prize. I am not going to fight you."

"I will give you no choice!" He turned around and eyed the half dozen lions—all males, that was going to be a fun group to hang out with—and said. "Do not interfere. This is between me and the bitch." He started stripping.

"Wait, you're going to shift for the fight that won't be happening?" I asked.

"It's only fair to use all the weapons at my disposal." He started the change. As I'd guessed earlier, it wasn't something that came easily to him.

"This is dumb," I told my companions. "We don't have to stand around and wait for this."

"They'll just follow us and attack when we're not looking," Raj said.

"I don't want to fight a lion cub for possession of my dead friend."

"Get it over with quickly," Florence said. "In the meantime, I'm going to sit down."

As I waited for my opponent to get into fighting form, I checked the knives in my arm sheaths to make sure I had firmly in mind which were silver then drew my sword. It took so long I considered going to sit with Florence and Petrina while we waited.

Finally, a fully formed lion stood in front of me. He roared, and although it was more impressive than anything else he'd done so far, I still couldn't muster even a tiny ounce of fear. "Let's do this, idiot," I said.

He rushed me; I stepped out of the way and sliced along his flank. I was careful to cut shallowly. I didn't want to kill him. He spun around, enraged, and made the exact same move. To play along, I did, too, and cut his other flank—a bit deeper this time.

He lost all sense at that point, crouched, and attempted to leap on me. I stepped out of the way and grabbed one of my iron daggers. He landed on it and the force of his weight combined with gravity dug it all the way in. He collapsed in a heap at my feet, then rolled and showed me his belly.

"Is he surrendering?" I asked. "It wasn't even silver."

"It looks like it," Raj said. "The rest of the lions have fled into the darkness."

"Did they truly flee, or are they waiting to attack?"

"They fled," Florence confirmed. "That doesn't mean they aren't waiting to surprise us with an ambush, but I can't sense them in the vicinity."

It was the most confusing fight I'd ever had. The lion was mewling in front of me, sounding more like a pathetic house cat than a mighty jungle king. "Change," I said to him. He shook his sparse mane and tried to back away.

The knife pulled out with a satisfying sucking sound, and he fell at my feet again, although the wound was already healing. Damn! Shifter regeneration was amazing.

"Change," I said, pulling from my mate bond to wield enough Alpha power to command him.

He shimmered and contorted for more than ten minutes before a sobbing, naked man cowered at my feet. "Get your pride in order," I said. "I never want to see or hear from you again."

"Yes, Alpha," he said.

I grabbed my pack and walked away.

A COUPLE HOURS LATER, Florence was visibly limping, and we were barely hitting two and a half miles an hour. I tried not to chafe under the slower than needed speed and bit my tongue every time I wanted to comment on it. She might be the most even-keeled, least ego-driven of this bunch, but that was a pretty low bar, and she was stubborn as fuck.

Raj, Petrina, and Florence all froze in place and their heads spun round to face the same direction. I didn't know what they sensed, but I knew enough that I ought to be facing that direction, too.

With a loud roar, Joey or Jimmy or Johnny or whatever his name was burst into my field of vision followed by a half dozen other lions. He must be running on fumes to have made a second change after the effort it'd taken to change to and from his lion form before. As I unsheathed my sword, I noted the other lions were American cougars although he was a maned type. Maybe that's how he got them to follow him—used his fancy hairdo to intimidate them.

I swung my sword a few times. Shifters were going to die, and it made me sad. They didn't deserve to be punished for being cursed with decades of poor leadership. Before I could develop a battle strategy in my head, Florence stepped forward and roared loudly enough to put any lion to shame. "Stop!"

They froze in their tracks—literally—some in mid-leap, which resulted in a sudden and loud drop to the ground.

"I have had enough of you. There have been plenty of opportunities to back down. Nothing you have done, either tonight or in your earlier association with your former pack, has been honorable. Do you hate losing to a woman so much that you cannot let it go? If Eleanor had been a man, would you be pursuing us now, or is it the humiliation of being defeated by a woman that goads you on now?

"You know in your hearts that if Emma and Eleanor had been men, this would've been dropped immediately. You are children. Children who were poorly raised and cannot comprehend a world where the strong, independent women are so very much stronger than you. Eleanor defeated you earlier with nothing but calm, her sword, and an iron dagger. Your temper runs too hot, and you feel too entitled. I will cool you down."

She muttered a word and made a flicking motion with her hand. For a second, nothing happened, and then they exploded. Every single one, one after another, like firecrackers on a string.

"What the actual fuck, Florence?" My jaw was hanging down to my chest, and I could barely get the words out.

"She cooled their blood," Raj said. He was laughing. "Florence, you are magnificent. If you weren't already involved with my daughter, I'd consider seducing you away from her."

I punched Raj. "Hey!"

He shrugged. "I suspect neither of us needs to worry about that being successful. In truth, she might be too scary for me."

Petrina was staring at Florence in awe. "You turned their blood to ice in their veins, didn't you? That is terrifyingly brilliant." She pulled Florence into her arms and kissed her with a passion that warmed the air around them. I took a step back, not wanting—at least not very much—to gawk at their private moment.

When they came up for air, Florence shrugged. "I watched a documentary once on trees exploding in winter if their sap got too cold. I don't have an opportunity to practice very much, but the theory is sound, and ice magic is a specialty of mine."

I was at a loss for words. "I'm glad you're on our side."

She grinned at me, but the amusement didn't reach her eyes. "You can burn people with a thought. This is no different."

Maybe she was right, but it seemed different somehow. Maybe my power was much less scary because I knew I was in control—much the same way that no matter how much I hated driving, I always felt safer when I was behind the wheel. There was a wee, tiny chance that I was a control freak.

"No!" Raj gasped. "You?"

"Cut it with the sarcasm, vampire," I said. "I don't need any comments on my baggage."

"I have a comment on your baggage," Petrina said. "We are not going to make it to Portland by the solstice traveling at this rate.

Particularly if we have to stop and fend off attackers ever other night. The packs are heavy and slow us down even further."

"We need those!" Florence exclaimed. "Not everyone can live on people."

"The people are already scarce," Petrina said. "We have to go farther and farther afield to find meals, and I'm starting to feel it. Father doesn't have to feed as often as I do. Ideally, with this physical pace, I should be eating every other night at the outside, although I'd prefer every night."

"What are you suggesting?" Florence said.

"I have two suggestions. The first is that I fly you and father flies Eleanor. He has a home in Portland where we can stay and recuperate. It's safe from prying eyes and will have every resource we need to recuperate while we're waiting for the final gate."

"No," Florence said, crossing her arms.

Petrina sighed. "There may come a point where you have no choice," she said.

"You said you had two suggestions."

"I don't think you will like this one any more than the first. I propose we cast about for horses and a cart. Someone around here must have something like that, if only for novelty purposes. We can make a little better time with horses than on foot, and it will give your feet time to heal. Also, I can find a couple humans, glamour them, and carry along our meals as well as yours."

"Your better idea is to steal horses, a cart, and kidnap and enslave humans for you to feed on?" Florence, the woman who'd just killed a half-dozen shifters by very dramatically exsanguinating them, looked horrified.

"I said you wouldn't like it," Petrina pointed out. "But you will not make it to Portland on time walking. If you insist on that method, we will have to leave you behind."

"You'd abandon me?"

I was beginning to wonder how far they'd gotten in their relationship talk before being interrupted by errant shifters.

"If you can't make it to Portland, Eleanor will need a witch who can help weave the weir that controls the magic release. I've watched you do it, and although I wouldn't be able to perform at the same level as you, I could absolutely do it satisfactorily."

Florence turned to me. "And you? Would you also abandon me?"

"Please don't bring me into this," I said.

"I want to know what you'd do."

"My idea earlier, if you'll remember, was for Petrina to take you in thrall long enough to fly you to Portland. I don't want to leave you behind, but I do want to get there on time. I'd also like to get there before all of our feet fall off. Petrina didn't want to do that because she felt it was a betrayal of your trust."

"And you?" Florence watched me through narrowed eyes.

"I think it's the best way to get to where we're going at the right time and with the minimum amount of emotional and physical damage to you. If she enthralls you, you won't be afraid. Based on her reticence to do it, I'm guessing she wouldn't be tempted to keep you as a thrall once it was no longer necessary."

Florence picked up her pack and headed to the highway. "I'll think about it. Now let's get going."

"If she hasn't made a decision by the time we get to Moab, I will decide for her," Raj said to me.

"How are you holding up with the food situation?"

"Better than Trina. She's right in that I don't have to feed as often as her. Every three to four days at this pace."

"Good," I said aloud.

"You've no idea how tempted I am to fly ahead and meet you in Moab," Raj said as we caught up to Florence. "My feet were not made for cross-country hikes."

"If I have to do this, so do you," I said. "Although if anyone wants to give me the go-ahead to turn into a dragon and scout ahead for other miscreants, I'd be delighted."

Raj and Petrina both laughed, but Florence maintained her icy silence.

I sighed. It was going to be a long couple nights to Moab.

CHAPTER SIXTEEN

Two nights later, we hobbled into Moab just before dawn. I was having second thoughts about the second 'f' in my 'bff' declaration to Florence. Petrina had decided to scout ahead to find us a safe place to sleep—although she was almost certainly merely looking for an excuse to stop walking. She met us at the edge of town.

"There's a hotel still renting rooms for cash. I booked two rooms there for the next two nights."

"We're already running behind—" Petrina held up a hand and interrupted me.

"We will get to Portland on time, but we must rest. All of us are depleted, some more than others." She glanced pointedly at Florence who tried to glare but gave it up in exhaustion.

I knew I ought to protest more, but I couldn't muster up any argument that outweighed a warm, soft bed.

"I took the time to heat the water before coming back," Petrina said.

"Show me the way," I said. The motels we'd squatted in over the last week hadn't had any water at all, and although Petrina could heat the water, she couldn't make it appear out of nowhere.

"Would you like me to carry you?" Raj asked.

That sounded amazing, but instead of answering in the affirmative, I straightened up, squared my shoulders, and started marching towards town. If Florence could make it, so could I.

"It's not a contest, you know," Raj said. *"You're allowed to ask for help. Your friend's stubbornness doesn't mean you also have to be stubborn beyond all reason."*

"You're right," I said aloud. "Please carry me. My feet are killing me."

He picked me up, got directions from Petrina, and whooshed me away.

I walked into the hotel under my own power and found the room that Petrina had secured for us. Nothing sounded better than peeling off my clothes, crawling under the covers, and falling asleep. Nothing except a hot shower. I couldn't decide.

"Either choice involved taking off your clothes," Raj pointed out. "Why don't you start there."

"You're just trying to get me naked," I said.

"Usually, you'd be right, but not today. I think we're both too exhausted for anything but rest."

My eyebrows crept up into my hairline in another futile attempt to appear quizzical.

"You caught me," he said, hands raised. "I'm never too tired for sex. You, on the other hand…"

"You're right. I'm exhausted. And filthy."

"We'll be here for two full days and nights. Shower now so you don't dirty up the sheets. I'll go find breakfast for you."

"Coffee?" I asked.

"Won't that keep you awake?"

"Nothing could keep me awake at this point."

"Coffee and breakfast it is, then. Strip. Shower. I'll be back soon."

The shower was the most miraculous thing I'd ever experienced, and the only thing harder than deciding to take the time to shower in the first place was trying to force myself to get out. A large cup of steaming coffee was waiting for me next to a plate of muffins and bacon. Raj was nowhere to be found, and light was seeping into the room through the cracks in the curtains.

I devoured my breakfast and hopped into bed. I was asleep before my head hit the pillow.

It was dark when I woke up, but there was another cup of coffee—that man was magic—next to me, along with a note informing me he'd be back soon and that dinner was waiting for me in Florence's room.

The aroma pulled me down the hall, and I had no trouble finding the right room. My mouth was watering so much I was afraid I'd start drooling if I didn't get food soon.

Florence opened the door before I could knock. I set my coffee down and stared at the two large pizzas gracing the small hotel table. My stomach chose that moment to growl loudly, and Petrina handed me a plate and got out of the way. I piled my plate as high as I could.

"This is amazing. It's been ages since we've had good, hot food."

"It's been a week," Florence said.

"That's, like, a year in Fae time," I declared around a mouthful of pizza.

"Don't talk to her when she's eating," Petrina said. "She always feels the need to respond before she's swallowed her food." She shuddered.

I swallowed, stuck my tongue out at Petrina, and grabbed my next slice. After I'd decimated both pizzas—allowing Florence to have a couple slices, of course—I leaned back, patted my belly, and sighed. "If only there were beer, this night would be the best in a while."

"Your wish is my command," Raj said, startling me enough that I yelped and almost fell off the bed. I was going to get that man a bell.

"Where are you going to hang it?" he asked, handing me a cold bottle of local IPA. I eyed it suspiciously and tried to fight the images he sent with his question so I wouldn't blush. "Does this even have alcohol in it?" I asked. "I thought Utah didn't have real beer."

"It's real beer," Raj said. "Drink."

I popped the top with the bottle opener he offered me and took a long, slow swallow. It probably wasn't as good as a Portland IPA, but those had been few and far between for the last months. No way was I complaining.

"We need to talk," Petrina announced, staring at Florence.

I double-checked the pizza boxes to make sure they were empty, then leaned back against the headboard. "Ready."

"We have a little over four weeks and eight hundred miles between us and the opening of the final gate. I had to peel Florence's socks off her feet last night because the blistering is so bad."

Florence flushed and opened her mouth, but Petrina held up a hand and continued. "I don't know what shape you're in, Eleanor, but even my immortality isn't protecting me from this trek. The landscape is unforgiving, and the nights are still cold. Eleanor, you will begin to have trouble resisting the urge to hibernate if we have to spend too many nights camping." She turned to Florence and took her hands. "Florence, I know you don't want to fly, but can you see a way to accepting that's the path we need to take? If you want the gates to open and you want Eleanor to be in the kind of shape to handle the magic that will burst into the world with the last gate, you may need to relent. An exhausted, worn out catalyst will be no good to anyone, and the shock could kill her, then where would your quest to save your sister be?"

Florence looked steadily over Petrina's shoulder and didn't say anything.

"Don't let stubbornness or fear or pride be our undoing," Petrina said. "Tell me what you need to make this safe for you. You are the bravest woman I've met in my three hundred plus years of life, and I know you're brave enough for this."

"I don't want you to drop me," Florence said so softly I could barely hear her. "When you're in a plane or a helicopter, there's a floor. If you carry me, you could let go, and I would fall."

Petrina cupped Florence's face in her hands. "I would never drop you. As for falling, I've already fallen enough for both of us. You are safe with me, I swear it."

I stood up and tried to edge out of the room without interrupting their moment. I knocked the pizza boxes off the table with my hip, then stubbed my toe and let out a yelp when I tried to catch them.

Raj smothered a laugh and Petrina shot me a half-hearted glare.

"Fine," Florence said. "Fine. I'll let you carry me."

"Thank you," I said. "My feet owe you a great debt of gratitude." I backed the rest of the way out of the room without further incident and headed out to take another shower.

WHEN I WOKE the next afternoon, Arduinna was sitting in a chair in my room paging idly through an old People magazine.

"Thanks for knocking," I said. I hated surprise guests, especially ones that arrived while I was sleeping. "How'd you slip through the wards?"

"Perhaps you were sleeping too deeply to be woken?" she suggested.

"Perhaps you might try your bullshit somewhere else."

She shrugged, smiled enigmatically, and leaned back in the chair, discarding the magazine. "I have my ways. Your witch's wards are not universal. Your magic regards me as a member of your group now and doesn't alert you to my presence."

"Why are you here?"

She sat up, all business. The witty banter portion of the evening was over.

"I came to warn you."

"So dire. I'm not ready for doomsaying—unless you brought me coffee."

Arduinna leaned over and grabbed a steaming cup of coffee that had been hidden from my view. She presented it to me with a bow. "Your coffee, Highness."

I slipped out of bed, grabbed the jeans that were crumpled by the bed, and pulled them on before grabbing the coffee. "I appreciate your consideration. You may now begin the doom and gloom."

"The regional governor of the northwest states knows you're here."

"And?"

"He's not happy."

"I'm going to need more than this, Arduinna. Why should I care that my existence in Utah is irritating the regional governor?"

"He blames you for what's happening in the United States."

"That's fair. It's not entirely my fault, but I am the reason it's happening now."

"He's human."

I cocked my head to the side and looked at her. "Spit it out, Arduinna. I don't know what I'm supposed to be getting from this. If you have something to say, say it plainly."

She heaved a sigh. "The regional governor, a human, blames you, a Fae, for the destruction of the United States and has made his view-points clear to the citizens of these states."

"Remind me which states this encompasses."

"Utah, Nevada, Idaho, Washington, and Oregon."

"Not California?"

"Not anymore. They've seceded and put up a magical wall to keep everyone else out—or to keep the Californians in. We don't know. There's no communication getting in or out of the state."

"Okay, so Governor Humanpants—"

"Pulsipher."

"Ugh, him? He's a douche. Fine. Governor Pulsipher, the stain of Utah, is telling the good citizens of this state that I am the reason for this destruction, and is making it clear that I am *not* human? And this is what is, in part, mobilizing the citizens of Utah to rise up and root out the evil in their midst?"

"Exactly."

"And he knows roughly where I'm at right now and may or may not be informing the uninformed mobs where to find me."

"Yes."

"So, any minute, we can expect pitchforks and tiki torches surrounding the hotel?"

"Not exactly," a man's voice answered.

I turned towards the voice and called out to Raj through our mental link at the same time. It must be nearly sunset, but if he was awake, he'd come.

A tall, objectively attractive man with silvering hair, strong jawline, and trim figure stood before me in a custom suit that radiated money. He held out his hand. "Allow me to introduce myself. I'm Governor Mitchell Pulsipher, the stain of Utah, and current regional governor of the Western States."

I ignored his hand and eventually he dropped it.

"What do you want, Mitch?"

A pained smile twisted across his face, probably at my informality and lack of manners.

"I wanted, first and foremost, to assure you that I'm not anti-supernatural as I've been portrayed by the President's aide here. In fact, I'd like to introduce you to my Lieutenant Governor." He turned and called over his shoulder. "Jerome, you can come in now."

A gaunt, lanky man with chalky skin and inky hair glided into the room. He looked like something out of a Vincent Price horror movie.

Mitch turned back towards me. "This is Jerome Worth, my Lieutenant Governor. As you can see, he is not human."

"Mitch, what do you and Nosferatu want from me? I've just woken up, I've had a long few months and have another hard month in front of me. I don't have time for bullshit right now."

Mitch seemed frustrated, and I wondered if he'd imagined the script a little differently. Perhaps I was supposed to be more impressed with him, but I'd met the vampire queen of the United States, was sleeping with the second most powerful creature of the night in North America and counted a number of powerful supernaturals among my friends. The bigoted former governor of Utah was not that impressive.

"I am here," Raj said. *"I will lurk in the shadows of the hallway like a proper creature of the night until you need me."*

Mitch sighed. "The reason for my visit is threefold. Firstly, I would like us to be allies. Someday soon, it will become apparent that the former United States will never be restored. You are rumored to be the natural choice for the throne. I would be an asset to you, and in return, you would keep me as chief among your advisors. I've been a politician my entire adult life. I have resources and contacts that can benefit you."

He paused as if waiting for a reply. "You said three reasons. Continue."

His grin was tight. I was apparently exceptionally irritating. "Secondly, I request your assistance to eradicate a troublesome group of demons terrorizing humans not far from here."

"Demons? Are you sure?"

"Demons or witches…does it matter what we call them? They are terrorizing the humans of a town in my territory."

"Are you also going to take care of the humans in Cortez that are terrorizing innocent groups of supernaturals passing through? Or is your ire reserved only for supernaturals?"

"You can take care of yourself, can you not? Us humans are helpless in the face of your powers."

Heat pulsed through my body. It was only a matter of time until I started smoking if I couldn't get my emotions under control. "A human killed one of my companions, Governor. I wouldn't call you helpless."

"Do you support supernaturals preying on humans?"

"Of course not. I don't support anyone abusing the power they hold over another group of people. However, I am not a mercenary for hire. If crimes are being committed, use legal avenues to investigate, arrest, and take the perpetrators to trial. Don't hire hitmen. That is tyranny, and I will not be a party to that. What is your third item of discussion?"

"I will leave that to my Lieutenant Governor to share. We were hoping your other companions would be here for this part."

"I grow weary of this conversation, Mitch. My companions will hear your words."

The vampire shuffled forward, and I struggled not to shudder. He was creepy as fuck.

"The vampires Raj and Petrina have entered my territory and haven't sought me out to declare their intentions. They've ignored centuries of protocol and have risked civil relations between our clans. I want them brought before me and forced to apologize."

"Wanna take this one?" I asked.

"Absolutely."

Raj walked into the room. Mitch's and Jerome's backs were to the door and didn't see him. I was not impressed with Jerome's powers of observation because he didn't even twitch when the most powerful vamp west of the Mississippi walked into the room.

"I'm masking my power."

"You can do that?" I was legit impressed.

"Hieronymus," Raj intoned. Jerome whirled around and became inexplicably paler. "I owe you no obeisance."

"This is my territory," Jerome said, but his voice was shaking.

"Governor," Raj said, inclining his head slightly.

Mitch nodded back.

"How was it decided that you would be the regional governor over the other five governors of the states in this region?"

"Well, I've been in politics longer, have better contacts, and am more powerful than the rest."

Raj turned his attention back to Jerome. "Wouldn't that make me, by default, the regional governor of the vampires in this six-state region?"

"I am the Lieutenant Governor. My power trumps yours."

Raj laughed, and every hair on my body stood on end. "Prove it, Hieronymus. Prove that you are more than delusions, more than mad visions. Prove that you can best me. I have five hundred years on you and have never been insane."

"I am a genius."

"No one said differently, but genius and sanity do not often walk hand in hand. I will not yield to you. I owe you nothing. Your territory is trifling, which is the only reason I let you keep it all this time."

"It is protocol!" Jerome was getting shrill, and Raj was sending out waves of irritation.

Raj grinned and showed his fangs. "Tell me more about your protocol? How do you welcome your betters?"

"Protocol!"

Holy fuck. Jerome was mad as a hatter. *Why are hatters mad? God, I miss Google.*

Raj's mouth twitched, and I knew he was trying not to laugh. He pulled himself together before anyone else noticed. His eyes blazed red, his fangs lengthened, and he roared, "Do not test me, Hieronymus!" Raj seemed to grow in stature until he towered over everyone in the room. This vampire was terrifying as fuck, and I didn't know how Mitch and Jerome weren't pissing their pants right now. The only reason I wasn't was because I was reasonably certain that the scariest guy in the room was on my side.

Jerome fell to his knees. "Apologies. You and your daughter may travel anywhere you wish without notice or permission."

Raj shrunk back into himself. "Leave me," he said.

Jerome started to Nosferatu himself out the room, and Mitch interrupted. "You can't tell my people what to do."

Raj turned to the Governor. "The vampires in this country are *my* people. Mine and my queen's. We know who you are, and you will be watched. You don't get a pass because you hired one supernatural into a position of power. Leave now."

"What about our alliance?" Mitch asked.

"We have no alliance," I said. "You are not the kind of man I'd ally myself with."

"Do you hate humans?" he spat. "You won't be a popular ruler if that gets out."

"I hate bigots," I shot back. "And I will not rule this country. Your rumormongers need new sources. I will rule, but it won't be here."

Mitch grinned. "Good to know, Fae. Good to know." He turned and walked out, snapping his fingers at Jerome. "Come."

Fuck.

"What have you done?" Arduinna demanded.

"I don't know," I said.

"You could've accepted his help now and not followed through later."

"I can't do that, Arduinna. It's not in my nature. He's slimy and gross. He hates everyone who's not white, rich, and male. Now he has a whole new group to hate. I won't pretend to be friends with a snake like that."

"He will harass you through the rest of your walk to Portland. He will send bands of human vigilantes after you with the promise of a bounty for your head."

"Was he behind the bounty hunter who killed Emma?"

"Who can say?" Arduinna said. "He is dead now, and can't reveal his sources. Governor Pulsipher is not alone in his prejudices. I am more concerned that your lover is setting himself up to take over."

I laughed. "What are you talking about?

"Did you listen to his words? He declared that by the rule the political leaders were following, he was more powerful than any other vampire save the Queen in New Orleans. He is setting up a coup."

Raj laughed, and I was relieved to see the red glow had faded from his eyes.

"Arduinna, you misunderstand me. I do not set myself up to be king. I set myself up to be the consort of a queen."

HOURS LATER, after we rehashed everything for Florence and Petrina, Raj and I found ourselves alone. Finally. I had questions as well as a desperate need for some food.

"I'll let you get your food and some sleep and see you in the evening," Raj said.

"Wait, what now?"

"If we're leaving for Portland via Air Vamp tomorrow night, I need to fuel up."

"Why are you talking like that? You're being weird."

He turned and met my eyes and the hurt in them was palpable. "I'm trying to give you some space and time."

"You've lost me, Raj. I don't understand what's going on, and you've shut me off from your mind. Please, just talk to me."

"I saw your fear and heard what you thought about me."

I wracked my brains but couldn't come up with anything that would've caused this kind of reaction. "I'm going to need a little more information."

"I scared you. *Terrified* you. You thought that I was 'pants-pissing terrifying.'"

"You are scary, but if you got all that, surely you must have heard that part where I was glad you were on my side? You know who else is scary? Petrina when she went all Queen of the Damned on those idiots in Cortez. And Florence when she exploded the shifters. And Florence when she impaled the necromancers. Florence might be scarier than you. I'm glad I have scary friends. I'm looking forward to not pretending to be hampered by non-existent magical bonds so I can join you all in the scary parade.

"I am in awe of you, Raj. I'm glad you're powerful and terrifying. I wouldn't want you any other way. You are beautiful when you're scaring the piss out of...please tell me that was Hieronymus Bosch. He's the only Hieronymus I know, and I need this to be true. Please?"

"I overreacted?" He looked a bit sheepish.

"You overreacted. Nice try on side-stepping my question. Is Jerome Bosch?"

Raj shrugged. "Who can say?"

"You, probably. Spill."

A smile ghosted across his lips. "Yes. That was him."

"Oh my god. Was he always a vampire? Is he mad?"

"Obviously he was once human. I don't know at what point he was changed, but I think he's probably always been a bit mad. We have more important things to talk about, though."

"Of course. Fine. On to the big things. What was that about being a consort?"

Raj shifted back a bit, and if I didn't know better, I'd say he was embarrassed. "That was probably unnecessary."

"You and Medb, then? Congratulations. When's the big day?"

"Don't downplay this, Eleanor."

"What else am I supposed to do? One of us is supposed to be dead in a month, and I'm betting it's going to be me. The throne is not something I'm worried about right now. I just want to get through the next few weeks, open the damn gate, and have both of us alive the next day. What we do next is almost incidental at this point."

"Not to me. I'm in this for the long haul, Eleanor."

"I'm not saying that I'm not, what I'm saying is the long haul might not be very long, so what's the point of digging deeper?"

"What's the point? The point is that we are two people in love, and that's what mature adults do when they're in love. They dig deeper and make plans for the future."

"Your plans include being my consort? That's kinda a big leap from 'we've been dating for five months.'"

"I don't want to fight with you, Eleanor. In the midst of my vampire intimidation, I said things that you weren't ready to hear, but it's out there now, and I won't take it back. We will figure this out, but the one thing I know for certain—as long as you love me, I'm not giving up."

"What about—"

Raj put his hand on my mouth. "No. You are my future. There's nothing else that needs to be hashed out right now."

"There are so many things that need to be hashed out right now! If we're going to make plans for the future, we need to—"

"Plan for every eventuality? Isn't it enough to say we plan to be together?"

"You're the one who started this whole relationship conversation, and now you're tabling it?"

"I merely want to set parameters. Those parameters are that this is a relationship, this is serious, and when you take the throne, I will be at your side."

"You're just in it for the crown," I accused, mostly in jest.

"It's good to be king," Raj said.

I couldn't help it—I laughed. "I guess you'd know."

"So, are we agreed?"

"I guess so, future Majesty."

"I love you, Eleanor."

I sighed. "Fucking hell."

"It'll be okay."

"I love you too, Raj."

CHAPTER SEVENTEEN

I sat on the front steps of Vista House at Crown Point and watched the sun rise over the Columbia River. Mt. Hood gleamed pink and orange in the reflected light, and the clouds hung low over the Columbia, creating the illusion that the river was made of pink cotton candy. The summer air was pleasantly cool as it often is in Oregon, and I shivered lightly in enjoyment.

Dragons rose over the northern horizon, flying in a wide vee formation like migrating geese. They swooped in and out of line, scales glittering in the early morning sun. I watched until they disappeared to the south, then turned my attention to the person sitting next to me.

"Why are you here?" I asked him.

"To see my grandfather, of course. This is what he was made for, and therefore why I exist. Also, I like fire, and you are living flame."

My first meeting with the erstwhile Dracula was as weird as I'd imagined it would be. "I meant, why are you here in my dream?"

"Are you sure you're dreaming? Maybe you've lost track of time. It's easy to go mad a little when you live forever."

There was no way I was having a dream argument about whether or not I was dreaming with Vlad the Impaler at sunrise, so I settled for a different line of questioning. "Was it worth it, what you got in exchange for the sword?"

"What sword?"

He might have been messing with me, but it was equally possible he had no idea what I was talking about. Drac was not playing with a full deck. At best, he had a few face cards and more jokers than were standard. "Raj's sword—the ruby blade. You gave it to Marie, but we don't know everything you got in exchange."

"She was so surprised when I gave it to her. It was a gift she couldn't have anticipated."

My fondest hope was that when all was said and done, if I lived, I would be able to surround myself with sane people who said what they meant and didn't create elaborate word dances. "And her gift to you? Was it everything you dreamed?"

"No. I wanted my love back. Marie agreed for one drop of my grandfather's blood. I asked him for his sword, and he gave it to me. He thought it was a loan, but I knew his blood, and the blood of his ancestors and his children was in the rubies, and that was better than a single drop, wasn't it?"

"Marie fulfilled her part of the bargain, though, did she not?"

"No!" He howled his grief to the sky. "Ilona didn't know me, didn't want me, didn't love me."

"Did you find her again?"

A sly smile slid across his face, and he regarded me out of the corner of his eyes. "Maybe I did. I wouldn't say, though, would I? You killed Rasputin. I am not going to tell you my secrets."

I looked away from him and watched the clouds slowly dissipate over the wide river. This was not how I wanted to spend my dream time.

"I'm coming," he whispered in my ear, hot breath moving wisps of hair. I shuddered. "See you soon!"

When I turned back to where he'd been sitting, Marie was in his place.

"This is so boring," she said. "I hate getting stuck in other people's dream sequences. I never learn anything interesting."

"Why are you here, then? I didn't invite you in."

She kicked something towards me. It was a bowling ball bag—heh—and it was unzipped. "He wants to talk to you."

"He what now?" I recoiled as Marie reached down and spread the mouth of the bag open. Rasputin—one hundred percent back to normal except that he was still just a head—looked out at me.

"You ruined my life," he said.

"That was the point of decapitating you." I was seriously talking to a head. A disembodied head. "And, in my favor, you were attempting to enthrall me for nefarious purposes when I did it."

"Not the point!"

If my next visitor was Jerome Worth, my triad of crazy vampires would be complete.

"That means a lot to me," Marie said, putting her hand on mine.

"What does?"

"That you don't think I'm crazy."

"Oh, no. You are sane. Scary as fuck, maybe, but sane."

She beamed at me, then looked down at the ball bag—heh—at her feet. "That's not what you told me you needed to say to Eleanor. I wouldn't have brought you along if it was."

He sighed gustily, and I wondered where the air to sigh and speak even came from.

"Fine. I wanted to look at her again, because I believed myself invincible and wanted to see the face of the woman who vanquished me. I also want to issue a warning. Do not trust anyone whose true name you don't know."

"That will be simple. I don't trust easily."

Marie zipped him back up, although I could still hear him protesting from inside the ball bag—heh. She looked around. "It is good to see where I'm going, though. Having a focus makes finding things easier. I hope you survive. You're not bad for a Fae, and I'd love to make good on my promise to deliver the head of the pretender to the true queen." Marie winked and dissolved.

Before I had time to process, someone new took her place—a stranger. A gorgeous stranger. She was staring at me as I stared back.

"You are not what I imagined," she said in lightly accented English. "You are younger and not as experienced as I would've hoped."

"Who are you?"

Her blue eyes were startlingly beautiful against her olive skin, and when she smiled, it was like being bathed in sunlight. "Don't you recognize me?"

"I've never seen you before."

"What do you feel, though? You have a gift of seeing to the heart of a person. You know who I am."

I'd held my magic so close for so long, that I'd almost forgotten how to release it. Once I did—it must be safe in my dreams, right?—I looked at her again. Her age and power were overwhelming, and I shrank back to create distance between us. "You're her! Raj's sire. I knew you were a woman."

She laughed, and the sound made me want to curl up in her arms like a child. "And do you know my name?"

"It's old. *You're* old. But yes, you're Sam—"

"Sam will do for now. I may not be Fae, but I'd rather not have my true name bandied about. I worked very hard to conflate my reputation with myth, and I don't want that work undone now." She added, almost to herself, "I'd forgotten about your true-naming talent. That is…inconvenient."

I had no idea who she was and hoped she wasn't getting that from me. I really, really needed Google. "Why are you here?"

"Did I not tell my son I would see him at the end of the world? I made him for you—for this. I do not have the power of prophecy, but I am gifted in other areas of mind magic. After I became immortal, I spent as much time with the great oracles—seeking them out based on only whispers on the wind—as I did playing the game of war. One oracle who refused to admit her power was declared mad and bricked up in a cave outside of town near where I'd grown up. The townspeople, not wanting her to curse them, brought her food and water every day as well as other small offerings from time to time. She raved, and it was hard to tell what was the crazed ramblings of a madwoman and what was true prophecy, so I stayed for five years and listened to everything. One thing she said over and over—that a man with a ruby blade would fall in battle to an oncoming horde, but if he could be saved, so could the world. As you can see, she gave me little to work with, but when I rode with Mahmud—oh, how he fascinated me—I saw Rajyapala and his sword, and I knew."

"And now what? He's to kill me with the sword to open the final gate, and that will save the world?"

"If the gate doesn't open, it will explode, and the flood of magic will be more destructive than you could imagine. Everything with a spark of technology will be destroyed. Anything created after the industrial revolution would be ripped apart in the wake of the magic. And in your homeland, the magic would flood out so fast that any creatures reliant on it to exist—those Fae creatures that are more magic than anything else—those creatures would also die. The Fae who have human blood would remain, but anything wholly of that world would be destroyed. The only way to save two worlds is for there to be one sacrifice. Blood must be spilled, and it must be spilled by a Fae blade decorated with the blood of generations of vampires."

"What if Raj refuses as he's threatening to do?"

"In the end, he will acquiesce. He may love you—a complication for which I wasn't prepared—but he is practical. He has loved before and knows he can love again. He will mourn you, gnash his teeth, tear at his hair, wear sackcloth and ashes, but he will still sacrifice you on his blade because it is the right thing to do. My Rajyapala is fiery—he loves too easily, too passionately—but he would not sacrifice millions for his own happiness. He doesn't have it in him, he never has."

"Have you watched him all these years?" I was fascinated with this woman and hoped asking questions would keep her here longer.

"Sometimes I would lose track of him for a few decades, but overall, I was always in the shadows. It helped that he gravitated to war. It was shameful that he usually gravitated to the losing side. I wish I'd been able to spend more time with him in the early days, but he needed to get strong quickly and wouldn't do it unless he was forced."

"Still, a rulebook might not have gone amiss," I suggested.

She laughed again, and warmth flooded my body. "You may be

right, but a thousand years and more have passed, and everything has worked out as well as expected. And now, I must go. But fear not—I'll see you again soon."

She stood and turned to walk away. "I was sorry to hear about the wolf," Sam said over her shoulder as she strode out of the parking lot. "I'd grown fond of her."

She left, and the world felt colder, even though the sun was well over the horizon by now. I looked around. I was at the site of the final gate—I could feel the magic all around me, and I wanted to let go, let it flow through me and around me, but it wasn't quite time. I needed to wake up soon, or I'd be tempted to see what I could do in this dream state.

I stood up, brushed off my backside, and pinched myself.

"You can't go yet," a voice behind me said. I whirled around and came face-to-face with Seth. He looked down at himself and scrunched up his face. "Why do you insist on forcing me into this form?"

"It's yours, isn't it?"

"One of them. I prefer to be Arduinna for you. Seth is more representative of the parts of myself of which I'm less fond."

"Why are you here? The others who've stopped by don't seem to have any real purpose, other than to say hi."

"They felt your presence at the gate site and wanted to find out where to go."

"How many people will be at the opening? Should I order hors d'oeuvres and champagne? Get some waiters?"

"It's not going to be that kind of party, Eleanor."

"Answer the question. Please."

"There will be approximately fifty people here. Representatives of each major supernatural group. I will be here with some other Fae. Petrina, Marie, and Vlad will be among the vampire representatives. I'm not sure if Rasputin counts towards their numbers or not. Florence will be one of many mages present, and there will be shifters as well—some familiar faces. Those who've met you got first dibs on filling the spots at the final party. It's a prestigious event."

"Why?"

"Witnesses. Regardless of how they felt about the gates opening, everyone wants to be there when history is made. Restricting the numbers to the bare minimum was difficult, but because the gates were closed due to the influence of so many supernaturals, we wanted to make sure there were folks here when they were reopened. Just in case."

"Just in case what?" My voice rose shrilly at the end.

Seth shrugged. "No one knows, but we're all fairly certain everything will turn out fine."

"Everything except the part where I'm opening the gate on the pointy side of Raj's sword."

"There are always minor complications to every plan."

I clenched my jaw to keep the words I wanted to say from spilling out. "Is there anything else you needed, Seth?"

"No—I'll see you soon." He walked off into the trees and disappeared.

"Fucking Fae," I muttered.

"I couldn't agree more," a silky smooth voice said. "My name is Connor, and I am first among the Fae at your father's court."

I turned and was met with a beautiful man with pointy ears, snow white hair, and a dusky complexion. He was holding a bottle and two glasses. "Would you care for some wine?"

I sat down again. This dream was out of control. "Sure, why not?"

He poured golden liquid into the glasses and held one out for me. I took a cautious sip. I wasn't much of a white wine woman, but I was pleasantly surprised. "This tastes like springtime!"

"Elvish wine is a miraculous thing. Something you can learn more about when you take your place at your father's side."

"Why are you here, Connor?"

"I wanted a glimpse of you before the big event. It's nice to get a feel for the competition, don't you think?"

"Am I the competition? For what?"

He winked at me and disappeared, taking the wine with him.

I looked around and waited, but no one else showed up. The

clouds on the river were starting to dissipate, but then I realized that it was me who was fading out. The world turned hazy then faded to black.

SOMEONE WAS KNOCKING on my door. Not urgently, but not politely, either. It was a constant, repetitive noise, like someone had been doing it for a very long time and was bored with the whole exercise.

I stretched, dressed, and took the time to splash water on my face. Whoever it was was being rude, and they could wait a little bit longer.

Arduinna stood in the doorway, hand frozen in mid-knock.

"What do you want?" I was not in the mood for this. I liked it a lot better when she only showed up begrudgingly when I called. All of the spontaneous visits were getting under my skin. I didn't trust her—especially not now that I knew she was a double—or was that triple?—agent.

Her smile was as stiff and insincere as was possible to have while still calling it a smile. "I want to not be here," she said under her breath. Then, louder, she added, "I have another message from Governor Pulsipher."

"Why are you his messenger all of a sudden? Don't you 'work for' President Murphy?" I made sure my air quotes were as sarcastic as possible.

"The President decided that it would be best if I were temporarily reassigned to the region in which all the excitement was due to happen, and as such, attached me to the governor as the federal liaison, to make it look more natural and less like I was here to keep an eye on you."

"So Pulsipher is supposed to think you're here to spy on him?"

"That's the idea."

"Do you think he believes that?"

"Possibly. He's a bit paranoid and thinks everyone is spying on him."

"Gosh, if only there was a way I could extend my visit to spend more time with him," I said. "You'd better deliver the message so you can get back to him and I can get out of here. Three visits with you in twenty-four hours is enough."

"This is only my second visit to your room," she said but didn't look surprised. I'd been hoping to trip her up to find out how real my dreams were, but apparently, she was maintaining the unflappable façade she usually sported.

"Come off it. I know it was real. Who is Connor, and why is he my rival?"

"I'm sure I've no idea what you're talking about. I know a few Connors, but none that are in Utah."

I wasn't going to get anything from her, was I? Damnit.

"Fine. Whatever. Give me the message from Pulsipher."

"He would like you to reconsider, particularly his second request."

"As I told him before, I am not a mercenary. If this group of supernaturals is truly terrorizing innocent humans and not defending themselves from overzealous mobs of ignorant bigots, which honestly seems a lot more likely, then they are breaking the law and should be handled through the legal system."

"He thought you'd say that and requested that I inform you that if you do not see fit to defend the innocent against powerful supernaturals, he will have no choice but to institute a travel ban on you and your companions, and you will not be allowed to leave Moab."

I laughed until tears streamed down my face. "How on earth does he think he's going to keep me here?"

Arduinna cracked a smile. "He knows you've been walking and that before that you were driving. He doesn't know nearly as much as he thinks he does."

"Tell him I'll take it into consideration. You can tell him I said I was worried, if it helps."

"Are you?"

"I worry about a lot of things."

She grinned again. "Are you leaving tonight?"

"I've been banned from leaving, haven't I?"

"Of course. See you in Oregon. Good luck."

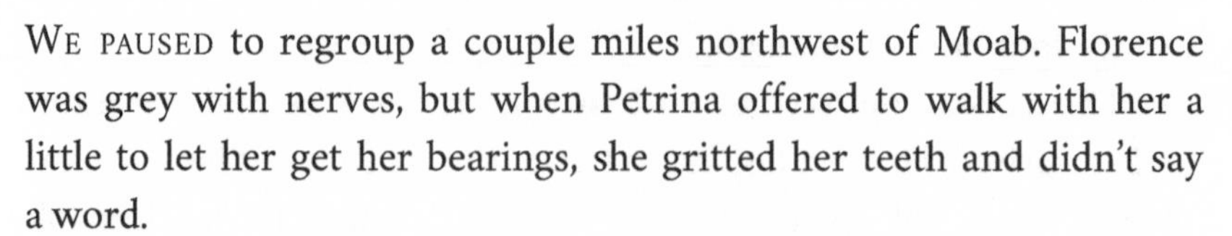

We paused to regroup a couple miles northwest of Moab. Florence was grey with nerves, but when Petrina offered to walk with her a little to let her get her bearings, she gritted her teeth and didn't say a word.

The others had been as amused as I'd been when they heard about our travel ban. Raj and Petrina flew us out and over the National Guardspeople stationed on the western edge of town, presumably to keep us from walking away. They didn't even look up when we flew over them.

"How far do you want to go tonight?" Raj asked Petrina.

"Not far. I've not done this type of travel with another person much, and I'd like time to get used to it. I can't skip through space the way you can, either."

"I looked at a map before we left. There's a town called Green River about fifty miles away. That might be a good first evening. It should only take a couple hours to get there."

Petrina and Raj looked at the map while Florence sat on the ground and breathed slowly and deliberately. I sat next to her. "It'll be okay."

"I do not like heights and have always hated flying. Even when I was on a plane almost every day of the week, I never learned to do more than barely tolerate it."

"Petrina would never drop you, and, as a bonus, she won't have engine failure."

"Logically, I know that, but my body's reactions are not in on the logic at the moment."

I put an arm around her and leaned into her. "It's almost over, isn't it?"

"This part, anyway. We still have a lot to do."

"If I die, I want you to know I'm sorry that I didn't get a chance to help you find Annie. And I also want you to know that you are the most amazing person I've ever met. I couldn't have done any of this without you. I've never really had friends, only close acquaintances.

You are the first and best real friend I've ever had. Thank you for being in my life."

I felt the gulf of obligation between us span wider as I thanked her. I owed her so much.

Florence reached down, found my hand, and squeezed it. "You have been a gift, Eleanor. I've not always been certain that I didn't want a gift receipt—"

"Hey!"

She squeezed my hand again, and affection warmed her voice as she continued, "but I wouldn't be anywhere else at the end of the world. You've brought so much into my life, and I'm proud to call you my friend."

We sat like that, hand in hand, until Raj and Petrina finished up their planning. "Ready?" Raj asked.

"As I'll ever be," Florence muttered as she stood and walked over to Petrina, pack in hand.

I stepped into the circle of Raj's arms, smiled up and him, and said, "Let's go places, baby."

The flight seemed slow, mostly because Raj usually took shortcuts when we were together, but he was holding back to Petrina's pace as she got used to carrying someone over a long distance.

"*It'll get faster as she grows more confident,*" Raj said. "*We'll be in Portland in a week, which leaves us three weeks to find the gate.*"

That's when I remembered that I hadn't shared my dream with the group. Arduinna's arrival had driven it clean out of my head.

"*I know where the gate is—and there's something else I should've told you before. I saw your mysterious S—*"

Raj stopped in midair and hovered, staring at me. "What?" he said. "How could you forget?"

"Arduinna showed up to threaten me on Pulsipher's behalf. It was so funny that I forgot about my dream. I was right, though. S— *is* a woman."

Raj started moving again and switched back to mental communication. "*Petrina was wondering where you were. Can you tell me everything now, or would you rather wait until we're all together?*"

"I wouldn't be so cruel as to keep you waiting any longer. The gate will open at Crown Point, overlooking the Columbia River. I dreamed I was there watching the sunrise, and I got all sorts of supernatural visitors. Arduinna was one, and she refused to confirm or deny the truth of what I saw."

"But you saw my sire?"

"Along with your grandson, Vlad the Insane and Marie. And Rasputin. And some elf named Connor who said he was from Eochaid's court and implied that we were rivals. But yes, I saw your sire."

"You can wait to share the rest of the information you received from your other visitors with the whole group, but I would be grateful if you could share what you learned of my sire with me now."

"She's Sammu-ramat, an ancient Assyrian queen. I don't know much about her, but she wants to be known as Sam. Said she'd worked hard to conflate her history with that of a legend, so that the truth would be lost to time, and didn't want me bandying about her name and messing things up.

She confirmed what we already knew—you must use the Ruby Blade to sacrifice me to open the final gate. It's why she made you. An—oracle foretold it. And she's been watching you for ages and following along on our adventure, too. She said she'd see us soon. I don't know if that means she'll show before gate day or not."

Raj was silent for a long time, and I was beginning to worry. *"I am okay; it's just a lot to digest. I know the history of Sammu-ramat, or at least what's believed now. I wonder if she really tricked her husband into naming her 'Queen for a Day' and then had him arrested and executed for treason so she could rule as regent for her son."*

"I sincerely hope so. That sounds awesome."

"We're nearly to Green River. I'm sure the others will be anxious to hear the rest of the story. For now, I have much to think about."

ISAAC

INTERLUDE

Isaac paced in his small cage. Diana, who guarded him regularly, and always without a partner, watched from the corner.

"She pulled from me," Isaac said. "I felt her pull on my Alpha power to force someone to shift."

"It was good you could give her what she needed," Diana said.

Everything was so ambiguous with her.

"My mind is cracked in so many places. If something hits it wrong, it could shatter into a million pieces."

"Still, you seem lucid today."

"The moons are new. It's easier when I don't hear her song."

"If I could, I would let you shift. But I am not in charge here."

"I know you're not, but you are more powerful than Michelle. Why do you do her bidding?"

"She is a guest of my queen, and I serve her, not the mad vampire. Because I've been commanded to be the head of security for the vampire, I do what she asks as long as it doesn't compromise her safety."

"And if it did?"

Diana shrugged. "Then I would be forced to ignore her orders to keep her safe."

Isaac tried to work out how keeping him chained with silver so he couldn't shift was endangering Michelle, but either it wasn't, or his broken mind couldn't figure out the logical argument.

"She will kill me, won't she?"

"It's hard to say. Already, she grows bored with you, but I believe she wants to see how far she can push you before you break completely."

"I do not want her to win."

"Then don't let her."

"How can I stop it? I'm already mad. Every full moon I feel myself break a little bit more. My dreams are insane, my connection to Eleanor fades in and out, and even the vampire Raj has stopped visiting me."

"But your tie to Eleanor was still strong enough for her to draw on your Alpha power," Diana pointed out.

"But it's fading as her bond to Raj grows stronger."

"How does that make you feel?"

Isaac thought about it before answering. "Sad. Not surprised, though. We had an instant attraction, but I was never her forever person. I'm not strong enough."

Diana asked, "Why would you say that? Aren't you an Alpha?"

"Yes, but she was stronger than me."

"And why would that matter? Surely, she didn't think you less because of that?"

"I don't think so, and I like strong women. I don't mind being the less powerful one. But Eleanor needs someone who can match her in strength. She didn't look down on me, but in time, I wouldn't have been enough. She may have loved me briefly, but only a prophecy convinced her to mate with me, and I was already starting to lose her to Raj before I decided to come here."

"Then she is a fool if she could not see what was in front of her face."

Isaac smiled. "And I was a fool to think she'd grow to love me more if we were tied irrevocably."

"Can this bond be broken?" Diana asked. "Or given to someone else?"

"If both parties agree to part ways under the full moon in front of at least one person who witnessed their mating, the bond is broken, and then each is free to tie their mating bond to someone else, but it can't be transferred."

"And when she finds you, as she's said she would? Will you offer to dissolve the bond?"

"I will insist. I know she worries. She doesn't want to betray or hurt me, but it'd be a worse betrayal for her to live a lie. It would hurt us both. But, I fear that is not something we'll have to worry about. It's far more likely that I'll be dead—either from my fracturing mind or at the hand of Michelle—long before Eleanor ever shows up to save me, if she even can."

"Do you want her to?"

Isaac looked down and refused to meet Diana's gaze. "I don't know."

CHAPTER EIGHTEEN

An insistent pounding woke me for the second evening in a row. If it was Arduinna knocking on my hotel room door, I was going to seriously contemplate stabbing her a little.

"It's another angry mob," Petrina said.

"Seriously? This is getting ridiculous."

"This one seems to be backed by the power of the National Guard," Florence added.

I rubbed my eyes and sat up. "Governor Jackass found us, didn't he?" We'd stayed up well past dawn talking about my dream, the final gate, and taking a detour to climb inside the World's Largest Watermelon slice and make Monty Python jokes about running away. I'd hoped to sleep in a bit. "Do you think Arduinna gave us up?"

"Either that or he has supernatural spies," Raj said. "We hadn't decided where we were headed until we left Moab. I was very careful about that—I didn't want to be overheard."

"No one should've been able to get close enough to hear us last night without one of us noticing," I said.

"Bugs?" Florence asked.

"That shouldn't work. My magic screws with technology at an epic level."

"Unless he's using a supernatural equivalent," Florence pointed out.

"Damnit. How would we know?"

"Lie," Raj said.

"But if they're bugging us, won't they know that's our strategy now?" I pointed out.

"It's not possible," Petrina said. "If there were such a thing, one of us would know. They must have found us some other way."

"Petrina says this is absolutely a possibility," Raj informed me, and hopefully Florence, too.

"You're right," Florence said. "I just don't understand how they could've found us so quickly and gotten the National Guard here, to boot."

"The how might not matter as much right now as what we're going to do about it," I pointed out. "Can we sneak out the back the way we did in Moab?"

Petrina shook her head. "We're surrounded, and it looks like that have snipers on the roofs of nearby buildings in case we go out by air. Raj and I are fast, but I don't want to bet your lives on whether we're fast enough."

"Do you think anyone wants to talk, or are they here to fight?" I asked. "If they're still willing to talk, we might have a chance of getting out of this unscathed. If it's a 'shoot first, ask questions later' situation, it might be best to take our chances with a roof exit."

"How do we determine their mindset?" Raj asked.

"I'm the most immortal. Nothing but decapitation will kill me," I said.

"Do you want to take your chances with whatever weaponry the military brought in? A few hundred rounds to the chest would be difficult for you to heal," Raj said. "Short of decapitation, nothing can kill me, either—not even a silver stake through the heart is guaranteed to kill me anymore—but I'm not excited to see what a firing squad with automatic weapons feels like."

"Fair point," I conceded. "Suggestions, then?"

"We could wave a white towel out the window and see what happens," Florence said.

"Isn't that signaling surrender?" I asked. "I am not surrendering to Governor Jackass."

"You're the one who told him to handle problematic supernaturals with his own forces instead of conscripting unwilling mercenaries," Florence pointed out. "And we're not surrendering. We're requesting a temporary truce for negotiations."

"There's nothing to negotiate. I am not his tool. I am not his ally."

"That may be true if you were still a human citizen of the United States, but it's very probable that he doesn't see you as anything more than a means to an end—whether that end is a mercenary or a stepping stone to power. You aren't human in his eyes; therefore, you don't have the same rights as a human. He believes that you are nothing more than a tool, and since you're in his territory, you're a tool he can use however and whenever he wants."

"If that's what he truly believes, then he can go fuck himself," I muttered. "Regardless, I'm not playing his game, so what do we negotiate?"

"Let's find out what they want and what they're willing to do to get it," Florence said. "No one said you had to agree to their terms. We need to find out how many people are out there, how many are willing to go to battle against us, and what kind of weapons we'll be facing. Once we know that, we can formulate a better idea of what to do."

"It's a good thing supernatural bugs are impossible," I said, remembering—a bit too late—that we might be being spied on in real time.

"Indeed," Florence said. She and Raj exchanged a look.

"You'd better not be keeping anything from me," I said to Raj.

"I'll tell you in a minute. Florence has a theory."

"I hate being in the dark," I groused.

"I know, but it'll be worth it. Patience."

I harrumphed loudly to signal my displeasure, then grabbed a towel from the bathroom and opened the door just wide enough for my arm to fit through so I could wave it around. I wished I'd liberated the giant watermelon slice from its tow wagon. Then we could sneak through their lines with no one any wiser.

"You can come out," a voice called. "We'll hold our fire."

"I'm going out there," I said. "I'm the one the governor wants, and I'm the least likely to die. Raj, if you'd like to accompany me, feel free. Petrina and Florence—if they even look like they're going to attack, kill them all."

"Really?" Florence asked. "They're humans."

I sighed. "I don't know. We've killed others who've attacked us. Vampires, mages, necromancers, shifters…why would their humanness make them more worthy of saving?"

"Are you coming?" the voice called from outside. I took Raj's hand and walked through the door.

Spotlights picked us up immediately and ruined any chance I had of getting an accurate count. There was no doubt in my mind that it was on purpose. Fuckers. I missed the other angry mobs that only had tiki torches for light. Mob two point oh was too well-organized for me.

I shielded my eyes with my free hand and tried to find the voice-in-charge. A uniformed man walked forward into my field of vision. "I am Major General Lewis Baker, Adjutant General for the Western States and Commander of the National Guard."

"Hey. I'm Eleanor. This is Raj. What do you want?"

"I have been instructed to use the full power of the forces under my command to apprehend you and bring you to Salt Lake City."

"What are the charges?" Raj asked.

"Excuse me?" General Baker asked.

"If you're apprehending us, there must be a reason. What is that reason?"

"You are dangerous supernaturals who are to be taken into custody."

I rolled my eyes. "What have we done that was dangerous?"

"Eleanor—you have done so many things that could be construed as a threat," Raj reminded me. *"That might not be the best line to follow."*

"You travel with two vampires and a witch—"

"They prefer the term 'mages,'" I informed him.

"—and there have been fatalities reported in every city you've been known to visit in the last year. You are a threat to regional and national security."

"I bet there've been fatalities in every city you've ever visited, too. What evidence do you have to tie any of this to me?"

Raj covered his eyes with his free hand. I might not be winning this negotiation, but the General wasn't pulling out anything concrete, either. I moved on. "What if I don't want to come to Salt Lake City with you?"

"I am authorized to use force."

"What kind of force? If we're a bunch of dangerous supernaturals, how are you going to force us to do something we don't want if you're also trying to keep us alive?"

"You're the only one I need to keep alive," he said. And there it was, the glint of madness I'd been looking for. He was a zealot as much as any of the less well-armed townsfolk.

"Do you know how to kill us?" Raj asked. "Because I can promise you, it won't be easy."

A tight smile spread across the general's face but didn't reach his eyes. "I know silver might not work on you, but I'm willing to try a firing squad of automatic weapons."

Huh. They did have us bugged.

The look of dismay on the General's face was immediate. He hadn't meant to say that. I wondered what Florence was up to.

"*Keep him talking,*" Raj said.

I cast about me for subjects but came up blank. "What's an Adjutant General, anyway?"

"It means I was appointed by the governor to be the chief military officer for the state—now the region. I command the Air and Army National Guards. Why am I still talking?"

"How is the Air National Guard these days?"

"Mostly grounded. Dammit!" He started clawing at something near his head. "Make it stop!"

Raj took a step backwards and pulled me with him. "Time for our strategic retreat."

He closed the motel room door behind us, and I felt Florence's wards—reinforced—go up.

"What the hell's happening?" I asked.

Florence held a finger to her lips then mouthed exaggeratedly, "Not done yet. Wait."

When the noises outside got weird—like an angry squirrel cage match—I glanced out through a crack in the blinds. General Baker, as well as a few other people, were in the spotlights. Feedback, like when the microphone gets too close to the speaker, erupted through our room, and I clapped my hands over my ears. The sound screeched, then dulled to a whine, then popped, and all that was left was an atonal ringing in my ears.

"We can talk now," Florence said.

"What was that?"

She grinned, and the mischievous glee on her face almost made me forget we were still surrounded by an angry mob—one probably made angrier by whatever had happened. "I found the bugs. I don't know who crafted them and how they got them in, but there were a half dozen in each of our packs. After I found the first one, it was easy to find the rest. They were all on the same magical frequency. Petrina and I did a little reverse engineering, sent a strong truth spell through the frequency to make sure we were on the right track, and then canceled out their frequency with our own until they imploded."

"So that bit with the pawing around their heads and faces?"

"That feedback we got right at the end? They got that right into their brains." She chuckled.

"Your laugh is a diabolical laugh."

She high-fived Petrina, looked at me, and said, "That's why you like me."

"We should probably figure out how we're going to get out of here," Raj said. "Now we know that they have no compunction about killing any of the rest of us, which changes the way the game is played. This is not a situation we can get through making it up as we go. We need a strategy. Fortunately, you are graced with the presence of one of the best military minds of all time."

I tried to keep my skepticism off my face but was unsuccessful. "I was talking about Trina," he said. "Military strategy skipped a generation, I guess. I captured a river once, but I'm no great general."

"I have an idea," Petrina said.

IT WAS CLOSE TO MIDNIGHT—NEARLY a whole night's travel was wasted because of these idiots—when the four of us crept to the edge of the motel roof under the solid shield I'd woven from air and darkness. It was the first time I'd consciously exercised this much magic since before New Orleans, and I was giddy with it. I wanted to light a few things on fire in celebration, but we were being subtle, so I restrained myself.

I'd wanted to take this one step further, turn into a dragon, and scare the shit out of everyone while Raj and Petrina whisked Florence away, but since my dragon self was still a secret—more or less—and wasn't invulnerable to flying projectiles, I caved to Petrina's superior strategery.

Florence tensed beside me, and the air temperature plummeted. Over the next few minutes, there were muttered curses that grew louder and more numerous as time went on accompanied by the clatter of dropped weapons. Florence was super-cooling all the metal in a fifty-foot radius around us, and from the sound of it, it was making it difficult to hold onto the guns. She couldn't get the steel cold enough to shatter, but she could get it cold enough to burn the hands of those holding the guns.

Raj encircled me in his arms and Petrina did the same to Florence. We started to launch off the roof, but a silver net was tossed at us. It didn't hurt anyone—vampires aren't sensitive to silver the way shifters are even if a silver stake through the heart can kill them—but it did make it difficult to fly away. Dammit. We were going to have to fight our way free.

I decided that it no longer made any sense to pretend I was still bound. I wasn't going to turn into a dragon and fry them all, but I didn't need to hold myself back anymore. I pulled on my connection to air, encased us in a visible air shield, and lifted the net up and off us. Then I jumped to the ground from the five-story roof, hoping that I could again control the air enough to soften my landing.

I heard Raj curse behind me, and he joined me on the ground a moment later. Petrina and Florence followed. I drew my sword, walked up to the first person I saw, and used the pommel to knock him out.

"Can one of you take care of the lights?" I asked. "They're too bright to see what I'm doing."

A couple minutes later, the lights pointed up at the sky. The area was lit, but no one was directly in the spotlight with impaired vision. After a deep breath, I strode forward and tried to amplify my voice. "We have done nothing wrong. We just want to leave so I can get on with my life. The only reason the National Guard is trying to detain us is because I wouldn't cut a deal with the Governor to take out hostile supernaturals, so he's attempting to make a point. We know now that General has been instructed to take me alive but has no such instructions for my companions. Are you okay with this? Would you shoot us because we won't be mindless tools for the new government?"

"You're freaks, ain't ya?" Someone shouted out. "Been killing us in our sleep for years! Why wouldn't we take the chance to kill you back a little?"

"Angry mobs are rarely made up of great thinkers," Raj said. "Are you really expecting to reason with them?"

"What else am I going to do? They're human."

"I might be a little old school—and a bit skittish about mobs, given my history—but I'm okay with fighting our way through the angry mob to freedom," Petrina said. "We can't talk our way out of this one."

"Now that we got rid of the net, couldn't we take off?" I asked. "We don't have to stick around here and wait for them to be able to pick up their guns again."

"What are you guys talking about?" someone shouted. We ignored her.

"I vote for taking them all out and salting the earth," Raj said.

I rolled my eyes. "We can't take out the entire Western States National Guard." Something wasn't sitting right, so I revised my statement. "We *shouldn't* take out the National Guard. It would be wrong. Petrina, what do you think?"

"I think we should take out the general and a few officers to teach the rest a lesson and then leave. It's too bad we don't have concussion grenades."

My companions were even more unreasonable than the angry mob. "Florence? What kind of blood-thirsty suggestions do you have?"

She shrugged, mouth in a grim line, and said, "I'd like to side with Petrina on this, but I think your idea will probably have the least fallout. Regardless of what we do, we need to do it soon. We've been waiting too long as it is, and there's not a lot of night left. If we flee without fighting, we'll need to get as far away as possible as we can so they can't catch up again. I think I got all the bugs, but I'm not positive, so we shouldn't discuss locations or destinations at all."

"We are overruled, Trina," Raj said. "Today we flee the field of battle."

"It's not much of a battle, Father. Few of the guardsman are of any worth, and the mob is nothing more than a brainless, spineless amoeba, squelching its way across the land."

"Do amoeba squelch?"

"Not the point, Eleanor. Let's g—"

Petrina's voice stopped before I heard the whir of something flying through the air, and she stumbled forward. A crossbow bolt protruded from her right shoulder, and her eyes were blazing red.

"Trina, no!"

She whirled around, but not before I saw her fangs lengthen. "Which of you did this to me?" she asked, and the timbre of her voice raised goosebumps on my arms. "Which of you cowards shot me in the back?" To no one's surprise, there was zero response. "My friends argued for your lives. Said that because you were human, you deserved more chances than I'd give another supernatural who tried to harm me. I don't know what she sees in you. You are cowardly, cruel, and afraid of that which you do not understand. You are sheep, easily led by a blowhard in a suit who wants to consolidate power by eliminating those he sees as threats. Yet, I was going to walk away because my friends believed you to be more than that.

"Tell me now, people of Utah, why should I stay my hand?"

The silence was deafening. I couldn't believe that there could be such total quiet with that many people, most of whom were still armed in some manner or another.

"We are leaving," she announced. "If any of you try to stop us, it will be the last thing you do." She turned her back on them, walked back to Florence, and then took off with her.

I backed into the circle of Raj's arms, and we followed them into the night sky.

A PALE BEAM of sunlight illuminated the end of the tunnel where I slept. I rubbed my eyes, shivered against the cold, and made my way out into the late afternoon sun. Florence had started a small fire and had coffee percolating. "You're the best."

"I thought you'd sleep longer."

"Me, too. The last three evenings, I've been woken up prematurely, mostly by idiots. Glad to see we're mob free!"

"Going the complete opposite direction and holing up in the mine-shaft of a ghost town seems to have fooled them—at least temporarily."

I was mostly tickled by the name of the town. We'd spent the day in Dragon, Utah. "What I wouldn't give for a chance to fly," I said. "My wings are cramped from disuse."

"That not how shape-shifting works."

"Maybe it does for Fae shape-shifters."

She shook her head and handed me a bowl of oatmeal. I grimaced but accepted it. Warm food and calories were more important than my taste buds. Stupid car.

As soon as the sun started going down, Raj and Petrina emerged from the cave. "We've enough light to read the map and take notes by," Raj said. Then he switched to mental communication. *"Petrina is still not feeling one hundred percent, but we should be able to go about a hundred and twenty miles tonight, and then two hundred or so every night thereafter. I'd intended to load up on supplies before leaving Green River, but I guess that plan's out now."*

Raj spread the map over the boulder we were using as a table and grabbed a notebook. After measuring various distances with a piece of string he produced from his pocket and making notations in the notebook, he turned the page, wrote quickly in his elegant script, and then shared with the class.

"May 15—tonight—Rock Springs, Wyoming.

"May 16—Jackson, Wyoming

"May 17—Sun Valley, Idaho

"From there, we regroup and replan, if nothing has gone amiss."

He looked around at us waiting for agreement.

"I'm not looking at the map," I said, "but that route seems a bit... non-direct."

"It is," he wrote. "We'll avoid population centers, not take any direct routes, and stay in the mountains as much as possible to discourage pursuit."

It didn't sound fun, but it did sound workable. We all shrugged our agreement. He and Petrina took a bit of extra time with the map while Florence and I packed up under the light of the rising full moon. Pain shot through me. It was the first full moon since I'd started this trip, excepting the ones I'd spent imprisoned in Marie's dungeon, that I hadn't been acutely aware of the moon phase.

CHAPTER NINETEEN

The last few nights hadn't been pleasant. Raj and Petrina were pushing hard to make up for the time we'd lost walking, being besieged, and detouring to throw our pursuers off-track. We were ensconced in a private home in Sun Valley—a friend of Raj's kept a place there, but seldom was in residence—where we planned to stay for a couple days to rest and recuperate. The blood-suckers in the group were running low on nutrients, and the food-eaters in the group—well me, at least—really wanted some variety in their diets. A variety of cheeses and meats with a carbohydrate delivery system sounded ideal.

The house had a giant fireplace in the main room and smaller fireplaces in each of the bedrooms. Even though it was nearing the end of May, I still hauled wood into the house and lit them all. It was chilly in the mountains. It was just after sunset on our second night in the house, when I heard a noise behind me. Everyone else had gone into town to get food of one kind or another, but I decided to stay warm and let them bring me things to eat.

"Raj?" I called. Maybe he'd come back early. We hadn't had a lot of alone time recently—at least not alone time on the ground when we both had a decent amount of energy.

"Apologies, child. It is not your lover. Rather, your mother-in-law has stopped by to visit."

Sam stepped into the room, and she was even more awe-inspiringly gorgeous, not to mention intimidating, in real life than in my dream state.

"That was also real life, of course," she said.

"Thank you! I was beginning to doubt myself after Arduinna refused to confirm or deny anything. How are you? Can I offer you a glass of wine?"

"I'd rather have whiskey if you've got any."

"I saw a bottle of 1965 Mortlach Scotch in the liquor cabinet. It doesn't look like it's been opened."

"Are you offering me a fifty-year-old Scotch from the home of your host?"

"Raj says we can help ourselves to whatever we want. I suspect that if his friend—who doesn't have a name as far as I can tell—raises a fuss, he can replace it with a two-hundred-year-old bottle of wine or something. The vampires I've met are collectors of old things."

She laughed, which wasn't comforting in the least, and said, "You've talked me into it. I'd love some Scotch."

After we had our drinks—I'd gone with what I hoped was a much more modestly priced Cabernet—we settled in front of the fireplace. I had no idea what to say to her, why she was here now, and what any of this meant. So, I gulped my wine, poured myself another glass, and tried to make small talk.

"Did you hear about the bands of armed militia attacking supernaturals?" I was so good at small talk.

"I have. I was impressed with the way you handled the Governor in Moab, but if you'd asked me for advice in the town with the watermelon on wheels, I would've told you to take out a few of the higher-ranked officers and maybe a townsperson with a big mouth and a small brain before taking off."

"That's what Petrina wanted to do, too. I didn't want to kill any humans."

"You've killed hundreds already, what's a few more?"

That information constantly resided at the back of my mind, jumping to the forefront at the least opportune moments. "I didn't know what would happen when I started, but I've worked hard since to mitigate the effects of the magic waves on humans. I know people have died as the grids have gone out all over the country. But just because I've been responsible for so many deaths doesn't mean that the possibility of causing more means nothing to me."

"Their lifespans are so short anyway, what's the difference if they live a score of years less?"

"Probably a lot to them. I'm only thirty-five, so I haven't yet had the opportunity to take the long view. Immortality doesn't seem real to me yet—ask me in a hundred years, and I might have a different answer. But I was raised human, and until eleven months ago, didn't know there was anything else out there. I might be a little more Fae every day but ending a life early just because their lives are short anyway doesn't feel right to me, and I hope it never does."

"You'll do, child."

"I don't suppose you want to tell me more about the sword and the sacrifice and what you know about it?"

"Didn't I tell you all you needed when we met at Crown Point?"

"I sincerely doubt that anyone has ever told me everything I needed to know. Supernaturals seem to take a perverse pleasure in withholding information for the sake of withholding."

"All will be made clear in time, but I would like Rajyapala to be present so that I only have to say everything once. Did you tell him we'd met?"

"Of course."

"And is he excited to see me?"

There's no real way to describe the expression I made at that question. My face scrunched up in confusion and disbelief, my head cocked to one side, and I attempted to draw my head back into my hoodie, like a retreating turtle. "I'm not sure excited is the word. It's not like you're a dear parent who's merely been on holiday and is returning to give him a hug and souvenirs. You're the sire he never met. The one who changed him without his consent. And the person who didn't stick around to guide him through his bloodlust or help him adjust to his new life. Or unlife. Whatever you want to call it. No. Excited is not the word I'd choose."

"Hmmm...is he at least interested?"

"Interested is a good word to describe how he feels. Curious. Maybe a tad resentful. I'm not sure. We are connected in a way I don't quite understand, but I don't get his emotions the same way I would get them through my link with Isaac."

"Of course not. Rajyapala is a vampire, not a shifter. It makes sense that your bond wouldn't be the same. He is also a very strong psychic and is probably better able to control what emotions flow through your link. He may not even be doing it consciously."

"Why are you here? Why now?"

"I wanted a chance to converse with my only son before the big day. Get to know him a bit. See how he turned out."

"You've been following him around for centuries and stalking us for at least the last few months. Don't bullshit me, Sam."

She cracked a grin. "I have instructions for him—instructions I couldn't give him until the time was right. Some of them I didn't even know until more recently, and some I've known since the beginning. There are things he needs to know that you don't, so don't try to weasel my secrets out."

"Why would I do that? Would you like some more Scotch?" I poured her another glass—a bit more generously this time.

"You can't get me drunk. It's nearly impossible to impair supernaturals unless they want to be intoxicated."

"I know, it's been a huge disappointment to me. No more drinking to forget."

"It's healthier this way. You'll live longer."

We both cracked up at that. Immortality jokes are funny, yo.

"If you don't mind, I'll give myself a tour and find a place to sleep—presumably there are plenty of bedrooms?" Sam asked.

"Help yourself," I said, waving in her general direction. "I'm going to have another glass of wine and see if I can remember how to get buzzed."

WHEN I WOKE, who knows how much later, I heard voices. Raj and Sam, and from the sound of it, they were arguing.

"...no way I can do that," Raj said. His voice was barely raised, but the anger was clear. "She is my love, my everything."

"You know as well as I do that love is fleeting, but the destruction of two worlds is forever."

"It's not fleeting when the people involved are all but immortal."

I'd fallen asleep on the couch in front the fireplace, mostly empty wine glass on the table next to me. I filled it up, stood, and tiptoed stealthily towards the sound of voices.

"You ask too much."

"I ask what is needed. This is what you were created to do. I sought you out and made you for this purpose. Everything rides on it. It has been foretold, more times than I can count. You have the sword, forged by Fae with rubies created from blood of your Fae and mortal forebears as well as you and yours. Which ruby is your blood?"

There was a silence interrupted only by the sound of Raj drawing his sword. Presumably, he was showing the ruby made from his Fae/human/vampire blood. I wasn't picking up anything from him about the surprise of having Fae blood. *I* was surprised.

"Focus on that ruby at the moment of the sacrifice. Never take your eyes off it. Remember that it was once part of you, and you will always be connected."

"What does that even mean?" Frustration rolled from him, and I tensed as a wave of anxiety crashed through our connection.

"I don't know." If anything, she sounded even more frustrated than he did. "I'm not a prognosticator, and I've never been able to keep one around to use as needed. Most oracles don't do well when they're on a leash, no matter how luxurious that leash is."

"You could say that about most people, and it'd still be true."

"That's a fair assessment, although I've had some companions who didn't mind being leashed to me." Sam chuckled low in her throat, and that voice did something to me. I'd never been turned on by a woman before, but this woman was powerful, and for some reason, that pushed my buttons.

"Back to the point, *Sam*." Raj spat her name like an insult.

"Why are you so angry with me? Eleanor said you wouldn't be excited to see me, but I didn't believe her."

"You may have stalked me for a millennium, but she knows me better than you ever could. You made me and abandoned me with a cryptic note written in a language I didn't even speak at the time."

"You figured it out, and here you are! You learned faster than you would've otherwise because you were on your own."

"Or I could've gone on an unrestrained killing spree the minute you let me out."

"Don't you see! My pushing you to early independence is what made you so powerful."

I knew eavesdropping was bad, but to be fair, if either of them had been paying attention, they'd have known I was awake and listening. Sam was full-on whack job with this, though. I fully expected her to bust out the last part of "A Boy Named Sue" to prove her point.

Raj started laughing. I guess someone was paying attention to me.

"You are always at the forefront of my attention, my sweet."

"Need a rescue?"

"Not yet, but thank you for the offer."

"Any time. I can stake her if you want. Just say the word."

"Your lover is awake, then?" Sam asked.

"And has been for some time. She's about as impressed with your arguments as I am. However, it is in the past. Bygones, as they say."

"No one says that anymore," I called from the other room.

"What is important now is moving forward. What other information do you have about me, Eleanor, the sword, and the end of the world that you haven't shared?"

"There is nothing else relevant."

"That wasn't my question," Raj said.

"Lying, if it's an option, is always better than prevaricating," I said, walking into the next room. I'd found my wine glass, a spare, and a new bottle, and filled it up. "Raj has spent too much time around the

Fae and is better at ferreting out a lie in truth than almost anyone I know."

"Rather than say I've spent too much time with the Fae, I'd rather you said I've not spent nearly as much time as I plan to," Raj said. He took the glass I offered him, inhaled the bouquet, then took a sip. "This is magnificent. Where did you find it?"

"Your mysterious friend has a lot of good stuff in the room with the bar. I found a hidden staircase that goes down into an honest-to-goddess basement wine cellar. I have decided this house is my new Earth headquarters. There are secret wine passages in it."

"She also found me a bottle of fifty-year-old Scotch," Sam offered. "It was incredible."

Raj groaned and put his head in his hands. "I am going to owe Katya so much money, aren't I? And that's not even taking into account what her…" he trailed off, and I eyed him suspiciously. Before I could ask where he'd been going with that, Sam interrupted my train of thought.

"I will pay her back," Sam said. "It's likely that Eleanor has no idea the value of this bottle of Scotch she opened for me."

"You said to make myself at home," I pointed out. "You didn't say the liquor supply was off-limits."

"I also knew you'd never go through her Scotch collection, so I didn't even think to ask you to be mindful of that."

I shrugged. "I'll find Katya—nice to finally have a name—another one."

"That might be easier said than done, but at this moment in time, it is irrelevant," Raj said. "What is relevant is what the point of Sam being here now is." He turned to face her. "If you're not going to give me anything more than 'think about the ruby' and what you told Eleanor during her visit to the last gate site, you could've left another note."

I settled back into a loveseat a few feet away from where the vampires were standing. I wasn't about to leave—this was much too interesting—but I didn't want to get in the way, either.

Sam sighed. "I have bits and pieces of prophecy, some of which may be real. For centuries, I searched out every rumor, every whisper, of oracles, whether they served the king of the day, were tied to a temple, or were considered the village madman who no one dared kill, just in case. I have volumes of the accounts I took, both from the scribes I hired to record their words and the thoughts swirling in their minds. I've worked on compiling and cross-referencing and attempting to make sense of what's to come, always afraid the end would approach faster than my understanding of what I'd been given.

"I was right to fear that outcome. All I have are guesses…conjecture. Nothing concrete, nothing that can help you. You know the basics of what needs to be done. The sword must be wielded. The catalyst must stand at the gate site. Blood must be spilled. And you, my only child, you must think of the ruby."

"That's it? Really?" Skepticism colored my voice. "Why don't you share some of your educated guesses and conjectures. As an exercise for the class."

She ignored me, fetched the bottle of Scotch, and filled the glass to the rim. The bottle was nearly empty. I knew she couldn't get intoxicated, but I was still impressed.

Sam glanced at her bare wrist where a watch would be, and said, "Oh, my, look at the time. The sun will be rising soon, and I grow weary." She placed her hand in front of her mouth and executed a not-very-convincing delicate yawn. "I will see you children in the evening."

"Aren't you Sammu-rammat and not Scheherazade?" I asked, more snarkily than I'd intended.

She smiled, "And why can I not be both?" She disappeared from the room before I could come up with a suitable comeback.

"Are you okay?" I asked.

He sighed. "I find her reappearance affects me more than I thought it would. I feel like an abandoned child rather than a thousand-year-old blood-sucking creature of the night."

"Awww, poor baby," I teased. "If it's any consolation, you're still my favorite ancient blood-sucking fiend."

He smiled at me, took my wine, and said, "I am well rested, find myself with plenty of energy, and was hoping you'd help me spend some of it. We have a real bed in a real house for a couple nights, and I've missed you."

I trailed my fingers across his jawline. "I could probably find a few ways to help you out." He kissed me and led me from the room.

I WOKE LATE the next evening and stretched, reveling in the lack of urgency. I smelled coffee and, after dressing, followed my nose to the well-appointed kitchen. Breakfast, in the form of pancakes, bacon, eggs, and coffee was waiting for me, all cooked on the surprisingly useful wood stove that sat alongside the more modern gas stove.

"I don't care about the final gate," I announced to whoever might be lurking. "I don't even care who made me this food. I am never leaving. This place is heaven."

I'd taken another bite of pancakes before my statement registered with me. "Holy shit. Is this heaven? Did I die? I mean, I might be okay if I did, I just want to know the score."

Florence came out of the next room with her cup of coffee. "You're alive and well. This house was prepared for every eventuality. Whoever Raj's friend is, they had everything stockpiled, supplies to last weeks, and cold storage that has been magically enhanced in the most amazing way."

"Are you reverse engineering the icebox?" I asked.

"Of course. Any new ice magic is of interest to me. I'm never too old to learn new things. Plus, once this is all over and Annie's home again, maybe I can set up shop and sell my services to fix people's refrigerators!" She grinned. Everyone was happy here. It was amazing what a couple of days of good rest, good, hot food, and lack of fear of being shot in the street could do to people.

"So, we're staying then?" I asked, shoving another strip of bacon in my mouth.

"Unfortunately, from what I understand, if the last gate isn't opened, we won't be able to enjoy this virtual paradise very long, anyway."

I sighed, washed down another bite with coffee, and said, "I guess you're right. Damn you and your pragmatism. Where are the others?"

"Out for breakfast, I believe. If we're going to leave tomorrow, they wanted to be as strong as possible."

"Sam, too?"

Florence pursed her lips, and I got the impression she wasn't impressed with our enigmatic and ancient guest. "Sam, too."

"Why don't you like her?"

"I don't know her well enough to make that kind of judgment call," Florence said.

"She knew I was listening and is very diplomatic when she wants to be. After all, for years, her career, her life, and the lives of so many rode on those skills, didn't they?" Sam said.

Florence tensed, and I perked up. Was I finally going to find out what Florence had been doing in the sixties and seventies that made her so familiar with so many government employees?

"Don't," Florence said. "It is not your story to tell."

Sam sighed gustily. "None of you are any fun. You won't share your secrets and won't let me have the fun, Rajyapala has shared too much already with the young one, here, and Eleanor has no secrets."

"You didn't mention Petrina," I said, as I was thinking back to what I knew about events that Florence might have been involved with that she didn't want me to know about. There was something tickling my mind about Pine Ridge in the early seventies, but I couldn't put my finger on it.

"Petrina is the best vampire in my line, and I've nothing to say about her when she's not around. If anyone could be said to have inherited my traits, it's her. She is brilliant, beautiful, and ruthless."

"Thank you, grandmother," Petrina said. "Those compliments mean so much from you when you knew I was within earshot." Petrina sounded more amused than annoyed, but I could see her expression. She wasn't ready to join the Sammu-rammat fan club that Sam wanted to start.

"It's interesting to me that you expected a warmer welcome than you're getting," I said. "Have you spent much time in the company of others recently? Or is spying on your undead descendants your only source of contact with people? You don't seem socially well-adjusted."

Sam's eyes flashed red so briefly that I wondered if I'd imagined it. Then she smiled, showing her fangs, and I knew I hadn't. "You live dangerously," she said, the ess elongating into an almost sibilant sound.

"You aren't going to kill me—I'm needed yet. You won't even hurt me because you don't want to force a confrontation with Raj—who is also needed. Calling you on your bullshit when there's nothing you can do to me isn't living dangerously. It's giving you a taste of something someone should've been giving you for the past however many thousands of years you've been wandering around stirring shit up."

"Stirring shit up?" She looked genuinely surprised and was still a little lispy. I hoped she didn't turn into a snake or anything like that. Other than baby snakes—and myself, obviously—I was not a fan of reptiles.

"C'mon, Sam. Level with me. If you couldn't find a good war, did you take a vacation, or did you stir the pot? A shot fired in the wrong place at the wrong time could push a nation to war, and then you'd get your fix. Tell me I'm wrong."

She laughed, deep and throaty, and again my body had that odd reaction to her. I didn't dare glance around to see if anyone else was having the same problem. I did not want to know. "You may be even more perceptive than I gave you credit for," she admitted. "I may have...helped things along from time to time. Nothing that wasn't already inevitable, of course. Just a nudge."

Raj strode into the room. "Unless you have something concrete to give us, I'm going to have to ask you to leave. You've passed on the information you deem most useful and refuse to share anything else. My understanding is there will be plenty of witnesses at the last gate, and that you will be one, so we'll see you in a few weeks. It was lovely meeting you."

Sam's jaw dropped open, and she stared at Raj.

"I guess your go at stirring shit up here is over," I said. "Meeting you was very interesting. Peace out."

Sam stared at us for a minute before turning and disappearing so fast that I had to blink a couple times to make sure she was actually gone.

"That was rather rude," I said to Raj.

"I don't care. She was annoying everyone, including me, and wasn't going to give us anything else to work with. Why stick around? She's bored and likes to cause trouble. Those traits are not welcome right now." He looked at Florence and Petrina. "Are you both still ready to go tomorrow night?"

After receiving affirmative replies, Raj added, "Then let's map our route—silently—so we can leave as soon as the sun sets. I'd like to get that over with so I can see what other treasures Katya has in her secret wine cellar."

CHAPTER TWENTY

The next two weeks could only be described as hellish. We did short jogs every night, all over the Pacific Northwest, trying to throw off anyone who might be on our tail and inclined to harass us. I never saw anyone, but the paranoid people in the group—aka everyone but me—assured me that the government was not to be trusted and better safe than sorry.

The upshot of their caution was that the four hundred or so miles from Sun River to Portland took fourteen days instead of four. When we arrived at Raj's house—or rather, mansion—in Portland, I didn't even bother to get the lay of the land, inside or out, before collapsing in the bed he pointed me towards. We had two weeks before the gate opened, I knew where the gate site was, and there was no way I was going to do anything before getting a good day's sleep.

Almost before I'd fallen asleep, I was woken by voices in the next room. "She's exhausted, I'm not waking her," Raj said.

"She's going to want to know; she hates it when she feels out of the loop."

I groaned, pushed my too-long hair out of my eyes, and stumbled out of the basement bedroom into the living room. "What do I want to know that's more important than knowing I want to sleep?"

"Your house is gone," Petrina said, matter-of-factly.

I gaped at her. "What do you mean, my house is gone? How do you even know where I live? Lived?"

Raj shrugged. "I have my ways."

"Gone how?" I asked again.

"It appears to have been overtaken by a very large hedge?" Petrina asked more than said. "The house might still be there, inside, like Sleeping Beauty's castle, but the laurel hedge that surrounds, including the top, is impenetrable, even to me. The hedge has swallowed the house."

"Huh. I knew that hedge was trouble. It was so sensitive to my emotions. I don't know if it became sentient, was connected to me no matter how far away I got, or blamed me—and the house—for something, but this makes sense."

"It does?" Petrina asked. "Because on the surface, it doesn't seem like it ought to."

"I don't suppose you could tell if the couple I rented it to got out or if they were trapped inside?"

"They got out," she said. "I talked to the neighbors. There was one in particular who knew everything that was going on. I got the feeling she'd been waiting to tell the story to someone new."

"It's handy living across the street from people like her," I said. "Nothing escapes them. I'm glad Hedge didn't kill anyone."

"I didn't say that," Petrina said.

"Oh? Hedge is homicidal, too?"

"I didn't see this for myself, so I can't confirm it, but rumor on the streets of North Portland is that if you walk too close to the hedge or decide that you're the young hero who can get through, the hedge will eat you."

"I didn't realize laurel hedges were carnivorous," I said.

"They typically aren't," Florence said. "What did you do to it?"

"Me? Nothing! It was a hedge on my property. I was trimming it last midsummer when the magic woke…oh shit."

Three pairs of eyes stared at me. I stared back.

"Go on," Florence said, gesturing emphatically.

"I was trimming the hedge last midsummer because it'd encroached a good five feet further onto my property than I liked and was getting tall enough to block the sun in the winter. I'd rented a wood chipper and a chainsaw and was taking care of business. The next morning, when I went to admire my handiwork, it'd grown back —and more. It kept growing, and I kept trimming it. Finn said it was responding to my moods, but what if, when I left, I left a carnivorous, angry hedge behind by mistake?"

"I think it's safe to say that no one could've anticipated that outcome," Florence assured me. "Was earth the first of your powers that manifested?"

"Yes."

"You woke the hedge the night the magic woke in you because you'd been so focused on it. It might've been better in the long run if you'd been harvesting dandelions or something, but then again, who knows what kind of havoc semi-sentient dandelions could wreak? They multiply so quickly, and if they were enormous?"

"This is all so fucked up," I whispered.

"There's nothing anyone can do about it now," Raj said. "Go back to bed. I'll ensure you aren't disturbed again."

A WEEK OF RESTING, eating, spending quality naked time with my boyfriend, and exploring the town I'd once called home was enough to restore me back to my energetic self. It didn't hurt that the gate magic was strong here, and every time I touched bare earth, it filled me up.

I'd gone to check out my house for myself, being careful to stay out of sight. I might appreciate my old neighbor and her penchant for keeping an eye on the neighborhood, but I didn't want to answer any uncomfortable questions. It was exactly as Petrina had described; only I had the impression that if I asked to go inside, Hedge would let me in. Since I didn't have the impression that Hedge would let me back out again, I resisted the temptation.

I was on my way to Forest Park, to the site of the first gate, and was taking the long way around from Raj's home in Northeast Portland. He lived in a ridiculous Gothic Revival Tudor that was as period as possible on the main floors, but neo-gothic in the windowless basement where his living quarters were. I'd borrowed a bicycle from the garage trying hard not to imagine Raj on a bike. It probably was one of his servant's, and not his, but I couldn't shake the image. In fact, I found myself adding details like a red-lined black cape billowing out behind the bike. I'd had to stop three times on my way to North Portland, overcome by giggles, and unable to stay upright.

I wandered for ages, up and down the streets of my North Portland neighborhood looking for signs that it was the same place I'd lived for over ten years. The houses that had risen out of mostly manicured lawns were looking more run down. Grass hadn't been mown, and trees weren't trimmed. Houses that had already been run down were falling apart.

The main street in my neighborhood had previously boasted several bars, bookstores, little restaurants, and more thrift shops than ought to be legal in one small neighborhood. Now, the bars seemed to be doing pretty brisk business, but everything else was boarded up and abandoned.

After leaving my old digs, I rode to the St. Johns Bridge—the quickest way to Forest Park. I'd started the upwards jaunt to get to the tall bridge spanning the Willamette River before I noticed something odd. I'd expected it to be devoid of car traffic. This close to the first gate site, nothing electronic worked. But I hadn't expected the one-hundred-year-old bridge to be destroyed.

There was a gap of about a thousand feet between the two towers that supported the suspension bridge. The parts that remained were covered in vines, and I could see the asphalt of the road cracking. I walked cautiously to the edge of the bridge and looked down two hundred feet to the river below. Something dark and impossibly long breached the surface, and I held my breath. I didn't think there was supposed to be anything that large in the river. I wasn't sure how I was going to get across it. A thousand feet was much too far to jump on the bike, no matter how much momentum I could get. I could wait until sunset and have Raj take me across. Or, I could stop pretending that I was someone else and take myself across.

It was too light, and there were still too many people to turn into a dragon in broad daylight. There might be river monsters, but I didn't want to incite any more fear than the locals must already be feeling. Instead, I carefully wrapped light around me, all but eliminating myself from view, and then let go of the wings that ached to be free. Certain that no one could see me unless they were looking for me, I walked back to the edge of the bridge and threw myself off. It took a heart-stopping couple seconds before my body and brain got with the program and started flying, but soon I was swooping over the Willamette, down low enough to trail my fingers in the water until a noise behind me startled me back up and away from river-monster grabbing range.

Enough of the exuberance of flying was out of my system, so I headed southwest toward the site of the first gate. Something was drawing me there, although I didn't know what. A few hundred yards away from the site, I landed, reluctantly returned my wings to wherever they were when they weren't out and unraveled my shields.

I walked the rest of the way to the clearing where I'd started it all and stumbled into a huge crowd of people.

"What the fuck?" I asked. "Isn't it a little early for Country Fair?"

A huge, burly man strode forward, and I took a half-step back before I caught myself. "I am Charles Robertson, Alpha of the Pacific Northwest Pack. Where is Isaac?"

I plastered a smile on my face. This was going to be great. "Isaac was my companion for the first four gates, but at the fourth gate, in Savannah, Georgia, Michelle—the vampire that previously lived in Portland and now resides on the Fae Plane, the same vampire who terrorized Isaac and your pack—offered him a deal. She offered him Emma if he would cross planes while the gate was temporarily open, and willingly surrender himself to her. He took the deal."

"Of course he did," Charles growled. "Always did have more

courage than sense, and he'd always felt responsible for Emma's death. You're telling me that Emma wasn't dead?"

I cringed a little bit more. I was not telling the story right. "She'd been imprisoned on the Fae Plane since Michelle used glamour to make you all believe she'd been killed. It was only a few months for her, and not the decades that'd passed here, but she was damaged."

"Where is she now? We'd love to have her back in our pack. She was such a beautiful soul."

I took a deep breath, resolved not to question the 'beautiful soul' comment, after all, she had been damaged by her time with Michelle, and what I was about to say was more important than clearing up any quibbles I had with their assessment of her personality. "She died after the last gate was opened. Have you heard of bounties being placed on the heads of supernaturals? She was killed by one such bounty hunter. She was amazing, though. I've never met a more powerful shifter, present company included. She should've lived a long, healthy life and led her own pack. I am sorry to have to bring you this news and make you mourn her twice."

"Have any shifters you've encountered lived to tell the tale?" he spat at me.

Christopher, Luis, and Rebecca strode forward. Rebecca laid her hand on Charles's shoulder. "You know they have. We have."

"And Isaac isn't dead," I said. "I can still feel him sometimes along our mating bond."

"He mated with you? He was supposed to be spying on you."

I shrugged. "It was foretold?" I offered. "But he is still alive, and I will get him back. Once this business is done, I have a lot of things to do on the Fae Plane."

Charles growled at me, but I could see the pain in his eyes and didn't take offense.

"It's best if you go now," Luis said. "I can't wait to catch up, though. I want to hear everything—especially about the vampire."

Christopher mock-punched Luis as Rebecca led Charles away. "Always with the vampire. A man gets jealous."

"I'd love to stay and talk, but..."

"Go—there'll be plenty of time later."

I didn't want to destroy their illusion that I'd be up for a chat after the last gate opened, so I smiled and left.

TOMORROW NIGHT, the last gate would open. I had one more night with Raj, one more day in my almost-unrecognizable city, and one more turn of the earth to agonize about what was going to happen. Raj didn't want to talk about it, but I knew he was as resigned as I was to the eventuality of the sacrifice.

Sam had shown up again yesterday and moved into one of the empty rooms Raj had, announced she'd be staying for a while and that the Pacific Northwest was her territory now. Raj shook his head, said they could discuss it next week, and walked away.

Much like the shifters had converged in the woods, the vampires were converging on Raj's house. So far, in addition to Sam, there were a bunch of vampires I didn't know, including someone introduced as 'Katya.' I smiled at her, expressed appreciation for her hospitality, and tried to look innocent and not think about all the expensive booze I'd had a hand in disappearing.

Marie had arrived a couple hours ago, complete with Rasputin in his bowling ball bag—heh—and immediately disappeared into a locked room with Sam, Raj, and Petrina.

Everyone else had wandered off into the city, presumably for dinner. Florence was who knows where getting ready to weave the big magics the next night. And I was here, alone, in a great big house with a great big bed, the night before my probable death. The whole situation made a girl feel neglected and more than a little grumpy.

"Self-pity doesn't suit you."

I whirled around, sword in my hand before I had a chance to think about it and came face to face with Father Clement.

"Phoenix," I said.

"Dragon," he replied.

"No one's supposed to know about that."

"I'm not no one. And you want me here, trust me."

"Why should I trust you? I know nothing about you. Except that your eyes are the lightest brown I've ever seen."

He grinned, winked, pulled two feathers from…who even knows… and handed them to me. "One for you, and one for the swordsman. Don't lose them and carry them with you tomorrow night. I'll see you around."

Then he burst into flames, flames so hot that I was uncomfortable, and try as I might, I couldn't quench them.

"What the fuck?" Raj said, bursting into the room. I tucked the feathers into a pocket and sheathed my sword.

"Father Clement came to say au revoir," I said aloud. "*Tell you the rest when we're alone.*"

"Leave, everyone," Raj ordered. They scattered, and he led me into our bedroom. I handed him a feather, told him of the ridiculously brief encounter, and then let him seduce me. Who knows, maybe it'd all make sense later.

CHAPTER TWENTY-ONE

I sat alone on the steps of Vista House at Crown Point with a newly opened bottle of wine. The last weeks had sucked. Raj and I had fought and fucked and fought. Petrina and Florence had fought. I wasn't interested in whether or not they were following the rest of the pattern Raj and I had set. Raj had roared for Arduinna in front of a stand of juniper trees until she showed up and reiterated everything she'd said before. He'd raged and threatened to leave and—short of stomping around in a snit—acted like a toddler in the midst of a tantrum.

And now it was time. It was an hour until sunset on June nineteenth. In less than twelve hours, it would be over. I crossed my legs and watched the sun slowly sink below the horizon. It was solstice eve. A year since these crazy wheels had been set in motion. I'd lost so much over the last year. Emma, with whom I'd developed a grudging friendship. My relationship with Finn. My blissful ignorance of the supernatural world. My mate. The internet and fast food. I took a moment to pour one out for Taco Bell.

Before I could get too sad about my losses, I took a few moments to think of everything I'd gained. At the top of the list was my stubborn vampire lover, followed closely by Isaac—who I could never do right by. It was stupid that I'd spent almost thirty-five years without a serious relationship and then in a year, met two men who had claim to my heart. The places I'd seen that I never thought I'd see. The people I'd met. Florence, Petrina, Emma, Rebecca, Christopher and Luis, Marie, and even those awful lion shifters from Chicago. I'd lived a lifetime in the last year.

I regretted the sheer number of lives lost. Maybe I couldn't have prevented it, but I would never know for certain. My only personal regret, though, was that it was the last year of my life, and I hadn't known it until recently. I cataloged my sins and found only one. I'd been too afraid, too hesitant to try new things, to trust new people. I didn't see a way out of what was about to happen, but I vowed to myself that if, by some miracle, I made it through June twentieth, I'd stop making decisions based on insularity and fear. I was going to go big or go home and fuck everyone who got in my way.

"I wouldn't mind getting in your way, if that's my punishment," Raj said.

I turned towards his voice and opened my arms. "I don't know if I can do this," he said, for about the one-millionth time.

"You have to," I replied for the one million and first time.

"I know."

For a few minutes, we sat entwined in each other's arms, not talking, not even thinking. Just reveling in the touch. Then I turned my lips up to his and waited for him to lower his lips to mine. He did, and it wasn't the slow build-up our love-making usually took. A spark took immediately, and before I could wrap myself around what was happening, he was on top of me, and our clothes were scattered around the concrete steps. He took my hand, led me inside to an out of the way alcove that was padded with blankets, and pulled me down beside him. He paused above me, ready to make that first thrust. I was aching for him and cursed at him for his hesitation.

"I'm afraid to start because that means it's the last time," he whispered.

"Raj," I pleaded. "I love you, and I need this. Now."

With a guttural cry, he plunged into me and then held still until I growled at him and he laughed. Then he moved against me, and I arched up to meet each thrust. I bit at the tendon above his collarbone, and he groaned and bucked against me. Our rhythm became erratic and frenzied, and I dug my nails into his back as he turned his head away from my flesh. I knew why he turned from me, and then I knew that this was what I could leave him with.

I reached up and turned his head towards me, kissing him fiercely. "Bite me," I breathed.

"No," he groaned against my lips.

I ran my tongue against his until he relaxed into me again. Then, I played dirty. I licked his fangs, deliberately nicking my tongue. The copper-warm blood trickled against his tongue and he—all of him—stiffened against me. "What did you do?" he gasped.

I laughed—low and wicked—then swirled my bleeding tongue through his mouth again, turned my head, and pressed his mouth to my neck.

"Bite me," I commanded again, sending him images of the pleasure I took from his bite. I wasn't playing fair, but it worked. He hesitated only a moment before plunging his fangs into my neck. I flinched at the first rush of pain before the pleasure receptors kicked in. Within seconds, I was writhing against him frantically, and he was drinking deep. I came with a cry, and he followed me over the abyss. As soon as we were still, he pulled out—of my neck and my still-throbbing center.

"You shouldn't have," he started.

I shushed him with a hand on his lips. "I needed to do that for you," I said. "Maybe now, you'll be a miniature dragon as opposed to a toy dragon." I couldn't help myself and let out an inelegant giggle.

"You are so annoying," he griped.

"But you love me."

"I do. I love you."

"I love you, too, vampire." I gathered up our clothes, and we dressed in silence before heading back outside.

"I'll do my best for Florence," he promised. "And then we'll find a way to free Isaac."

My breath caught in my throat. "Thank you," I choked out.

"How much longer?" he asked.

"Less than five hours," I said.

"Not enough time to tell you how much I love you," he said.

"Not nearly enough."

Raj and I whirled around to confront the voice that floated towards us in the darkness.

THE VOICE DIDN'T SOUND familiar, but I knew it had to Finn.

"It's not Finn," Raj said.

We stood in tandem and linked hands to face this new threat. I knew Petrina and Florence were nearby, but I also knew they'd be out of earshot, not wanting to hear our good-byes.

"*They could be here in an instant,*" Raj's voice whispered in my head.

"That won't be necessary," the stranger said. He stepped forward far enough that I could see the shape of his face, and more importantly, the shape of his ears.

"Connor," I said.

"Even so," he agreed.

"What do you want?"

"I am here with the others to observe. The rest will be here soon, but I wanted a look at our sacrificial lamb before it was too late."

"Who are you?" I asked at the same time Raj demanded, "What others?"

Usually, Raj didn't ask a lot of questions, preferring to pluck the information he wanted out of people's minds. I tilted my head to look up at him while keeping one eye on the elf outlined in darkness.

Raj shrugged slightly, and I turned back to the interloper.

"Answer the questions," I said.

"Or what?"

"Or I'll kill you," I said.

"You kill so easily now?"

I hesitated. He was right. I wouldn't kill a stranger just for interrupting my romantic moment. I was a defensive warrior, not an offensive one.

"Even if she doesn't, I do," Raj said. "I've had centuries to practice."

The elf laughed. "I was old before you were born, and I'll exist long after you're ash. You cannot kill me."

I sighed. I had only a little bit of time left before I shuffled off this mortal coil, and I didn't want to spend it trading threats and insults with an unknown elf.

"Please answer our questions," I said with as much politeness as I could muster. "I'd like to know why you're here and who are the others you spoke of."

He smiled flashing too-white teeth. "Was that so hard?"

I gritted my teeth. I might not want to kill him, but I was beginning to have a burning desire to punch him in the face.

"So violent," he crooned. "How is it that two community college instructors ended up with such a violent child? I guess that ends the debate on nature versus nurture, doesn't it?"

"You are seriously getting on my nerves," I ground out through gritted teeth. "Either say what you came to say or get the fuck out of here." I held up one finger to forestall any denial. "Don't deny that you want to talk. If you didn't, you would've stayed out of sight."

"Violent yet perceptive. People will always underestimate you." His gaze raked my body, and I had a feeling that his night vision was a lot better than mine in human form. I felt Raj tense beside me. He might not be possessive, but he *was* protective, and the strange Fae eye-fucking me was igniting every one of his protective instincts. At least I'd dressed. I didn't need another naked confrontation.

I took a deep breath, striving for control. Then I turned my back on the elf and slid my hands up Raj's chest. "We don't have much time left, and I don't want to spend it tense and angry. Will you sit with me and help me finish this wine?" I gestured at the half-full bottle a few feet away.

I saw the tension start to drain out of Raj and was impressed by his iron self-control. "It would be my pleasure, my sweet."

We walked, hand-in-hand, to the bottle I'd set down when Raj had appeared earlier. We didn't have glasses, and even though it seemed a bit trashy, we drank straight from the bottle.

The stranger strode up and sat without invitation. "May I?" he asked.

"No," Raj answered.

"It's okay; I brought my own." The elf pulled a flask out of his jacket and unscrewed the top. "Drink?" he asked, offering the flask to me.

"No thank you," I said, although part of me wanted another taste of his elven wine.

"You'll need to learn some etiquette if you're going to take the throne."

"I'm not planning on taking the throne," I said. I didn't add that I wasn't planning on living through the rest of the night because even though we were almost to go-time, I didn't think Raj would appreciate it.

"Don't be ridiculous," he said. "Of course you'll take the throne. You're the true heir. There's no way to get out of this."

"Pretty sure even in Faerie dead people aren't allowed to wear the crown," I said.

"Well, no, of course not. That's why your vampire, for all his Fae blood, could never rule. But you, my child, are not dead."

I felt Raj twitch. "I'm not dead yet," I said.

"Oh!" he clapped his hands together in a macabre imitation of childlike glee. "We're having a Monty Python quote competition! Give me a second to come up with something appropriate." I just stared at him. This dude was creepy as fuck. "I know, I know! 'Strange women lying in ponds distributing swords is no basis for a system of government.'" He looked at Raj. "Where'd you get that sword?"

"It's been in my family for as long as I can remember."

"Not too long, though, right? It's Damascus steel, and you're a thousand years old. How much older than you can it be?"

Raj was cold. "It is a family weapon, tempered in the blood of my ancestors and fed with the blood of me and mine."

"It is a Fae weapon," the elf said. "Forged by dwarves and set with gems of demon blood. Also, I think it spent some time in the possession of a moistened bint." He laughed, and the sound raised goosebumps on my arms.

I was tired of this. "Do you have a point or are you just trying to be the third wheel?"

"It is your sword, Ciara nic Mata. It is your birthright, and this sword will be all the justification you need to set up your brand of government, watery tarts or no."

"Sooo…after Raj sacrifices me with this, I'm going to stage a coup and take Medb's throne?"

"Exactly." He stood gracefully in one smooth motion. I'd been trying to do that for years. Damnit. He looked at Raj in silence for moment and then he was gone.

"Well," I said, staring at the place he'd just been. "That was weird."

We didn't speak of it, but rather sat in silence passing the wine bottle back and forth. When it was empty, I scooted close to Raj and pulled his head to mine.

"There are others arriving," he said.

"I guess we have an audience, then."

"How much longer?"

"Not much. I can feel it," I said. "I don't want to leave you."

"I don't want to be left."

"Are you ready?" I asked.

"I will never be ready for this."

"Got your feather?"

He nodded and patted his pocket. *"You?"*

"Yep. I guess it's time."

He stood and offered me a hand. I pulled myself up with his aid and then looked around. We were surrounded—at least as far as I could see. I walked around the circular house. Yep—figures on all sides. The waning quarter moon was rising, and between the moon and the Milky Way, there was enough light to make out some faces.

To the north, on the river side, was a coven of mages, with Florence at the center. They were holding hands in a semi-circle and chanting. In the west in the light of the setting sun, a line of vampires with Sam at the center and Marie and Petrina on either side of her stepped forward, hands joined. The northernmost vampire reached out to the westernmost mage, and the semi-circle became a half-circle. To the south, with their backs to the rising hills, Rebecca stood in the center of a line of thirteen shifters. I looked for other familiar faces and saw Christopher and Luis and the odd bobcat shifter, Extra Grady, that we'd met in Asheville. Luis waved slightly, and Rebecca smiled and winked, then her line joined hands and linked to the vampires. In the east were the Fae. I recognized Arduinna in the center, and at her right hand was Connor. She nodded to me and then the semi-circle of Fae clasped hands and then fully joined the circle, releasing a surge of power.

I faced Raj, and he looked at me. He pulled his sword from the sheath at his waist and waited for my word.

I could feel the power around us and the gate building in front of me. I shivered in fear and anticipation. "I love you," I said to Raj.

"I know," he said back. Fucking Star Wars geek.

He raised the sword. I swallowed, trying to steel myself for the blow. I started to bend my head, and then everything went to shit.

Raj gasped, and I looked up, just in time to see the light starting to fade from his eyes. He slumped forward and the sword continued the momentum he'd started, and plunged into my abdomen. He collapsed into my arms, pushing the sword further into me, and we fell. I had enough time to see Finn standing behind him holding a stake that glinted silver in the moonlight. Finn's expression was one I couldn't recognize, and before I had a chance to try, everything went dark, then erupted in a blaze of flames.

The last thing I heard was "Oh my goddesses, the volcanoes."

EPILOGUE

"It is done, Majesty," Finn said, bowing low before Medb's throne.

"She is dead?"

"I saw her disemboweled on the vampire's sword with my own eyes."

"And the vampire?"

"I staked him with silver."

"Did you see him turn to ash?" Medb asked.

"No, but the old ones don't so easily," Finn replied. "His body was still there, on top of hers, at daybreak."

Medb drummed her fingers on the arm of her throne. "I guess that will have to do, but in the future, I require that you bring me the heads of my enemies."

"As you wish."

"Give me the sword."

Finn risked a glance up at her, trying to figure out if she wanted his sword or something else. "What sword, Majesty?"

"The sword that the pretender was killed with. Are you stupid?"

"I…uh…didn't know you wanted it. There were so many people that I thought it expedient to remove myself as quickly as possible and let the sword stay buried in the dragon bitch's guts."

Medb stilled, and Finn mentally cursed himself.

"What did you call her?" Medb's voice was low and quiet and terrifying.

Finn didn't answer. He didn't have to.

"How long have you known?"

Finn stayed silent and prostrated himself in front of the dais. He felt her heel, razor sharp, pierce the skin on the back of his neck. "When you had her bound, you knew you were binding, not just the dragon queen but an actual dragon?" Medb asked.

Finn tried not to whimper.

"When I made the deal with a treacherous Voodoo Queen to have her bound again, you knew she was a dragon?"

The heel pressed further into his neck, and he felt it hit bone. He gagged then and started vomiting.

"Answer me," Medb hissed. "If you want to live."

"Yes," he babbled. Anything to make her stop. "I knew, but I wanted to protect you."

"Ignorance is not protection," Medb said. She withdrew the stiletto from his neck in a smooth motion that left him gasping in pain and retching again. Funny that Medb and Eleanor shared similar opinions on that, at least.

"You will live," Medb pronounced. "But if you fuck up one more time, I will feed you to my wolf, one piece at a time." She whirled to the person standing deferentially behind her. "Get him out of here."

"With pleasure, your Majesty," the forest Fae said, bowing from the waist.

Hours earlier...

Isaac was floating in the weird in-between world where he spent most of his time. It was an escape from the pain he could still feel, but not an escape from the torture of knowing that Eleanor was out of his reach. As always, when he thought of her, her feelings came to him in sharp relief. He concentrated and felt her fear and resignation.

"No!" he yelled. He didn't know what he was railing against, but she felt…final.

Then he felt the sword pierce her belly and twist. He felt her pain and shock and grief. He felt everything until there was no more pain.

And then, Isaac opened his eyes.

As always, there were a half-dozen guards in the room in which he was chained. They were usually slumped against the wall. After the first few months when no matter what he'd done, he'd failed to free himself from the silver chains that confined his body and his beast, they were no longer on alert and afraid.

Now, however, they looked up and whatever they saw on his face scared them.

He heard the sound and sudden stench of urine and knew at least one had pissed himself.

Isaac laughed. He loved their fear. He would consume it.

One of the guards ran out of the room, leaving the door unlocked and open. The others drew weapons and approached him.

Isaac howled his song of rage and grief and drew on the power of the moons of Fairyland he shifted.

When next he came to himself, he was running through the forest outside the prison in which he'd been kept, bathed in Fae blood. For a moment, he contemplated changing back to his human form and looking for a gate back to Earth, but then he scented the vampire who'd captured him, bound him, and tried to break him. Isaac's eyes flashed yellow, and he howled again, this time in anticipation of the hunt and the kill. He was out for blood, and woe betide any who got in his path.

THE LOST CHILD

ELEANOR MORGAN BOOK FIVE

The first thing I became aware of was a searing pain in my midsection. The second thing was a heavy weight on my chest. And the third thing was the fire.

I opened my eyes slowly and glanced around, being careful not to move my body - not that it seemed likely that my body was going to move any time soon. I could see fire arcing over me in a dome. It was noonish—or thereabouts. I could see the sun high overhead through the orange flame curtain and I was baking into the granite stone steps beneath me—although whether that was due more to the sun or the fire, I wasn't sure.

I looked down towards my chest to determine the source of the weight. The only thing I saw was the sword. It was no longer piercing my midsection, which was probably good. However, its weight didn't seem to explain the pressure I felt. I reached cautiously towards the sword and grasped the hilt, moving it off my body. Once it was by my side, the weight vanished. The discrepancy between how heavy it felt when I picked it up and how heavy it felt when it was on top of me was something I might need to chalk up as one of life's little mysteries —at least until I figured out what was going on.

I was naked—because of course I was—but my questing fingers didn't find any external signs of my recent disembowelment. I was certainly feeling some internal signs, although probably not enough to actually account for a disembowelment, but I was definitely more sore than that time I'd decided to try P90X the same day that I took the AB-racadabra thirty-minute ab class at my local gym. I'd almost passed out every time I'd sneezed, laughed, or thought about moving for a week.

It was likely that I was going to need some assistance to get out of here and figure out what was going on. I tried reaching out to Raj in my mind. He probably wasn't the best person to help me right now because vampire, but he'd at least know what was going on. I hit a brick wall and that's when I remembered.

Finn.

That motherfucking bastard of an elf had staked Raj just as Raj stabbed me. Fear gripped me and I saw the flames intensify in reaction to my emotion. I tried to tamp it down—both emotionally and literally. It'd be a pretty crappy end to survive a ritual sacrifice and then become a victim of accidental self-immolation.

I concentrated on the fire. It wasn't being particularly responsive, but I wasn't sure if that was because I was weak or because the flames had an external source. Those phoenix feathers must have been there for something, after all. If I was reborn from the metaphorical ashes, then it made sense that I'd be naked. And Raj had had a phoenix feather, too, I reminded myself. He might not be here, but he'd had a feather, and that damn phoenix had known something. And so had the elf. *Connor,* I reminded myself.

There was no help for it. If I was going to get out of here, find my vampire, and see how much of the world I'd broken, I was going to have to sit up.

Pulling from the five yoga classes I'd gone to in college, I rolled over onto my right side oh-so-slowly and then pulled my knees towards my mid-section. Once the stars and chirping birds that accompanied the pain of movement had mostly dissipated, I propped myself up on one elbow and attempted to breathe through the pain.

I don't know how long it took me to move into a sitting position. It seemed like hours, and I was sweating from more than just the summer sun and the omnipresent flames by the time I was upright and cross-legged. I pulled the sword onto my lap to help me focus, and again the weight of it was astounding. There was something odd about it, but I didn't have time to investigate right now.

There'd been four groups of thirteen surrounding me when the sacrifice had happened—one group for each of the four major supernatural contingents in this world. Their circle had been right about where the fire's perimeter was now. I hoped no one had been injured when flames appeared. I didn't see any bodies. It's possible—probable even—that the watchers had wandered off after the gate had opened leaving me for dead. I was supposed to *be* dead, after all. The only one who'd had any doubt about my imminent demise was the elf I'd spoken to shortly before sacrifice.

I needed to concentrate now instead of reliving the immediate past. There was seldom much to gain from dwelling in the past. I closed my eyes and reached out with my other-senses to the fiery dome surrounding me. I wondered briefly if the spectators had believed it to be my funeral pyre and then shut down that line of thought before I could get too much further.

I centered myself—finding the spot inside me that allowed me to feel balanced and whole—and then reached down to my connection with the earth, grounding myself. This was usually instinctive, but I was injured, tired, and confused, and I didn't want to make any mistakes.

I opened my eyes and looked—and then *looked* again with my magical sight. The fire was definitely coming from me. It must have been instinctive self-preservation. I hoped that Finn had been caught in the firestorm, but knew I could never be so lucky. He'd likely teleported out of there the instant Raj had collapsed.

I found the source of the flames and shut it down. The fire flared once and then died, so suddenly that my ears popped and the silence that followed nearly deafened me. I looked around again now that my vision was unimpeded. I didn't see another living soul. Even better, I didn't see any dead people, either.

I tried to redirect the energy that had been spent in feeding the flames into healing me enough that I could stand up. With a groan, I remember how badly my feet had hurt during the epic hike portion of my journey and spent a moment trying to decide if dying of exposure on Crown Point was better than going forward on still-tired feet.

Then I remembered that I could fly. There was no reason to walk out of here now. I was alone. There were no rules that I was aware of. And the magic had returned. I'd stay away from populated areas, of course. No need to panic a populace already freaking out from whatever changes they'd experienced over the last year.

I pulled myself slowly to my feet, laid the sword down on the ground, and went within to find my dragon self. I closed my eyes in pleasure as I felt my body shift and change and then I screamed in pain as my injured abdominal cavity moved to accommodate the difference between human and dragon anatomy. I was gasping in pain by the time I finished my change and if I'd been able to sweat in my dragon form, I knew I'd be dripping.

I picked up the sword with my front claws and prepared to launch myself into the sky. My first priority was to find Raj. My second to find Florence and Petrina. My third was to find Finn and see how he liked being stabbed.

I took off and flew in increasingly large circles around the area. It occurred to me that I didn't know how much time had passed since I'd been stabbed. It felt like less than a day, but the healing I'd experienced indicated that a lot more time had passed. I wasn't sunburned or starving, though.

I decided that not more than a day or two had passed and that if I didn't find a real-life person to talk to soon, I might just go mad. I tried to use the Force to figure out where Florence was. We'd shared magic and it seemed logical that I could find her that way. I didn't hit a brick wall like I had when I attempted to kindle my connection with Raj, but I didn't find anything that would lead me to her, either other than a subtle pull to the northeast.

After circling further and further east the area for an hour or so and confirming that it was even more uninhabited as it had been prior to the final gate opening, I flew towards the Interstate and located a small town that seemed a likely place for me to spend the night and make some plans. I landed outside of town and changed back to my human form so as not to alarm any remaining townsfolk. Although since I had no clothes and no supplies, maybe my dragon form would be less alarming than my naked woman form.

I reminded myself that I was really at my best naked and walked into town.

On my first pass down the dusty main street, it seemed as if the town truly was abandoned. There wasn't a lot to the town that the sign posted at the edge of the collection of buildings proclaimed to be "Warrendale." There was a small diner called "Jo Mama's" next to "Papa Joe's" gas station. I walked into the restaurant/gift shop, hoping that I'd be able to find some shelf stable food and a t-shirt to call my own. I found the latter, but not the former, and I kicked myself for not heading back to Portland instead. I wasn't sure what had drawn me east instead of west, but whatever it was probably could've waited until I'd been fed.

The town—if you could even still call it that—didn't have any other buildings and it showed signs of having been abandoned a long time ago—way more than the year since the world had started changing. I found a case of Coca Cola in a storage room and decided that would have to do for dinner. I was exhausted. Between being stabbed, generating a long-lasting protective fire, healing, and flying about, I was running on fumes. I hoped the caloric content of the Coke would be enough to get me somewhere with food—and maybe even a bed—tomorrow. Tonight, I was sleeping at Jo Mama's.

I WOKE with a start and rolled off the padded booth I'd decided would be a better bed than the gray and sticky floor. I banged my head on the table trying to stand up, and only realized once I crawled out from under the table and stood in a defensive posture, sword at the ready, that my abdomen had barely twinged at all the motion. I did a couple experimental torso twists to verify things, but I felt mostly healed up. Apparently it's good to be the Queen.

Body check taken care of, I pushed my attention outward. Something had started me. It was dark and even with my enhanced eyesight, there was so little light available that I could barely make out the shapes of the tables and chairs scattered haphazardly throughout the room.

I walked as lightly as I could towards the outline of the door, straining my ears for any sign that I wasn't alone. I banged my hip into a table, tripped over a chair, and fell noisily to the ground. "Motherfucker!"

So much for stealth.

"Eleanor?"

I shot upright, hitting my head *again,* and asked hesitantly, "Florence?"

Before I could register what was going on, I was caught up in a hug so hard that I felt my ribs creak. "Ow! Florence! Put me down."

"Oh, I am so sorry," she said. "You must be injured still. Did I do any damage?"

"I'm mostly better," I said. "You just have a very strong grip."

She laughed. "I knew you wouldn't die."

"Did you? You might have shared that with the class. It might have made things easier for me and Raj if we'd known." I faltered. Raj. I felt tears spring to my eyes.

Florence must not have been able to read me—or was deliberately not reading me—for she continued blithely on. "I wasn't one hundred percent certain and didn't want to give false hope. Also, if you'd known, you might have done things differently and we wouldn't have the result we have today."

"And that is?" I couldn't see her, but I sensed that she was staring at me blankly. "I woke up naked and alone and covered in a dome of fire. I don't know what happened."

"What's the last thing you remember?" Florence asked.

"Raj stabbing me and Finn staking Raj." I flinched again as I said his name. I couldn't ask yet, though. I wasn't ready for finality. I'd lost Isaac. I couldn't bear to lose Raj, too.

"I didn't see Finn," Florence said. I hated not being able to see her face.

"Can we go somewhere with some light?" I asked. "How did you find me? Where are you staying? Is Petrina with you?"

"So many questions," she said.

"Like I said, I woke up naked and alone."

"Are you still naked?" Florence asked.

"You can't tell?" I asked. That didn't seem right.

"It's very dark in here and my magic is working unreliably at present."

That must be why she wasn't reading my mind. Lack of ability and not interest.

"I am wearing a t-shirt and some novelty boxers," I said.

"Have you eaten?"

"No." My stomach growled loudly to emphasize the point.

"Okay," Florence said, decision made. "Let's go to where Petrina and I have made camp. There is lantern light there, and I have your things so you can change. Once you've eaten and dressed, we will fill you in. And then you will answer some questions for me."

"This is the best plan ever," I said fervently. "I don't suppose you have any beer? I feel like I might deserve a drink after the last...how many days has it been anyway?"

"Five weeks," Florence said.

I stopped moving. I felt my jaw unhinge and couldn't muster up the will to close my gaping mouth.

"I'm sorry," I squeaked. "Did you say five *weeks*?"

"Yes," she said. That was all I was able to get out of her. "Just wait," she said. "What's a few more minutes when it's been more than a month?"

I grumbled but was left with no other choice but to follow her out in silence.

We followed the interstate west. It was eerie walking on the wide expanse of highway with no cars and no light. The moon was a barely visible sliver in the sky, but I couldn't tell if it was waxing or waning.

"Waning," Florence said. "Tomorrow's the new moon."

Apparently her mind-reading skills were improving.

"There was something odd in that place," she said. "It blocked me from reading you or using much of my magic at all. Fortunately, it was a small town and you are a very loud sleeper. If I'd had to search for you or rely on my own magical senses, it would've taken me much longer to find you."

So much for my attempts at stealth.

"You fell off a table or something within the first seconds of sensing my presence," Florence remind me. It sounded like she was trying not to laugh. "Stealth was kind of moot at that point, don't you think?"

She had a point, but I refused to vocalize it for her. I was feeling a little grumpy. I'd gotten cold sleeping in nothing but a t-shirt and boxers, and my central processing unit seemed to be a big sluggish. I changed my wish from a cold beer to a gallon of hot coffee. Lattes. Americanos. A large Stumptown drip with a dollop of cream.

And pancakes. I would cheerfully kill someone for a short stack. No—I corrected myself as my stomach rumbled painfully—a tall stack. A dragon sized stack. And five pigs worth of bacon. Or just five pigs would do. "Do you think there are any farms around here?" I asked, trying to sound casual.

"I'm not loosing a dragon to terrorize the countryside and carry off the farmers' prize flocks," Florence said. "It's just too cliché."

"How far are we walking?" I asked.

"We're holed up in motel in Troutdale. It's about twenty miles up the interstate from here."

"There'll be food and a bed and coffee?"

"All of those things," Florence assured me. "There's also beer."

"I take back all the mean things I was thinking about you," I said.

"I know you didn't mean them. A hungry dragon queen is a cranky dragon queen."

"Are we really walking twenty miles, though? I'm not sure I can do that on a five-weeks empty stomach."

"Have a little faith, Eleanor," Florence said. "I can teleport us there once I get a little further away from Warrendale."

"You can? You can do that?"

She didn't answer, but I could almost hear her smug smile. After walking for about twenty more minutes, she stopped. "This is far enough."

There was a flare of light and Florence was lit up like a roman candle.

"Holy fuck, Florence! What the hell?"

She smiled and I hoped it was my imagination that she appeared a little bit sinister. "The magic is back."

ABOUT THE AUTHOR

AMY CISSELL IS an urban fantasy and paranormal romance writer. She grew up in South Dakota and received her BA in English Literature from South Dakota State University. That degree has carried her far in her career as a financial administrator.

Her first exposure to fantasy was when she picked up her father's copy of The Hobbit while in elementary school and an enduring love affair was born. Although Amy reads anything and everything, her first love is fantasy.

Amy is the author of the Eleanor Morgan series. Visit Amy online at www.amycissell.com and sign up for her newsletter. In addition to receiving deleted scenes and excerpts from her upcoming releases, you'll get the newsletter-exclusive serial following the origins and first millennium of Raj Allred—everyone's favorite sexy vampire.

facebook.com/acissellwrites

twitter.com/acissellwrites

instagram.com/acissellwrites

ALSO BY

The Eleanor Morgan Novels

The Cardinal Gate (February 2017)

The Waning Moon (June 2017)

The Ruby Blade (October 2017)

The Broken World (March 2018)

The Lost Child (February 2019)

Oracle Bay

It's Not in the Cards (October 2018)

First Hand Knowledge (November 2018)

Belle of the Ball (December 2018)

Wing and a Prayer (January 2019)

Made in United States
Troutdale, OR
03/09/2024